OFF TELEGRAPH

A Novel of Berkeley in the Sixties

Joseph Rodricks

Victor Press
Arlington, Virginia

Ring the bells that still can ring. Forget your perfect offering.
There is a crack in everything.

That's how the light gets in.

"Anthem" by Leonard Cohen

CHAPTER 1

When Getz was certain his last experiment had failed he locked up his laboratory and headed home. A cool and windy Friday evening accompanied his slow walk across the Berkeley campus. He seemed unaware of his surroundings and at one point took a wrong turn and had to retreat. When he reached Telegraph Avenue, with its processions of hippies, students, and assorted street people, he hurried his pace, found a way off it, and took another route home. The frivolity of the Avenue's gathering night life was not bearable. He jogged the last few blocks to his apartment.

Gina was in the kitchen pouring herself a glass of wine. She smiled as Getz entered and quickly reached for a second glass. Getz smiled weakly and then collapsed without a word onto their ragged sofa. He snatched up the pack of cigarettes that was on the old wood crate that passed for a coffee table and lit up as Gina approached with two glasses of wine. She knelt on the bare floor and offered Getz a glass, which he seized.

"Did you eat?" she asked.

He nodded that he had, then said that he hadn't. He quickly downed the wine, got up and went to the kitchen for more, and returned to the sofa.

"Did you just come from the lab?"

"Yeah. It was a very long day."

Gina rose and started to move to the sofa where Getz was sitting, then turned away and sat down across the room, on one of the chairs by the small table they used for dining. The table had been one of Gina's contributions to the small apartment on Durant they had been living in for nearly a year. Gina had been in her first year of graduate school when she first met Will Getz, who was then in his third, and they had decided to move in together after only a couple of months of dating.

"I guess things didn't go well," Gina said, in a barely audible whisper.

Will lifted his head to look directly at her and, after a pause said, "No, a disaster… I can't explain what I'm seeing. It's impossible to understand."

Gina took a sip of her wine, and turned away from Will's gaze. She understood the frustration he was feeling. She understood that the long research journey he had traveled was apparently at a dead end. After a few moments, she spoke and said there was no food in the apartment and asked Will if he wanted to go out to eat. Will nodded yes, put out his cigarette, and rose to put on a jacket. Gina did the same, and they locked up the apartment and began a slow, chilly and silent walk up Durant to Telegraph. As they walked, Gina thought about the dismal situation Will was now in. She knew it totally dominated his life and had pretty much displaced her.

Gina knew of Will's problems with reproducing his initial and apparently successful research results. She understood the seriousness of his setbacks, the extra time it would now require to complete his doctorate, the possibility that he would have to begin again in some new area of investigation. She knew enough about Will's research to recognize that the research problem he had chosen under the guidance of Professor Alden Jensen was exceptionally challenging. He had elected to work on the laboratory synthesis of a chemical substance found in nature, a compound present in a plant found in areas of South and Central America. Some early studies on the compound suggested it might have use in medicine, as an anti-cancer drug. The problem was that it was difficult to isolate the compound from the wild plant in sufficient quantities, and in sufficiently pure form, for practical use in medicine, or even in laboratory testing.

The compound was called pfaffadine, from the scientific name, *Pfaffia paniculata*, of the plant from which it came. It was a complex molecule and contained certain bonds between its atoms that were uncommonly difficult to create by laboratory synthesis.

Jensen had received a grant from the National Cancer Institute to attempt laboratory synthesis of pfaffadine. He had over the years published extensively on the lab synthesis of relatively simple compounds containing the same unusual chemical bonds found in pfaffadine, and the NCI approved his grant on the assumption that Jensen was uniquely qualified to attempt the synthesis. The NCI wanted a reliable source of pfaffadine so it could get on with its testing program. Will Getz had eagerly taken on the pfaffadine synthesis project when it came time for him to develop his doctoral research program. If he could carry off the complete synthesis, that in itself would give him quite a name, and if the compound also proved to be successful in the medical clinic, he'd quickly be elevated to the upper echelon of the ranks of medicinal chemists.

Under Jensen's guidance, Will had spent several months putting together the plan for pfaffadine synthesis. The plan was a kind of chemical road map that depicted a route from a relatively simple and readily available chemical compound through a series of increasingly complex molecules, and ending with pfaffadine. As you moved along the route each new molecule you encountered looked, in its molecular

3

architecture, more like pfaffadine. The Getz plan had 12 steps, from the first, simple molecule to the product resulting from step 12, the pfaffadine itself. Each step consisted of a different chemical reaction that would, if it could be made to work as planned, change one molecule to the next one on the road map.

Developing the plan of synthesis took a combination of knowledge of the underlying science and high creativity, the ability to imagine a succession of chemical alterations that, in the end, would lead to the specific set of chemical atoms and bonds that were found in pfaffadine, and in no other molecule. Will Getz's plan had won praises from Alden Jensen, who blessed it and then sent Will to the lab to execute it.

Of course, the road to pfaffadine was one no one had ever traveled before. It was a road into unknown territory. This was research, and the successful completion of a research project like this one was necessary to earn a doctorate. But there was no guarantee that even the best experimental chemist on earth could move along the proposed pathway to pfaffadine without encountering impenetrable barriers. At any of the steps along the way it might be found that the plan was not going to work - - some molecule along the path could not, for a large number of possible reasons, be forced to change into the next one. If this type of problem turned up at step 2 or 3 or 4, not much time would be lost, and Will would have gone back to the drawing boards to come up with a new approach. There were many possible ways to get to a desired product. The creative part of planning came in guessing at the one route that was most likely to work, in the least number of steps. Will Getz's plan, if it could be made to work, was highly ingenious.

Unfortunately, he had discovered, at a very late stage, after he had put in a long, arduous effort, that the stumbling block - - apparently one that could not be overcome - - was at step 12.

Over the first year of lab research Will had had good luck. He proved to be a skilled laboratory scientist and brought off the first nine steps of the planned synthesis with relative ease. He didn't worry much about maximizing the efficiency of each step; he had only to ensure that each planned chemical reaction produced the desired intermediate molecules in quantities sufficient for use in the subsequent steps of the synthesis. Only if the ultimate synthesized compound, the pfaffadine, proved useful as an anti-cancer drug would it be necessary to worry about maximizing the efficiency of the synthesis. That would be someone else's problem.

The second year of Will Getz's research proved to be far more difficult than the first, but he was able to move through steps 10 and 11 of the synthesis and, after a dozen false starts, was able to develop about five grams of the compound that was, according to the plan of synthesis, the immediate precursor to pfaffadine. For simplicity this precursor molecule Getz and Jensen called pre-pfaff. The pre-pfaff molecule looked very much like pfaffadine --one alteration in its molecular architecture should cause it to become pfaffadine. The chemical means to produce this specific alteration involved the type of reaction Jensen had specialized in and which his previous students had successfully applied to other molecules, much simpler ones than pre-pfaff.

Will's first attempt at this reaction, step 12, appeared to work. He had evidence that he had created a few milligrams of pfaffadine, beginning with about half a gram of pre-pfaff. Most of the tiny amounts of this first product had been used up in various studies to show that it was, in fact, chemically identical to the natural, plant-

5

derived pfaffadine. As the two walked up Durant Avenue, Gina recalled how they had celebrated Will's success by going out to Berkeley's most expensive restaurant.

But then Will had to repeat step 12, using more of his limited supply of pre-pfaff. He had to repeat the conversion of pre-pfaff to pfaffadine both because demonstrating reproducibility was a requirement in the practice of science, and also because he had to develop a couple of grams of pfaffadine to deliver to the NCI. Three attempts over a four-month period, all apparently identical to the first, had yielded no product identifiable as pfaffadine. This was a mystery. Perhaps the first apparently successful attempt was a fluke, perhaps the product he obtained was not, in fact, pfaffadine, a case of mistaken identity. Or perhaps there was some unknown factor in the chemical reaction critical to its successful completion that had been present the first time, but was somehow missing in the succeeding three attempts.

This last failed attempt, confirmed just a few hours ago, was devastating because it had depleted Will's supply of pre-pfaff. To repeat the entire eleven-step synthesis of this precursor molecule would take six or more months of very tedious work. He had no will to take it on, but without more pre-pfaff, Will could not experiment further with the last step of the synthesis. He also knew that even if he were to start all over and make more pre-pfaff, it was possible he would never be able to get it to convert to pfaffadine. Based on his experience of the last several months, it was not just possible, it was likely.

"Does Jensen know?" asked Gina, as they turned onto Telegraph Avenue and approached Rafael's restaurant.

"He's been away for three of the last five weeks. I've told him nothing. As far as Jensen knows I've got the product. He thinks I've just been repeating the initial work to produce the few grams NCI wants. He has no idea about these failures."

"Shouldn't you let him know? How do you know he hasn't already broken the news of success to NCI? Maybe he's told them you have a successful synthesis. Wasn't he there, in Bethesda, a couple of weeks ago?" Gina remembered seeing Jensen flying out of the Chemistry Building, suitcase and briefcase in hand, telling her that he was off to NCI for a meeting.

"Maybe Monday. I'll tell him the bad news on Monday. Let's get something to eat."

Schaefer and two others were huddled around several pitchers of beer in the large corner booth at Rafael's. Will wasn't in the mood to join them but he and Gina did so when Schaefer called out and waved the two of them over. Gina slid in beside Schaefer, who was an Assistant Professor in the Department of Anthropology, and Gina's thesis adviser. Will took the other end of the seat, beside Peter Weiss, a graduate student in the Philosophy Department. Will had first met Weiss at the seminar where he had also first met Gina. Schaefer was giving a talk on his travels in Central America and his search for plants used by the locals for medicinal, religious, and recreational purposes. Schaefer had done his own graduate work under Wilhelm Heidt at Columbia, the investigator who had first brought *Pfaffia paniculata* to the attention of NCI. Will had taken a seat between Gina and Peter and the three got into a heavy discussion on something to do with medical botany while waiting for Schaefer to make his appearance. Will and Gina had immediately connected.

Preston Schaefer was a bear of a man, heavily bearded and generally unkempt. He was considered brilliant by a few, a visionary of sorts, but was too eccentric to be taken seriously by many. His research record was small but considered to be of high quality, enough to make his position and future at Berkeley relatively secure. He was apparently averse to frequent bathing and so usually smelled foul, as he did this evening, but Gina was used to it.

David Zaretsky, another student of Schaefer's, was spouting off about the evils of the war in Vietnam, and something about an upcoming protest march in San Francisco. Schaefer and Weiss were sipping at their beers, apparently ignoring David's rambling monologue. Gina and Will ordered some food, and just sat in silence.

Will was occupied by thoughts of his failures in the lab. Where was his out? Was he buried here indefinitely? He had hoped to be through with the lab work by about now, and to begin writing it all up for his doctoral defense, which he once thought he would have by the end of summer. He'd also been planning a job search. He knew Gina wasn't close to completing her work, but he hadn't worried much about the possibility that he'd have to leave her behind, at least for a while, if he took up a post on the East coast, which is where he wanted to be. He even had his eyes on a research job at NCI, on the campus of the National Institutes of Health in Bethesda, Maryland, near the nation's capital. He hated the government's involvement in the war, but that wasn't enough to dissuade him from taking a position, using Jensen's assistance, at the leading cancer research center in the world. All this, because of his terrible setbacks, was now a quickly fading dream.

Back in January, when he was certain he had completed the pfaffadine synthesis, he had felt an enormous sense of accomplishment. Although this was, he had thought at the time, the greatest of his life, Will Getz had behind him a long string of accomplishments. He had navigated his way through high school back in Boston, college at Columbia, and the first years of graduate school at Berkeley with an unbroken record of high achievement, and it all seemed to come with relative ease. Not that he didn't work hard - - Will Getz had always been a serious, hard-working student. The ability to do hard work, to persevere, came easily to him - - his father's influence, no doubt - - and he thrived on it and prospered from it.

The unsuccessful struggles of the last four months, the attempts to harness the chemical bonds in the pre-pfaff molecule and force them to rearrange to become pfaffadine, were like none he had ever engaged in. Never before had he worked so hard and never before had he failed so utterly.

The pfaffadine molecule had become to him a kind of demon that he had been unable to slay. His sense of frustration had grown to mammoth proportions and now seemed to grip him totally. Only once before in his life, when he was a boy and had to wrestle with another kind of demon that had interrupted the flow of his life, had Will felt such hopelessness. Anger and hopelessness, at once.

But the boy had found a way to overcome that earlier demon and now the man had to find a way to overcome the new one that blocked the path to his future. His father, he knew, could not help him this time.

Like Will, Gina had avoided any involvement with Schaefer and the others at the table. She picked at her food and gazed across the table at Will. He looked miserable, completely unconnected to anyone at the table, including herself. Gina certainly had sympathy with his plight, but thought he had taken his losses a little too hard. After all, what he was experiencing was inherent in scientific research. She understood that Will was not accustomed to failure, that his recent defeats were not easy for him to handle. But she also understood him to be dedicated to a life in science, and she thought it odd that he'd reacted so badly the first time he had encountered the frustrations and defeats that were inevitable in any scientific undertaking. She'd begun to think the chasm that had opened between them must have some cause other than his research setbacks.

Will and Gina, trying to ignore what seemed to be a political shouting match between Schaefer and Zaretsky, and the usual weird stares from Weiss, managed to get through the tacos they had ordered, and left the restaurant with nothing more than hand waves. They hurried their way down a crowded Telegraph Avenue, and then turned off it at Durant.

On Monday Getz got to the lab around eleven. He'd had a long cup of coffee, four cigarettes worth, at Capp's, and then wandered through Sproul Plaza and Sather Gate, and up the eucalyptus-lined path to Chemistry. Over the weekend, he had made up his mind to reveal everything to Jensen. He wasn't sure his adviser would be in, but planned to break the bad news as soon as he could locate him. Where this would lead, he didn't know, but guessed that Jensen would direct him to go back to square one. No other path to a completed doctoral thesis seemed available. There was a chance Jensen would agree that the work done so far was enough, but this seemed unlikely. At least one more stab at the pre-pfaff -to-pfaffadine conversion would be necessary, and for this he would need to go through the agonizing and drawn out process of synthesizing more pre-pfaff, probably lots more. The only alternative would seem to be the development of a totally different path of chemical synthesis, an even uglier prospect to contemplate.

Getz ran into his lab mate, Bill Kane. "Will, where you been? Jensen was here looking for you. I think he's giving his organic mechanisms lecture, but he'll be back around noon."

Kane was pretty cheery. His work was proceeding very well and was yielding results that he was getting ready to present at a regional American Chemical Society meeting, coming up in a month in Los

Angeles. Kane was a superb experimentalist and his skills at the bench made up for a lack of theoretical savvy. Kane relied heavily upon Jensen's thinking, but he could take the professor's ideas to the bench and turn them into reality with great artistry. Getz was nearly the opposite, brilliant at the blackboard but a plodder at the bench.

Getz went through the pages of his notebook. He hadn't kept particularly clear or complete notes on his last three experiments, so no one reading his notebook could tell that they had gone nowhere. On a piece of scrap paper he had drawn the complex molecular structures of pre-pfaff and pfaffadine, and the details of how the conversion had been expected to take place, how a certain pair of atoms had been expected to link up with another pair located in a different portion of the complicated pre-pfaff molecule. That particular conversion, the one Jensen had discovered when he had worked on much simpler molecules, should have taken place under the conditions of the planned experiment. There was no reason for the failure, it didn't fit with prior experience with similar compounds. Getz should have had a vial full of pure pfaffadine to show Jensen, with complete documentation of its identity. Instead he had a relatively empty notebook, some dirty reaction flasks, and a residue of pre-pfaff that was too small to be useful. This is what he'd have to present to Jensen in an hour. He left the lab and shuffled to the student lounge for a smoke. He couldn't stop smoking.

Dr. Elaine Callahan was in the lounge and was also smoking. She was a post-doctoral fellow, out of Northwestern University, where Jensen had himself studied.

"Hey Getz, I want to show you something. Come to my lab," Elaine exclaimed. Getz dropped his cigarette and silently followed her to the large corner lab where she had set up an elaborate experimental system. She had been working on a new method for isolating natural compounds from plant products and for purifying them, all in one continuous process. Her plan was highly innovative and she had had some early successes with it. Elaine showed Getz her recent results involving a series of so-called alkaloid compounds found in a wild relative of the common potato plant. She had apparently isolated and separated from each other five alkaloids in one continuous process, a pretty remarkable achievement.

"I've already started on your favorite plant, to see if I can isolate pfaffadine in sufficient amounts for the NCI. Jensen told me to do this last week. He told me it wasn't meant to compete with your work, but just to test my system. I don't think we have much of a chance here, because I'm guessing pfaffadine is going to degrade under my isolation conditions. They are really suited only for certain classes of compounds, and I don't think pfaff is one of them."

Getz was a little stunned by Elaine's revelation. Had Jensen already guessed the lab synthesis of pfaffadine was going nowhere? Jensen had promised NCI two grams of pfaff by June, and it was now early May. Maybe Jensen thought that he could deliver the natural product, if Elaine's system worked, and that would fulfill his immediate obligation until synthesis was successful. Maybe he thought Elaine's system would make synthesis unnecessary. Getz didn't know what to think, and didn't know what to say to Elaine. His eyes had dropped and he found himself staring at Elaine's feet. Elaine sensed he was upset and reached out to touch his arm. Getz smiled, told Elaine he was impressed with her system, and then left her, to return to his lab.

At noon Getz was at his desk writing madly in his notebook. He had just filled a vial with about two grams of a compound he had prepared early on in his research, in connection with a small project Bill Kane had been working on. Kane still had about 30 grams, and wouldn't miss the amount Getz removed, because the compound was no longer relevant to Kane's work. Getz now labeled the vial containing this compound "Pfaffadine. Synthetic. Sample X-4A. 2.2 grams. 5-3-67." He recorded in his notebook full descriptions of his last three experiments. He pulled from his files the various tests he had run on the product obtained in the first and apparently successful run. Those various tests, elemental chemical analysis, mixed melting point, infrared and nuclear magnetic resonance spectra, and mass spectra, had all shown that the product he had obtained, in very small amounts, one-tenth of a gram at the most, in the first experiment, was identical to natural pfaffadine. The first product, labeled Sample X-1A, had been subjected to these various tests on January 13.

On each of the spectra and documents obtained from tests on the apparently genuine product, Getz changed the sample number from "X-1A" to "X-4A" and the date from 1-13-67 to 5-3-67. This was not hard to do. Within 20 minutes he was ready to represent to Jensen that the two grams of compound in the vial labeled X-4A was genuine, synthetic pfaffadine and that the various successful test results had been obtained on it. He was not sure where the idea of doing this came from, and never stopped to ask himself. By twelve-thirty he was ready to talk to Jensen, with a new and grand message.

How could this fraud work? Easy. Jensen would obviously not go back and repeat these tests himself on the fake product. He would accept Getz's findings. He would accept that Getz had had three successful runs, and that the contents of the vial were the combined results of the last three experiments. The stuff would be shipped off to NCI, with supporting documents of its authenticity. NCI might rerun some of the chemical and spectrographic tests, that was the risk, but with supporting documents from Alden Jensen, they'd probably not do this. They needed to conserve as much of this valuable product as possible. They would just go ahead with their screening tests for anti-cancer activity. The fake pfaffadine would flop, and that would be the end of NCI's interest.

A successful completion of the total synthesis of pfaffadine, enough to get Getz his doctorate, and soon. And a finding at NCI that the compound was not effective for anti-cancer activity, no big loss there. This would also mean that no one would ever attempt to repeat his synthesis, there would be no practical need. His work would be published, it would represent a fine achievement, but the lack of any practical use for pfaffadine would mean it would all end there. There was some risk to Getz here, but not a lot.

He took a deep breath, managed to put on a smile, gathered up the vial of fake pfaffadine, his notebook with the phony experimental details, and the revised test documents, and walked confidently to Jensen's office. No one except Gina knew of his failed experiments, not even Kane, who'd been recently preoccupied with his own successes. This was easy. Small risk, large reward. Plans back on track. All he needed was a way to explain to Gina this sudden reversal of fortune.

CHAPTER 2

On the following Sunday, the day after the huge anti-war march in San Francisco, Gina left before Getz awoke and drove back into the city to her dad's house and studio on Green Street. She arrived about noon and found Marco cooking in his small kitchen, which also served as a storage area for some of his art materials. He'd expanded his studio after the death of Gina's mother in an auto crash in 1960, seven years earlier when Gina was seventeen, but it was still too small to contain all the supplies he needed. Marco's work was now selling at an all-time high which, unfortunately, was still pretty low. He made enough to get by and to support Gina's studies, but had little spending money beyond that and nearly no savings. But all he knew was in his paintings, miniatures and maybe old-fashioned by today's standards, but still, at age forty- seven, he maintained a level of faith that some day he'd catch on in a big way. More than twenty years of evidence to the contrary was behind him.

Marco loved to cook and there was no one he loved to cook for more than Gina. Although he had had close relationships with several women since Teresa's death, only Gina truly captured his heart. He could imagine no limits to what he would do on her behalf.

They downed the fish stew, his homemade bread, and some wine made by his best friend, Aldo Marcino, who had emigrated with Marco from Italy in 1946, when they were both in their early twenties. Aldo now owned a small and successful Italian restaurant and coffee house in North Beach, where Marco was always a welcome and non-paying guest. This had been the tradition for twenty years, the result of which was an endless display of paintings by Marco Antinori in Aldo's Trattoria. Aldo's food had been a big help for Marco and his family through their toughest years, and Gina's pictures of family meals served at the large round table in the corner were a big piece of her memory.

"You are not happy today, Gina. Not happy." said her father, his wine glass aswirl in his hand.

Gina was silent, and stopped eating.

"Your ol' man sees some pain in your face. I would like to paint it, if it were not yours."

"I don't think I want to talk about it, today at least. Maybe we could take a walk after dinner. It's really nice outside."

"I accept. Both your requests." He laughed and sopped up his stew with a large slab of bread.

Later they walked on Green, all the way to Columbus Avenue and then headed down to North Beach. They decided to have some coffee at Aldo's and found him in enormous good cheer on this beautiful Sunday in May. The restaurant was crowded, some tourists, but mostly the local crowd of artists, writers, and their hangers-on. Gina spied Peter Weiss, the philosophy student, sitting in a corner, sipping coffee and reading from some very fat volume. A guy she did not recognize was seated next to Peter. She left her father to say hello and told Peter she'd be back to talk with him later.

The music in Aldo's juke box was great, mostly operatic with some jazz and folk, a unique collection that reflected its owner's style. Aldo was terrific fun, a happy and robust greeter who seemed to like everybody. He scolded Gina for not coming by more often and then hugged her with every ounce of strength in him. She was a small person and could take Aldo's great bear hugs for only a few seconds. She loved him but not his hugs, which she had suffered for as long as she could remember.

They ordered coffee and when Marco became engaged in conversation with some real old guy at the next table, Gina moved over to sit with Peter and his friend.

"What on earth are you reading?" she asked, pointing at the enormous book on his table.

"I'm not really reading, just scanning. It's a collection of materials related to the work of Madame Blavatsky. You have heard of her? A major figure. Theosophy. Unparalleled insights into the human mind. By the way, this is Chris. Chris meet my friend Gina." Peter Weiss was a slight fellow, delicately featured with fine, sandy-blond hair hanging to his shoulders. He always wore white cotton shirts that looked as if they were made in India, white trousers, and sandals. Year-around, it seemed. Gina thought Peter had an interesting face, but he was definitely not her type. He wouldn't appeal to most of the women she hung out with, but she knew that many must be attracted to him. He seemed to be smart as hell, but because he never said much it was hard to be sure.

"What are you doing here?" she asked. "I've never seen you here before."

"I don't know why not. I come here a lot. I have a good friend who lives nearby. I had lunch with him."

"Were you at the anti-war march yesterday? I didn't see you."

"I was, certainly. I stayed in the city afterwards, spent the night with my friend."

Peter closed up his big book and stared into Gina's eyes. She had felt his stares on other occasions and was half-intrigued, half-upset by them. She couldn't imagine what he was thinking when he stared at her in this way.

"How is Will? Where is he?"

"He's fine. Sleeping off last night's party. We all got together at Kay's place after the march. I came to visit my dad, the one over there talking to that very old guy."

Peter's stare evaporated but he continued questioning Gina. "I detect that all is not well with you and Will. If I'm out-of-line, let me know."

Gina didn't know what to say, then offered a weak, "No. It's ... it's fine."

"He was having dissertation troubles. Is he over them?"

"Yes, definitely, he had a big break last week. Jensen - - his adviser - - has told him to go ahead and write it up." Gina stumbled over these words, trying to understand why Peter and his questions made her nervous.

"Are you pleased for him?"

"Of course, it's great."

"What will happen to the two of you when he finishes up then? You have several more years --aren't you at least a year behind him?"

"I am. And I don't know. We'll work it out." Her voice had taken on a slightly angry tone. Peter only smiled, and drank the last of his coffee.

"This is my friend, Chris Swift. Say hello to Chris, don't be shy, Gina. Gina is very shy, Father. You see, Gina, Chris is a priest. You would never have guessed that I would be pals with a priest, a Catholic priest. But Father Swift is no ordinary priest." Peter was staring again and Gina had to turn away.

"My good friend is trying to change the church. His boss is the holy Cardinal McIntire, king of the L.A. diocese. He wants to get rid of Chris, so Chris ran away. Maybe to take some time to collect his thoughts. Isn't that right?" Weiss' sickly smile intensified under heavy cigarette smoke. The alleged philosopher somehow always managed to convey the impression that he knew everyone's most hidden thoughts, but maybe it was only Gina who perceived this in him.

Gina finally spoke in Chris' direction, "You don't wear a collar."

"I usually do, but I'm kind of hiding. McIntire hates me. He's never met me, wouldn't stoop that low, but he gets reports. I went into the church to do some good. McIntire's only interested in power. He's been in power twenty years and all he's done is build Catholic schools and hospitals, mostly real estate development. He's reactionary. I'm not the only priest he's trying to pull the trigger on."

"What'll you do? Can he throw you out?" Gina pretended to be only mildly interested, but she was intrigued, and when she finally looked closely at the priest she was almost startled to discover his extraordinary good looks. Priests aren't supposed to look like this, she thought.

She guessed that Chris Swift was the kind of priest who might have been able to hold on to heretics like herself. She still had at least an emotional attachment to the church, but the death of her mother had caused her eventually to doubt; she couldn't trust any God who could allow such unexplainable evil, who could allow all the other evils that were found in the world. But when the church captures you at birth, its grip is nearly impossible to break completely. Her father was still a believer, and often hinted, in the gentlest of ways, that she should return to the flock.

Chris started to respond to Gina's question, but Peter interrupted and asked, "We are driving back to Berkeley. Do you need a ride?"

"No. My car's back at my father's place."

"See you soon. Say hello to Will for me. I missed seeing him." He patted Gina on the shoulder, more a caress than a pat, and slid gracefully away. She and Chris exchanged smiles, and she watched while the two men exited.

When it was time for Gina to say goodnight to Marco and return to Berkeley, she finally said out loud what she had carried in her thoughts all day. They were standing outside his house on Green Street, in the late Sunday coolness, with no one else in view on the long block between Fillmore and Webster.

"It's happening again, Daddy."

He put his hands on her shoulders, gripped them tightly. In the light from the nearly vanished sun she saw, suddenly it seemed, how much age he showed in his eyes. Maybe it was also the intense sadness that quickly overcame him when she uttered those words, words she had used many times in the past half-dozen years, each time the dread returned to haunt his only daughter. It arose from nowhere, it seemed, would plow into her life, and then would unaccountably lift away for several months. The doctors understood nothing.

"When did it come?" he asked.

"Over the past week or two, I felt it most last night, or early this morning. Will and I were walking home from a party. He has been very quiet lately. His research was just shitty, but a few days ago he recovered a lot and things are bright for him at last, but you'd never know it from his behavior."

Marco was pleased she was able to talk, at least a little. Sometimes in the past, though not since she had met Will, she would go weeks without engaging in real conversation. Marco had been highly distressed when Gina had first told him she was moving in with Will. He knew this to be sinful but, because he trusted his daughter's judgment, he had let it happen without attempting to interfere. He knew this kind of behavior was increasingly common in Gina's generation, and that a lot of it reflected a lack of discipline and loose morals. He knew his daughter well, and could accept that her relationship with Will was a responsible one. He'd grown to like and respect Will, and was pleased with the young man's positive effects on Gina. At least that's the way it seemed for a time.

"His mood does this to you."

"No. I don't think so. Maybe, but this is my own thing too. You know that, Daddy."

"And your school?"

"I'm hanging on. Actually better than that. Courses are easy for me and I'll be working up a Ph.D. research plan this summer. I'll hold on to Will, he's a great person, really bright. I love being with him. But these moods hurt us, I know it. My energy fades for a while. Oh, I don't know what I'm saying. One day I'm fine and then I'm sinking away from life. This is stupid, isn't it? I don't make any sense."

Her dad smiled, holding back small tears that made his old eyes glisten. He pulled Gina close and held her to him. He had no other words. These were feelings that he could paint about, not talk about.

"Look, I know school's over for you next week. I want to go visit Uncle Tony and Aunt Grace, up in Seattle. You haven't seen them for a long time. How about making the trip with me? I'm thinking to stay about a week, maybe more. You always said you liked my brother so much ... and Aunt Grace's pizza. What do you think?"

Gina smiled, hugged her father, whispered that it sounded like a good idea, and turned to find her car. She drove back to Berkeley, stopping on the way to do some grocery shopping.

Later that evening Gina entered her apartment and was surprised to find it in total darkness. When she managed to turn on some lights she could immediately feel Will's absence. Three drab empty rooms. A few dirty dishes in the sink. An ashtray full of cigarette butts. Her desk cluttered with books and her study materials. Will was nowhere in sight, but she found a note from him on her pillow.

Dear Gina,

I need some time alone. I need to get my thinking straight. I am going to the mountains for a few days, maybe until next weekend. I'm not sure where. I've taken our gear. Please don't worry.

W.G.

CHAPTER 3

He had set up camp near a small stream about three miles from the Motahwa Trail entrance, where he had left his car. The old wreck had barely made it up into the Sierra foothills, so he had decided not to drive to higher elevations. The six hour drive from Berkeley to this area just north of Yosemite had put him at the trailhead at about seven o'clock in the evening, and he had managed to get his gear and supplies up the trail to the camping area in about two hours. A full moon made his setting up easy. He hadn't eaten all day, but was in no mood to cook, so he ate some dried fruit and nuts, drank some water, and crawled into his sleeping bag. No fire. Just the moon above, its light beaming down through the spruce and pine, accompanied by the music of a mountain creek rising from just below his campsite. The slight hunger that remained after he ate actually felt good. He liked the lightness in his head and the emptiness at his waist, as long as there were no pangs of hunger in his stomach. He was not able to sleep for several hours, but when it finally captured him, he remained bound until the morning sun was so high that its rays awakened him.

He was alone. This little campsite was one he'd occupied a couple of times before, the last time with Gina, last fall he thought it must have been. They had given it their own name - -the Refuge they had called it. Now he was alone and maybe he would find the kind of solitude he needed to sort things out.

He had created a crisis in his life. No one else had created it and no one else knew about it. Clarity of thought was needed. Gina was no help, she couldn't be. He had not had much difficulty in explaining his sudden "success" to her. On the day he had faked his results - - 5/3/67 - - he had remained in the lab until late in the evening. He had then explained to Gina that he had discovered that he had been misrecording and misinterpreting test results on the product he had been obtaining these last several months and that, he now knew, he had actually succeeded in producing pfaffadine. There was no way Gina could know that such mistakes were highly improbable. She had accepted his lie, and congratulated him on his achievement. Will knew that what he had done, if she ever were to learn of it, would be incomprehensible to her. She would no doubt simply tell him he needed to admit his lie and get back on the right path before it was too late.

Too late. Too late? What did that mean? It was too late the moment he lied to Jensen. The moment he left Jensen's office with the big lie left behind. No, not left behind. It would be with him as long as he lived. Confession would do no good.

Getz cleaned up his site after his light breakfast. He should have been famished, but he felt satisfied in his body, and decided to pack up a sack of dried fruit and nuts, a canteen of water, and set off up the Motahwa Trail. It rose through the ponderosa pine and mountain spruce forest and leveled off at about 9,000 feet where Douglas fir took over. There he'd pick up another trail that wandered at about that altitude for five or six miles. He'd then catch a downward trail that, he was sure, would take him to a spot about half a mile above his campsite. Maybe ten miles altogether, an easy day's jaunt for Getz's well-conditioned body. He decided to leave his cigarettes behind, at the camp site. Jesus, he had to give them up, they were destroying him.

For the entire morning's hike Getz was able to focus entirely on his surroundings. The alternating patches of sun and shade and the quiet of the forest seemed to nourish his body. He strode powerfully and gracefully. His physical movement was a thing of beauty. Gina always loved to walk behind him whenever they were out on the trails, so that she could watch the strength and grace of his fine legs. She also loved to see the sweat of his back drench his shirt and make visible the movement of his muscles.

He hiked without stopping. In the early afternoon he entered a large shadeless area, and plowed ahead under a brilliant blue and nearly cloudless sky, the sun's rays seemingly directed only at him. He thrived on the heat they brought to his flesh and the strength they seemed to impart. He felt he could move like this forever.

At about four o'clock, on the downhill trail, and into deep shade, he decided finally to stop for awhile. He thought he'd seen a large animal, but couldn't confirm it. He dropped onto the earth and all of sudden felt a little tired. He realized he'd barely eaten all day, and wolfed down all the food and water he'd brought. It felt unexpectedly warm in the deep shade of this exceptionally beautiful spot, so he lay back and relaxed into it. He thought he might fall asleep here, but he soon became aware of the fact that his inner world was not inhabited by the kind of peace and order that was everywhere around him. His swirl of inner agonies did not belong in these mountains. These magnificent creations were not here to bear witness to human folly.

He was somehow changed when he discovered be had failed. At first he was high on his success. Somewhere in him, maybe for the first time ever, he had felt that he was on the trail to some kind of position of power, at the top of his profession. He was on the trail to big time science. He had never realized how much he had been gratified by that first feeling of real importance. And then came the crash. He was off the path in a matter of a few weeks, and then he just kept tumbling down. Jesus, he just hadn't been able to get up after that crash. He'd tried a couple of times. He couldn't get up. He knew he was no great hero, but he thought he was at least honest and could always persevere. So how could he so easily have become the worst kind of fuck up?

He thought of the time he had spent these past two years on the anti-war movement, and before that, in college, on civil rights campaigns. He'd spent several weeks during the summer of '61, after his sophomore year at Columbia, participating in a freedom ride through Alabama, and had come close to getting his brains beaten out of him by some local rednecks. His commitment to these causes did not come out of a desire to be fashionable, to fit in with the kinds of people he wanted to be with; his commitment was genuine. In his heart, he knew that was true. JFK had crystallized a lot of his thinking, but before that, growing up in New England, he had come of age at the time the civil rights movement was blossoming in the South. The news from the south had moved him, he had felt immediate sympathy for the cause. He knew what was right and that change was coming and, somehow, he wanted to be in on it. This was never quite as important to him as his science, but he'd managed to spend whatever spare time he had trying to help. Will Getz was a serious person.

He hated racism, militarism, imperialism, and every other craven, irrational quest for power. That's what all this was really about, power. Mad men in Washington, in Birmingham, in every place on earth, hungry to dominate others. But truth and justice should be the goals, not power. This is how he had come to think about the world. This was how most of his friends, at least those whose boundaries were cast wide, thought about the world. Some were more radical than he - - Zaretsky, Schaefer - -and others less, but the complacent '50s, all tied up in quests for money, security, and a place in the suburbs were not for Will's generation. A revolt was underway and the weak points in the foundations of American society were cracking up.

Will saw the process by which science pursued understanding and truth to be similar to the process by which the need for social change could be understood and its course planned. This was how he saw the world. Now he had done something completely contrary to everything he held sacred. It was not comprehensible.

Will saw that the sun was sinking fast and that he needed to move to get back to camp before it was too dark. He quickly resumed his earlier pace and was back at the campsite in time to collect wood for a fire and to cook some of the food he'd brought. When he'd finished the first sizable meal he'd had for two days, he cleaned up and turned in, again in his sleeping bag set out under the mountain's trees.

On Thursday Will opted for another trail, one that was poorly marked. It took him to much higher elevations and by noon he was bushed. He had no idea how many feet he had climbed in the three hours of hiking but his exhaustion signaled that it had been more than he'd bargained for. He dropped his knapsack on the ground and pulled a sweater from it. The sun was bright but the temperature was low enough to support icicles on the face of the cliffs that rose from where he'd stopped. Will found as much shelter from the wind as he could locate along the trail, which had become fairly narrow between cliffs that fell to his left and rose to his right, almost perpendicular to the ground. He decided that, after some food and rest, he would not proceed further, but turn around and retreat down the trail which he had just ascended. He was uncomfortable in the cold, but at this location it seemed to him that he was completely alone in the world, that he had achieved a state of perfect solitude.

His father, Will Senior, had taught him the joys of this kind of wildness. The two had spent many hours together in the mountains of New Hampshire, hiking and camping, and taking in the glories of the natural world that Will Senior, biology teacher and amateur naturalist, understood so well. Especially the birds - - by the time Will was ready to leave for college at Columbia, he had mastered the identities of most of the birds of the East. For that gift and for many, many more, Will felt infinitely grateful to his father.

Since his wife, Will's mother, had left him, Will's patient, shy, hard-working father had devoted his every free hour to his son. Will remembered little about his mother because she had left his father when the boy was eleven, or rather just as he was turning twelve. He recalled only that she had always seemed displeased about something, and was often visibly angry. Will Senior was a calm, quiet person, happiest when he was teaching or reading, or out walking with his son. Angela, that was her name, was just the opposite, impatient, ambitious for something Will could not possibly comprehend. She seemed to be at peace only at mass in the huge old church in Brookline, just across the street from their small house, where she would take Will every Sunday. After she left, Will's father had cured the boy of what he called the "disease" of religion, and Will remained disease-free, another blessing from his father.

One cold winter day, the twenty-first of December in 1953, two days before her son's 12th birthday, Angela packed two bags full of her clothing and a few other things, and left, never to return. Neither Will nor his father had heard from her since. She hadn't even left a note. Will Senior, his sadness as well concealed as he could possibly make it, tried to explain her actions to his son, but none of it made any sense. Will recalled only that, all of a sudden, their small house on Collins Avenue seemed to be a much quieter place, where everything seemed more subdued, even the colors of the rooms and the smells of the kitchen. Will Senior did everything he could to comfort and reassure his son - - "Nothing," he would say, "will change for you" - - but the boy knew that he had been transported to a different place, and that some massive emptiness had grown within him. It had taken him a long time, many months, to restore his wholeness.

He did it by finding some way to explain his mother's cruel act. He did it by discovering that she was an evil person who had grievously betrayed his father. Will's "discovery" was, in fact, a complete fabrication - - he came to imagine that his mother had gone off with another man and he even imagined he had once seen her with this other man - - "They were kissing," he had told his father. At the time the young boy did not understand he had made up this story, it somehow had seemed real to him, it was explanatory, and it had had its effect of convincing his father that he had been betrayed by a bad woman. The boy and the man came to accept this myth and had somehow been healed by it, and thereafter the two had become closer and the boy had grown under the man's influence to become an excellent student and, now, an exceptional scientist. Or so it had seemed before 5-3-67.

All of a sudden Will felt as if he must be on Mount Washington, in New Hampshire, in the dead of winter, the coldest place in the United States, a small but rugged peak he had once climbed, in the middle of summer with his father. He needed to get off this icy perch and retreat down the trail he'd climbed. He shivered as he packed up to go, and for a brief moment wished that Will Senior had been there to help him find his way.

Will stayed on at the Refuge for two more days. He tried to read - - he had ambitiously brought a copy of *Moby Dick* with him - - but made no progress. He was increasingly preoccupied, alternately, with thoughts of Gina and of what he had perpetrated in his laboratory, and whether out on the trail or just sitting at the campsite or trying to sleep, he could not eject them from his mind. Neither could he advance his thinking on either subject; his mind was aswirl with the dilemmas he faced and he could achieve no clarity or resolution that satisfied his heart.

When he had first met her and for many months after, he had felt an emotional attachment to Gina that was new to him, and immensely satisfying. He had known many women who were bright and who could challenge his intellect, and he had often been intensely drawn to them - - smart, assertive women, provided they were physically attractive, were sexy and desirable, and usually available to him for the asking. Gina, small dark-haired Gina, with the prettiest of faces and eyes that were like soft magnets, was exceedingly bright, but it was not easy to find that out. She was shy and as unassertive a woman as Will had ever met. Somehow, as he discovered more about her, he had become captured by her as he had been captured by no other woman. In her quiet, unassuming way she had led him into places he had had little experience of - - music, art, literature - - and had allowed him to discover what he came to call the "softer" places in his heart. He had always directed his energies to understanding and mastering the outer world, the world of science and nature and, to a degree, the world of social action. Gina's whole life had been far more sheltered than Will's, had been dominated by her father and his art and her mother's music and reading, by her school life - - almost straight A's everywhere she had been - - and, at least until her mother's terrible death, her church. So as Will came to appreciate and maybe even love this young woman, she followed him into the world he understood and began to uncover parts of herself that had never before stirred. It was for Gina, however, a difficult and slow process of change.

Even as Will grew fonder of Gina, he found himself increasingly disturbed by certain aspects of her behavior. In social gatherings she would rarely speak, even though she had opinions and could speak clearly and even forcefully about them. He knew this because when they were alone together she sometimes did so, and often challenged him to ascend above his own level of understanding. He also came to see that, in many ways, she was passive, a child of the 50's who seemed to be satisfied with the role society assigned to women: although she was pursuing a doctorate, her only ambition was to be a teacher, like her mother. Gina talked little about things such as marriage and children, but Will always suspected they were the only other aspirations in her life. Her love of art and music would no doubt continue, but simply as high-toned hobbies. Will thought he sometimes saw glimpses of higher ambitions in her, and he knew she had the intellect to achieve great things, but he felt disappointed that she showed little sign that she had the will to pursue them. Gina did not have the strong will that was increasingly evident in some of the women of his generation and that he found so attractive.

All this had its effect, and Will found himself losing interest in Gina. He still liked and respected her, at least some part of her, but he was pretty certain he did not love her. As his troubles in the lab grew he increasingly withdrew from her. If he was to be helped through his crisis, he needed someone much stronger, someone who would not passively watch him drown. Of course, now that he had overcome his failures, had found his "success," he was perhaps ready to carry on in the way he had always felt most comfortable, at least since he had left his home and father, and that was as a solitary voyager.

On the fourth day of his stay in the Sierras, Will Getz came to a certain kind of peace. He somehow came to accept that what he had done in the laboratory was not only undiscoverable, but also harmless. No blemish on the body of science would be visible, his betrayal of science would never be noticed. This somehow came to seem certain to him. For the first time during his five days of solitude, he came to rest and felt as if a wrong had been righted. That night, as he watched a bat circling above him, he fell into a completely peaceful sleep, high in the mountains where the trifling sins of man made no difference whatsoever.

CHAPTER 4

David Zaretsky and Gina were camped out in Preston Schaefer's office. As usual Schaefer was late for the meeting he had asked for the previous Saturday, at the post-march party. The professor had been away all week at some meeting in St. Louis, but had been expected at ten o'clock. It was now nearly eleven and no Schaefer sightings had been reported.

David, wearing his usual dirty denims and sporting a new pair of rimless glasses, was in Gina's eyes, a not very attractive man. His hair was an unbelievable tangle and he sported a one- or two-day old beard that grew in splotches over his pock-marked face. He chewed constantly at his fingernails and never looked directly at the person he was talking to. Gina could not understand how Kay Hooper could stand to be around this guy. Kay, divorced and now a newspaper reporter for the East Bay Gazette, shared a house with David and three or four others. Gina had a hard time believing she and David could be close friends. Kay was highly intelligent, and rational and clear in her views. David often seemed incoherent - - radical, to be sure, but because he usually spoke in such a disjointed, rambling way, he was hard to follow. Gina found herself tuning out on the guy when he started in on subjects he considered to be serious - - politics and political action, the horrors of capitalism, racism, and the greatness of

Preston Schaefer, which was David's topic when the professor finally burst in and plopped down at his desk.

Schaefer's enormous desk was piled high with books and papers and was unimaginably disordered. His office was as messy as the rest of his life. This was the way he lived and worked. The outward signs were a little deceptive, though, because his work did have some semblance of order. He specialized in the cultural and religious life of the natives of a climatically unusual region of the Guatemalan highlands, and had over the years spent many months among them, people called the Maryanta. He'd made some perceptive observations regarding the origins of many of their practices and beliefs. They lived in areas of nearly incessant rainfall and had adapted to this condition in some highly unusual ways.

As was the case for many so-called primitives, the Maryanta found medical and ceremonial uses for some local plants, and Schaefer and two of his students had, on one of their trips, collected and brought back dried specimens of several of the more interesting species. One was *Pfaffia paniculata,* known among the Maryanta as "walking dream plant" because consumption of its leaves brought on a state of relaxation accompanied by a feeling of great physical strength and clearness of mind. Schaefer had personally verified this property many times over. Plants like this one were not the principal concern of his studies, but did provide some pleasurable side benefits.

Schaefer had sent samples of *Pfaffia paniculata* to a friend of his, Joel Atkinson, who was an assistant professor of pharmacology at UCLA. Atkinson had isolated and chemically identified the structure of the compound he eventually named pfaffadine, a so-called alkaloid present in the leaves and seeds at small concentrations. Atkinson had also given some crude extracts of the leaves and seeds containing pfaffadine and a number of other, unidentified compounds, to an associate at UCLA who subjected them to the anti-cancer screening tests that ultimately got the National Cancer Institute interested in the plant and in the compound that might be the active anti-cancer agent.

Those findings had led to Alden Jensen and NCI's quest for sufficient amounts of pfaffadine for more complete and definitive anti-cancer testing. Schaefer had also turned over his entire stock of dried leaves and seeds, about a kilo, to Jensen, who now had more use for it than did the anthropologist. The anti-cancer possibility had nothing to do with the natives' use of the plant.

"I wanted to talk to you two about two things. First, you both need to write up proposals for your dissertation research. I'm expecting them by the end of the summer. Second, I want to talk about a possible trip to the Maryanta area, in Guatemala, this fall, maybe for six weeks. I plan some investigations that I'd like you both to be part of, and that should help form the data base for your thesis. I've got funding for the trip lined up and I think you two, along with Tom Silva, are the best support for this work." Tom Silva was another graduate student of Schaefer's.

Gina and David were both surprised by Schaefer's proposition. Neither had expected that field work would be coming up so soon. But both reacted positively and eagerly. Gina paused for a moment and reflected on what this separation from Will might mean. She also knew that their separation might come earlier, for other reasons. She had no idea whether Will would even care about her leaving for such a period of time. She quickly left these thoughts behind and joined in the discussion of objectives for the field trip already underway between Schaefer and David.

During this Elaine Callahan appeared at Schaefer's door. Schaefer stopped his speech about the Maryantans and turned to greet the visitor.

"Remember me?"

"Certainly. Come in. Grab a seat. I assume you came to see me, whoever you are?" Schaefer beamed.

"Elaine. Elaine Callahan. I'm a post-doc with Alden Jensen. You gave us your supply of pfaffia, last fall. We need more. I'm isolating the active principle from it. I think I've got a really good method for extracting and purifying the compound. But I need more plant material to get more compound. My system looks great. We're thinking about growing the plant in the Botany Department's hothouse, so I can isolate really large amounts of the stuff."

"Why do you need so much?" asked Schaefer.

"We think it's got anti-cancer activity. We're supplying NCI, the National Cancer Institute. They want to put pfaffadine through a whole series of tests. I thought you knew that."

Gina interjected. "I thought Will Getz had just synthesized the compound and made enough to satisfy NCI."

"You know about that?" asked Elaine, surprised by Gina's comment.

"I live with him."

Elaine wondered about that. She's pretty, Elaine thought, but a little mousey for the likes of Will Getz. He might enjoy a somewhat hardier woman. An actual woman, maybe. She stopped this line of thought, and replied. "Yeah. He says he's got a synthesized product. That's great. We'll send it in for testing. I'm on a different approach. If my isolation system works as well as I think it does, we'll be able to produce more compound faster. Course, we'll need to be able to grow lots of the plant and hope it keeps making the active compound when we grow it here, in these temperate regions. It should, if we can do it in the hothouse. But we need more plant product now, and also some seeds to culture. What do you ..."

Schaefer broke in, "I don't have anything left here. I gave you all I had. But I can get my associate in Guatemala City to collect some more for you. He'll have to dry it all there, and package it up for shipping. The USDA worries about introducing weird plant diseases into the U.S. If we dry the plant and ship it for research purposes we're okay. I'll write today. No problem. I don't know how soon Perea could get out to get plant. Viable seeds, I don't know about. But Perea can check that, too. Glad to assist." Another beaming smile emerged through Schaefer's huge beard.

Schaefer managed to get Elaine to join him for lunch and they left together. David left without saying goodbye, and Gina walked over to the library with the intention of spending the afternoon researching some of the available literature related to Schaefer's work.

She spent the afternoon in the library but couldn't concentrate. She would drift into a kind of numb reverie, then turn back to her reading, but with little success. The research would be great. The research would be boring. She had great heights to climb. She wanted to go nowhere. Her father was proud of her. He was disappointed in her. Will loved her. Will was somewhere else. She was everything to him. She was nothing to him. Schaefer prized her work. Schaefer would just as soon drop her. Fragile person she was. Small. She thought of that Jefferson Airplane song, about the white rabbit, that was now so popular. One pill makes you taller and one pill makes you small. She knew which pill she was on. She remembered that Will had talked about Elaine. How the guys swarmed around her. Will did not find her attractive. Will was drawn to her. She was strong. Gina was weak.

When she reached her apartment that evening Gina found another note from Will.

Gina,
   I'm back. I'm at Rafael's. I was hungry and wasn't sure when you'd get back. I'm with Peter. Come if you want.
W.G.

The guy leaves a note and disappears for a week, she thought. Then, another note when he gets back. "Come if you want."

He was hungry, but not for her. Gina called her father. "Daddy, when are we going? To Uncle Tony's. I'd like to go soon, maybe tomorrow or the day after. I can drive. The VW's in good shape."

CHAPTER 5

He'd never had a woman like this one. Her hunger was beyond anything he had experienced. She'd made him shower first, told him straight out she couldn't take his foul odor. She wasn't going to bed with him unless he cleaned up. He did this and couldn't believe her reaction. He loved that red hair and the way she tore at him. He had even doubted he was capable of meeting her demands. He worried she'd be repulsed by his beefiness, his large belly, not overly fat exactly, but broad. None of this seemed to concern her. They'd spent Friday night eating out together, talking, getting a little drunk, and planning to meet again on Saturday. Schaefer had no idea she was ready to have sex with him, although he knew she had taken to his style, his intellect, found him interesting. Elaine had this way of probing that made him eager to respond, to make himself interesting, or rather to work hard at revealing to her just how interesting he really was. And Schaefer was that. Because he was slovenly in his dress and personal habits, it was easy to get the misimpression that he had little to offer someone, like Elaine, who treasured men with high intelligence and a will strong enough to do something with it.

Preston Schaefer had not only begun to make a name for himself in the academic world, but he was also involved deeply in social and political issues. He was a radical, which was not in itself unusual in Berkeley in 1967, but he had also contributed significantly to the growing literature of New Left radicalism, on a national scale. He'd become a respected contributor to and member of the editorial board of a San Francisco publication called *Breaking the Hold,* which was devoted to examining the mechanisms used by America's elite to maintain its grip on the social, political, and economic structures around which the nation pivoted. The journal had gained a surprisingly large readership and influence in the New American Left, and Preston Schaefer was given significant credit for its success. He read incessantly and widely, could synthesize and integrate ideas in novel ways, and in addition possessed a lively writing style. He was also active in several antiwar organizations, and had in the late 1950's and early 1960's, while a student at Princeton and later at Vanderbilt, earned high marks as a contributor to the civil rights movement. He'd even had the opportunity to meet Martin Luther King and spend a few moments chatting with him at a meeting in Birmingham, Alabama, back in 1963.

If everything Schaefer said about himself was to be believed, this was a guy present at the creation of just about every major social, cultural, and political event of the past decade. He had been at Port Huron, Michigan, in 1962, when Tom Hayden and other student radicals had drafted the so-called Port Huron statement, the manifesto of the Students for a Democratic Society. Schaefer did not go so far as to claim a significant role for himself in the drafting of the statement, but he did claim he had ties to Tom Hayden, and was frequently contacted by him for advice.

Schaefer, if he was to be believed, had also met and talked to Che Guevara, during one of his trips to Guatemala. Since leaving Castro in Cuba, the Argentinean doctor and revolutionary had been traveling through Central and South America, giving advice and encouragement to local insurgents. The area in Guatemala where Schaefer worked, and which he had visited four times in the past six years, was in the heartland of Guatemala's thirteen-year old rebellion, and Schaefer - - so he said - - had become friendly with the Guatemalan revolutionaries. Guevara, he also said, had visited the area during one of Schaefer's trips, and he'd had a long talk with the great man about the need for worldwide revolution. The story was probably true, because Schaefer had written a piece about it for publication in *Breaking the Hold.*

Cultural revolution was as important as political revolution, and Schaefer's interests in ancient religions, mystical practices, and especially the use of psychedelics had taken him, among other places, to the religious ashram called the International Federation for Internal Freedom that Timothy Leary, the ex-Harvard professor turned LSD prophet, had created at a mansion owned by the wealthy son of and heir to a millionaire industrial kingpin. Schaefer had spent several weeks one summer studying Eastern meditation and the ancient wisdom found in *The Tibetan Book of the Dead.* He, of course, became a close friend of Leary, and was present when the great man had first come up with his famous "tune in, turn on, drop out" slogan.

All this - - if he was to be believed - - and a significant record of academic achievement, was enough to hold onto a position at one of the country's top universities. On top of all this Preston Schaefer managed to maintain a healthy social life. He was not very much into the recreational drug scene - - his drug use was more selective and esoteric - - but he took every advantage he could of what was coming to be called "women's liberation." He was always ready to foster the movement, especially when it had to do with sexual matters. The "pill," of course, had removed a major impediment to a woman's ability to explore at will, and it was no longer a secret that women had as much sexual desire as men. Schaefer was always on the make, but this Saturday's prize was astonishing to him.

Elaine, pale-skinned and red-headed, completely naked, pounced back into the bedroom carrying a large bag of potato chips and a couple of beers. Schaefer was under the covers, a broad smile peeking through his beard. Elaine sat cross-legged on the bed, munching and drinking away, looking pleased. Schaefer had seemed to satisfy her the first time they had sex, he recalled the extraordinary aggressiveness with which she had sought him, the wildness of her responses. As she sat before him now, a couple of hours later and after a short snooze, he could feel desire in his loins, but Elaine seemed more interested in food and drink. She dropped the bag of chips, and lit up a joint.

"I love this shit. And it's going to make me even more hungry than I feel now. I mean for food. Let's go get something."

They arrived about ten p.m. at a small Mexican restaurant a couple of blocks from Schaefer's apartment on Hearst Avenue. Chico's was one of his favorite spots and he spent a lot of time there entertaining friends, studying, writing, and satisfying his stupendous appetite. Schaefer was truly a bear, six-two, probably two-thirty. He'd played football at Princeton and still considered himself a jock, although he wasn't in great shape. He always had plans to drop about thirty pounds but never got around to it.

After they ordered he asked Elaine to tell him about her research, what she was doing, where she was going. "You got me talking about myself, and I love that, but I haven't learned much about you."

"It's not that interesting. Pretty specialized. I fell into a technique for efficient isolation of natural products, like pfaff, and I'm trying to perfect it. It's not really why I came to do a post-doc with Jensen, but it's such a potentially useful technique that he asked me to change directions and to follow up. It's not that interesting as an intellectual matter, more practical."

"You did your Ph.D. at Northwestern? That's where Peter Weiss did his undergraduate."

"Yeah, I know. I was in Chemistry. I flew through there, had great luck. Jensen did his Ph.D. there and still has attachments with the faculty. That's what got me here."

"No regrets?"

"No. I'm happy here. But I am worried about something."

"Tell me." Schaefer wolfed down half a taco and swilled down half a glass of Dos Equis.

"Well I shouldn't. I'm not sure yet about it, so I shouldn't. In fact, I won't."

"When you're ready. I'm easy."

"I'll say you are. You're a nice guy, Schaefer. I like you. No steady woman in your life?"

"No. Nothing like that. There once was, my first year here, in 1963. Her name was Grace. An actress who spent most of her time waiting tables over in the city."

"What happened?"

"I'm not sure. She just said goodbye one day, after about six months of pretty steady stuff. She did a lot of drugs. Her father was a beatnik, fancied himself a poet, lived on next to nothing. Had the greatest pad I've ever seen, in North Beach. Her mother was long gone. Grace Perry. I really liked her. I don't know where she is."

"Nothing like that since?"

"Nothing."

Schaefer hoped that Elaine would come back to his place to spend the night, but she begged off. "I need to go to the lab tomorrow. I've got something cooking, I want to get there early. But thanks. Thanks for a great day. I'll see you soon."

She walked away and left Schaefer wondering if she meant that last remark. She had truly made an impression on him and later, as he drifted off to sleep, he imagined the smell and taste of her heat, there in the bed beside him.

Elaine showed up in her lab at about eight on Sunday morning. No one else was around anywhere on the fourth floor. She put on her lab coat, made some coffee, and went to work.

Several days earlier she'd ground up about half a kilo of dried leaves and seeds, and extracted the powder with ether, a solvent that would remove pfaffadine, along with many other natural components

40

of the plant. Her isolation system was fairly complex, and involved a series of glass columns packed with certain inert materials that would selectively adsorb components of the ether extract, and ultimately separate them from each other. This was not an easy task, and the technique she had accidentally come upon was surprisingly efficacious. If it could be perfected and scaled up, it could have wide application.

It had taken her only two days of work to isolate about three grams of pfaffadine from 500 grams of dried seeds and leaf material. She had matched her product to some of the very small amount of authentic pfaff Jensen had obtained from its discoverer, Joel Atkinson at UCLA. She had verified that her three grams was also authentic pfaffadine, no question.

After lunch on the day of her success, which was the previous Thursday, she had gone to see Getz. His lab had been empty, so she went to his desk to leave him a note saying he should come to see her. "Two victories in the past two weeks, yours and now mine!" As she started to leave she noticed a small vial on Getz's desk labeled "Pfaffadine. Synthetic. Sample X-4A, 2.2 grams, 5-3-67." This was Getz's synthetic stuff. She picked up the vial and examined its contents. The crystalline form looked different from hers, but that was probably attributable to the different solvents that they no doubt had used to crystallize their products. His stuff looked pretty pure, no tinge of color. Hers carried a slight tinge, probably a trace of impurity, not unusual for a natural product. Still, Getz's synthetic product looked surprisingly good.

Elaine put down the vial and searched around Getz's lab for an empty one. She was sure he wouldn't mind if she took a few milligrams so she could make some comparisons with her own natural product. She carefully opened his vial, and with a spatula removed a few milligrams. Since the vial contained 2.2 grams, which was 2,200 milligrams, Getz couldn't possibly notice that any was missing, and he'd still have more than he needed to supply NCI. Besides, Jensen was also going to be able to supply NCI from the product she had now isolated.

She decided to add to the note she left on Getz's desk that she'd taken about 5-10 milligrams of his pfaff to compare with her own product. She was sure he wouldn't mind, but at the last moment, before she left his lab, Elaine decided not to leave behind the note she had written. She decided she'd talk to Getz directly on Monday.

She had taken Getz's sample on Thursday. She'd done a little work on Getz's product on Friday, and what she learned worried her. She had then decided she would follow up on the weekend. That was when she had left the lab to visit Schaefer and to ask him to get her some more plant material.

CHAPTER 6

Preston Schaefer was holding forth on the role of anthropology as a force for social and political change, how anthropologists were going to be instrumental in revealing just how arrogant was the white man's view of his own superiority over the darker and so-called "primitive" races of the earth. That arrogance created the wicked legacy of racism and colonialism. In Schaefer's view, it all led back to the development of science and technology in Western white society, because science and technology were primarily means to exert power over the lesser peoples of the earth. Maybe there were a few side benefits, but science and technology were primarily tools of imperialism. Anthropologists needed to be more active in demonstrating just how false and arrogant the white view of the world was.

"Our goal is not just to understand the world, but to change it! Right, Preston?" shouted out one of his colleagues from the anthropology faculty who was standing in the doorway to Schaefer's living room. Schaefer's small pad on Hearst Avenue was jammed with the usual collection of students and junior faculty and an odd assortment of other people. Word had gotten around that Schaefer was hosting a beer and wine smash on Saturday night, and many more had shown up than the good professor had anticipated. He didn't care. He just sent out for more food and drink, his treat. He loved this. He especially loved the young female students, who were often completely stoned, and who showed up looking to rub shoulders with distinguished faculty members. As he spewed forth his sermon, he cast his eyes about in search of some especially flavorful specimens.

When Elaine Callahan squeezed through the pack and waved to him, Schaefer cut short his search. He'd tried a couple of times to reach Elaine after his extraordinary night with her a week ago, but had been unsuccessful. He was pretty sure she thought of their tryst as just a one-nighter, but he left an invitation note at her apartment anyway. Now she was here, and smiling at him. He struggled to his feet and pushed and shoved his way over to her. She seemed friendly and gave him a weak hug.

Will Getz witnessed this from his perch on Schaefer's kitchen table. He wondered how it was Elaine and Schaefer knew each other, then recalled that it was Schaefer who'd been involved in the Guatemalan search for pfaffia. He guessed that Elaine had received plant material through Schaefer for her pfaffadine extraction work. This brought to mind his own problem with pfaffadine. He was intensely interested in Elaine's progress, and actually hoped she'd made none. If she was able to extract enough natural pfaffadine for NCI studies, Jensen would probably send her stuff along with his phony pfaff. This was a problem, or at least it was a problem if Elaine's stuff proved active in the anti-cancer screening test and his phony stuff didn't. If they both flopped, no problem, because all of the NCI interest in pfaffadine would evaporate. But the prospect of NCI figuring out that his stuff was phony frightened him. It would mean the end of his career - - science has zero toleration for fraud.

Will had spent the whole week in the lab, writing, or at least organizing to write. Jensen had stopped in on Wednesday, the day Gina had left town with her father, and told Will he'd like him to submit an abstract of his work on the pfaffadine synthesis to the American Chemical Society, in preparation for an oral presentation at the next national meeting, in Atlantic City in September. He also told Will he wanted to write up a short communication of his work for submission to a journal, maybe *Drug Chemistry*. Will couldn't disagree with these requests and told Jensen he'd get to it. Jensen also mentioned that he was going to Bethesda in two weeks, and that he wanted to carry Will's synthetic pfaffadine with him. He patted Will on the back, and smiled approvingly. "We also need to talk about getting you a position for the fall. I'm ready to help."

None of this was welcome news for Will, but he should have known it was coming. He'd dug a deep hole for himself, and he didn't see any way out. Again, if the stuff failed at NCI, pfaffadine would go down in the annals of chemistry as just another interesting natural compound. Will's synthesis would be remembered as an achievement in its own right, and would be enough to get him a name in the field. His so-called "synthesis" - - only he would know there was no such thing.

Surely his fake pfaff would fail the NCI test; it was, after all, just a simple synthetic compound with no functionality expected. It was the prospect that Elaine's work would succeed, that she'd get enough authentic compound for NCI, and that her real pfaff would not fail the anti-cancer screening test. It would then be known that Will's compound was not pfaff. NCI might believe it was just a mistake. Jensen would know the truth.

By Friday morning Will had somehow gotten by these worries and was actually writing. He finished the ACS abstract and put it on Jensen's desk for approval: "The Total Synthesis of Pfaffadine, a Papaverine-Related Alkaloid from *Pfaffia paniculata*." A.M. Jensen and William Getz, Jr., Department of Chemistry. University of California at Berkeley. May 31, 1967.

Elaine was standing by his side, wine glass in hand. Will was smoking and drinking beer, and was mildly startled when she said hello.

"You know Schaefer." It was a statement, not a question.

"Yeah. Remember. He brings pfaffia from Guatemala. I actually didn't meet him face- to-face until a week ago. I went to ask him to get more plant material for my work."

Will had never noticed how long and luscious Elaine's red hair was. He didn't think she was all that pretty, certainly not as pretty as Gina, but he suspected her body was spectacular. She was looking directly at him, smiling, those pale green eyes enticing behind her rimless glasses.

"You've been out .... how's the separation work going? Jensen didn't mention it to me." Will looked away and saw that Schaefer was heading their way.

"I'm just about out. I think I was able to isolate a little from a half kilo of dried leaves. There's a higher concentration in the seeds. What I've got isn't all that pure. I came to see you about the solvent system you used to crystallize your synthetic stuff. You weren't around and I never came back."

The party was getting loud and someone had turned up Schaefer's sound system to maximum volume. There were probably two dozen people squeezed into the small apartment. Schaefer appeared and brushed up against Elaine. "I've had to send out for more refreshments. I never expected so many. You two acquainted?" Schaefer's rough beard was moist with beer and had bits of potato chips scattered through it. "You got a cigarette?" Schaefer begged.

All three lit up out of Will's pack of Winston's. "You're both in chemistry. I knew that. Will's item is one of my students. You know Gina?"

"I met her in your office a week ago, remember?" said Elaine.

Will returned his gaze to Elaine's face, and he carefully scanned it as she chatted with Schaefer. He wondered where she was on her purification system. It sounded as if she'd made progress, but it also seemed she'd not be able to do much more until she was able to acquire more plant material. How long would that take? How much did she have? Maybe what she had wouldn't be enough for NCI. Maybe his own fake stuff would go in, fail the cancer screening test long before Elaine would be able to produce enough natural pfaff. Then Jensen would have no reason to send her material to NCI. He'd have no reason to believe that Will's material was not authentic pfaff and that pfaff had no anti-tumor activity. Will relaxed a bit, took a draw on his cigarette, and spoke.

"Gina's away. She's in Seattle. Went with her father, some family stuff. I'm not sure when she'll be back." He wasn't sure why he mentioned this, but he wanted to get in on the conversation.

Elaine begged off to go to the bathroom. When she was gone, Schaefer turned to Will and asked about Gina.

"Is she okay? Seems to me she's been unusually withdrawn lately. Some of her students actually complained to me the last week of classes that she seemed to be ignoring them. I didn't say anything to her. What ...?"

Will interrupted. "I'm not sure. She's always been a little depressive. Off and on. I've noticed it too. I don't think it's anything unusual. Maybe the trip with her dad will help. She's anxious to get started on her research. She really likes working with you."

"You know I asked her to go to Guatemala with me and Dave Zaretsky and Tom Silva this fall. She didn't seem eager. It's pretty important for her research, if she plans to work for me." Will didn't respond. He had no recollection that Gina had mentioned this trip to him.

He was hoping Elaine would return soon and that Schaefer would find something else to do. Within five minutes he had his wish. "You had enough here? How about going down to Rafael's or someplace else?" It just came out, and Elaine's eyes brightened. "I've only been here a half hour. But it is pretty crowded. Why not? Let's go," she said eagerly.

They made their way out. Preston Schaefer was back on the living room floor and lecturing loudly to a group of apparently infatuated students. Will guessed he didn't see them leave, though they did run into Peter Weiss in the hallway. They exchanged hellos briefly and left. Peter, dressed in his usual all-white costume, noticed that Elaine had put her arm around Will's waist as they descended the stairs to the street.

"My place is across campus, on Piedmont, a couple of blocks up from Telegraph." Elaine offered this invitation as soon as they hit the street. Will hesitated only a few seconds. "Lead the way."

A half hour later they settled into Elaine's sofa, which took up a large part of her studio apartment, and she rolled up a joint for them to share. This and some red wine, pretty bad stuff that improved greatly after a few puffs of the magic weed. "I really like natural products." Elaine teetered, taking a big draw. "That's why I came to work for Jensen."

"You did your degree at Northwestern, right? That's where Jensen came from, maybe fifteen years ago?"

"Right." She drew another puff, then left to put an LP on her stereo. Will wasn't sure what the music was, but it sounded pretty exotic. When Elaine returned to the sofa she let herself fall virtually onto his lap. This led to where they both now wanted to go.

They made love deep into the night and into the early morning hours. Elaine always suspected that Will Getz would be perfect for her in this way. She loved that long, lean look and his deep set eyes. The way his dark blond hair fell to his shoulders. His hands were large, but his fingers were slim and graceful. She noticed that he had some trouble becoming erect, maybe some guilt here, but it was only temporary. Her nakedness fired him up, he was completely taken with her body and the long red hair that swept down her back. They couldn't stop. Lust overtook them both. They reveled in each other's sex and made love several times before they fell asleep, near dawn, in Elaine's small bed.

Will awoke first, late on Sunday morning. He pulled the bed sheet over his body and spent a few moments gazing at Elaine's hair and her naked back. He couldn't help but think of Gina's small body, pretty in a way, but not voluptuous like this one. He also immediately felt guilt. Gina's away four days and I'm already cheating, he thought. Jesus, what a shit I am. I cheat at everything.

Will Getz had had his share of women. His college years at Columbia were in fact rich in sex. No steadies to speak of, and he wasn't, like a lot of guys, just out to get screwed at any opportunity. He was a serious student, put in long hours at study and even held several part time jobs. But an attractive woman who seemed available captured his attention pretty easily. He'd had some hot nights but this one with Elaine seemed special. She stirred a little and gave him a glimpse of her breasts, prettier under the daylight than he had remembered from his first glimpse of them the night before. She had the most seductive eyes he had ever seen.

This was his first act of infidelity toward Gina. He'd not been with another woman since the first time he'd slept with Gina, almost two years ago. What brought this on, and so quickly? He was pretty sure he knew, and it was not just the sex.

Elaine turned toward him. "You're a beautiful man, Will Getz. You smell of sex. I've never smelled so much male sex. You got a cigarette?"

He rose, naked, to fetch his Winston's, and brought the pack back to bed. "I'm not sure how we got here so fast, but that was an incredible night."

"Don't run off. Please, stay awhile." There was a slight pleading in her voice.

"I'm okay. I'm going nowhere soon."

They eventually got at least partially dressed and managed to make some coffee and toast. They made small talk, kissed and caressed each other often, and by midday were deep into sex again, then fell into a quiet time. "I've always had my eye on you, you know." Elaine seemed a little uncertain as she spoke. "But I shouldn't say that. You're not ... you've got a woman in your life. I met her. She seems sweet."

"I'm not sure she's still in my life. I think she's falling away from me."

"You're not being honest. That's not true. You're making excuses."

"No, that's honest. That's why she's gone off to Seattle, to think this through."

Will was lying over Elaine, between her thighs, his head buried in her neck and hair. They were silent for a few moments, he kissed her deeply, and then rolled away to her side.

"What are you saying? You're finished with her?"

"I'm not sure. I'm just saying I think she wants out." He knew he was lying.

"What about you? What are you feeling?"

"It's hard to figure. I've had a lot else on my mind, my research, so I haven't spent much time thinking about her and me."

There was little more to be gained here, Elaine thought, so she changed the subject. "So what is next for you?"

"You know I'm writing up. I've got a finished project. Jensen wants me to present the work at the ACS meeting next September."

"You think you really have synthesized pfaffadine?"

"I know it. I've got more than two grams."

Elaine didn't respond. She turned and stared at Will for several minutes. He continued. "I'll be done by fall. I'm not sure what's next. Maybe a post-doc. I'm thinking of applying for a position at NIH. Or maybe do the reverse of what you've done, a post-doc at Northwestern, where Jensen's got connections. He'll support that."

They dressed and went out for lunch. Elaine asked Will about his past, and as was usual for her, she was able to get him talking with unusual ease. She was good at this, at least with men.

"I took to science real early. By eighth grade I was hooked. I haven't wavered since. My Dad taught biology in high school. He never pushed me in this direction, at least not with a heavy hand. He was great." He paused a few seconds. "My mother skipped out on him. Ran off with some guy. I haven't seen her since I was twelve."

"So you lived with your Dad?"

"Yes. He's still back in Boston, still teaching. I try to get back once a year. He's never remarried. I think he's never even been out with other women. He was really hurt when she ran out." Will's memory of his mother was dim, but the memory of his own feelings of defeat, of failure, when she had vanished from his life, was anything but. Only his recent struggles with the demon chemical had been comparably defeating. He remembered what he, as a young boy, had done to rescue himself from his defeat.

"My family's broken, too," Elaine said softly. Will liked the way she looked at him when she spoke. Her glasses seemed to amplify the sexiness of her pale green eyes. There also flashed through his mind what he knew about her sex life, what everyone seemed to know. He was one on a long list. A slight pang of - - what? - - jealousy shot through him. She was very attractive, her face if not beautiful, was pretty interesting, her body...

"Where did you grow up?"

"I'm from Baltimore, a suburb of Baltimore. My parents split when I was small. I shuffled back and forth between them for years. I don't go home much. Only once, I think, all during graduate school." She reached across the table and ran her hand over his long fingers. He didn't pull away, instead squeezed her hand.

Through lunch they talked on and on, mostly about him. She learned he was by no means one of these "techies" she hated, scientists who cared for nothing but science. She was struck with his devotion to the outdoors, and smiled as he described his passion for the wilderness, his dream of doing some serious mountaineering. Will grew more interesting to her as the afternoon wore on. He showed no sign of wanting to leave, and after lunch they spent several hours walking and lying out on the campus green. Will felt some guilt and couldn't get

Gina entirely out of his mind, but did not have any intention of leaving Elaine anytime too soon.

Back at her apartment, they had sex again, and then laid together into the Sunday dusk. Much later she spoke. "Will, I need to ask you something. I'm hesitant, but I'm worried."

"What are you talking about?" He took up a cigarette and offered her one. She declined.

"I want to ask you something about pfaff."

"Pfaff. Okay. Ask me. You want to purify your stuff, recrystallize it. I used methylene chloride. It works fine. I'll help you."

"That's good. Thanks." She was quiet again, got up, and slipped on her jeans and a tee shirt. Will took in her body as she dressed. It was not easy to....

"I took a few milligrams of your synthetic pfaff. I went to your lab a week ago Friday, looking for you. I took a few milligrams."

Will was still focused on her body, and didn't respond.

"Did you hear what I said?" she asked, as she put on her eyeglasses, returned to the bed, and sat down. Will was propped up against some pillows, ashtray in one hand, cigarette in the other. "I took a few milligrams of your synthetic pfaff. I think it's not what you think it is."

Will was stunned, but didn't respond. He didn't expect anything like this. He wasn't sure what she could have done to find out. "Yeah, it is. I know. I've got plenty of spectroscopic data - - IR, NMR, UV, I've got elemental analysis, I've got melting point. Direct comparisons with Atkinson's original isolate. There's no mistake." He paused, then asked, "Why did you take my stuff without asking? What did you do?" He showed some anger, he was even trembling a little, and put out his cigarette. Elaine remained calm.

"I wanted to compare it with my isolate. I took a mixed melting point. It was greatly depressed from what it should have been if the two compounds were identical. I then worried that my product wasn't really pfaff. So I took an IR of your stuff, it took only a couple of milligrams. The IR of your synthetic bears no resemblance to pfaffadine. I repeated the IR with my isolate, and it's identical to what's in the literature in Atkinson's original paper. You've made a mistake, Will." Elaine sounded confident. Will moved out of bed and dressed. He sounded perturbed when he finally spoke.

"You've screwed up. I don't know what you did, but you fucked up or are trying to jerk me around."

"I'm sure of what I did, Will. I'm not trying to screw you. This has been worrying the hell out of me for the last week. I'm just trying to help. I really like you, I admire you, but there's some mistake here."

"You've screwed up somewhere."

"Come to my lab tomorrow. I'll show you what I did."

Will persisted. "You took the wrong stuff."

"No. I took it right from the vial labeled "Synthetic Pfaffadine." It was on your desk. I didn't make a mistake. You did. I'll help you figure it out. You can't send that material, whatever it is, to NCI."

Will paced the room, but remained silent. He felt his heart pounding in his chest. He didn't know what to do or say. Elaine couldn't be bullshitted, he knew that. There didn't seem any way out. He thought she might believe that he'd just made an error, put his product in the wrong vial or mislabeled it. No, she couldn't be fooled about that. Now he'd have to turn over to her what he claimed was the "real" stuff. She would expect him to do that if he continued to claim she had made an error. She would ask to check his stuff again if he argued she had gotten it wrong. Why had he left his vial out on his desk? Incredibly stupid!

"Why didn't you ask me for it?" He seemed calmer now.

"I'm sorry. I didn't think you'd mind. Please, Will, tell me what's going on, there's a mistake here somewhere."

Will started to leave, Elaine begged him not to go, to stay and talk ... This was no way to end such a wonderful day ... I'm sorry I brought this up now ... I was going to do it tomorrow ... I have been worried ... don't go Will.

He hesitated a little, then turned to embrace Elaine. "I'm going. I need to go. We'll talk about it tomorrow. I promise. This was one of the most perfect days of my life. I'll talk with you tomorrow. Here. Can I come here?"

Elaine returned his hug. "I have to see Jensen first thing tomorrow. I'll see you here about noon, okay?" She smiled and then kissed him.

It was only a ten minute walk from Elaine's place to his apartment. It was about ten on Sunday evening when Will Getz opened the door to the darkness of the rooms he shared with Gina. He didn't bother to answer the ringing phone and prepared for bed with thoughts of Elaine Callahan, her beautiful body, and the knowledge she carried in her mind of Will Getz's big lie.

CHAPTER 7

Will was out running, at dawn, into the Berkeley hills. He climbed slowly, trying to focus entirely on his movement and his breathing. He wore no shirt, just skimpy running shorts and shoes, so that he could maximize his body's contact with the cool, sweet breezes of the hills. A run up these hills was rough and painful, but at its end it brought a physical pleasure that was not unlike that brought by sex. It also brought a sense of mental peace and clarity, and on this early Monday morning, on the day he was to resume his discussions with Elaine, there was nothing he needed more. Elaine knew the truth, or at least an important part of it. She knew his little vial of synthetic pfaffadine contained a completely different substance. What she didn't know for sure was why.

Will rested at the top of his climb, in a small park on Canyon Road. The sun was bright and directly in his vision as he faced east, toward California's great central valleys. Behind and below him was the campus of the state's top university, and beyond it, across San Francisco Bay, lay the great city, whose tallest buildings were just now catching the first rays of the morning sun. Will's back was toward the campus; he turned his back on this great center of learning and discovery, a place he'd worked hard, very hard, to get into. The enormous frustration brought by his failures in the laboratory had turned him upside down, had brought out some inner weakness that had simply eradicated the kind of person he thought he had become.

He had no explanation, except the possibility that he was, at heart, dishonest. With his father's help, he had broken with the church of his youth, and he had by the time he reached college discovered the dishonesty and lies that underlay all religious belief, and he had thrown over those lies in favor of the rational, objective truths of science. He had been courageous enough to accept the tentative truths that science, with a painstaking commitment to honesty, could reveal in favor of the absolute, invariable but baseless dogmas of religion. The more modest understanding of the world and of human life that science could offer was far preferable to the grand but phony wisdom offered by those who claimed to possess special, revealed knowledge.

But now, somehow, Will Getz had sinned against science. He could excuse his disloyalty to his church and his hatred of religion, because they were directed against false beliefs. He could see no way to excuse his sin against science. Now someone had discovered his error and that someone was damn smart, smart enough to guess what he had done.

Will started to stroll down the Berkeley hills to his home, to prepare to return to Elaine's place. His whole situation had become complicated by the fact that he'd slept with her. Not just slept. They had had incredibly passionate sex. There was something about Elaine Callahan that excited him immensely, and he sensed the feeling was mutual. In fact, he feared it might be more than sex on her side, that she might already be hung up on him.

This could complicate matters more. And until he could work out something with her about his research situation, he knew he'd have to stay pretty close to Elaine. He couldn't afford just to drop her - - who knows what she'd do then? He was in one fucking difficult situation, a quagmire of his own making. There was no way he could lie to her about what he'd done. She couldn't be fooled. Would she go to Jensen? Not likely. But how, he asked himself, does my shit affect her own work? I send my phony crap to NCI. They test it. It's useless. She's got authentic pfaff and a novel way to isolate it, I guess. I don't know if she'll have enough in the near future to send to NCI, but the failure of my stuff will mean there's no reason for her to continue. She's got other products to work on. Her target is to perfect the isolation technique, she doesn't need to use pfaffadine; there are plenty of other natural products to work on. That's all true, but how does she just drop her concern over me? He didn't know.

Will hadn't made any progress in his thinking by the time he got to Elaine's apartment at about noon, although he'd had additional concerns about how he was going to deal with Gina when she returned from Seattle. First things first, though, Elaine first.

Elaine had arrived just a few moments before Will, back from a meeting with Jensen. She smiled when Will entered and moved to embrace him. He returned the embrace, but only weakly, and then backed away to light a cigarette. He dropped to her sofa and a brief memory of her naked body kneeling before him at this very spot flashed in his mind. Elaine did not sit beside him, but took a seat opposite him, at a table. She continued to smile, but said nothing. Finally, after a few moments, she asked if he wanted some coffee. He nodded and she got up to make him a cup of instant.

She returned with the coffee a few moments later and placed it on the table in front of him. She then knelt on the floor and spoke. "I loved my time with you, all of it."

He didn't expect this, at least not at first. He took up another cigarette, and began sipping the coffee. Then it just came out.

"I deliberately faked my research. I know the stuff's not pfaff. It's just a compound I'd made a year ago as a possible starting material for an alternative synthesis. But all the spectra I have, the NMR, the IR, the UV, and the elemental analysis are real. I made pfaff last January. I completed the synthesis. I had no question about it. Then I needed to repeat the last step, from pre-pfaff, the immediate precursor compound. My first try yielded less than half-a-gram, and I used it all up in testing it out. I went back and tried it again with two grams of pre-pfaff. I couldn't repeat it. The last step's a ring cyclization that

Jensen had worked out with other compounds. I made it work once, I couldn't do it again. I tried again, and used up more pre- pfaff. No luck. Again. No luck. My pre-pfaff is all gone. I'd have to go back and make some more pre-pfaff. That's an eleven-step, and very tedious process, probably five or six months. It's also likely I'll fail again to convert it to pfaff. I'm sure I got it the first time. I'm positive, it wasn't a spurious result. But there must have been some factor in the reaction conditions that was critical to success, and I don't know what, or why it was missing my next three tries. So I cheated. You can look at all the spectra I got on the first batch if you don't believe me when I say I got it. I got pfaff on my first try."

Elaine just stared, first directly at Will, then down to the floor. He then sat back in the sofa, seemingly relaxed. He just looked at Elaine and waited for her reaction. She got up from the floor and returned to her seat by the table. It was time for her to smoke.

"Will, I guessed something like that was going on, but I couldn't believe it of you. I've heard you talk about your work, your love of this science, everyone on the fourth floor knows you're Jensen's brightest. Jensen adores you. What you've told me isn't consistent with anything I or anyone else knows about you." She looked anguished.

"Apparently, I'm not what I've appeared to be. Even to myself." He paused, then spoke as he looked away from Elaine. "What will you do? Now that you know. What will you do?"

"Will, you've got to do the right thing here. You've got to go to Jensen and tell him you've made a mistake. You can't do this to yourself. You'll ruin yourself."

"I can't do that. I've been through the results thoroughly with Jensen, twice. There's no way I can make this seem like a mistake."

"Then tell him the truth. Tell him what and why, just like you told me. He's going to carry your pfaff, your fake pfaff, to NCI next week, or the week after. What then?"

"It'll just fail the NCI anti-cancer screen. That'll be the end of it."

"Will, you've lost it ...what are you thinking? ...NCI ... aren't they going to check your stuff, chemically, to see that it's real?"

"I don't think so. Jensen will tell them its authentic, he'll go over the spectra and my other results with them. They'll just put it into solution and do their anti-tumor assays."

Elaine lit another cigarette, and turned away. She seemed to be in tears, or at least her eyes were moist. She was highly distressed. Will just sat. His body was limp, his mind a blank. He seemed emotionless, lost in the moral swamp he'd created for himself, helpless to get out. Was he looking for help from Elaine?

"What do you think I should do?" she asked quietly. "Will, I just spent two glorious days with you, you've been in my mind continually, I don't want to hurt you, just the opposite. Let me help you. I'm not going to go to Jensen. I don't want to do that."

Will felt a small measure of relief when she said that. He had an urge to go to her, but held back.

"I thought of never raising this stuff with you, but I didn't see how I could live with it. Now I'm sorry I brought it up. I should have just buried it. I thought for a while that you'd simply made a mistake, and that I should just drop the whole thing. I wish I had." With this Elaine went to him and sat beside him on the sofa. She took his hands in hers, those graceful, strong fingers that had touched her so deeply. They sat in silence for a very long time.

"What about us?" Elaine spoke at last, in a whisper.

"I don't know. I'm really ..." Will stopped, unsure that he should say what he was thinking, or rather feeling. There was another long silence. "Gina's still away, will be for at least another few days, until Thursday. I don't know where her head will be when she gets back." He paused. "I like being here, just like this."

Elaine smiled and kissed his cheek, then put her arm over his shoulder. She thought back to the meeting she'd had this morning with Jensen. Preston Schaefer had been there, to tell them that his associate in Guatemala, Perea, could easily get them several kilos of dried pfaffia material, probably by the end of summer. It was no problem. She saw then that she'd easily be able to produce 20-30 grams, maybe more, of authentic, natural pfaffadine by mid-October, assuming she could repeat her extraction and isolation procedure. If pfaff turned out to be effective in the anti-cancer screen, they'd turn to her technique to isolate the natural stuff for further evaluation; this would be far more efficient than any lab synthesis. The prospect excited her, not only because of her contribution to a possible cancer treatment, but because her novel isolation system would get wide recognition, and a lot more attention and use. She'd even talked to Jensen about getting some patent protection for it; she'd only need to prove it was novel, a new invention - - which it was - - and that it had utility. She was, with her pfaffadine isolation, well on the way to proving this.

She'd left Jensen's office with Preston Schaefer. He immediately began asking why she'd not called him; he'd tried to reach her several times since their night together, had left notes in her mailbox. She'd left his party so soon after her arrival he'd not had a chance to talk to her alone. Was she interested in spending more time with him? Hadn't she had a great time with him? He'd pursued these themes all the way across campus. Elaine hadn't responded until, as they parted, she promised she'd meet him for dinner at Chico's on Tuesday evening. Schaefer was satisfied with this, and left with a large grin under his tangled beard. She wanted no more of Preston Schaefer, but she did like him and didn't want to entirely break their relationship. She knew well how guys who wanted to screw her took to the "just friends" approach. Shit, she'd have to find some other way with a guy like Preston Schaefer. The guy she really wanted was here, close to her, but lost in this terrible trap he'd built for himself.

"Will you stay with me tonight? I'll cook something for us. We'll just watch TV or something. Not even go out. Stay with me, Will. I want to help you out of this. I put you into it, in a way. There was no reason for me to let on about what I knew. Now I've put you in a corner. We'll work together on a way out. Stay. Will you?"

Will said nothing at first, felt an urge to leave, felt that if he just walked away she'd do nothing, just cover it up. But he still wasn't sure. Maybe she'd react badly. Revenge. No, she didn't seem the type.

"Okay, I'll stay. I'm not hungry. Let's just sit, maybe take a walk later."

In the late afternoon they went out and at Will's suggestion decided to walk up the hills of Berkeley. It occurred to Will that no one who knew them was likely to see them if they took this route; except for David and Kay none of their friends lived up in the hills. Will didn't yet want to have to deal with the Gina problem, and so preferred to keep Elaine a secret for the time being.

After about an hour of mostly silent walking, they arrived at the same Canyon Road park where Will had rested after his morning run. He told Elaine about it, and she remarked that she'd guessed he was a runner, or some kind of athlete. His body was really beautiful.

"I can return that compliment, and double it," said Will, the first smile of the whole day on his face. "You have truly one of the loveliest bodies I've ever seen. No bullshit."

"And you've seen ... how many?"

"A few. Not as many as you, I'm guessing."

"Where did *that* come from?" she responded quickly.

"I don't know. Stories. It's no secret you're a free spirit sexually, as they say."

"Oh? Just what have you heard?"

"Let's talk about something else. Tell me a little more about yourself. How'd you get into chemistry?"

"I'm not sure. Probably my high school chemistry teacher got me excited about it. I went to a Friends school, a Quaker school, in Baltimore. By the time I got to college at Penn I knew exactly what I wanted. I was the only female chemistry major in my college class, and one of only three in the doctoral program at Northwestern. Women don't go into science, but that's starting to change."

Will asked Elaine to tell her more about her broken family. "My father cheated on my mother, all the time I think. I hated him. I once caught him screwing some young thing right in the living room of our home. I'd come home early from school. I also didn't care much for my mother. She was really weak, scared of life. I haven't been home since my first year of graduate school."

She abruptly changed the subject.

"I really wanted to get into medicinal chemistry, right into some major drug company. Jensen's got connections at several. That's where the most interesting organic chemistry's going on. My isolation technology was not the reason I came here to work with Jensen. It was kind of an accident, how I discovered it. But it really looks good, so I'm going to pursue it. I'd hoped pfaff isolation would continue to be my major effort. If your stuff goes to NCI and fails the screen, Jensen'll probably ask me to switch to some other product. But maybe not, it's still useful to demonstrate the value of my isolation technique."

They talked some more about their experiences in the lab and of their respect for Alden Jensen, but no more about Will's problem. They returned late to Elaine's apartment, ate peanut butter and jelly sandwiches, and went to bed. They lay close, naked, but neither initiated any sexual activity. Elaine kissed Will lovingly, ran her hands over his chest and belly, and then the two fell off into sleep. In the middle of the night Will awoke, startled by something in a dream which vanished quickly. A woman, unrecognizable. He sat up in the bed and immediately turned to view Elaine's lovely body, deep in sleep, next to him. He smoked, and thought a while about Gina. He wasn't sure how he felt about her now. He'd gone through many months of intimacy with her, and he knew that she was probably still drawn to him. Will was entranced by her quiet beauty, a beauty that was in part physical but that mostly arose out of her sensibilities. She had not been very experienced when he met her, because of the enduring influence of her Catholicism, and he knew that part of her appeal to him lay in her sexual naivete. He loved to look at her, her dark oval face was quite beautiful. Her body was small, not voluptuous like Elaine's, but it seemed perfect for the kind of person Gina was.

Gina's shyness, in some way, also appealed to Will. He realized that she often slipped into moods of mild depression, that her sometimes long periods of relative silence were not just periods of excessive shyness. Will knew that her mother's death had been devastating in its effect on her, and he guessed the despondency he perceived had its origin in that dreadful event. But he wasn't sure, and it was something they never talked about.

Will glanced at Elaine as she turned under the sheets in a way that revealed her breasts.

Not once had he experienced with Gina the pure physical lust that he'd felt with Elaine. Gina was not, for some reason, very physical in her lovemaking, and seemed to become less so as their time together passed. But, he thought, maybe her unresponsiveness was nothing more than a natural reaction to his emotional paralysis.

Will put out his cigarette, pulled the sheet up over Elaine and himself and tried to sleep. He also tried to put into words how he now felt about Gina, but couldn't. He knew something significant had been lost. Maybe it was due to his own failings. Maybe he now felt that he did not deserve someone with Gina's qualities. She would be completely shocked if she were ever to learn that he was a cheat, probably more shocked by his infidelity to science than by his sexual infidelity to her. That's a laugh. Who was he kidding? He drifted into an uneasy sleep.

At dawn Elaine awoke first. She slipped the sheets away from Will's body, and began to caress it. She immediately felt the need to have him inside of her, she knew she would quickly be ready to receive him, she moved to make him ready and then she made long deep love to him. Will could think of nothing else for the rest of the morning.

That evening Elaine met Preston Schaefer, as promised, for dinner at Chico's. He had been there for quite some time before she arrived. He actually rose to greet her, and noticed that she didn't appear to be enthusiastic about seeing him. She ordered a beer and the two sipped and made small talk for a few minutes. Schaefer finally got to the subject.

"So, I thought we'd really hit it off weekend before last. I've been wanting to see more of you. You fascinate me. You're a strong person. I like that in a woman.

"It was fun, Preston, but it was just that. You know that. We hit it off for a few hours, and got to like each other. But I'm not into steady things. I don't want to start anything now. I like you, you're really interesting, I'd like to keep a friendship, but I'm really not interested in anything more than that."

"Jesus, I couldn't have guessed that after our time together. That's your mode of operation, a quick fuck when you feel like it, then go on?"

"That's pretty crude, Preston. I don't think of these things in that way."

"A liberated female. Wow! An authentic one. I've never met an authentic one. The ones I know who say they're liberated, they go to bed with you and then expect you'll be around. It's like they are still looking for a return for the favor. Not Elaine, you're different. Is that right?"

"Right. I'm not looking for anything in return. But I don't want to make this a big problem, a cause of hostility. I hope you're not the angry or vengeful type." Elaine thought of Will still back at her apartment, probably worried sick, in agony, and here she was having to deal with this nuisance. That's unfair. Schaefer's not that, but she just didn't have time for this now.

Schaefer looked puzzled, as if he didn't know how to react. He was usually in the position that Elaine was now in. He recognized that anger or pleading or argument would go nowhere. He thought he'd just drop the issue and hope she might be of a different mind sometime soon. But he didn't stay with this thought.

"You left my party early. You stayed about 15 minutes. Someone told me he saw you leave with Will Getz."

Elaine paused, then responded. "I did. We thought it was too crowded. We went and had a beer. What's that got to do with anything?"

"Just thought you two might have something going. Maybe that's the reason for your rejection of me."

"Well, we don't. And your so-called rejection isn't that at all. I just don't want to carry on in anything more than a casual friendship mode. My work is what occupies me, not Will Getz or anyone else." He thought she was protesting too much, but there was nothing more he could say on this topic. He didn't want to be a pest. She did seem uncomfortable when he mentioned Will.

They parted with a handshake and a promise from him that he'd keep after his friend, Perea, in Guatemala City, to acquire the plant material she needed, and he also mentioned that Perea was talking to a botanist he knew about how to collect seeds or shoots that might be used for cultivating the plant. He also told her she'd be invited to a small dinner he was having in a couple of weeks. She said she'd try to come, then turned and hurried home.

Will was completely stoned when she got back. He'd gone back to his place and picked up his stash. He was really whacked, and also ready for sex. Their night was as passionate as their first night together, maybe even more so for Elaine, who truly could not seem to get enough of Will Getz.

They stayed together all week. Will returned to his apartment to get some clothes and do some laundry. On Wednesday evening he was there when Gina called to tell him she'd be back in a week, on June 15th, a week from Thursday. They didn't talk much, but he was relieved to learn he'd have more time to figure out how to deal with her than he thought he'd have. In his present situation, locked up with Elaine, tied both to her sexual power and the power she had to destroy him, there was going to be no easy way to deal with Gina.

It was on Friday evening that Elaine revealed to him the plan she had contrived to help him. They'd taken another walk into the Berkeley hills to the park and as soon as they sat on the park's only bench, she started.

"Will, I have a way to help you. I think it's foolproof. I believe you when you say you were successful the first time you tried to convert pre-pfaff to pfaff. If you hadn't been, you probably wouldn't have wasted all of the pre-pfaff in the later tries that failed. I understand your frustration. Here's what I want to do. I have more than two grams of pfaff isolated using my system. It's not pure enough for the NCI screen, but I think it only needs to be recrystallized with the right solvent system. You can help me do that. I'll get about two grams of pure stuff. You can have most of it. Give it to Jensen to take to NCI. Use it as if it's the pfaff you synthesized. That way, when NCI does its chemical identification, which I'm sure they will, there'll be no problem. I should never have brought this matter up to you. I put you in a box. Now I'll help you out. I'll have tons more plant material by September. I'll be able to turn out many grams of pfaff in a matter of a few weeks. I'm that confident in my isolation system. If the anti-cancer screening test is successful at NCI, and more pfaff is needed for further evaluation, NCI will turn to Jensen and Jensen will turn to me, not you. The synthetic path is too inefficient. You'll never have to repeat the synthesis, and no one else will either. It'll just go into the literature as a great piece of synthetic chemistry. And my isolation system will become famous. That's what I'm looking for, along with a way to keep you ... I mean to help you."

Will was stunned. At first he wasn't sure he'd heard right, but as she talked - - slowly, deliberately, as if the whole speech had been carefully planned, except maybe that last sentence - - he came to understand clearly what she was offering. A truly foolproof way out.

He wanted to yell out - - yes, yes, yes, that'll work, Elaine, that'll work, it's perfect - - but he held back. She was proposing to participate in his fraud. She was willing to join him in his reckless action, and to put her own career in jeopardy. She ...he could not ask her to do this. Impossible. He would have to be an even bigger shit than he thought he was to allow Elaine to bring herself into this mess. He noticed that she was staring directly into his eyes, looking for his response. Her eyes were very seductive.

"Elaine. Jesus, no. That's ridiculous. I can't accept ... I can't believe you would do that for me. Why on earth would you do that for me? No, no way. I'm in this alone, I'm not bringing anyone else along on my descent into hell."

"But I brought myself along. I'm the one who pried. I had no business taking a sample of your stuff. I should have just shut up about it. I'm doing this because I believe you when you said you had been successful the first try. I believe that. I'm also doing this because you're too good to ..."

"Bullshit. I'm not too good for anything. I'm not deserving of anything like this. I deserve to be discovered, to be driven out of the priesthood, but I'm a coward and I'll try anything to keep from being discovered. Anything except pulling you into it."

"I'm already in. I want to be. I've thought about this night and day since Monday. You help me recrystallize my pfaff. We can go to the lab Sunday. Jensen won't be around, and if we go early in the morning no one else will either. You said you had a good recrystallization system."

"Yes, I used it with my first batch, I recrystallized the three-tenths gram I had, easily. Methylene chloride's the key. I picked it up from Atkinson's paper on the chemical structure of pfaff. I'll help you purify, but I'm not going to take your stuff. Besides, why hasn't Jensen suggested that your material go into NCI along with mine? What if he asks? You won't have enough left for another NCI test." Was he starting? Was he thinking seriously about her proposal? He couldn't do this.

"I never told Jensen exactly how much pfaff I'd isolated, or how pure it was. I'll just tell him I don't have enough for NCI, if he asks, which he won't. Or I could say I lost half when I recrystallized. That's believable. Besides, he doesn't want to waste the compound. There's no need to test the same stuff twice. He's totally convinced yours is real and real pure. He also knows I've got lots more plant material coming and that I can turn out large amounts with my system if NCI needs it in the future."

They walked slowly down the hills, back to Elaine's apartment, the great Berkeley campus spread below them in the late spring dusk, the long rays of the setting sun beaming through San Francisco to the west, across the great bay, and coming to rest on this great East Bay university. Will had not agreed to Elaine's plan, but Elaine knew he would. She had found a way to save him, at very little risk to her. She also knew it was bound to bring them closer to each other, this secret that she was sure could not now be discovered by anyone. Held between just the two of them forever.

It took them about six hours on Sunday to recrystallize Elaine's sample of natural pfaffadine. They produced nearly two grams of highly purified compound, sufficient for the NCI screening test. Without talking about it, they both knew by then that this substance would go into the vial labelled as "Synthetic Pfaffadine," and that Will would pass it off as the product of his own research. On the walk back to Elaine's apartment late Sunday afternoon Will turned his thoughts to his problem with Gina. She'd be back Thursday. He decided to leave her a note, telling her it was time to separate, that he was sure she'd also reached that conclusion. They would have rent due through their leasing period which ended on the last day of August. He would leave her his share of three months' rent.

Elaine had said he could move in with her, she'd love it. He knew he had to be in Elaine's life now. It was a little cruel to Gina, but there was no choice, no better way. Of course his note to Gina did not explain where he was going or the real reason for his departure.

That Sunday night he and Elaine drank some beer and then went into a night of almost ferocious sex. Will was more aggressive at it than he had ever been. They drowned in each other's lust, lost in each other's sins.

CHAPTER 8

During the first week of September, Atlantic City was invaded by a horde of chemists, more than 6,000 of them, for the 1967 meeting of the American Chemical Society. They came from universities and colleges all over America and many came from Europe and a few from Asia. They came from the laboratories of pharmaceutical and chemical companies. They came from government research laboratories. They came together to share knowledge and to discuss the intricacies of their science. They talked about atoms and their properties, and about how they came together in seemingly endless variety to create molecules. Chemical reactions were at the heart of most of the work described, the factors that influenced them, their products, and how they could be manipulated to achieve desired results. Chemical science filled that gap between physics and biology, and was expected by many ultimately to provide the bridge between the two.

Practical applications also occupied many of those present - - new drugs, new materials for industrial and consumer uses, fibers, plastics, on and on the list went. Most of the scientists were there because they loved the subject, wanted to learn about its progress, wanted to contribute somewhere, and wanted to gain the respect of their colleagues.

A small number had already earned that respect. The big names in the field, when they lectured, drew huge audiences. Many notables were there to review whole fields of work, not to present new results, and up-and-coming scientists flocked to hear these grand syntheses of knowledge. There were also hundreds of sessions on special topics, convened in hotel meeting rooms up and down the Boardwalk, where scientists presented the latest research results, where the work of a year or two had to be summarized in 15 minutes and on a half-dozen slides. Every conclusion that seemed a bit extreme, that seemed to go beyond the data presented, was almost certain to be challenged. Most presentations offered little in the way of novel results, but there were always a few that woke up the audience, that caused some excitement, that seemed truly unexpected or original. Occasionally, very occasionally, came a "break through," a finding that really shook up thinking. This was the way all of science crept into the future - - tiny steps, an occasional small jump forward, a rare leap, and then synthesis of a whole field by those whose experience gave them a perspective that most did not have. Revolution? Once every generation, at best.

Will Getz was the last speaker of the morning in his assigned session on Medicinal Chemistry. He'd sat since nine a.m., with Elaine at his side, listening to a string of fairly interesting presentations on the isolation, identification, and laboratory synthesis of molecules of astonishing complexity and variety that were, for one reason or another, thought to have some potential for use as pharmaceutical agents. The session was fairly well attended, with maybe 50 scientists in the audience. Many were from pharmaceutical companies, looking for new opportunities. Most of the others were from academic institutions, who were there because they were working on similar projects and were interested in advances in their disciplines, and in who the competition was.

Will nervously took to the podium at his assigned time of 11:45 a.m. This was his first presentation at a national scientific meeting. He'd given several talks at seminars back at Berkeley, and felt he did a decent job at this sort of thing. He'd prepared eight slides that demonstrated the total synthesis of pfaffadine. The first described the origin of knowledge about the compound and the second its chemical structure, with a reference to Joel Atkinson of UCLA, who had worked out the arrangement of atoms in this relatively complex molecule. Getz's third and fourth slides focused on Alden Jensen's earlier work on structurally similar molecules and on how that work figured into the design of the synthesis, the sequence of reactions predicted to lead to pfaffadine, that Jensen and Getz had planned. On the last three slides Getz presented the results of his execution of the twelve-step sequence of reactions. Some of the early and simple steps Getz described very briefly, and then slowed down to cover the last few, exceedingly difficult steps. Alden Jensen was in the audience, sitting just behind Elaine. Getz recognized no one else there among the 50 or so present for his talk. As he approached the last slide, with only two minutes left in his allotted time, he suddenly grew anxious. He recalled how difficult it had been for him to prepare this slide, to draw the structures of pre-pfaff and pfaff, and the arrow depicting the conversion of the one to the other. The lie. Or maybe not such a lie, because he was still sure he had actually accomplished this conversion the first time he'd tried it. Now he had to describe it out loud to the professional community whose blessings he sought.

He looked toward Elaine. She was smiling, she knew he was about to lie, she who had, since June, been a party to his lie, she who was also his lover. She smiled. Alden Jensen looked a little anxious, he was no doubt wondering about Will's pause before the climax of his talk.

Will finally got to it, but had to hurry the ending, because the session chair told him he was out of time. No time for questions, Will hoped, and got his hope. He was finished. The Big Lie was out, and it was given an unusually enthusiastic applause. No one present could possibly know that he had just lied about the findings. Elaine and Jensen stood to congratulate Will as he stepped down from the speaker's platform. As the room cleared, Will noticed someone moving toward him from the dark rear of the room. There, smiling and advancing slowly, was his father William, looking shy, as always, apparently waiting for Jensen and Elaine to leave.

Will immediately excused himself and walked over to his father, who reached out and embraced his son warmly. Elaine guessed who the tall stranger was and was struck by the fact that the man and his son were exactly the same height. The father, William Senior, was much slimmer and it was obvious that Will must have inherited his other features, his good looks, from his long departed mother. Will urged his father toward Jensen and Elaine and as they approached Will said, "Professor Jensen, this is my dad, down from Boston. I wasn't sure he was coming, and I never even noticed him in the audience. Also, Dad, meet Elaine, Dr. Elaine Callahan, a post-doc in our laboratory who's also working on pfaffadine."

William Senior just smiled, shook hands, and at first didn't say a word. They decided to find some lunch at the hotel's coffee shop.

"My dad's a biology teacher, at a high school in Brookline. Mostly sophomores and some seniors, I think." William Senior nodded as he sipped his coffee. He'd ordered only a tuna salad sandwich and just nibbled at it. He finally spoke, "I didn't understand much of the talk, but I'm thrilled I was able to come down. They didn't even charge me a registration fee when I said I was a high school teacher, here just for the one talk. I need to go soon. I drove down yesterday after school and didn't get in 'til nearly one a.m. It's about 8 hours by car, plus I got a little lost. I found someone to handle classes today, but I need to be back for tomorrow. I guess your work's exciting, huh ... is it really an anti-cancer drug?" He nibbled some more at his sandwich.

Alden Jensen chimed in with, "We don't know for sure, yet. It's been undergoing some tests at the NIH. I'm meeting this evening in Bethesda with the people who've been testing it, to get the initial results. Even if it doesn't pass muster as a drug, I can still tell you, Will's done a great piece of work. He's really good. He can conceptualize a solution and then work it out in the lab. He'll go places. I just wish he'd finish writing up his thesis. He's been at it since June,

but I don't see much progress. Will, this could have been all written up
by now. What's holding you back? You should be going through your
oral defense as soon as possible, and on to some post-doc work. I've
told you I can arrange a good spot for you at NIH, in Virgil Goode's
lab. You'd love it, and it's really exciting work he's doing, on a whole
range of biologically active natural products. You could be there the
first of 1968, if you'd just finish up!"

"And you'll be back on the East coast," his dad broke in. "I
miss seeing you more often."

Elaine could see how attached the father was to his son, and,
though Will spoke of him only rarely, she knew that the son loved the
father. She also knew that, though he hadn't seen her for many years,
Will still resented deeply his mother and what she had done to William.
Will never mentioned how his mother's departure might have hurt
himself. She compared her own family history to Will's. When her
parents split she ended up hating them both, and she had little interest
in reattaching herself to either of them. The fact was that she'd
probably lost that attachment long before her parents split up. With
Will, the break-up brought him closer to William.

Jensen departed first, to prepare to leave for Bethesda. Will
fervently hoped that pfaff had failed in the NCI screening tests, and
that the compound would never he heard of again. He knew he'd have
to get his thesis written and a complete paper ready for submission to a
journal for publication. He had worked off and on over the summer
but the writing was not going well, and he knew why. Elaine, into
whose life and apartment he had moved in June, had encouraged him
to complete his work, had even offered to help. (He'd rejected her
offer with a half-caustic remark that she'd already helped him enough.
She hadn't liked that.)

Will's dad left after lunch, with an invitation for Will to come
visit, perhaps at Thanksgiving, and with the hope that he'd complete
his Ph.D. and move back East. William asked nothing about Will's
personal life, although it was apparent that he wanted to learn more

about Elaine and about Gina. Will's letters used to mention Gina and William had always wanted to meet her. With Elaine present he was inhibited from asking about her. He made a mental note to write to Will about the matter.

Later that afternoon Will and Elaine went to the beach. They had planned to stay for some sessions on Wednesday, and then to fly back to San Francisco. With Will's talk past, the stress he was feeling dissipated and they camped out with a six-pack, some cigarettes, and a couple of cheap paperbacks. Will loved the way Elaine looked in her two-piece, and even admired the fact that she exhibited no inhibitions about her fabulous body. He still wasn't really sure how he felt about her. No question about their physical relationship, it remained intense and there was a powerful attraction between them, chemical, no doubt. She was smart as hell, much more so than he'd imagined, and there was also a sharpness about her that sometimes drew him closer, but which also distressed him. She was ambitious and maybe even domineering. She'd sucked him further into his lie, but at the same time had helped him make the fraud virtually undiscoverable. She had become a party to it herself. She couldn't reveal what she knew without implicating herself. Even so, he knew that if he broke from her, as long as she still wanted him - - and there was no sign that she wanted any other man - - his control over her and the knowledge she possessed would be diminished, completely lost even. This thought, which he'd had many times since his fall into Elaine's life, still caused him anguish.

He tried to read but couldn't. Gina was now in his mind. His cowardly note to her to end a nearly two-year relationship flashed in his mind. He lit up, and opened a second beer. What a shit he was. Gina had never tried to contact him. This was just like her. She'd have presumed that if he wanted out, that settled things, and there was no need to talk about it. He suspected that, at some level, he still loved her, or was at least attached to her the way he had been early in their relationship. The kind of feeling he once had for Gina he did not have for Elaine, nothing like it. It seemed, he'd discovered over the past year, that he must need something different in a woman. Why, he couldn't say. Maybe his loss in self-confidence, self-worth even, over his research failures, and the compounding effect of the terrible way he had chosen to deal with those failures, had something to do with his loss of feeling for the kind of woman Gina was ... or is. He'd become the kind of man who wants the kind of woman Elaine Callahan is. There's a lot to desire in the strengths Elaine has.

"Jensen's really pissed you haven't written up. I can tell he's not pleased. What is it, Will? You say you go to the library every day. Maybe you don't. It's been nearly three months. I've seen your writing, maybe sixty pages, just the literature background." Elaine was lying on her side, looking up from the book she'd spread open on the beach blanket. Something by Vonnegut.

"It's just hard. I'll get it."

"You don't find writing that hard. Something else is going on. It's not hard to guess."

Will looked away, toward the ocean. The sun had started to fall behind the monstrous old hotels that dominated the landscape behind the Atlantic City boardwalk. A slight chill settled on the beach and many started to pack up and leave.

"Will. Speak to me. I'm not, like, just some kind of physical object in your life. Or am I?"

That comment startled him a bit. He started immediately to object, but then held himself back. Instead he said, "This talk I just gave will make it easier for me to write. I've said it all out loud. No need to hold back now."

"You can be out of Berkeley by the end of the year. Take the post-doc at NIH. Jensen says it'll be easy. There's lots of positions there now. I'll apply and I can quit my post-doc by next March. I'll join you. D.C. is a pretty good place. We'll do well at NIH, it's top-notch."

"What about pfaff? What if NCI wants more?" Will knew that Elaine wanted to be with him, maybe permanently. He wasn't sure, but he couldn't say no. Besides ....

"My way. My isolation system works, and it'll be easier to get pfaff that way than through synthesis. You're not on the spot." She ran her hand over his shoulder and then down to his waist. Her knee moved up to brush against his bathing suit. He could feel the sex in him beginning to respond.

"What about the plant material? You still don't have it from Schaefer, from his buddy in Guatemala."

"I'll call him as soon as we get back to see where it is. He said it was no problem. I can then isolate plenty of pfaff."

"I hope it doesn't work, that it fails the anti-tumor test."

Elaine scowled, and moved away from Will. She didn't understand why he seemed so scared by all this. Their plan was foolproof. They were together in this. Pfaff would be available, if necessary, from her isolation system. They hadn't played by the rules, sure, but there were much bigger things at stake --their careers. Together, they'd go places. She already had a name for her isolation system, and when she would finally publish it, she would rise to the heights. Will had made pfaff, the first time, he was sure of it. So where's the problem? His work gets him to Virgil Goode's lab; what a great place to establish his credentials. They'd fly high, together, if he'd just get his ass in gear. And if pfaffadine turned out to be a big deal in the anti-cancer therapy market, all the better. Why is he so anxious for pfaff to vanish? "Will, it's okay. Nothing can go wrong. Just get moving."

No. Nothing can go wrong. Except inside of him. He was no scientist. He'd proved that to himself. How silly of him to want to maintain the facade. Just dump her, go back to Gina. Hah. "It's getting cold. Let's go."

That night, while they were making love in their hotel room, the phone interrupted. It was Alden Jensen. "Will, your stuff was very active in the NCI screen. Very active, comparable to the best compounds they've seen at this early stage. They want more. They want to move on to the next level of testing, and also get some toxicity data, to see what the downside might be. They're very excited. When I get back, next Monday, you and Elaine and I will meet. We're either going to recommend that we get more using Elaine's isolation system, or that the NCI repeat your synthesis in their own labs. If Elaine's system is ready, that'll be a lot faster, probably. This is more reason for getting your work written up. This is great news. See you next Monday, nine o'clock sharp."

CHAPTER 9

Gina had moved into Kay's large group house at the end of August, when the lease on the apartment she'd shared with Will had expired. When Gina had finally let Kay in on her situation, in July, nearly a month after she'd found Will's pathetic note, Kay immediately offered her the room. Gina could barely have afforded to stay on in the apartment on her stipend, and didn't want to anyway, not without Will.

Her reaction to Will's note on the evening of her return from Seattle had surprised her. Anger. Just plain anger. This was so unlike her, but something in her seemed to have changed during her trip, or rather because of the time she'd spent away from Will. His note was unbelievable. She'd thought it one of the most cowardly acts she had ever seen.

She had spent the next several days trying to understand how the man she had once known and loved had become such a cowardly, dishonest shit. Wanting out of their relationship was one thing, maybe even understandable, but this way out was unforgivable. She puzzled over the events of the past six months and Will's gradual withdrawal from her, his darkening moods. He'd never been a wild man, but he'd always been interesting, intellectually and physically active, eager to learn, to master his craft, to understand hers. Something had caused all this to dissipate. Maybe his research failures could have accounted for these changes ... but then he'd finally had success! Why hadn't that lifted his spirits? And this final act with her ... she had no way to understand it, and it was not in her to go to him seeking explanations. She didn't even know where he'd gone.

She told no one until a week later when she went to visit her father in San Francisco. Marco was all excited when she arrived, and immediately told her about a small project he was hired for, two murals inside a restored mansion on Nob Hill. It was real money, which he always needed. He had also agreed to teach some drawing classes at UCSF, for a little extra income. His paintings still weren't bringing much, but he couldn't stop. His attic studio was full to the bursting point with his canvases.

Gina did not tell him about Will until she was near ready to leave. She didn't say how Will had departed. Marco had a good image of Will and she didn't want to destroy it completely. She assured her father that she was handling it just fine. He offered that she could come stay in her old room for a while, if she needed to, but she declined. Marco embraced his daughter, looked for signs of distress in her eyes, that sadness that had been so often visible there, but did not see them. She seemed composed, solid. He didn't know why, but he was happy to see it. He hoped it was real.

For the next month Gina avoided much social contact. She talked a couple of times with Preston Schaefer about her thesis, and was able to begin putting her plan together. It involved a trip to Guatemala in October to visit and study the villages of what remained of the Maryanta Indians. She planned to go with Schaefer and David and Tom Silva, assuming Schaefer really had enough money in his grant to accommodate all this. Otherwise, she wasn't sure how she'd carry out her investigations. It would probably work out.

She didn't see David much during this time. He was to have spent July and August getting a plan together, but she had seen him in his office only once, and at the library not at all. She had run into Kay in early July, and then had met her for lunch a few days later. It was at the lunch that she'd finally filled in Kay about Will, and that was only after Kay had asked several times about the two of them. Gina told Kay the whole story, even the story of Will's note.

"You haven't tried to see him? Where the hell is he?"

"I don't know."

"Isn't he still in Chemistry. He has a lab. You could go find him there!"

"I don't want to. I don't need to."

Kay was dismayed at first, disappointed in Will because she'd admired and liked him. She also had seen strength in Gina's reaction to the situation and she liked that. That was when she'd asked about Gina's living arrangements, and had invited her to live in the group house, the house Kay called the Manse.

Gina had enjoyed the two weeks she'd spent in her new abode. She had not yet attempted to get to know the four or five other residents, or the half-dozen non-residents, who came and went everyday. She spent most of her time either alone in her small but wonderfully comfortable room, or with Kay. David wasn't much in sight, and Kay had simply said that he was involved in some political work in San Francisco, with the Bay Area Chapter of the SDS. But Kay was worried he was on his way into some extremely radical anti-war efforts, groups far more extreme than the SDS.

It was a Saturday evening gathering at the Manse when Gina decided to socialize for the first time since Will's departure. The fall 1967 semester had begun two weeks earlier, and the usual combination of post-docs, graduate and undergraduate students, some faculty, including Preston Schaefer, had all come on board for some drink, music, and laughs, and maybe smoke some pot and other fine pharmaceuticals. People of unknown status were also in abundance. As was usual, guests brought their own drink and the hosts supplied food, most of which was chips, dips, cheap cheese, and the like. Smoking of all kinds filled the Manse, and the more sensitive partygoers had to escape to the back porch or the front lawn. The music was loud and set the tone.

"Berkeley is really full of crazies. Smart as hell, most of them, but nuts. Don't know where they're going. They hate the worlds they come from, and want to create this kind of world. Crazy dreamers. Now, all summer long, we've had these lost kids, teenagers mostly, drifting into San Francisco from all over the place. Summer of Love. Hah. Who made up that slogan? I think it's kind of sad, all these kids who hate where they come from, and have no place to go." Kay Hooper was sitting at the kitchen table. Gina was there, along with David and two guys Gina didn't know and who had not been introduced to her. Kay seemed to know them. One was bearded and was as thin as a rail. The other was completely bald, large, and muscular. They drank tea. People streamed in and out of the kitchen, pausing to say a few words to Kay and David and usually looking for something. The kitchen was the one relatively quiet room in the house.

"Don't mistake the weird dress and behavior with a lack of seriousness. There's a revolution in the works. This fucking war is a symbol of everything that's wrong with America and it's got to be destroyed. We are the destroyers," exclaimed the skinny, bearded guy.

The muscular, bald guy spoke up. "Most of these people are here for a good time. They want pleasure. The old world they want to destroy is the one where people are made to conform to a code. No behaviors outside these limits permitted." He held his hands up in front of him to display the boundaries he was talking about. "These are people who want social change, cultural change. They want to do what they want to do. No artificial constraints. So, if there's a revolution it's about personal behavior. It's only a few people, the same old few, who still think about revolution in the larger sense. Let's just get out of our social rut, get free of that. All the rest will follow."

David interjected. "It's more than that. Look, you've got the black revolution. You've got people who are ready to fight this ugly, imperialistic war, to the death. Maybe you've got women coming out of the woodwork at last. Maybe all kinds of groups of people whose behavior is considered abnormal, antisocial. Jesus, there's so much going on, get with it." David seemed exasperated.

"Don't forget the sources of all this repression you are trying to destroy, David Zaretsky." Peter Weiss had appeared. Preston Schaefer was close up behind him, looking a little fierce, eager to speak.

"Repression. That's what you are trying to destroy, isn't it, David? Forces of repression that are built into our power structure. They make the non-conformist feel weak. They make the non-conformists feel guilt about their non-conformity. They are repressed. You need for people to overcome these forces of repression and liberate themselves first. Only after self-liberation comes social liberation." Peter Weiss, slight and soft-spoken, commanded attention. He sounded wise. Schaefer pushed in front of him.

"Power. That's what it's all about. Their power. His power. Our power. Clashes of power. The powerless have power in their very powerlessness. That's a source of power. Look at Mr. M.L. King and his henchmen. Where's the cheese? I'm hungry as hell."

Gina was thrilled by all this conversation and even Preston Schaefer's bluster. These were people that she liked, although she still felt intimidated and never thought to participate. Schaefer she still didn't quite follow, but he did dominate the talk for the next half hour, mostly because he talked so loud and didn't mind interrupting. He was soon, somehow, onto his favorite topic, and he made it clear that his ideas on it were entirely original. For Schaefer everything evil turned on Western science, its unique way of uncovering knowledge. The method that had developed since the seventeenth century was powerful, and what it uncovered about the workings of the material world gave unprecedented power to those who understood this, the elite of Western society. In fact, for Schaefer, Western science was no better at uncovering the truth about the world than were a hundred other ways of knowing, including the ways of the so-called primitive peoples of the world, the ways of religion and art. The ancient wisdom. Western science was simply better at getting at those particular truths that could be used to develop tools that could in turn be used by the Western elite to dominate. This was his ultimate conclusion. When he started on this topic Schaefer was unstoppable. To Gina, his tone was fanatical, but she could see how it could be persuasive to people who wanted to believe the West was decadent. Gina thought she understood what Schaefer was saying, but his views seemed so extreme she wondered about his sanity. She again didn't speak up, perhaps because she didn't wish to buck her thesis adviser, but Kay did.

"Schaefer, where do you get these ideas? You mistake science and the knowledge it acquires for its uses. Its uses may be politically driven and put to bad ends, but how you can knock its method, its way of getting to the truth, and equate it with the irrational, or non-rational, ways of religions is beyond me. Sometimes I think you say these things just for dramatic effect."

Schaefer didn't respond right away, and Peter broke in to defend him. David seemed impatient with Schaefer and left the room, as did the two guys whose names Gina still didn't know. Peter and Kay went at it awhile, but Schaefer seemed to lose interest, and turned to Gina.

"Where's Will?"

Gina hadn't really prepared herself to begin explaining her situation to all of her friends. Schaefer had asked about Will a couple of times before, when she had visited him in his office, but had not persisted when she didn't respond. Tonight he persisted.

"Are you two in a break-up? What's going on? I used to see him fairly often, or you'd talk about him. Is everything okay?" Schaefer opened another beer and started downing it, with half the first gulp ending up in his beard and on his belly.

Kay was looking at her, silently urging Gina to talk about Will and what had happened. Gina felt comfortable near Kay, and finally told her story, or at least most of it.

Schaefer listened intently, never interrupting. He expressed what seemed to be sympathy and his only comment was that Will's behavior seemed out of character. "Must be something really pressing on him. Any ideas?"

The room was quiet until Kay spoke. "He's in some trouble. Or he's just a shit we never suspected. Gina won't try to talk to him, or even contact him. Maybe she's right not to."

Much later that evening when most of the crowd had dissipated, Gina found herself seated on one of the sofas in the huge living room. Peter had dropped onto the sofa next to her, smoking as usual, and carrying a bottle of red wine and two glasses. He offered one to Gina; she accepted, and he poured for both of them. "Preston told me your story. About Will and you. I was not surprised. In fact, I knew about it, or strongly suspected." Peter could not seem to avoid smiling, and as always, he displayed the kind of smile that seemed designed to suggest that he possessed some secret knowledge and that he wanted the listener to understand that.

"How could you know?" Gina stared straight ahead, but sensed the warmth of Peter's body and his eyes staring into the side of her face. She heard a Doors song coming to an end on the stereo across the room, and then quiet conversations from among the half-dozen stragglers filled the air. It was nearly two a.m. She looked for Kay but she was not in sight.

"I saw him, about three weeks ago. He was not alone. On campus, in the eucalyptus grove near the Campanile. He was sitting talking to someone. I stopped and we chatted. I asked for you but he talked about something else. I detected that the person he was with was close to him. You know her, I think."

Gina's heart pounded in her chest. She didn't want to hear this. Why was this guy doing this? She had never liked Peter very much, had always thought he was mean, maybe dishonest. He finished his glass of wine and poured another. Gina had consumed none of hers.

"Maybe you know all this. I could be wrong, of course, I'm just guessing." He moved closer. "I need to talk to you and Kay about something. Where is she?"

Gina turned to look directly at him. "Who was he with? I don't know where he is, I haven't tried to find out. It's over, that's the way he wants it."

"Her name is Elaine. I don't recall her last name, though he introduced her to me. I'd seen them together before, at a party at Schaefer's, a couple of months ago. I remember it, because I expected to see you when I saw Will, but this Elaine was with him. Or at least they left together." Peter's sickly smile broadened behind a cloud of foul-smelling cigarette smoke.

Gina had no immediate reaction to Peter's remarks. She set her wine glass aside, and got up. "I'll find Kay." She walked hurriedly out of the living room and then through several other rooms before she came across Kay in the hallway, saying good night to some guests. Gina grasped Kay by the arm, and asked her to come to the living room.

"What do you want to ask?" Gina said to Peter, Kay at her side. She sounded perturbed.

"I have a favor to ask. Do you remember Chris Swift, the priest, my friend?"

Kay had never met him, but recalled Gina's mention of him. Gina had had thoughts of him since her return from Seattle, and was immediately pleased to hear his name. She said, "I know him. He left L.A., some trouble with the Bishop. What's he been doing? Kay hasn't met him, but I think I told her about him." Kay nodded, and Peter went on.

"He's been living with me since May. He's attached himself to some Catholic church here in Berkeley. The priest there is glad to have him around to help out. He still has no idea what do to with himself. He sometimes thinks about going back to Los Angeles and making amends with the Bishop, and behaving like the gentle lamb of God he's supposed to be. But he knows how difficult it will be for him to keep silent on matters he feels strongly about. He remains committed, I think, for the time being. But who knows? He's in a tough spot. He works part time at a coffee house on Shattuck, and barely survives. I think he prays a lot. Anyway, I'm clearing out of here. I'm leaving Berkeley, going to live in San Francisco. I'm just not driven to study anymore. There are other things I want to do. So Chris has no home, or won't have soon. I was going to ask if you could put him up here for a while, any corner will do. He has no money, but he's willing to work, be your housekeeper ...."

"What are you going to do?" asked Kay.

"I'm going to study Zen Buddhism with the hope of joining a monastery for a time. There's a center in the city for this kind of study. It's much more appealing to me than what I am studying here, this dry analytical philosophy, so completely heartless. I'm tired of learning how to dissect language. I want to dissect the soul." He seemed a little drunk, though it was hard to tell how to read that endless smile. Gina thought what he was telling them was probably pure bull.

Kay didn't answer right away, and then spoke, "I'll have to bring it up with David and some of the others. But it's probably okay if it's not indefinite. Maybe we could handle this for a couple of months. Not more."

"I'm sure that's okay. I'll tell him. Can he come by tomorrow to talk about it? Will you be here?"

"Yes. I'll be here."

"Me too," said Gina quietly. She retreated to the sofa while Peter went on talking, and tuned him out. In her mind she heard only Peter's earlier comments about Will.

Gina went to bed at about four a.m., after cleaning up with Kay and two other residents. Gina said nothing during that time and Kay sensed that something serious was on her mind. Just after Gina crawled into her bed, Kay knocked on her door. Gina's room was dark, but Kay could make out Gina sitting up in her small bed. Kay sat down next to her. Gina was moved by Kay's presence but said nothing. She raised her arms and wrapped them around Kay. The two women embraced in that way for a few moments, until Kay felt Gina's quiet sobbing and the moisture of her tears. Kay gently pushed Gina back onto the bed and then lay down beside her. They embraced again, and lay this way into sleep, there in that small room in the very large house in the hills of Berkeley.

CHAPTER 10

On Sunday morning, while Kay and Gina slept, Will Getz was out running. In fact, at about ten a.m. he ran by the very large house, and had a passing thought that he might stop in on his return to visit with Kay and David. On his flight back from Atlantic City, just three days ago, Will had committed to take up running again, and to stick with it. He needed the kind of physical pleasure and clarity of mind running brought. He determined to work his way through his crisis, by tapping the strengths of his intellect and the power of his will, and using them to overcome the weakness he'd displayed these last several months. Elaine was right. He'd chosen a path for himself. He had chosen it. No one else. He had to live with it, and he was not going to squander his talents and destroy himself by retreating. Elaine was right, they could be highly successful together.

He had not been pleased with Elaine's recent prodding, her constant attacks on his apparent weakness, his inability to write up his work, claim his doctorate, and move on. His way of dealing with Elaine's attacks was to clam up, but this didn't deter her, she seemed oblivious to this behavior of his. She still was passionate about him, no doubt about that, and brought out passions in him that continued to astonish him, notwithstanding his distaste for her pushiness and his uncertain emotional attachment. The heart is a trickster.

Right now his heart was working at full capacity as he pounded up the last hundred yards to the Canyon Road park where he always rested. He'd been out three times since their return home, and the run seemed more difficult each time. It would take three or four weeks to get back into tip-top running form. He sat a few minutes on the park bench and immediately began to go over his plan for dealing with Jensen on Monday. He and Elaine would convince him that her isolation system was the only way to go. Synthesis was too laborious. She'd contact Preston Schaefer right away about the status of his friend's plant collection efforts in Guatemala. She was confident that she could run several kilos of plant extract through her isolation system and produce 20 to 40 grams of highly pure pfaffadine in a matter of a few weeks. If it was successful with the pfaff isolation, if she could repeat what she'd done before, she would be ready to publish. She would make a name for herself, no doubt. The Callahan Linked-Column Reverse Phase ... something like that. Jesus, if pfaff was really anti-tumorigenic and not too toxic, both Elaine and Will would be in the news.

But they had to bury the synthesis of pfaffadine, Will's phony work. They had to convince Jensen that it was too inefficient. Will would promise to get all his work done by the middle of October, one month away, and would ask Jensen to arrange an interview for him at NIH, with Dr. Virgil Goode.

Repetition. Elaine could repeat her work. The key to progress in all of science. If one could not repeat one's own work, no one else could be expected to do so. What gets published is that which can be reproduced, by anyone with the requisite technical skills. Will would write down the specific reaction conditions that he had employed the first time he converted pre-pfaff to pfaff. These conditions - - time, temperature, solvents, reagents - - would be written down in detail, as would the method of isolating pfaff from the reaction mixture and the method of its purification. Enough detail so that another trained chemist could repeat the work, get the same result, repeat the entire sequence of reactions. He could describe perfectly, from his very well organized lab notes, the first successful try. But he also knew that the next three tries, under apparently the same conditions, led nowhere. Why? Who knows? Some uncontrolled and unknown factor, missing the second and third and fourth times? Was it really possible that he was wrong the first time, that it was not pfaff that had been produced? No, he had good spectroscopic evidence of several types. Jesus, he couldn't understand what had happened. Reproducible results. Nothing else counts. He was just lucky that, he was now pretty sure, there would be no need for him or anyone else to go through the whole, tedious synthesis. No practical need. The work would stand based on the strength of the published results. No one would have a reason to believe they were wrong, and no one would possibly choose to try to reproduce the synthesis just out of curiosity, or to see if what Will reported was correct. Far too much work for no real purpose.

Elaine's system. Jesus, she'd better be right about her system. She was the most confident woman he had ever known. He ran, at blazing speed, down the hills, the cool September breezes, laced with the perfume of eucalyptus, bathing his body. He was finally master of his fate. No more wavering.

He slowed at the sharp corner near David and Kay's house, then dropped his pace to a walk. He was three houses away and spotted Gina on the raised front lawn. She was dressed in jeans and the light green sweater she loved so much. Her hair was tied in a bun. She carried a large bag and was picking refuse off the lawn. Will stopped. His heart was beating audibly as he moved to the side of the road, out of Gina's sight. He could still see her, but she would not be able to see him unless she came down the walk to the street. He was astonished. Why was she here? He'd never thought about where she might be living, just assumed she would have remained on Durant. He should have known she could barely have afforded to keep the place. Was she living here? Just visiting, probably, but why was she cleaning the lawn? Barefoot. She stopped working a moment, and turned in his direction. He could see her face clearly. He saw there the kind of soft beauty that had attracted him in the first place, that still attracted him. A kind of beauty that was nowhere in the coolness of Elaine's face. He shuddered a little, and backed all the way to the corner, and looked for an alternative route home, or rather to Elaine's apartment.

By late Monday morning, Elaine and Will had convinced Alden Jensen that pfaffadine was going to be easy to get in abundance using Elaine's system. The only hold-up was the lack of plant material. Preston Schaefer, she reminded Jensen, had contacted his friend in Guatemala in late May and got assurances of a shipment. She'd go see Schaefer right away and pin down an arrival date. It would take her only a couple of weeks to process the material. Jensen knew that a repeat of Will's synthesis would take several months, and that scaling it up to produce 30 or 40 grams of the compound would not be easy - - it would be the kind of scale-up pharmaceutical firms might attempt if they were interested in producing pfaff by synthesis. If the compound looked really good in the next set of NCI tests, attempts to obtain FDA approval and commercial production might be appealing to a good firm. For now there was no question that isolation from the natural source was the way to go. Will again promised Jensen he'd complete his thesis write- up soon, interview with Virgil Goode, and take his orals. The oral defense of the thesis before three or four faculty members would be the last step in the acquisition of his doctorate, save the actual graduation ceremony. He also promised Jensen that he'd write the first draft of a paper for publication as soon as the thesis was written.

Elaine immediately called Preston Schaefer at his office and caught him in. He would be happy to see her, how about lunch? She agreed and left Will to meet Schaefer at Chico's. Will went off to the library to write.

"You look great, where've you been all summer? Let's order first."

Schaefer looked as if he'd lost some weight, although his general appearance was as unkempt as ever. His tone was pushy and he seemed a little angry. He'd taken Elaine's arm when she appeared at the restaurant, and virtually shoved her toward a table. The place was busy and they'd taken the only remaining table, a small one jammed in a corner. Schaefer could barely squeeze into his chair. They ordered and Elaine got right to her subject.

"I need to know when my plant material is expected from your buddy in Guatemala. I think it was late May or early June we talked about it. I've been busy with other stuff, but the compound looks promising as an anti-tumor agent. NCI needs more. I've got to have a date for the plant material." She was all business.

"I've heard you're with Will Getz. Like, permanent. Living together? How'd that happen?" Schaefer was already on the second of his three tacos. He was guessing that what he'd heard from Peter Weiss was true.

Elaine was surprised by this. She and Will hadn't tried hard to keep their living arrangement a secret, but they hadn't gone out of the way to make it known, either. Will had not seen or talked to Gina, as far as she knew. Maybe Gina had guessed and mentioned it to Schaefer. How else could he know? She saw no reason to hide it from Schaefer.

"Yeah. We're together. It was all over between him and Gina several months ago. But that's all irrelevant. I need some idea about the plant material."

"Perea, his last letter to me, in early August, said his associates had already collected and were sun-drying the stuff. He thought it would be ready to ship end of August. I haven't heard any more." He spoke hurriedly, then paused a few seconds. "You never gave me a straight answer about us. You jumped right out of my bed into his. Never even talked to me about it."

"Can you contact Perea right away, find out?"

"You are not easy to get out of my head. So I persist. We spent a night and a day together, you really hit me hard. I thought I'd done something similar to you. And then you just vanished. Now I know where to, but I don't understand."

"That's my business. I don't think I owe you an explanation. I've known Will quite awhile, my lab's just three doors from his. I had a chance with him, just as he was breaking with Gina. It just happened, it was good. It just happened at about the same time you and I ..."

"Wow. Easy for you to hop from one life into another?"

Elaine could sense a mounting fury across the table, but she wasn't intimidated.

"Preston, come on, I was never in your life. For Christ's sake, can we talk about the plant? I'm really desperate here." Elaine was finally eating something. Schaefer wasn't deterred and was calling the waiter over to order dessert.

"Look I'm ready to help. I just really need to be convinced about us. I know I couldn't have been all wrong after our day. I contacted you once, you brushed me off. But I still think about us. I'm working on a couple of great ideas now and planning a trip to Guatemala in October with some grad students. I've got a lot of work on my plate. See, I'm developing this whole new idea about science, I think I'm onto something great ... it'll make my name, worldwide. You'd love life on my side of the world. I could tell when we talked that Sunday. It was a beautiful day for me. To say nothing of the night before. I can't get those hours out of my mind." He had finally moved his plate aside and stopped chewing while he talked. He looked directly into her eyes, no longer angry, more sad, pathetic even.

"Preston, look I'm somewhere else now. I'm with someone I really like. I'm not interested in anyone else. I like you, believe me, you're damn interesting, one of the most stimulating people I've met, but that's not enough right now."

"Maybe it's my physical self. I'm not in great shape, but I once was. I could get back ..."

"Please, tell me you'll contact Perea, right away."

Schaefer paused, not sure what to say. Elaine had a passing thought that he might want something in return for his efforts with Perea. No, that seemed unlikely. She had no reason to believe he was dishonorable in that way. He was pretty gruff at times, pushy, domineering, impolite, at worst. He wasn't going to try to bribe her.

"I'll call Perea today, or at least wire him. That might be easier. I'll get you an answer today. Where can I call you?"

"Don't you have my phone number? Just call me there."

Schaefer squeezed out of his corner, threw some money on the table, and left. His anger had returned, she could see that. But he wasn't going to take it out on her.

He phoned her apartment at about six that evening. He'd reached Perea. Twenty kilograms of dried plant material had been put on a cargo ship and would arrive in San Francisco on September 20. It was good stuff, dried leaves and seeds, no extraneous woody material. It was addressed to Schaefer, so he'd have to go pick it up. Elaine could go with him.

Elaine really didn't want to accept the invitation, but saw no way to refuse. He was doing her, and Will, a tremendous favor. The twentieth was a week away. She'd arrange to meet Schaefer as soon as they could learn the exact time of the ship's arrival. Schaefer said nothing else, just hung up abruptly.

When Will arrived later that evening she gave him the good news. She said nothing to him about the rest of her meeting with Preston Schaefer. Later that same evening they engaged in a long and heated bout of sex, unlike anything they'd experienced for several weeks. It wasn't gentle in the least. Both lovers seemed to approach it as a battle, as if each was hoping to achieve sexual power over the other, as if each was trying to offer a degree of sexual pleasure to the other that could never be found elsewhere. All spoken purely in the languages of their perfect bodies.

Elaine didn't fall asleep until long after Will had dropped away. She had uncomfortable thoughts about Schaefer, and couldn't dump them for a long time. She remembered his awkward thrusting at her the night they spent together, and couldn't help but to compare it with what she'd just felt with Will. She wished she had no need to depend upon Schaefer. Well, they'd get the plant material on the twentieth. That would end it.

CHAPTER 11

On the Sunday morning Will had been out running, and had seen Gina raking the front lawn of the Manse, Kay awoke late and alone in Gina's room. She remembered lying down with Gina in the early morning hours, after the party at which Gina got the news from Peter about Will and Elaine. Kay recalled Gina's quiet sobbing, her tears, and the feel of her small body against her own. Gina was something of a mystery to Kay. Her reaction to Will's odd and cowardly departure had seemed strange from the beginning. On the one hand it appeared she was a passive, timid, and powerless female, and on the other it was as if she was above it, strong and independent, and unneeding of whatever Will had meant to her. Now that his unfaithfulness was clear, Kay could not guess how Gina would ultimately be affected. Kay arose, went to the window and looked out to the west, over the campus toward the bay and the city. She then looked down to the front lawn and saw Gina moving about with a large garbage bag, collecting the party's refuse. Kay felt sorrow for her and also some kind of love. She was also drawn to Gina's quiet beauty. Quiet because you understood and appreciated it only if you took the time to be with her and to study her features as you would a painting. Gina possessed beauty of the most subtle kind. Kay also loved the way Gina moved her body, her gracefulness seemed completely unconscious, so unlike Kay's own, awkward, lumbering self.

Kay broke from her reverie and made her way downstairs, to the kitchen. David was there munching on some toast. He'd started a beard and, although it was probably as full as it would get, it was not attractive. It was scraggly and erupted from his face in too many directions. They exchanged a few innocuous greetings and Kay made herself some coffee. She sat down at the table opposite him.

"Well, are you coming or going? One night you're here, the next night you're not. You don't talk to me anymore. What in hell is going on? It's been a month or more like this."

David was silent, pretending that he hadn't been listening. He got up to get some more coffee, and then walked out of the kitchen, through the dining room and onto the front porch.

Kay hesitated a few minutes, then decided she had to clear this up. She followed him to the porch and sat on a bench next to him. Gina was now raking the small lawn, probably distant enough so that she couldn't hear their conversation. She waved and then returned to her work.

"Okay. I owe you. I am moving out. I've got some serious things I want to do. Really serious."

"Where are you going?"

"There's a group house in the south side of Berkeley, near Oakland. A kind of cell is being organized there. They asked me to join."

"What kind of group? Who are they?"

"Two were here at the party last night. Remember the two guys. One was bald, the other had a big beard, real tall, thin. Curly and Moe we call them." Kay remembered them. She waited for more. "There's a few others. We don't have a name for the organization yet. We all think SDS is a drag. It's just too soft, a lot of mental gymnastics, not enough action. We think more radical action is needed to end the war. We are going to work at that. It's what I need right now."

98

"What more radical action are you talking about? Are you talking violence? Or do you mean just more craziness, drugs and cultural shock, that shit?"

David rose and paced the front porch, looking nervous and like he just wanted to leave.

"Jesus, David, what is in your head? For God's sake don't do something dumb. And what about school, your degree?"

"I'm not giving that up. I haven't been working at it the way I was supposed to, but I have an appointment with Schaefer on Monday morning. Gina does, too." He pointed to Gina, who was now walking toward them. She seemed relaxed, happy even.

"What are you guys doing?" Gina was looking at David.

"David is moving out. Soon." Kay smiled faintly.

"Yeah, I'm moving to another group house."

Kay got up and stood next to Gina. She asked, "Do you want to take a walk? I'm in the mood for some huevos rancheros, down at Enriqueta's. Come on, I'll buy." The two women moved off the porch, hand-in-hand.

At breakfast, Kay asked Gina about Will and any reactions she'd had to the news of his infidelity. Gina said that she felt worried about Will, couldn't believe that an involvement with Elaine Callahan was the whole story. After an initial sadness at hearing the news from Peter, her reaction had been only one of worry for Will's well being. This was strange, maybe, but it meant she was really beyond him, she had other people in her life, Kay foremost among them. Gina had prepared well for the trip to Guatemala that would be the cornerstone of the data-gathering phase of her doctoral thesis. She also mentioned that, as far as she knew, David had done little or nothing to prepare. Gina did not see how Schaefer could support a trip for David.

On the way back from Enriqueta's a rain shower overtook them, and Kay and Gina crouched under a small grove of eucalyptus on Dwight Way, about three blocks below the Manse. The rain was very light and lasted only a few minutes, but the two decided to sit for a while on the log that was used as a bench.

"When is Chris Swift coming?" Gina asked Kay in as casual a way as she could. She had continued to have thoughts of the wayward priest, and upon hearing that he would be moving into the group house, she had been unable to get him out of her mind, notwithstanding the news about Will and Elaine. She had awakened in bed with Kay, but with Chris in her thoughts; he had been there all morning.

"Oh, Jesus, I forgot. He's supposed to come by today, around four o'clock. I guess there's plenty of time."

Father Swift did not show up on Sunday evening. He finally called at about eight o'clock and told Kay he was tied up, but would come by on Monday. Kay told him to come for dinner, around seven.

On Monday morning Gina showed up at Preston Schaefer's office at nine-thirty. David and another third-year grad student, Tom Silva, were already seated on Schaefer's ragged sofa. The man himself was on the phone and seemed to be in no hurry to get off. The three students sat in silence, Silva reading and David and Gina looking nervously at each other. After about ten minutes Schaefer turned to the three and began in his usual gruff way.

"Guatemala's on. We leave October second. There's a problem though. I can take only two. It'll be Zaretsky and Silva. Money's part of the problem. This trip's expensive and my grant just won't carry four people. Also, there's guerilla warfare in Guatemala, involving some of the very native indians we plan to visit. Perea warned me about this a few weeks ago. He said it's getting worse. The indians are severely repressed by the American-supported government, a bunch of beasts, puppets of Johnson, and Kennedy and Eisenhower before him. I can't let a woman go into that. I'm pretty sure you guys'll be safe from the guerillas, they'll know through Perea we're with them, we're

100

sympathetic. Some of them know me from previous visits and they know I'm sympathetic. But I must warn you, there's some chance the friggin' government forces will give us trouble. Gina, you'll just have to wait 'til next spring. There's plenty you can do here to get started on your work. Also, I need you to stay behind for some teaching assistant work. I want you to take over Tom Silva's 101 lab section in his absence. You, David, I haven't seen your project write-up. You'll need to get that to me by the middle of next week." Schaefer turned away and picked up his ringing phone.

Gina was flattened by the announcement. She couldn't believe what she'd heard. David hadn't done a thing to prepare. She had turned in what she knew was a good plan of work and Schaefer hadn't even mentioned it. And her safety, God that was no more an issue for her than it was for the other two. What was the bastard saying - - she couldn't go because she was a woman! She spoke up.

"Preston, this will slow me down by months. I'm ready for this trip. I've done the background work. You sound as if you haven't read it. What am I going to do until next spring? I'm being treated unfairly."

"Tough decision for me. There's nothing I can do. You've got course work to complete, haven't you?" Schaefer talked into the phone and told the caller to hold on.

"I've finished requirements. I'm taking 390, a seminar, just for interest. And what do you mean about safety; why am I any more at risk than these guys? My grade point average ...."

He cut her off to talk to whomever was on the phone. He seemed intensely interested in the call, and in nothing else. David and Tom were sitting quietly, neither looking at her. Gina knew it was useless to argue with Preston Schaefer. She got up and left.

She walked the campus for about an hour trying to grasp what had just happened to her. Her thoughts soon ran out of control, shifting from Preston Schaefer's leering and uncaring face to David Zaretsky's blank stares, from thoughts of Will, Will's pathetic note, Will and Elaine together, Will and Elaine making love, or having sex, then to her memories of lying naked under Will's body. A brief image of Father Swift, and then back to the ugly and humiliating meeting in Schaefer's office. At one point she remembered her mother and the grief that followed her mother's death and as these and all the other images raced through her mind, she accumulated feelings of anger and self-pity and self-hate and for reasons she did not understand at all, confidence in her ability to persevere, to fall never again into the depressive life she had once known, to walk away forever from her shyness and the self-loathing that had often accompanied it. This screwing over by Schaefer would be overcome, just the way she had overcome Will's faithlessness. And then she wondered whether she had really overcome Will and what he had done. She ended her wandering on the campus and walked purposefully down Bancroft toward Shattuck. She turned off onto Royce and found Saint Christopher's church. It was almost time for the weekday noon service, and she climbed the steps to the front door and went in.

Gina had spent little time in churches since early in her college days, when her faith, which had been shaken by her mother's death, began to be further eroded by her increasing awareness of the secular world and the hollowness of the church's dogma. Her loss of faith was deeply disturbing to her, but she saw no way simultaneously to remain honest to herself and to the beliefs the church required her to hold. The emotional power of the church and its rituals waned far more slowly than did her faith, and she came to understand that it would probably never completely release its grip. She sat as the mass began. Because it was a weekday, attendance was very low, maybe twenty people, most of them elderly. She did not pay much attention to the celebration of the mass, but simply sat and tried to assimilate the emotional peace it conveyed.

How many defeats could she suffer? Yet, except perhaps for the death of her mother, she had not suffered greatly, her setbacks and defeats were not much different from those most people experienced. It occurred to her for the third or fourth time that Schaefer's dismissal of her was born out of sexism. That bastard. So in this respect she was maybe like others of her gender. The great progressive professor is as sexist as the worst reactionary. The world doesn't really know yet how much of this kind of thing goes on.

Will was in trouble, she knew it. A soft prayer for him, here where she had prayed so much for her poor mother's soul, at least for a time. Now she was not convinced anyone had a soul, let alone one worth a prayer to an unknown, unknowable, maybe nonexistent, God. Another male, this God, to honor? Where was Chris Swift? She thought she might see him here, assisting at the mass. He was not present. She felt sourness in the pit of her stomach, but then fell into the rhythm of the mass, listened to the prayers being uttered, focused her gaze on the host being raised by the priest. It brought tears.

She left during the communion, raced out into the bright September sun and the cool breezes reaching up from the Bay. She would beat this, she would not be defeated, she would make a place for herself in this university, in this city, in this country, in her time. It was a good time for a visit to her dad.

CHAPTER 12

Marco was painting when she arrived. After his hugs and kisses he immediately told her about a show at a gallery in Palo Alto where he would be the only featured artist. He'd been working night and day to complete a couple of old paintings and to add a couple of new ones. He excitedly pushed her around his studio and showed her the two dozen or so canvases he intended to show. She had not looked closely at his work in recent times, but now took some time to contemplate this collection over which her father was so enthusiastic. His range of colors seemed to have expanded and, although he maintained his abstract style, this group of paintings seemed to speak more directly than any she remembered. Several seemed to begin in chaos, usually at their centers, and grew to order, at the edges. Maybe her imagination was overly rich, but that's what she saw. She told her father, who had not had a one-man show for ages, and whose income had always been meager, that he seemed to have reached some new plateau, that his time may have arrived. His show would begin October sixth, a Friday when she was to have been in Guatemala.

After the excitement brought on by Marco's potential good fortune, they sat and had some tea. Gina had told him in July about Will's departure and her planned move to the Manse. She now told him about life there, and a little about Kay Hooper. Finally she told him about Schaefer's incredible villainy. That was the word that leapt out of her mouth - - villainy.

"At least you won't have to worry all October about my safety. I know you hated that part of my career choice, the field work in faraway places." Gina managed a smile, and Marco took her hands in his.

"I am happy about that, I must admit. But I do not understand this professor of yours. It means you will have to spend several extra months, unless you change your project. Maybe you can do something else?"

Gina explained that this would not be easy to do, as long as she was working for Preston Schaefer. She still wanted a career in anthropology and his territory appealed to her. She admired the work he had done, although her admiration for the man had declined considerably over the past several hours. The father and daughter talked quietly about her experiences of the past few months and how she seemed to have weathered them better than in the past. Marco could see this in the way she talked, the words she chose. She told him more of Kay and of her ability to think for herself, to stand for something without being dogmatic about it.

"Your mother, I always thought, was like that. It was part of the reason I loved her. She was really smart, had her own mind. She never got where she should have. A high school teacher. If she had been a man.... I don't know. Who knows? She might have gone on to something more. Who am I to say?"

"Dad, I want to ask you something, okay?"

"Ask me. I can always say I don't know." Marco smiled and poured himself some more tea.

"Mom died in an auto accident. That's what I was told. She went off the highway somewhere in Marin, I forget where. You refused to show me. She was traveling fast, must have been, because she went a long way off and down a very steep hill. She must have been traveling very fast. Was that like her? I never could picture her driving like a madwoman."

Marco sipped at his tea, put his cup down, and spoke. "No one knows for sure. The police think she was over the speed limit. How much, no one knows. No witnesses nearby. She just lost control."

"Were things okay between you two at the time? I mean you weren't angry, or anything like that, with each other at the time? I always had this vague feeling something was wrong between you two, but I couldn't tell. And afterwards I could think of nothing but the fact of her death. But ever since I have wondered about her state of mind. God, I don't know how I got onto this topic. We have talked for a long time, it's nearly six o'clock. I've got to go, and you've got tons of work to do." Gina did not seem to want answers to her questions, and Marco didn't offer any.

"Yes, okay, you go. We can talk about this some other time. I hope you do not get too sour on your schoolwork. Time is not all that important. You will get where you want to go. You are really smart. Just stay on course. Do not retreat when times are bad. Oh, before you go, I must ..." Marco rushed away to his bedroom, and returned a few moments later carrying a case.

Gina immediately recognized it as the case that contained her violin. She had left it here when she finished college. She had minored in music at Mills and had played all four years in the college's orchestra. She never made first chair, but for her last three years had been in the first row. The fact that she never made first chair was not a male-female thing, because Mills was all female; she didn't make it because she wasn't quite good enough.

Music and her violin had been extremely important in her life until she'd decided to take up anthropology at Berkeley. She had majored in history, but had always been tempted by a career in music. For some reason, once she'd made the choice, she put away her violin and not looked back. Part of her planned study in Guatemala, so cruelly foiled by Schaefer, concerned the musical traditions of the Maryanta.

"I was clearing some space in your bedroom, to store some old paintings, and I came across it. I always wondered why you left it here. Why don't you take it? You always found solace in music, especially when you made it yourself. At least when you were not practicing what you hated!" Marco smiled warmly, lovingly.

Gina took the violin case and opened it. The instrument seemed a little different from the way she remembered it when she had last closed its case more than two years ago.

"I don't know, Dad, I don't have time now." She chuckled. "Well, maybe I do now that my career's on hold." She closed the case, stuck it under her arm, hugged Marco with her free arm, kissed him on the cheek, and departed.

When she arrived back at the group house she decided she was neither hungry nor in a mood to talk with anyone, not even Kay, so she went straight to her room. She was hungry enough to eat a banana she had in her room, and then turned on her radio. The campus station was doing some folk music she was in no mood for, so she switched to San Francisco's classical music station. They were broadcasting some piano music, twentieth century, maybe Shostakovitch. She listened intently, but could not clear her mind of thoughts of the day's events, or even the weekend's events. She thought some more of Kay and of how easy it was for the two of them to be together. Kay was ... she wasn't sure what, exactly. But important to her, no doubt. She needed to talk to Kay about Schaefer. There was no one more important for her to talk to, but she'd wait until tomorrow.

The radio announcer told Gina she was right about the Shostakovitch. She had stopped listening to music the way she used to - - Will had not been a big fan, he preferred literature as his diversion - - but she knew that it was deeply embedded in her soul. Gina had never become truly enamored of the pop music of her generation. Like so much of the new culture - - the manner of dress, the so-called art, the uninhibited life styles - - it remained at the periphery of Gina's life. Her music was the music she had been brought up with, the music of her mother's soul. She opened her violin case and took up the instrument. She loved its feel, its weight. She could hear the sounds that could miraculously arise out of this box of wood.

She began to play. She made no conscious decision about what to play, the music just came. It was the piece she had played at a recital her junior year at Mills, the recital that had put her on the front page of the college newspaper, and that made others notice her like nothing else in her life had. Bach's Sonata for Violin, Number One, a piece about ten minutes' duration, which seemed to her to harken back to some ancient time when man first recognized the power of his intellect and creativity, and started to celebrate the good that power could do. A short piece that never seemed to end. Her playing was far from technically perfect, but it satisfied her completely. She ended it and collapsed onto her bed just as someone began to knock gently at her door. She sat back up a little startled.

"Who's there?"

"Can I come in? It's Chris Swift. I heard the music. Is that you, Gina?"

Gina leaped from her bed and opened the door. He stood there smiling and as handsome to her as when she first met him, maybe even more handsome. Thinner, definitely thinner, maybe too thin.

"Kay said my room was across from yours. I heard the music and came out and stood outside your door. It was beautiful. I almost cried. What was that? You play beautifully. I had no idea. Bach, I guess."

Gina stood in silence, the violin and bow still in her left hand. It took her a minute or so to respond. "Yes, Bach, a sonata, one of the simpler ones to play. I haven't played for a couple of years. My father found my violin recently and just gave it back to me. I'm not serious about it. I'm not accomplished. I ..." She was nervous and showing it.

"Can I come in?"

"Oh, sure, yes, come in." Gina waved him in and closed the door behind him. There was a chair at the desk in her room and the priest took it. Gina sat on her bed.

"So, you're here. I heard you were moving in. Peter Weiss arranged it. He's going off to some Buddhist thing. What is that? He left you homeless." She was still a tad nervous. She noted he was wearing jeans and a tattered gray sweater and some old slippers. His black hair was a little longer than she remembered, but still beautiful. He could not be a priest. Priests don't look like this.

"I don't have anything to offer you, no drinks here. I'm sorry."

"It's okay. Maybe we'll go down to the kitchen in a bit. I'm really lucky to have a good place to hang out awhile. And I'm more than lucky to run into you again. I enjoyed those few short moments we had together. Peter told me you were here, that you broke up with your boyfriend. I'm sorry." He was sitting backwards on the little chair, his arms folded over its back. Gina sat upright on the bed, her legs crossed neatly beneath her, now appearing completely relaxed.

"Yes, it's true, but I'm over that I guess. I'm going on my own way now. And you? What have you been doing? I thought you were an escapee from the Bishop in Los Angeles. Don't you have to return there sometime? How can you remain a priest unless you're attached to a parish or a monastery or something? I never heard of free-lance priests, at least while I was still a Catholic." Gina smiled, shifted her position, and finally put down her violin.

"It's a long story. I still feel I'm a priest. I took the vows. I have the collar. I attend mass almost every day. I've been volunteering at St. Christopher's, here in Berkeley, do you know it? Father Sullivan is really great, he's trying to help me. He thinks he can get me reassigned to a parish somewhere around here. He's made an appointment to see Bishop Sperling in San Francisco. I think it's near the end of September. If that works, I'm back where I belong. And want to be. I'm in love with the church. I think lots of what it does is wrong and needs to be changed. I'm with Pope John the 23rd on that, a great man he was. His reforms are badly needed and I want to fight for them. And there's still so much in the church that's good, its concern for the poor, for social justice, its anti-war ...."

"Sure, maybe, but there's so much irrational, life-smothering stuff. You know, the unbelievable guilt trips. I went to Catholic schools, all the way through high school. St. John's in San Francisco. It took years, my college years, to unburden myself of all that, and it's still not gone. You must know what I'm talking about."

Chris smiled then lowered his eyes to the floor. He didn't respond for several minutes, and Gina thought she must have offended him.

"You think you could never return to the church?"

"Maybe, when they bring in some women priests. Sorry, no offense."

"I'm not offended by that. In fact I favor it. Look, the church has a hold on huge numbers of the most wretched souls on earth. Just think what an impact, if some of us could turn the church more firmly in the direction of liberation, so that it becomes a leading force for social change, just think ...."

"First you've got to get it off its view that all we need to care about is preparing for the great hereafter. No need to change social conditions in the here-and-now. Just remain obedient, docile, good sheep, and you'll get to heaven." Gina was amazed she was able to speak out like this before a priest. Maybe because there was no way this guy could be one. She fell back against a large pillow on her bed, sure that something sexual was awake in her. Jesus, where was Sister Elizabeth Jean tonight, and what would she think about this?

"How about some more music. I loved what you played. Maybe play it again.... Sam. You know that line? Play it again, Sam. I went to see *Casablanca* at the Telegraph, part of a week long Bogart thing. It was truly wonderful. It's there a couple more nights. If you've never seen it, we could go."

Go out to the movies with Father Swift. She guessed that would be a kind of date. Well, she hadn't been out on one since before Will. Why not? Besides you can't date a priest, for God's sake. "Sure, maybe tomorrow evening. I've never seen it, *Casablanca* that is."

Kay poked her head in the door. "I'm not disturbing anything, I hope. I thought you'd be eating. You guys eat? Come on down, I'm starving." Kay was dressed the way she'd gone to work that morning. Gina had seen her leave at about eight a.m., and here it was more than twelve hours later, and Kay was just returning. Long day. Gina hopped up and took Kay's hand, leading her out of the small bedroom. Chris followed.

While the three scrounged up some dinner, Kay quizzed Gina about the Preston Schaefer meeting. Gina went through it all. Chris put down the tomato he was slicing and spoke.

"God, Gina, that's an abomination. How could he? Is it like him to do this? I've met him, through Peter. I thought he was some kind of leading social progressive. This sounds like pure sexist stuff."

"I'm sure it is," Kay interjected. "Schaefer has a few interesting ideas, and a lot of radical-sounding but actually quite regressive ideas, I think. Even nutty ones. But I didn't think he was sexist. I don't know what else this could he. David was not ready to go, he admitted that ...what bullshit. Sorry, Father."

"Look, priests are not innocents. And I'm Chris to my friends. What will you do?"

"I don't know. I don't think protests will help. I thought of going to the Department head, but he's not going to overrule one of his faculty on something like this. I don't know." Gina sat and started at a piece of bread. Kay opened and poured some wine.

They talked late into the night. They talked some more about Schaefer, and about David's new plans. They talked about Gina's dad and his upcoming show in Palo Alto. Even a little about Peter.

"I found him very interesting, actually very learned. It takes a while to learn this," said Chris. "He has read widely and he really knows his philosophy and can explain things well if you give him a chance."

"That may be true, but there's something weird about him, even scary," said Gina. "It's like he's always wanting you to think he knows some deep secrets of yours, when you speak with him he seems to want you to think he believes you're lying to him, hiding something. And it's like he knows what it is. Does that make any sense?"

Kay didn't respond, and Chris simply said that he had not experienced that. "He's going to spend several months, maybe a year, at this Buddhist study center in San Francisco. I think his parents support him. I think his family's got wealth. He's from Chicago. Anyway, he may even go to a monastery in Japan. I think he thinks Western philosophy has gotten pretty sterile, all language analysis, no soul. I must say he also reads a lot of very esoteric stuff, fringe things. He's fascinated with the mystics and all sorts of what I think of as weird cults. But I still think he's really smart."

As Kay and Chris went on chatting, Gina's thoughts turned again to her mother, Teresa. Too much wine, Gina thought. Jesus we've just finished the second bottle and Chris is opening another one. Bread and cheese and wine and two good friends, one very sexy. Jesus. Teresa. How beautiful my mother was, maybe I am nearly as pretty.

They ended up on the front porch, the three pretty plastered, laughing, telling some jokes, Kay even telling a mildly dirty one that Chris didn't seem to get. Gina wondered if he had ever had sex. God, he must get propositioned a lot. Kay passed out around midnight, completely exhausted from her long work day. Gina and Chris lugged her off the porch and up the stairs to her bedroom, where they tucked her in. Gina was pretty drunk, and asked for help from the priest to get her to her room. She wrapped her arm over his shoulders as he crouched a bit to offer assistance. She felt somewhere under her alcoholic fog sexual desire, but it was unfocused and dissolved as she collapsed onto her bed. Chris Swift covered her with a blanket, opened her window, and staggered away toward his own room. He didn't like the feelings that had grown in him. They were not what he was about. He knelt to pray.

CHAPTER 13

"The son of a bitch won't let up." Elaine was in a rage as she opened a beer and then lit up a cigarette. Will was seated at the kitchen table reading a letter from his father. The letter was full of congratulatory remarks and words of pride in his son's accomplishments. It was a very long letter in which Will Senior described some of his own early ambitions to become a research scientist and how he had been diverted from his goals. He was, he said, now fulfilled, in a way, by his son's achievement. Will could barely read the letter through. "What's the matter? Who're you talking about?"

"Schaefer. I went with him today into the city, to the docks, to pick up the shipment of plant material from Guatemala. It was shipped to Schaefer from his buddy in Guatemala. This is the stuff I can now put through my system. We'll have, I estimate, 30 or more grams of pfaffadine in about two weeks. You watch. It'll work like a charm. We'll be out of this mess ... clear air flying for us." She paused, then went on. "Schaefer was okay on the way over, but he really started coming on to me on the way back. I mentioned this to you before. He's got this thing, I don't know where it comes from, but I'm beginning to think I've become an obsession. We dumped the pfaff plant packages at my lab, and he even began pulling me back into his car, wouldn't let me walk home like I wanted. I'm getting worried as hell. Thank God he's leaving the country soon. He's going to Guatemala, a field trip, in early

October. He and two grad students."

Will immediately thought of Gina and was happy for her. He had no knowledge of what Schaefer had done to her. The image of her raking the lawn at the group house came to his mind. He'd like to talk to her, it had been several months. He hadn't felt much for her during their last half year together, but maybe all that was due to his failures in the lab. Could he be missing her?

"Gina's not going. He told me he didn't have enough money to support her and that there were significant dangers in Guatemala, guerilla fighting and a seriously repressive and violent government."

Will was disturbed by this information, but felt he had to turn his attention to Elaine and her problems. "What're you telling him? Didn't you tell him you aren't interested?"

"Of course, Jesus, Will, what do you think? He's a pig. I used to think he was an interesting person, but now I think he's just a bully who gets pissed when he doesn't have his own way."

"So how did he get so interested in you? I didn't think you knew him that well."

"I don't. A few meetings at parties. A few talks about getting the plant material." She paused. "I had lunch with him once. He invited me after a meeting in his office." She finished her cigarette and went for another. She was dressed in tight jeans, a tee shirt, and a leather vest. Will stared at her breasts and the nipples that were clearly visible through her tee. It wasn't unusual for her to dress this way, braless, it was the trend, at least in this part of the country. But why did she dress this way when she knew she'd be with this horny old lecher who apparently had a real hard-on for her? There's more than lunch behind this, Will thought. He didn't really care. Well, maybe that wasn't true. Who the hell understands all this?

He looked again at his dad's letter and his eyes settled on the words at the bottom of the next-to-last page:

... your mother disappeared, you were almost 12 years old, and left me to care for you myself. From that moment on that's all I cared about, making life right for you. I hope I have succeeded. Of course, I know there's something a mother gives that a father just can't. I hope the fact that I never found another mother for you (I think that would have been impossible) has not left some deep wound, an emptiness in you.

Will felt immensely sad at that moment. Never had such a deep sadness found its way into him. Never. Maybe his twelfth birthday was like this, he couldn't remember.

Elaine tossed off her clothes and was prancing around naked. Will stared at her superb body and wondered what part of him this woman touched? Jesus, he hoped she didn't want sex now. He couldn't. No. She headed to the shower, maybe to get rid of the Schaefer grime.

Later, when Elaine had dressed and calmed down, she made some dinner, one of her very good mushroom omelets. Will hid his father's letter in some of his lab files, he didn't want Elaine to read it. He would have to write back, but what in the world could he say in response?

As they ate Elaine brought up, for the first time since the beach day in Atlantic City, the question of Will's writing progress on his dissertation. He'd been in the Chemistry Department library everyday, as far as she could tell. It was now the twentieth of September, and he had had ten full days at the desk. She knew Will could write well and fast when he wanted to.

"Okay. It's okay. Not real fast. The details of each of these reaction steps are complex and very tedious to write up, to say nothing of the evidence supporting the structures of each reaction product. Maybe step seven, five to go."

"What about the background, the literature review, explaining the basis for the synthesis design?" Elaine seemed pleased with Will's response. It was the first indication she'd had that he was making progress. He seemed down most of the time, and she assumed he was still fighting the monster he'd created for himself. But Elaine still believed that what she had done to help him was the right thing to do, that he'd crawl out of this pit, and that he'd want her right by his side. She still had a hearty passion for him, he had reached parts of her she'd never known. When Will was at his most withdrawn he was still more exciting and interesting to her than anyone she'd been with in the past. The future would be great, what a powerhouse team they'd be. A year for Will at NIH; she'd join him when her year was up at Berkeley in March of '68, and then the two of them would move on. Maybe a drug company, maybe a top-flight university, maybe someday their own company - - drug development. They had the scientific skills, the right level of ambition, the strength of personality. The demons would be banished.

Will didn't answer Elaine's last question, and she didn't pressure him. They did the dishes together and then read for the rest of the evening. Elaine had more thoughts about the pig. She just had to avoid him at all costs. Tomorrow she'd unwrap the dried pfaffia plant material and begin the Soxhlet extraction that was the first step in the isolation. She'd run the whole thing through, starting with a trial batch of about two kilos of dried material. By the end of Monday, the 25th, she'd complete her run of that batch. If all goes well, she'd be ready to go to about 6-8 kilos, which would yield the maximum amount of extract she could put through her lab-scale system. Two such runs, she estimated, would yield at least 25 grams of pfaffadine, enough to keep the NCI running through the next two test batteries. If the compound still looked promising at that stage, the NCI would probably contract with a pilot-plant facility to procure very large amounts of plant material, and to operate the Callahan isolation system on a scale sufficient to produce enough pfaffadine to determine how toxic it was and, assuming it was not excessively dangerous, to move into the clinical setting, into cancer patients. This would be tremendous.

She needed to talk to Alden Jensen about getting patents for her invention.

Elaine slept well that night, though Will's sadness remained with him and prevented him from sleeping. He wished he could explain things, explain his actions, to his dad. God, how impossible to contemplate. What was there to explain? Why he had cheated? How some weakness in him had taken control during a period in which he had lost confidence in his abilities? He should have confessed to Jensen way back. Even Elaine had suggested this at first. Now he was way past that. He had presented his work to the community of chemists whose own activities were closely allied to his. The big lie had come out of his mouth, there on that small platform in the dark meeting room in Atlantic City. Why had he accepted help from Elaine? She had put herself in jeopardy by helping him to cheat the system. Why? Was this out of love? She couldn't have loved him then, they'd barely known each other. Who was she? What was she to him? Schaefer. He thought she must have slept with Schaefer, though he didn't know why. Maybe not. Schaefer was a pig, and Elaine didn't need him. Will finally fell off to sleep, but it was Gina he thought of as the darkness descended.

The next afternoon Will sat at his desk in the chemistry library and attempted to write down the exact experimental details of the last step of his synthesis. The first eleven, up to pre- pfaff, were nearly done, more near completion than he had suggested to Elaine. The pre-pfaff-to-pfaff step was going to be the tough one to record. He had his lab notebook open to the relevant pages. He had all the analytical and spectroscopic data that had suggested that, after his first try, the few milligrams of material he had isolated from the reaction system was indeed pfaffadine. It seemed to check out on every count. He studied his results in detail for the hundredth time. He had had it! But he could not repeat it. He could not demonstrate that he could repeat this last step. And then the pre-pfaff was nearly gone, and he had in him no will to repeat the long, tedious synthesis of pre-pfaff. Jesus, what a loser he was. No character. He should quit. He left the library and walked out into the cool September afternoon.

Where could he turn? Who could he turn to? He was completely alone in this sin. Even Elaine was innocent, she was blameless here.

He walked quietly across campus, by the Campanile and through Sather Gate to Sproul Plaza, where a crowd had gathered to listen to and cheer on several anti-war speakers and a Black Panther representative. He thought he saw David Zaretsky standing next to the black speaker who was in a rage about the indifference of the mostly white students who crowded the Plaza. He couldn't be sure it was David, because the guy up there was wearing a beard, a pretty scraggly one. Will stopped and studied the guy's face for a while and decided it was indeed David. He wondered if he was going to speak, but decided not to wait to find out.

Will skirted the crowd, found his way to Bancroft, and started uphill. He'd left his sweater behind in the library, and was feeling the chill of the late September afternoon, the first day of fall. Fall. His favorite season, his father cheering him on at the high school football games; the New England autumns that are so special and like no other ones. Berkeley was still all green and brown. No seasons here, no yellows and reds. In ten minutes he was standing a block away from the group house where Gina now lived. The winds were now quite strong and a serious chill was settling in. Will was cold. He stood and stared, shivering. The lawn where he had seen Gina raking up trash was deserted. The house seemed deserted. A small sports car raced up, and the good-looking woman at the wheel gave Will a smile and a wave as she flew past him. Will Getz stood for several minutes in the late fall afternoon wind, peering at Gina's home, wondering which room was hers.

CHAPTER 14

Chris Swift had agreed to meet Peter Friday night for a beer at the Crow Bar on Telegraph. He'd been to the movies twice during the previous week with Gina, both times to see *Casablanca*. They'd spent a lot of time together, talking about the church and about other aspects of their lives. He'd found Gina to be thoughtful, quiet but firm in many of her views. He had never talked in such depth with a fallen Catholic, and had never felt so challenged in his thinking. He was awkward around women, though he knew they found him attractive. It had been that way since high school. He'd wanted to spend tonight with her, maybe cooking up some food together, but felt he had to keep his promise to Peter, who was coming over from San Francisco.

Chris got to the bar at about eight, and spotted Peter at a table with Preston Schaefer and David Zaretsky. The priest was disappointed to see Schaefer and was not anxious to be around him after the events of last summer. Peter greeted Chris and poured him a beer from one of three large pitchers at the table. The place was crowded and noisy as hell, standing room only. It reeked of beer, cigarette smoke, and marijuana. As usual Preston Schaefer was holding forth. Chris's arrival didn't cause the slightest pause in his delivery, and the big guy gave no indication he even noticed the priest.

"I've got this commitment to finish an essay for *Breaking the Hold* by the end of the month. I'm having a hell of a time, I know what I want to say, but can't get by the first paragraph." He swilled down nearly a full glass of beer, and went right on.

"You know I've been exploring this angle on science and the power structure in this country. Or in the West, Europe too. I've come to believe that science is the source of the power the imperialists hold over the rest of the world. The method of science. It's fucking powerful, makes claims about getting to the only real truths. I think that's bullshit. Science does get to a certain kind of truth that provides incredible power, technical power, to those who possess it and believe in it. But its way of getting at the truth is in fact no better than a dozen other ways. It just seems better because the so-called truths it finds give enormous power to those in possession of them. The nation states of the West. I've got to learn how to say this clearly, structure the argument. I know it's true, you know it's true, and it's got to be heard by the world outside our little group." He grinned, then laughed. "The root of evil, modern evil, like Faust, huh? It's the model of science. Maybe Dr. Frankenstein is better!"

The big man continued. "When I publish this thesis, wait and see, I'll be famous overnight - - it's a startling original idea, I'll change the world! - - then we'll hit 'em with our other plan!"

"Preston, man, slow down, or change the subject, please. We all know your ideas here, we've been hearing them all summer, all of us. You know we agree. You just need to take the time to write them up. Our group is tuned in already," exclaimed David, as he refilled Schaefer's beer glass.

"You are on to something we all agree," said Peter. "But you could benefit from a little exposure to Zen, you know. It turns these Western ideas about truth upside down. Or maybe it's better to say it just shows they are irrelevant."

"Irrelevant! God no. My insight explains a lot about the behavior of the imperial powers. You've got to understand their source if you hope to change those behaviors. Father Swift, how the fuck are you? You back in our group? You've come to see the wisdom of my ways?"

Chris flinched and said nothing. He just stared nervously at Peter.

"So, what about women, Weiss-man? Are these Buddhists you're with like the Catholics? No pussy? Sorry, Father," Schaefer blurted out. "God I couldn't take that. I can't believe you don't get any. Father Swift, sit, don't go. God, the women must be crawling all over you."

Chris felt the warmth of a blush come over him, and hoped it wasn't visible. He began to feel he should leave. He hadn't expected to see Schaefer, he had had enough of this guy.

Schaefer turned to Peter and spoke. "I could never figure you. Always talking about women, at least to me. But never about yourself and women, always about others and women. And sex. Who was screwing who. Or whom. I figure you for a virgin, Weiss. What about it? Real interested in other people's sex lives. A voyeur? What about it?"

Peter was silent. His smile turned to a weak frown, which he immediately covered in a cloud of smoke. "Don't talk to me about women, Schaefer. I know your weird habits real well. Undergraduates. You know the tricks to get them to drop their pants for you. Get them stoned, make them think you're a big deal professor of everything. Fool them. Very honorable." Peter was smiling again. So was Schaefer.

"Come on, Schaefer's no fake. He's a top-notch mind, an important figure in our cause. Women find his powers intoxicating," David offered.

"Not women. Little girls, high schoolers. Freshmen. Just girls looking for daddy."

"Weiss why are you attacking me like this? Getting your kicks talking about my sex life!" They ordered two more pitchers of beer and listened to Schaefer carry on about a young woman standing at the bar and how he'd like to impress her.

"What about Elaine? Whatever her last name is. You talked about her and how great she was. Next thing I knew she was living with Will what's his name, the chemistry guy. She left you real quick.

Too old for you Schaefer? She was maybe past 22? You thought she really had a thing for you. She vanished fast." Peter was not going to let up, not going to let Schaefer get back into a position of dominance on this topic. He knew the subject of Elaine would put Schaefer on the run.

"Will, you mean Getz, who used to be with Gina, who's now living with Kay up at my old house?" David asked. "I'd heard Will had taken up with someone else and left Gina high and dry. Gina's okay, but I can't figure Will on this. So you had a thing with her, Elaine I mean?" He turned to Schaefer.

"I don't wanna talk about her." Schaefer tilted his chair back, and turned his head away from the group.

Chris listened with intense interest to this last exchange. He knew a little about Gina and Will, but not much. Gina had only mentioned Will and that they'd lived together for quite awhile. She said only that their relationship just weakened and when it had completely petered out they'd separated. A mutual thing, she'd hinted. Chris wondered now about this Elaine, and whether Will had actually left Gina for her. Gina had never mentioned this other woman.

"You won't tell us what happened? Come on, Preston, you're not generally shy about these things. Will Getz is a really good looking guy. You are not. So, for all your manly charms, you still can't compete with really good looks! I met this Elaine, I've seen her. She fits better with Getz. You probably never had a chance. Schaefer in love!" Peter smiled and took up another cigarette, at least his fifth since Chris had come in.

"Look, I don't want to discuss this. So shut the fuck up about it. There's more important stuff to talk about. Zaretsky and I, for instance, are getting ready for a trip to Guatemala. Some research. Warfare. We're walking right into the middle of a guerrilla war down there. The very indians we're working with are in full-scale revolt against a bunch of puppets of the old U.S. of A. I'm personally scared shitless, but still excited about going. 'Course this is right up Zaretsky's alley, now that he's gone and joined a bunch of wild ass warriors in Oakland. Armed revolt. Good for you, Zaretsky. You'll piss off your old liberal parents, pacifists I'm sure. I'm going to teach you yet the value of sticking with me."

A roar came over the crowd as two young girls climbed up onto the bar and started to dance to the music that was blaring from the juke box. They were encouraged by the roar of the crowd and went into a kind of frenzy. The four at the table turned to watch, and then all except Chris stood up as it became apparent that the two were going to strip. No one interfered and they were soon completely naked. They dropped off the bar when the music ended and disappeared into the crowd. The three sat.

"Too much for you, Father?" Schaefer chortled and Chris felt another blush. "How can you resist that, a guy like you? Don't you get it? By the way are you going to find a home somewhere, some church? Aren't you out of work? Maybe you can be priest to our group? A true priest should love my ideas and plans, one with any balls, anyway. We already suspect you have no balls, don't we?" Schaefer then glared at Chris, and a fierce grin poked through his beard. He drank some more of his beer and then spat out, "You freakin' coward. I thought you wanted to change the world - - I give you the chance and you run away. You freakin' coward." He turned away from Chris in disgust.

The priest was shaken by Schaefer's outburst, and got up to leave, but Peter grabbed his arm and told him to sit down. Chris complied.

They spent the rest of the evening in small talk with Peter continuing to harass Schaefer about Elaine. At around ten o'clock, Chris said his good-byes, promised to visit Peter in the city, and then began to take his leave. He was anxious to see Gina. At that moment, it occurred to him that he'd not said to Schaefer what had been on his mind since he saw him when he first entered the bar. He sat down and turned to look Schaefer, who was sitting next to him, directly in the face.

"You know, you really were unfair to Gina. She's seriously wounded in her heart over this Guatemala thing. Your actions don't make sense. I wish you'd change your mind, or give her a better explanation. You really disappointed her. She's thinking about getting out, from anthropology." Chris had no idea whether this last statement was true, but he'd inferred it from some things Gina had said. It also didn't seem to be true that she had been wounded. She was angry and disappointed, but not in despair. But why not make Schaefer feel guilty, if that was even remotely possible?

Schaefer said nothing. Peter said, with feigned sarcasm, "Schaefer, you beast. What did you do to the poor woman? I thought she was going, I heard her say that just a couple of weeks ago. What did you do? Did she refuse to put out for you? Is that it?"

This was too much for Schaefer, and he lurched across the table, grabbed Peter by the lapels of his jacket and bellowed, "You asshole. What's with you tonight? What are you ..."

David and Chris grabbed Schaefer and with much effort were able to get his huge body back down onto his chair. He was furious. "You fucking asshole, you goon. You take your virginity out on me, is that it? You can't get it up, it just hangs like a little worm?" Half the people in the bar heard this, and Peter was visibly shaken by the ferocious outburst. He quickly rose from his seat, grabbed his cigarettes from the table, and disappeared into the staring crowd, heading for the door. Chris dropped a five-dollar bill on the table to cover his drinks, and followed after Peter. He was nowhere to be seen when Chris reached the sidewalk, so he decided to go home.

Up at the big house, Gina had spent the evening with Kay, first at dinner and then in Kay's large bedroom. They'd lugged a large jug of wine up to the bedroom and drank and gabbed about everything under the sun, including the devil Schaefer, Chris' apparent aimlessness and his many compensating charms, Marco's big exhibit, and Kay's interview that afternoon with a black activist and feminist named Angela Davis, who'd come up from Southern California to lecture and participate in Bay area organizing events on behalf of several black groups.

The two women were talking politics and agreed on the need to rescue Hubert Humphrey, a good man, from Lyndon Johnson, when Chris burst in.

"I'm for Humphrey." Chris spoke as he entered the bedroom. He poured himself some wine and sat down on the edge of Kay's bed, where the two women were lying. He couldn't help noticing how beautiful Gina looked, her long dark hair spread out over the large pillow she was lying against.

The three chatted and drank into the early morning hours. Kay was the first to fall asleep. Gina and Chris continued to talk in a whisper until he collapsed into his own slumber. Gina gazed for a long time over these two wonderful people who had come into her life. In quite different ways they brought new life to her. Kay made her think about social and political issues in new ways; she was able to make her ideas incredibly clear and she could also put them into larger contexts. She was progressive, yet balanced, a radical in the true meaning of the word, she got to the roots of things. She tried to interrelate and integrate things. Kay Hooper was no one- dimensional character like so many people who claimed to be on the left. Chris Swift was no deep thinker, but he was someone whose commitment to the good she found very attractive. Gina had a lot of doubts about the church and thought Chris's views on many subjects were pretty naive, but his commitment to the church and to bring out the best the church had to offer - - its devotion to the poor, the ill, the least of God's creatures - - overrode most of that. Besides, Gina was stuck on him in other ways, she couldn't deny this, especially when this wine haze permeated her thinking. He is really beautiful, and I have this desire for him, she thought, that grows every time I'm with him. He surely likes me, but he's never...

With that thought Gina moved across the bed and laid herself beside his sleeping form. She moved her head above his, and lowered her lips to his. A light kiss, though long. He did not respond, so she continued, without any thought about what she was doing. Kay turned and opened her eyes to see the kiss. When she realized what was happening, she sat upright, a little startled. Gina turned to look at her. Kay, looking puzzled, got up from the bed, turned off the light, and left the room, to go to Gina's room for the night. In the dark, Gina turned away from Chris, Father Swift, beautiful Father Swift, and just lay wondering where all this might lead. And down the hall, in Gina's room, Kay Hooper undressed and crawled into Gina's bed, shaken not for the obvious reason, but because she knew what she felt for Gina was even more forbidden than what she had just seen. She caressed Gina's pillow, smelled it, imagined her lovely face there in her hands, and wept because the reality was so remote from the desire.

CHAPTER 15

Will and Elaine were in her car and driving up to Alden Jensen's house for a gathering of his grad students and post-docs. The hills above Berkeley were unusually cold for early October, and rain was coming down in torrents. The driving was slow. Elaine had been quiet all evening, but as they were nearing the Jensen residence she started in.

"The bastard left me a long letter, left it on my lab desk yesterday, right out in the open. I think he's either insane or evil."

"You mean Schaefer? I thought he was leaving the country."

"He is, this week. I think maybe he left Monday. He'll be gone 'til the middle of November. David Zaretsky and some other guy are with him. But you should read this letter."

"Do you have it? Why didn't you show me it earlier?" Will wasn't really that interested, but he pretended he was. "This is Jensen's house, we're here. We have to go in. We can't talk about this now."

"I know. I just wanted you to know. It will explain my mood this evening." Elaine put out her cigarette, and the two hopped out of the car and made a dash to Jensen's porch. They rang the bell and were almost immediately welcomed in by Betty Jensen, the professor's wife.

The living room was filled with familiar faces. Alden Jensen had six graduate students in addition to Will and three post-docs, including Elaine. All seemed to be present, most with companions or wives. Elaine and Genevieve Florian, a graduate student, were the only females in Jensen's group. Most had put on their best clothes for the occasion, and presented quite a different picture than the one they presented in the fourth floor labs.

The conversations were wide-ranging, from the inevitable discussions of the latest Vietnam tragedies, to expectations for the 1968 elections, to the recent race riots in Detroit, to the dismal U.C. football record so far this season. There was even some shop talk, mostly about Bill Kane's recent defense of his thesis and his plans for a post-doc at Stanford. The bright talk continued through the buffet-style dinner the Jensens had laid out, food that was at a qualitatively different level than anything these students were accustomed to. Much of the discussion was political, but it wasn't very heated because most in the room held the same, liberal views. Only a graduate student named Lochsley stood out, because he was firmly in the pro-war camp and wasn't the least bit shy about defending his views.

During the coffee and dessert, Alden Jensen spoke out. "I just wanted to say a few words while we're all gathered together. In the day-to-day grind of research we rarely have a chance to talk much about the larger enterprise we're all involved in and the goals we're trying to accomplish. I can say honestly and without exaggeration that in my nearly 20 years of experience at this great university, I've never had a brighter, more dedicated and hard-working group of students than I have now. I've had in the past a few individuals, Roger Wilford for sure, maybe John Greene and a few others, who were extraordinary talents, but never a whole group at your level. The country, the city here, the campus, are suffering through some turbulent times, and we can't ignore them. We're not just scientists, we're also citizens. I hope though that the outside world is not such a huge distraction - - and I don't think it is - - that we ignore or give short shrift to our science. I grew up in an era that was just discovering how important science is to our civilization, and you people have had that idea drilled into you since at least high school. It's true, not just because science gives us technologies that make life better, but because it teaches a way of knowing about the world and a way to understand the wonders of that world. I'm beginning to sound like a preacher, and maybe I am on this subject. Everyday we're doing something in the lab that is going to teach us something about the world in a way no other method can match. Keep that idea in your heads as you work. It helps especially when you think you've lost your way, can't get what you're looking for ... go back to fundamentals and stick with them. The scientific enterprise has been enormously fulfilling for me, and it will be that way for you and for the society you're serving. Enough. Let me congratulate Bill Kane for his achievement and wish him the best for his next step. Also, Elaine, for your isolation system which looks great - - I understand you've just completed a successful repeat of the pfaffadine isolation - - and Will for his pfaffadine synthesis, which you've all known about since last summer. We've got several more equally remarkable achievements, and we're going to produce a flood of publications next year. You've all made me very proud, and I'll do my damndest to help you all take your next steps. To my scientific children!" Jensen raised a glass of wine in toast to his group as they in turn gave the professor a round of applause.

Will took a seat in a corner of the living room to avoid the various conversations that were underway. Jensen's words echoed in his mind.

Will had immense admiration for Alden Jensen, and from his first encounter with the professor, he had fixed in his mind that Jensen was the type of scientist he wanted to emulate. Jensen had an excellent record of achievement in natural products chemistry. His work centered on compounds, such as pfaffadine, that might have use in medicine. Most of the major pharmaceuticals were of natural origin - - plant products such as morphine and quinine and fungal products such as penicillins - - or were close chemical relatives of such products, modified by chemists to improve their efficacy or safety profiles. The research in this area was, to Will, highly exciting chemistry and its excitement doubled because of its potential value to medicine. Experts like Jensen also did very well financially because they were in demand as consultants to pharmaceutical firms. That's why Jensen spent so much time away, on the East coast.

Now that pfaffadine had passed NCI's first level of anti-cancer screening, it was possible that it might ultimately make the small, select list of effective cancer drugs (though effectiveness, he knew, was a relative term, because even the best, FDA-approved cancer drugs had pretty small margins between the effective dose and the toxic dose). Ordinarily someone in Will's position would be thrilled at this prospect. Instead Will was only terrified that NCI would for some reason turn to his "synthesis" instead of Elaine's isolation system to produce more pfaffadine and then the truth would come out. God, what a horrifying prospect.

Will glanced up and saw Elaine talking with Brad Mitchell, the newest post-doc. She was standing very close to him and was apparently completely absorbed by whatever he was saying. She flirted with anybody halfway good looking and Mitchell was very good looking. He thought, "Bitch. She's got more pfaffadine. Her system works. Our fraud is now completely undiscoverable. Or at least there'll be no reason for anyone to try to repeat my synthesis, so my deception, my fucking lie, will not be discovered."

Will hated what he had done. He hated himself for being the kind of person who could do what he had done. He hated Elaine for helping him complete the deception, and for trapping him into this relationship so that he could ensure she wouldn't reveal his lie. He hated what he had done to Gina. He hated all this self-pity, too. Jesus. I need to end this ... his mind went blank and the next thing he knew Elaine was tugging at his arm, urging him to leave the party.

Will managed to thank the Jensens for the great evening and silently thanked Alden for not asking about progress on his dissertation. The rain had ceased but it was intensely cold, so he and

Elaine ran to their car and got the heater going. They sat for a few minutes in silence as the car warmed up.

"You were pretty glum all night, you hardly spoke. I'm the one with this idiot Schaefer hanging over me. You should read his letter. I'm the one with a reason to be glum."

Will didn't respond, but was captured by his own thoughts. Maybe this woman, this woman who is really smart, does not understand the seriousness of my crime, or even of her own participation in it. Could she be so dumb? Didn't she hear Jensen's words? Or maybe she just doesn't give a shit. She's ambitious as hell, and won't let anything in her way. Ambitious not only professionally, but also in her desire to have me in her life. The shameless bitch will do anything. Will put the car into gear, and drove off toward the apartment that was his prison. Angry now. Really angry.

As she prepared for bed, Elaine Callahan avoided Will as much as possible. She knew he was angry and that he had not gotten past his problem. His anger was now even directed at her, maybe for getting him in deeper. She knew her need to have him was deep, although she didn't equate that need with love. Love was an unclear idea for her, need was much clearer, she could feel it at her core. But she was at a loss, was becoming increasingly incapable of dealing with Will and his beast. It seems he cannot overcome it. She knew he was paralyzed. He couldn't just keep going to the library and staring at the walls. She had to think of some other way to get him to move on. Her clear success with isolating pfaff this past week should have helped, because it made his synthesis irrelevant, but he had not reacted to the news in a positive way, at least after his initial smile.

She thought she'd better not get into bed with him tonight. The last time they'd tried sex it was a failure. Will was not interested, and it was hard to see what might come next. Elaine curled up on the sofa and pulled a large blanket over her body. She was not ready to give up on this man and she fantasized about some future with him that was all power and influence and sex.

On Sunday morning Will awoke very early. He quietly made himself some instant coffee, lit up a cigarette, and sat at the small kitchen table. The window above the table faced east, and the first rays of the sun beamed up from behind the Berkeley hills above him and began to light up the apartment. He thought about running, the one thing he had managed to pursue consistently for the past month. He then saw the letter Elaine had talked about laid out on the table before him, along with some other papers. He read the letter.

1 October, 1967

Elaine:

I am off to Guatemala next week and won't be back until November 12 or 13. I won't have a chance to speak directly with you, but I wanted to give you something to think about.

You led me to you. You placed yourself in my path. You offered yourself. You showed me something that most women I have known do not have. You showed me power, strength, high intelligence. I have not known these things to be present in women who also have the ability to entrance, to charm, to please. I have cast off more women than I can count. I have glimpsed in a few some of your characteristics, but you showed me everything.

I am not the kind of man who can release such a bounty. You led me to your arms. You cannot just drop the kind of man I am.

And what kind is that? You know. I watched as you sat with me, saw that you understood. I have a will like no man you have known. I couple my will with more intelligence than you can now understand. I shall lead. I have within me the skill and understanding of what we need to do to create the society we need to become. My academic work is useful to my project, but is only a step. If you study my political and social writings you will see where I am leading. I have new, completely new, ideas that will change society forever, and I have a project to implement them. An amazing project.

You can join in my project. I need people like you. I also need the woman you are. I shall not fail. You will find ecstasies of mind and body that are beyond anything you have known!

I have academic as well as political goals in Guatemala. I will tell you about these when I return. I am not the kind of man who lets irrelevancies stand in his way. I know that person to whom you now think you are attached is a weak creature. I understand this from a friend, you may know him, a certain philosopher. I shall return.

Preston Schaefer
The Future
Your Future.

CHAPTER 16

Chris Swift and Gina headed south out of San Francisco on Highway 101, toward Palo Alto and the Fulton Gallery's showing of Marco's paintings. It was opening night and there would be some refreshments served to the group of invited guests and a chance to meet the artist. Marco had not had a show of this size for several years, and had never been the sole artist exhibited. Gina was truly happy for him and prayed it would be successful beyond anything he'd previously known. Her beloved dad needed this in his life, which was fast approaching late middle age. Funny how he still looked to her the way he had always looked, handsome and kindly, a touch of sadness and loneliness in his eyes.

"I heard from Father Sullivan this afternoon. He's talked to two assistants of Bishop Sperling in San Francisco, to see if I can get attached to a parish up here. This Bishop's pretty liberal, unlike the reactionary McIntire in L.A., the one who ran me out. But no dice. No luck. No home. He said I should go back to L.A., apologize to McIntire, and return to my assigned parish. I can't do that. Maybe the church isn't for me. I'm really feeling lost. I can't just continue this way."

Gina turned off the freeway as they neared Palo Alto and looked for the Mountain View highway.

"Jesus, Chris, I'm sorry. Isn't there some other ..."

"Not really. In the Church you get assigned; you take what you're assigned. They put you where they think you're needed. Maybe I should just go back to L.A., ignore McIntire. Do my thing. I can serve the parish and also spend some time on the types of activities that I think the Church should be pursuing - - antiwar, anti-poverty, anti-racism - - there's plenty of opportunities. But McIntire is really right-wing. He squashes nuns and priests who are out there on these issues, at every opportunity. God, I wish he'd just go."

"Maybe you should forget the Church. Get a job to just get by, and get in with some activist groups in the Bay Area. You don't have to be a priest to do good things."

"Maybe." He paused, and then read off some directions to Gina. "What about you? You've been so disappointed over Schaefer's thing. You were even talking about dropping out of anthropology. You haven't talked much about this lately. What've you been thinking?"

"I have been talking with Kay. I'm just becoming more and more interested in what she's doing. Not journalism. That's not for me. But working on social issues, political stuff. I'm no radical. I could never be, but I think we're in a time for great social change. Kay's got the right attitudes on how it should come about. How we should forget about ideology, but work to unify all these different forces for progress. The New Left's wrong in its approach. It's too divisive. I'm really learning a lot from Kay, and what she's given me to read."

They pulled into a lot next to the Fulton Gallery and parked the VW. It was dusk, and they got out of the car and approached the gallery. "Law. Maybe law school. That's what I've been thinking about. Lawyers have tremendous influence in America, and they don't all have to work for large corporations or big law firms. There's plenty of room for making real change through the legal system. Kay's right. You can talk all you want about race riots and marches in the street, but it was the Supreme Court's decision on school integration - - you know what I mean, the Brown case in the 50's - - that really had an effect. I hate Lyndon Johnson's war, but think of all these civil rights laws he's passed. Think of the opportunities for change by working through the legal system." As soon as she uttered these words she recognized that there must be some new Gina emerging under the influence of Kay, and maybe because of Chris, too. She had thought about matters such as these in the past, and had discussed some of them with Will - - only Will - - but they had always seemed unfocused and incoherent and irrelevant to her life and future. Kay, it seemed, was definitely having an influence. "The more I think about it, the more I ..." They were in the gallery and immediately Gina was in Marco's embrace.

"Having you here is the most important thing to me, dear Gina," and he kissed her on the cheek. He noticed Chris and asked about him.

"A friend. Chris Swift. Actually, Father Chris Swift. No collar tonight. A friend I met a few months ago. He asked to come along when I told him about you and the show."

"A priest! Well, I'm glad to see you have such friends! Come, I will take you around. Oh. Get some food and some wine. It's very good."

The show was a real treat for Gina and she was overwhelmed with joy for her father. She displayed a heartfelt smile all evening and spent a lot of time observing the other guests and how they seemed to regard her father's work. She noticed by closing time that three of the two dozen paintings had been marked as sold, and she wondered if it was possible that most or all would be sold by the time the show closed in November. She and Chris spent a long time absorbing one very recent work that she thought was outstanding; something in it moved her deeply, drew her from the extraordinary chaos of colors and shapes buried at its center to the vast and clear peace that formed its border. She imagined it on the large bare wall of her small room.

The evening closed with Marco, in a state of elation and perhaps drunkenness, thanking them for coming and inviting them to his place for dinner on the upcoming Sunday. Gina said they might be able to come, and she'd call on Saturday to confirm. Marco walked them to the car and they exchanged goodnights.

"That was great. I really liked the paintings. I might have guessed you'd have a father like that. What about your mother, where's she?" They pulled out of the lot and headed back toward 101.

In all their time together over the past month, the subject of her mother hadn't come up. In fact until tonight neither had said much about their families. They'd talked mostly about their own pasts in school, their beliefs, their likes and dislikes. Gina didn't feel like talking about her mother just then, but felt she had to say something.

"She's dead. An accident, an auto accident, about eight years ago. My father never remarried."

"Oh. I'm sorry. We haven't talked about parents 'til now. I never guessed. I'm sorry. That must have been really hard on you. You were what, sixteen? God. I can't imagine."

Gina wanted to change the subject. "Yeah, I was a long time getting over it ... but it's okay now. What about you? Your parents? Where are they?"

"They're pretty ordinary. Like you, I am an only child. My mother was, or is, very religious, very devoted. I think she once thought about becoming a nun. But she met my dad, Christopher, when she spent the summer after high school graduation working at a camp near Ojai. He was a carpenter, working there at the camp. He still is a carpenter, works construction all over the Orange County area. They married about a year after they met. My mother, Agnes, just takes care of the house, and helps around the parish. They lead a very quiet life, same house they moved into the year I was born, 1940. I don't think you'd find them very interesting."

"Most people are more interesting than we give them credit for. You have to take the time to get to know them."

"Maybe. I'll bet Marco is. I wonder why he's alone. I'd think he'd be very attractive to many women."

"I think the same about you." Gina wasn't sure where these words came from. There was a long pause, and then she decided to pursue the matter. "You're very attractive, that's no secret. I find you very attractive in many ways. I sometimes wonder how you could possibly escape all the temptations that must have come before you. You did take a vow of celibacy, n'est pas?" She was slightly tipsy and feeling spunky. She remembered kissing him when he was asleep, and lying beside him all night. He can't be a virgin.

"Alright. I'll tell you. I did take a vow like that and I've kept it. I had relationships in high school, but once I got into seminary, I didn't." He seemed to be embarrassed.

"Really, nothing for all those years?! What's that, maybe eight or nine years! I find that hard to believe, someone like you."

"You can't seem to understand my commitment. I kid around sometimes, and maybe seem superficial, but I'm very firm in my beliefs and in my dedication to God. I'm not sure where this came from, but it's in me. God, and justice on earth. I haven't been really focused this whole time since I left LA, but it'll happen again."

"Doubts? You must have had doubts. You spent all that time with Peter. He's some kind of cynic, or maybe skeptic. Buddhist now, right? Boy that's weird. Maybe he's that but he'd think the kind of spirituality you're talking about is pretty juvenile." This type of free and easy conversation with a man other than her father was exciting to Gina, new even. It had occurred in the early days with Will, but this somehow seemed different to her.

They traversed the Bay Bridge toward Oakland and then turned north toward Berkeley. Once near the campus they decided to get some coffee and something sweet. They parked on Durant, walked up to Telegraph, and found their way to the Telegraph Avenue Cafe. It was crowded, standing room only, but they got some pie and coffee, and squeezed into a spot at the stand-up counter that ran along one wall. Gina was for some reason famished and dug into her large serving of pie and ice cream. Chris had decided against dessert, and just stood sipping his coffee, and looking at Gina. As she got about halfway through her dessert, her eyes opened wide, as if in shock.

"Jesus."

"What's the matter?"

"Will. That's Will over there, sitting in the corner. You know. Will Getz, the one I told you about." Gina recognized the woman with him. Elaine what's-her-name? His lover. Gina turned so that Will could not see her face if he were to look up. She wasn't sure, but there was no sign he had noticed her. Chris could see that she was disturbed in some way by Will's presence. Or maybe Elaine's. He wasn't sure what to say. Gina stopped eating, and stood quietly, staring down at her dessert and coffee. Chris finished his coffee, and asked if she wanted to leave.

"Yes, let's go." She turned and led Chris by the hand across the crowded room, and then directly up to Will and Elaine.

"Hello, Will." Gina stared directly into his eyes as he raised his head. Will, startled, leaned back in his chair, and inadvertently knocked over his coffee cup, which fortunately was near-empty. Elaine turned to look at Will, and then turned toward Gina. She also took in Chris.

"This is Chris Swift, a friend. Will and, Elaine, right?"

"Right, I'm Elaine Callahan."

Will said nothing and did not extend his hand to Chris when the priest offered his.

"You look fine. You finished with your thesis? Ph.D. yet? What's next?"

Will didn't speak, but Elaine wasn't shy. "He's still writing. He'll be done in a few weeks. Not sure about the next step, maybe back East."

Gina saw that the situation was difficult for Will, so she decided to cut off the discussion. "Good to see you. Good luck." She led Chris out the door and onto Telegraph. She was shaken by the brief confrontation, but glad she'd gone through it. She had continued to think about Will from time-to-time, had tried to understand his odd behavior, but had come up with nothing that satisfied her. She also knew that her interest in him had not completely dissipated. There may even have been a small flare up during their brief meeting. She gripped Chris' hand hard as they headed back to the car.

They didn't talk during the short drive up to the Manse. The house was mostly dark. Someone was watching television in the living room but otherwise the house seemed deserted. Kay was away for the weekend, visiting a friend down in Santa Cruz. Chris and Gina climbed the stairs and headed down the hall toward their rooms. As Chris started to say goodnight, Gina reached for him and pulled him toward her. "Please, can you stay with me awhile?" He hesitated, then smiled and followed her into her small, dark room, lit only by the faint glow of a nearby street lamp. Chris closed the door and took off his coat. Gina turned and put her arms around him, burying her face in his shoulder. He wrapped his arms around her small shoulders, and gently pulled her closer. They remained in this position for several moments, until Gina turned her head and then moved her lips to his. He seemed unresponsive at first, but soon returned her kiss. He pulled her closer, and their kiss and embrace took on more passion. Gina's desire for this person was growing quickly, and she half-consciously hoped that it would show in her kiss and touch, and that this would ignite something deeply submerged in this beautiful man. This priest. The thought did not deter her. She had never been this aggressive with a man.

They fell to her bed, and went through several moments of awkward but impassioned fumbling. Chris turned away at one point and seemed to want to stop. She ran her hand over his chest and then down to a place under his sweater and then up over the bare flesh beneath the sweater. He turned toward her again, and they kissed. Finally, he spoke.

"Gina. Gina. No, I can't do this. It's not you. I'm not made for this. I'm not ..." He seemed anxious, confusion and fear were in his voice. She thought he might fall to his knees and start praying, and this made her laugh, inside. She reached for the belt to his trousers and undid it, and then opened and unbuttoned the trousers. He did nothing, just lay there. She pulled down his zipper, and without hesitation ran her hand beneath his undershorts and found his penis. My priest, my lover, what am I doing?

Chris sat part way up and tried to understand what was happening to him. He looked into Gina's face and found a smile, found two eyes glowing, so pretty, in the reflection of the street lamp.

"Come into my bed. Come into my bed."

They embraced naked under the sheet and blanket. They had lowered the shade and the room had become very dark. Kisses and embraces, her small, lovely body against his lean, maybe too lean, body. She thought his face was as beautiful as a man's could be, and she filled with desire for him as she had for no man since the early months with Will. She ran her hand over his bare chest and moved her body over his. The priest was almost immobile. He returned her kisses and caressed her back, but did little else. She could feel his penis against her thigh, soft and unresponsive to her.

They lay together, talking quietly deep into the night and then into early morning hours. He started several times to apologize because he could not rise to Gina's loving caresses, but she insisted it wasn't important. He was very nervous, at once frightened by the experience and drawn powerfully to it.

Sometime in the early morning darkness they slept, but not for long. As the dawn's light began to penetrate the small room, Chris awoke and turned to gaze upon Gina's face and bare shoulders, her long dark hair spread over the sheets and his own naked chest. He sat up and after a moment's reflection had the urge to leave this sinful space. But he knew within seconds he could not leave this woman and her bed. He slid down between the covers and took her into his arms as she awoke.

"You're still here. I'm so glad."

"We didn't sleep much. It's still early, like 7:00 am."

"Kiss me."

"Yes." And he did, in a full embrace. He slid over her body and she opened her legs and his hips fell between them. In this way, Gina made love with the priest as he finally grew hard against her moist center and she reached to guide him into her body. It was a brief joining, but complete in every important way. He collapsed over her, and she was amazed at his lightness, as if he were only partly flesh. They fell into sleep and did not rise until nearly noon.

Gina and her priest lover spent the rest of the day together, eating, walking around the city and campus, going to a movie. They spoke little about their wonderful night together, but talked more about Gina's ideas for law school and Chris' future in the Church. On this cool and windy Saturday evening, as he walked with Gina up toward the group house after the movie, he wondered if it were still possible, or even desirable for him to continue to seek a place in the community of priests. His parents, his mother especially, would just die if he were to abandon his vows.

Late Saturday night, around midnight, again wrapped together in Gina's bed, Chris spoke.

"I have not known these feelings. It's true Gina. I went out with girls in high school, we did some things, but never this much ... except one, her name was Allison. I was frightened by it though. I don't know why. I never understood this in me. I would have these sexual feelings, but whenever opportunities arose, I ran ..."

"You must have had plenty. You are very good looking. I was drawn to you the first time I saw you." She kissed him, hoping he was ready again to make love. She loved these feelings that seemed to diffuse through her whole body. She had never felt so uninhibited with anyone.

"I'm confused. You are wonderful. I don't know what to do with these feelings. Peter used to ..."

"Do we have to bring him up? I never understood why you two, or how you two ..."

"I came to San Francisco after the confrontation with McIntire. I moved in with an old friend, Bobby White. He's a librarian, lives in the city. I stayed with him awhile. He introduced me to Peter. I thought this guy was really interesting. I still do. Though ... he kind of scared me too. I wasn't displeased when he decided to leave Berkeley."

"What do you mean? What did he do?"

"Well. I shouldn't ... it's embarrassing. He..."

"What? He always gives me the creeps. Tell me."

"Well, he's ... I guess ... a homo, they call it. He tried to get me. He got into my bed once, actually twice. He was undressed and tried to get me to ... you know."

"I can guess. I don't like him, but that stuff has nothing to do with it. That's his business. Maybe it explains a lot. I thought he disliked me. Maybe it's all women? It's like he always knows some secret about you, that smile he always has and those beady eyes. Maybe he's just hiding his own secret. Can we talk about something else?" She moved against Chris and raised her thigh over his hips.

"I once, more than once, thought I must have been. Peter must have thought it about me."

"Must have been what?"

"You know, like him. I had certain desires."

"But did you ever?"

"No. That's the truth. And Peter was okay when I didn't respond, he stopped. He wasn't aggressive about it, and we remained friends, not close, but still friends. But maybe now I know, with you, my real ..." but her kiss cut him off. Gina wanted him, deeply, and she became aggressive, almost attacking him, urging him in every way to come to her. She sat above him, felt him grow, and she lifted him to her center. Gina made love to her priest and was filled with joy.

On Sunday the two visited Marco. He'd prepared a feast for them, a pasta with a perfect marinara sauce followed by a roast of garlicky pork, accompanied by Swiss chard fried in olive oil, and bread that was just out of the oven. All this came with the best wine Marco had in his basement, a bottle Gina's favorite aunt had brought from Italy on a recent visit. The three chatted about a dozen different subjects, told jokes, laughed, and then listened to a couple of recent additions to Marco's jazz record collection. At dusk as they started to leave, Marco put his arms around Gina and held her close. He seemed to want to speak but didn't, just held her and smiled at Chris who was standing outside the entrance to the house. Marco never spoke, and Gina kissed him on the cheek and turned to leave.

The two walked by Saints Peter and Paul Church, where Gina had gone as a child. She showed Chris the nearby Catholic school she'd also attended. He smiled, began to walk toward the church, but then stopped. In the cool Sunday twilight in the beautiful city by the Bay, Father Swift realized with full force the betrayal he had committed against his Church. The guilt stung at his core, but when the woman beside him, the small, dark-haired beauty, took his hand and led him away, he followed without hesitation.

CHAPTER 17

Elaine sped across the Bay Bridge in her '61 red Ford Mustang, the car her father had bought her because, she always thought, he felt some guilt about being the shit he was. She had agreed to meet at a coffee house in the Haight at three, and it was already ten of. She had asked for the meeting so it wasn't good that she was going to be late. It was not a meeting she was looking forward to, but one she thought was necessary.

Will hadn't said a thing to her about the Schaefer letter, except that he had read it. That was more than three weeks ago and not a word had come out of his mouth. In fact neither had he talked about much else. He was going nowhere on his dissertation, and nothing she could say would motivate him. He languished. Her own success in isolating significant amounts of pfaffadine from its natural source gave him the perfect cover, because no one would need to repeat his work. He could go on to great things if he'd just finish. Jensen could not understand Will's lack of progress, and was getting more and more impatient. He wanted Will to get out and move on, and he wanted to get a paper on the synthesis submitted for publication. Will was stuck in the mire he had created for himself, but didn't have the stomach for extricating himself. Elaine had thought Will was a strong man. This was part of the attraction for him she had, but was now losing. Their romance was pretty dry, and he didn't want to do much. He ran, almost everyday, read a little, hardly talked. Their sex life was dead. She still got aroused looking at him and thinking about him, but his behavior was beginning to turn her off. And there was the specter of Preston Schaefer still hanging over her. He'd be back in a couple of weeks, and she needed to do something to fend off the obscene advances he was sure to make. Hence this trip into the city.

It was mid-Sunday afternoon and the coffee shop was near-empty. He was seated at a corner table, already sipping coffee and smoking. He'd let his hair grow longer, a lot longer since she'd seen him last, during the summer, the night she had left Schaefer's party with Will, then about three weeks later when they'd met for a beer at the Crow Bar in Berkeley, and then a couple of times after that in early August.

Elaine had met Peter for the first time five years earlier, the fall of her first year of graduate school at Northwestern. Within a week of her arrival at the university she had met another chemistry student, Viktor, a Dutch, last name now forgotten, who was a second-year graduate student. They had quickly entered into a sexual relationship, and for a couple of weeks they had spent every spare moment screwing. Elaine found the Dutchman sexy as hell and he was a tireless and able lover.

About a month into her academic year, Viktor had introduced her to Peter Weiss, an undergraduate student who was, at that time, considerably better-looking than he was now. He had been muscular, fuller, not shrunken and weak-looking. Elaine, for all her experience in sexual matters, was still shocked to learn that Viktor and Peter were lovers. Viktor was a specimen she didn't realize existed, a true bisexual. Elaine was at first repulsed by the idea, but the image of these two good-looking men locked in sexual combat began to intrigue her, and by the end of the first semester she'd been to bed several times with the two of them. She had found herself enormously excited by the sight of the two muscular men having sex, and was doubly excited when she and Viktor displayed their own passions openly in front of Peter. Peter was gay only, he seemed to have no sexual interest in Elaine, but he did love to watch.

Homosexuality was not talked about openly. The two men had kept their secret well- guarded, for fear it might jeopardize their enrollment and future careers. Elaine knew their secret, as did a couple of other women who had been in Viktor's life. But each, including Elaine, swore to hold this knowledge to herself.

It wasn't long before Elaine learned that Viktor had a serious drug problem, and that he was experimenting with all kinds of weird shit, much of it supplied by Peter. Viktor and Peter tried several times to get Elaine hooked, but she opted for nothing stronger than a little hashish. The three would sit around in Viktor's room, the Dutchman completely stoned on God-knows- what, Elaine in a hash haze, and Peter whacked out and listening to the strangest music Elaine had ever heard, some Indian stuff that seemed to go on forever. Peter said little, but seemed to know a lot. Elaine got increasingly jittery around the guy, but couldn't exactly say why. By the end of her first year of graduate school at Northwestern, she opted out of this bizarre relationship.

Peter stayed in touch with Elaine during his final two years at Northwestern and then left for graduate school at Berkeley. Their relationship was not especially friendly, and they saw each other no more than half a dozen times during the two-year period. As far as Elaine knew, Peter's secret remained a secret, and he did everything he could to keep it that way. He came from a wealthy Chicago family - - his father was CEO of some big company - - and Peter wanted to make sure the money kept flowing in his direction. Discovery of a queer son, he would say, would surely queer the money flow.

Elaine had actually helped him make a contact at the Berkeley philosophy department, a guy she had known at Penn, who was now an Assistant Professor there, but by the time she had completed her Ph.D. and was ready to go West, she had forgotten about Peter.

He had not reentered her life until the night of Preston Schaefer's party in June, a few months after her arrival, and he apparently recognized her immediately when she was leaving the party with Will Getz. She hadn't recognized him right away, because of his much slighter figure, but she did place him just a few moments later, and hoped that the brief encounter they'd had on the stairs was all they'd ever have.

Peter had, however, come to the Chemistry Department a few weeks later and looked her up. She'd made the mistake of welcoming him with apparent friendliness and of agreeing to having lunch with him. They'd spent a couple of hours at the Crow Bar, eating, drinking beer, reminiscing. Peter had not changed and he told her he hoped she would not reveal what she knew; he was still secretive about his orientation. The money flow had not been interrupted and he wanted to keep it that way. He was unusually inquisitive about the course of her life and, reluctantly, she told him of her recent liaison with Will and was somewhat startled to learn that Peter knew Will, at least a little, through his relationship with Preston Schaefer and the latter's relationship with Gina, Will's woman, or former woman. Elaine's tie to Schaefer, because he was Jensen's link to Guatemala and plant material, seemed to connect her to Peter, in unexpected ways. This had not been welcome news for her, but it was a minor issue.

She'd met Peter a couple more times after that, in August, just to keep him from pestering her too much at the lab and because she got a minor thrill listening to some of his weird interests. She'd also asked him not to say anything about her thing with Will. She mentioned that they now had little secrets about each other that would be best kept that way. Peter seemed to get the hint. Elaine told no one, not even Will, about her contacts with Peter, because she didn't want to risk raising the past and also because she didn't think he was worth mentioning.

"Sit. Will you have a cigarette?"

"No, thanks, just some coffee. Are you still getting thinner? Jeez, you trying to disappear altogether?"

"I'm pretty penniless, you know. My parents still send money, but not much. They got angry when they learned I was leaving graduate school. To pursue frivolous things, in their bourgeois minds. And you, you're looking a little haggard."

"I'm okay, just working hard in the lab."

"Still with Will, I take it. A happy couple, no doubt."

"Yeah, still with Will." This she said with no enthusiasm, and Peter picked up on it.

"Ah, so love evaporates, as always."

"Who said? I didn't say that."

"I smell it, in your breath."

"Wise ass. And who are you making it with? I worry you're too skinny to attract the pretty boys."

"I get what I need. I always will. So why are you here? You have not before gone out of your way to see me. You are not overly fond of me, so you must need something from me. N'est-ce pas?"

Elaine drank some of the too-hot coffee, spit it out, and wiped her lips and chin. She was dressed in a heavy turtle neck and jeans, her hair was in complete disorder, and she was dog-tired. But not too tired to be irritated at Peter's "n'est-ce pas," which he always said when he felt he understood some secret about you. She reached for Peter's French cigarettes, and lit one up for herself. The coffee house was deserted except for the skinny, hollow-eyed waitress and one smoker at a corner table huddled over a newspaper and a mug. Elaine felt cold, and took some more coffee.

"You're a buddy and disciple of Preston Schaefer ... n'est-ce pas?"

Peter hesitated at the unexpected question. He responded, "Off-and-on. Now it's off. We had a little disagreement a couple of weeks ago, before he left the country. I have not seen him since. He's away, in Guatemala. But I am sure everything will be fine with us when he returns."

"Yes. I need to ask you... has he said anything to you about me? Before he left?"

"He mentioned you to me several times. He believes you are quite ...shall we say ... desirable. I understood you had something going with him. I thought this odd, because I know you live with Getz, since he left Schaefer's student, Gina. Quite a tangle, with you at the center. But of course, strange relationships are not new to you."

"We had nothing, he's just obsessed or something. He won't leave me alone. I need your help to call him off. I've told him in no uncertain terms to back off. He keeps coming on and when he returns, it won't stop. You should see the letter he wrote me. I thought you could work on him. You can influence him. He respects you. Won't you do this for me?"

"Why should I? I do not owe you anything. You have hardly been a friend."

"Come on. I got you a good contact at Berkeley, remember? I've shared my life with you the times we've met. We know some pretty deep secrets about each other. Course you've more to hide than I do." She was immediately sorry she'd made this last remark. She didn't want to antagonize him. On the other hand, she knew he was crazy to keep his sexual orientation hidden.

"I thought you came to talk more about Will. His troubles."

She had let on at their earlier meetings, more or less indirectly, that Will was having trouble getting his thesis done, and that she was worried about him and their relationship. Peter had probed to learn more, but she'd not said much at all. The note from Schaefer, with its reference to Peter, suggested that he had drawn some inferences from her remarks about Will. She had no intention of telling the guy more about the nature of Will's - - and her own - - predicament.

"How about Will? What does he know? Can't he protect you?" Peter asked as he took up another cigarette. "Or are you on the road to nowhere? He's a weak person, I surmise, he's not up to your standards. Schaefer is not weak, he's a formidable figure, incredible intellect, a will like a god. I used to tell him he's like Nietzsche's Übermensch, you know, the bridge to the future. Ha!" Peter coughed through a cloud of cigarette smoke, smiling at Elaine the whole time.

"Will is not weak. He's just in a difficult ..." She cut it off, and turned the discussion back to Schaefer. "Look, if he was really such a person as you say, he wouldn't be out of control like this. I'm really afraid he'll do something drastic, or maybe violent. He's out of control. Can't you talk to him, at least? He respects you."

"Maybe. I always suspected he was not telling me the whole story about you. He doesn't like to take no for an answer to anything he really wants. He's a determined fellow. You might be surprised where he could take you, but I guess you have some reason to stay where you are.   I shall speak to him when he returns. We had a little spat before he left, but I suspect he will forget it, or already has."

Peter rose from the table. "I assume you have no reason to speak to him or to anyone else about me. You understand my situation is sensitive."

"I'm not intending to. But, you know, it's not such a big thing anymore, especially here in the Bay area. It's not so hidden."

"My parents. They continue to support me. My father is wealthy, and I am the only child. He is also very conservative, smugly religious. He'll cut me off in a minute. No risks."

The two separated without further exchange or even "good-byes." Elaine headed directly for the Bay Bridge and Berkeley. She hadn't got much satisfaction from Peter, but it was probably all she could have expected.

As she approached the long bridge her thoughts turned to Will. She flashed back to the brief meeting with Gina and her friend - - damn good-looking friend - - at the coffee house a couple of weeks back. Gina seemed more at ease than did Will. The guy is either still feeling guilty about what he did, or he's still hung up on her. She never tried to get him back, just accepted his leaving. Elaine would never have just collapsed that way. She was still wrapped up in Will Getz, and needed to find a way to lift him out of his funk. He has nothing to fear.

While Elaine was with Peter Weiss, Will had driven to Muir Woods, the redwood sanctuary in Marin County dedicated to the great naturalist. Will spent a couple of hours wandering about in the grove of redwoods, captivated by these mammoth beauties, but unable to clear his mind of the ugly situation he had created for himself. He had given up trying to understand the deep flaw in his character that had allowed him to perpetrate such a crime, and to continue to cover it up. Among these magnificent trees, in this darkening October wood, in the cool winds from the Pacific Ocean a few miles to the west, Will Getz felt only disgust for what he had become.

He sat for awhile on a log, away from the main trail and the handful of other visitors who were ambling along it, in apparent peace. During these moments, Will Getz resolved to go to Alden Jensen and to reveal what he had done. Will Getz resolved to end this life with Elaine Callahan. He resolved, and shuddered at the thought of the consequences. Jensen would have to have him dismissed from the graduate school. No Ph.D. No future in science. He'd probably not even be able to teach high school, like his father. His father would be absolutely devastated. Will's success was the man's whole life. He recalled his father's visit in Atlantic City, and the letter from him.

Will had attended a lecture on Friday. The lecturer was R.B. Woodward, Harvard University, Nobel Prize in chemistry in 1965. The prize was awarded for achievements in "The Art of Organic Synthesis." Woodward had devised and successfully completed laboratory syntheses of some of the most complex molecules known. His syntheses were considered masterpieces, the pinnacle of this branch of chemical science.

Will had spent endless hours studying the great works of chemical synthesis, the masterpieces of the science. As in the case of pfaffadine most of the challenges related to natural products, and were taken up after these compounds were isolated and purified, and after their molecular structures were established. Determining molecular structures was itself an enormous challenge, but once these structures were worked out, it took in many cases real daring to even attempt the reconstruction of these molecules in the laboratory. Once Will understood that organic synthesis was what he wanted to devote his life to, he went back to the original publications of the geniuses in the field, and studied their approaches, the strategies they used, their failures and successes. He began with Richard Kuhn's astonishing work in the 1930s on vitamins A and B, Carl Djerassi's brilliant work on cortisone and other steroids, and, back in Cambridge at MIT, John Sheehan's extraordinary synthesis of penicillin, a truly tough molecule to master. And the work of Woodward himself, a true grand master, beginning with quinine and then strychnine and other exceedingly complex molecules, was beyond remarkable. Will studied all these syntheses, and many others, and he knew most by heart - - he could go to the blackboard and diagram Woodward's elegant synthesis of strychnine without pause. He loved the art of this science.

Will's own "synthesis" was difficult, and the plan he and Jensen had devised for it quite artful, but not in the same league with the least of Woodward's. And, of course, Will had not really completed the synthesis. Will left Woodward's lecture, a model of lucidity, before the Q&A session. He realized fully that what he had once aspired to, the kind of work and achievement he had just listened to, was not in his future. Even if he could get away with his fraudulent work, he would know what he had done, and he knew he would never feel joy in any future accomplishment because of it.

Elaine did not understand his attitude, which he could not hide from her. A confession from him would immediately raise the question of where he had gotten the pfaffadine for the shipment to NCI, and Jensen would know it had to be Elaine. Shit, she'd be brought into it. Will had no idea what Jensen would do about Elaine. She'll be pissed beyond belief. She helped him and now he was going to betray her, if that was the word for it.

Will walked slowly out of Muir Woods as a deep autumn darkness descended. He made his way to his car, resolved to rehabilitate his character. He had given up his future in science the very moment he fabricated results and recorded them in his notebook. His fate had been sealed then, back in May. He was not the kind of person who could live with such a mark on his conscience. He supposed that if there was any positive aspect to this decision he had now come to, it was the realization that he was not the kind of person who could remain dishonest for long.

The drive back to Berkeley was long and slow, purposefully slow. He would tell Elaine of his decision immediately. He must not waver. Who was the guy with Gina? Will knew him. The priest! There would be no return to Gina. Maybe he should try to see her, to explain his actions. Yes, he should tell her why ... but that would mean she would know about Elaine's role and her grip on him as the real reason he had left Gina. God, maybe he should skip Gina ...No. No, he would clear it all from his conscience. Just the act of telling all to everyone he hurt....

"Jesus, are you fucking out of your mind?" were the first words out of Elaine's mouth late that Sunday evening when Will told her what he was going to do. She had started to get ready for bed and was sitting half undressed on the edge of their bed when Will told her he was through with his deception, he was ready to clean the slate.

"Will, I'm sorry, I didn't mean to shout out like that. But, man, why? This will completely destroy you. And Jensen, he'll have to go around retracting. Think of that. It'll threaten his grant from NIH. He'll be blamed. You'll get kicked out of here ..."

"I know. I've thought of all that. But I can't live with myself. I cannot write my thesis. I cannot write the paper Jensen wants. He knows there must be something wrong, he knows there's some problem or I wouldn't be taking all this time. It's the end of October."

"Christ. What about me? What's this going to mean for us?"

"I don't know. I guess I'll leave Berkeley. I don't know where I'll go. Maybe back home, to Boston. I'll have to face my father."

"Will. Will. Why? There's no threat you'll be discovered. No one's going to ... and what about me? You'll have to tell Jensen that I was the source of the pfaffadine! He'll want to know. What will you tell him? I put my ass on the line for you, actually for us. We're a great pair if you could just get by this. Will, think again. There's no need for this. It will be just a path toward destruction." Elaine pulled a heavy red flannel shirt off of a pile of dirty clothing near the bed and slipped it on. She felt cold. And seared. She rose and walked to the side of the chair Will was sitting in. She took his head in her hands and pressed it against her breasts. She raised a leg and rested her knee on the arm of the chair. Her bare thigh lay against Will's chest. He did not resist her embrace.

"Will. Will. This is not a way out. You made the choice last summer. Remember what you were thinking then. Remember how we came together. We're good together in every way. You can't back away from that choice. Think of how much destruction. Jensen, your dad ... me ...and the worst will be for you. You've got greatness ahead. I want to be there ..." She pressed his head more firmly against her breasts. He sensed she might be in tears. He sensed the tenseness and fear in her body. His stomach seemed to twist inside of him. His mind went blank as he ran his hand over Elaine's perfect thigh and up to her hip, there in the small dimly lit apartment in the Berkeley hills.

CHAPTER 18

Gina spent Thanksgiving Day with Marco. The two passed the morning preparing a small feast for themselves. It was a cool and rainy day in San Francisco, a good day to stay inside, eating and drinking. Marco was in a good mood as they prepared the food, and talked with pride about the critical success of his recently concluded exhibit and the substantial amount of money he'd made from the sale of all but three of his paintings. He let Gina pick one of the remaining three to take with her, and she welcomed the offer enthusiastically.

While the turkey, the smallest one Marco could find at the market, was roasting, the two sat together in the living room with some wine and cheese, and put on a record. It was one of Gina's favorite pieces, Beethoven's great Violin Concerto, played by Yehudi Menuhin. The music brought memories of Gina's mother, because one of the last evenings the two spent together was at a San Francisco Symphony concert that featured the Beethoven piece. That had been more than eight years earlier, but the memory of that evening came back vividly as Gina listened. Marco probably didn't recognize the connection Gina had to the piece, but sat with his arm around his daughter's shoulders, listening, apparently completely content.

At dinner Gina talked at length about her evolving plans for law school and how she would manage the transition. She seemed to Marco to be more enthusiastic about the potential this choice held out for her than about any possible career path she had ever mentioned to him. He had always had a feeling that anthropology had never been a passion for her; it seemed to be a kind of default choice, maybe influenced by a close friend of Gina's at college and some reading she'd done of the works of Margaret Mead.

He listened intently as she now poured forth on the need for women to pursue more aggressively career choices that would offer them more potential to change social conditions, to lessen the domination of the white, mostly waspy, male power elite. She explained the phrase to Marco, and it was apparent to her father that she'd spent a lot of time reading and thinking about these matters. After about an hour of listening to his daughter talk about what the choice of law could mean for her future, Marco finally smiled and told her he would find a way to support her as much as possible. He had spent most of his life in the world of art and the world she was talking about he had no practical experience of. But he seemed to understand. Marco, though by no means a political or social activist. clearly had progressive sympathies. He'd come from a family of Bolognese left-wingers who had fought and suffered under the Fascist government in Italy during the thirties and forties. He understood that America was going through a time of social ferment and that the forces of progressivism were more active now than at anytime since the Great Depression. His daughter had obviously been captivated by some of these new ideas, but he knew her well enough to guess she was no slave to them. She could think critically and could discriminate what was humane and rational in the movements of the sixties from that which only appeared to be progressive but which was, not far below the surface, as irrational as the system it was trying to overturn. Marco was not capable of articulating these thoughts about his daughter, but he understood them intuitively, and it gave him trust in her decision.

They cleaned up a bit after dinner, talking very little. Marco peered out the kitchen window, saw that the rain had reduced to just a mist, and recommended a walk. They put on raincoats, took a large umbrella and set out. Dusk was beginning to envelope the great city by the Bay. The streets were very quiet, with virtually no automobile traffic and only a few walkers. They walked arm-in-arm for about half an hour and when they approached a small park, Marco asked Gina to sit with him awhile.

The father and his daughter sat without speaking in the cool, dark Thanksgiving evening. Gina was pleased about the way the discussion about law school had gone, and was lost in thoughts about the future. She'd finish up her teaching commitments under Schaefer in January, sign up for a couple of courses for the spring semester, look for a part-time job, and make formal application for the fall of 1968. She'd be out in '71. Who could know where she'd end up? She thought about getting an apartment with Kay in January, and decided it was a good idea. Chris. What about her priest? He needed to make some decisions about his own future, and soon. She wanted to break off the sex thing, any hint of a romance. She sensed his real commitment would always be to the church, and, although she liked him, found him physically attractive, admired his attitudes, their time together had not created in her the romantic attachment she at first thought might exist. Not like those early times with Will. Never like that.

She found it remarkable, though, that she could have enjoyed the sex so much, the pure pleasure that came from making love with someone who was so physically attractive. God, could she have also enjoyed it so much because he was a priest? The added excitement that came from doing something so forbidden?

"I need to say some things to you, Gina. This is maybe not the right time, but I fear there is no such time." Marco spoke, interrupting her thoughts, but so quietly she was unsure what he'd said. She was beginning to feel cold and wanted to go back to the house. He spoke again.

"Gina. I need to tell you. I am ill. Very ill, I fear."

"What? What do you mean?" She felt immediate panic and turned to her father.

"I have a diagnosis of cancer. It is in me, in my pancreas. I have known this about a month, and I cannot wait anymore to tell you. You need to know."

"What? Daddy, what ... are you sure? How do you ...?" She felt tears beginning to form. He explained he had been diagnosed by specialists at the University of California Medical Center. There wasn't any doubt. He held her close and felt his own tears emerge. A few minutes went by.

"What can you do? What can they do? How bad is it? Are you getting some treatment?"

"They have used radiation and I've had one treatment with some drug, anti-cancer drug. I was real sick with the treatment a week ago. I'm feeling better today. But you need to know this. It is, Dr. Barrett tells me, and other doctors too, a very bad cancer. It is fast-acting. It is one of the worst cancers and there is little hope I will survive. Not more than a few months." He got it all out, slowly, in his quiet and gentle manner. He held his daughter close in the night air that had fallen around them.

The two eventually returned to the house. Gina decided to spend the night. Her mind had received the news but had not found a way to absorb it. It remained quiet, blank almost. She and Marco listened to some more music, and both fell asleep on the sofa. At about midnight, Gina awoke. She rose from the sofa and decided not to waken Marco. She lifted his legs off the floor and got him into a horizontal position on the sofa, covered him with a blanket, and went upstairs to her old bedroom. She crawled under the covers and buried herself in the silent darkness.

On Friday morning Gina got up and raced downstairs. Marco was in the kitchen, finishing the clean-up from Thanksgiving. He immediately poured a cup of coffee for his daughter and offered her some freshly made muffins. Gina did not think about what Marco had told her until she was into her second cup of coffee, but it then hit her hard and the fear returned. She didn't know what to do or say. She put aside the coffee and half-eaten muffin, and stood to help Marco finish washing the dishes. The sun had returned to the city, and through the kitchen window the two could just see the sparkling reflection off the very top of the partly visible Golden Gate Bridge. It was the kind of day that brought everyone out of their houses and onto the streets.

The father and daughter spent the day together roaming the city. They shopped a little, had lunch at Aldo's Trattoria, visited the City Lights bookstore, and strolled around Fisherman's Wharf like a couple of tourists. They spoke about Marco's illness only at the end of the day, when they returned to his house.

"I am not prepared for what will happen to me." Marco was sitting at the kitchen table, clad in his favorite black turtleneck. Gina had always loved it that her father was so handsome, yet also so kind and gentle. To her his good looks had not deteriorated with age.

"I am not prepared to leave this earth, and especially I am not prepared to leave you. But I guess there is no time when I would feel prepared. Maybe not. Maybe when you are very old, very very old, there comes a time when you feel ready ..."

Gina had no response. She held his hands and looked down at them, the hands that had created so much beauty. She recalled the first time she had really noticed these hands and wondered at their power to create. She had been sitting in the living room. She was maybe eight or nine years old. She saw her parents sitting together on the sofa, listening as usual to some recording. Marco's hands rested in his lap and one of her mother's hands was caressing them, loving them. Teresa, her mother, who died, died quickly, not slowly and with some great, painful mass growing inside of her body. Gina would be alone, truly alone. Could she deal with this? No, that wasn't the question. The question was how she could help her father deal with this. Maybe it wasn't inevitable, people recover from even the worst diseases. Where could this come from? She thought of Will and his new anti-cancer drug. Maybe it would work here. She should ask Will? Will. She would like to have him nearby during this.

"I need to say more to you, Gina. I must prepare myself. There is something in me that hopes, it keeps reappearing. But I know that what my doctors say must be true. So ironic, is that the word? My first real recognition as an artist ends with this. That is the word, ironic. God is a great ironist. I have difficulty accepting that there is a God who plays with people in this way, but what else can I believe? Is this punishment for something? Hah."

Marco got up and opened a bottle of wine. "I'm not supposed to drink this, because of my medicine. But wine is a great joy in my life. My daughter, my wine, my paintings, my little home, my friends, my books, the streets of my city, music ... it is so difficult to accept that they will simply vanish. God cannot replace these things, they are not in heaven. We learn to love so many things and people, and then they vanish. I guess we vanish, and they stay. That's more the case. There will be others to love these things, always."

Gina was sad to hear this, but in some way felt good that Marco could talk in this way. She wondered again how she could help him. Words were useless, or at least any words she could possibly find would be useless. Maybe listening. Maybe just being around to listen was the most useful thing.

"I promised myself I had to reveal to you one more thing. I don't want to wait any longer, I could become too ill to say what I want to say, in the way I want to say it." Gina took the wine he offered and turned to listen to whatever it was he had to say. Marco sat, took a few sips, and then told Gina about her mother's death.

"I must clear away something from my soul before I die. This will not be pleasant for you, but I cannot leave this earth without some confession. Telling some priest is not enough. You have become a strong person. I trust you. You had a very difficult time after your mother died, but you eventually overcame your grief, or at least learned to live with it."

Gina should have felt nervous, but she didn't. Just curious. She had felt for some time that she did not know the whole truth about her mother's violent death, but had never pushed Marco to tell all. He seemed prepared now to do this.

"This is perhaps selfish on my part. I tell this to clear my own soul, or at least try to. It will cause you pain, and for this I am sorry. In the long term, for you, the pain will fade, become part of who you are."

Marco paused a few moments, but Gina simply sat, waiting, anxious to hear his story.

"You once said to me you wondered whether your mother and I had a good marriage, whether there were some difficulties that might have caused her to end her life. I avoided an answer, but will not anymore. Your mother's death was not an accident. She deliberately drove off that cliff, at great speed according to the police reports. I know it was deliberate because she left me a note, a letter really. I do not have it anymore. I burned it, so I cannot show it to you. But you will believe me, because I have no reason to invent such a story.

"I found the letter on a Friday morning. You were in school. Your mother left the house very early, I'm not sure when, and took our car. I did not have any idea she left and was surprised when I woke up to find her missing. I found the letter in which she described her plan to end her life. I did nothing. I sat and read and reread the letter a dozen times. You came down for breakfast and I made up some story to explain your mother's absence. You went off to school, and I just sat, stunned and frightened. I had no idea when she would go and how she would do it, or when, except some time that day. I thought about calling the police, but I didn't. I did not do this! I just sat and let it happen. The police perhaps could have found the car, and prevented this. I did nothing!"

Marco had to stop a few moments and regain his composure. He seemed angry, which was a rare mood for him.

"You see, your mother ... I forced her to do something she hated doing. I told her ... this was about two months before her death ... that she had to do this or I would turn her out, and I could have done that. I threatened her, told her she would never see you again.

This must sound mysterious."

Marco was in distress. This was difficult for him in the extreme. Gina could not guess what he might be talking about, but still did not feel any fear about hearing more. She held her dear father's hands and urged him on with his story.

"I shall just say it. Your mother had an affair. She became pregnant. She wanted to have the man's child. She wanted to be with him, but he left her, refused. He didn't know about the child. I reacted badly when she told me all this. I became angry, even out of control."

"A baby? Do I have a brother or sister somewhere? What happened? What happened? Where is ..."

"I told your mother she had to get rid of the child. I refused to accept another man's ... I forced her to get rid of it. She hated this, she could not ... she did it, I arranged it through a doctor I know. It was a miserable thing, but I would not stay with her unless she did this. And she did, one dismal day in that summer when you were 16." Gina moved close to Marco and wrapped her arms around him. He could not say more for several minutes.

Abortion? Her mother had had an abortion. Another man's child? A lover, her mother? She loved her father so much. Gina was sure that was true. When? How? Abortion was a crime, it was murder. My God, how could this have happened?

Marco finally regained enough composure to go on. "She went through with it, but it affected her strongly. This was against her moral sense in every way. But I threatened to turn her out and to keep her from you if she didn't ... I was willing to forgive her infidelity, though it was very difficult, I could do that. My love for her was very strong."

"You must have been heartbroken. How could she? That seems so wrong ...so impossible for me to imagine." Gina turned away from Marco and collapsed onto a kitchen chair. Marco stared at his daughter, looking for her reaction. He was surprised that her first reaction was to question her mother's act of infidelity, not what he had said was his own offense.

"My ... Gina ... don't you see? My insistence that she do something completely hateful ... she could not live with that. Her note, the one I burned, did not blame me. She blamed herself for the affair and for the ... murder of her child. Those were her words."

"Who was the ... father?" Gina asked, almost in a whisper.

"It's not important. Gina, what's important is that you understand what happened to your mother. Nothing about it involved you. You blamed yourself, I know you did, but never could find a reason. I am going to die. I have no time left to tell this to you. I owe this to you. I cannot take my sin to my grave without confessing it to you. I knew my actions would hurt your mother ... not drive her to her death, I never imagined that ...but ... still."

Gina stayed with Marco the rest of the weekend, and returned to Berkeley early Sunday evening. Nothing more was said by either her or her father about her mother. They talked some more about Marco's cancer treatment and his schedule for hospital visits. His pain was only occasional but he knew it would get worse, much worse.

Gina could not help thinking about her mother's abortion. It was an illegal act in America, and Gina could only imagine the horror of going through that kind of thing. She became distracted a moment as she thought about her own state. She'd gone off the pill in early September, when it looked for sure like Will was not returning. Gina had never been overly keen on taking it, and welcomed a break from it. She hadn't imagined jumping into sex with anyone else for at least a few months, and Chris was a completely unexpected sexual partner. Father Swift. She'd maybe risked pregnancy with him, although they had had complete sex only about three times, and based on the timing she wasn't too worried. It was over, too, she needed to talk to him when he got back from his Thanksgiving visit with his parents.

That night in her room, Gina wrote down what she had heard from her Dad. She felt some need to record it, to have her father's and mother's actions down on paper so she could analyze their motives. Why did her mother have this affair? Why did Marco react the way he did? Why was that not what he should have done? Why should he feel guilt? Writing it down did not cause an explanation to appear. She now understood for the first time the cause of her mother's grief. She confirmed what she'd always suspected, that her death was suicide, not an accident. Gina did not blame Marco. Not on this night, as she wrote, seeking to understand, knowing in her heart that some things would always be beyond comprehension.

CHAPTER 19

It had been nearly three weeks since Will had resolved to confess to Alden Jensen and to take the consequences, but he had failed to do it. Elaine's pleading was part of it, his own fear another, and the fact that Jensen had been traveling for about half the time made Will's delay easier. Each day Will agonized, reworking in his head the need to come clean, and imagining all the devastating consequences. Oddly, his relation with Elaine seemed to have strengthened a little. He somehow began to see her more as a victim of his own actions than as someone who, by her own act to help him perpetrate his crime, had made him captive to her will. He'd spent more time with Elaine, their sex life returned, with surprising force, and they had even planned a trip together for the Christmas holidays.

Elaine was confused. She thought Will had dropped his plan to confess, but she saw no sign that he had resumed his thesis writing or that he was making plans to apply for a new position. She decided not to push him to do these things, but instead talked to him only about his incredibly bad decision to confess and ruin himself and her as well. Her apparent success on this subject was the most important thing. Elaine knew, however, that Alden Jensen's patience must be about to run out, and that he would come down on Will very hard in the near, very near, future. He had to. What this would bring was uncertain, but there was nothing she could do about it. So, while she was happy about Will's renewed interest in her, she rode that happiness anxiously. Will too, she knew, was under incredible stress, and she had no idea where it would end. Better no thesis, no Ph.D., for lack of effort, than the destruction that would come with a confession.

The Sunday after Thanksgiving was an unusually warm day, and Will took advantage of the weather. He ran that morning at the University track for more than an hour, at greater speed than he thought he could ever muster for such a length of time. His running had continued to improve since the summer. It had become a compulsion, almost, perhaps because during it and for a few hours after he was relatively free of his anguish. Running was better than any pill.

At the end of his long, exhausting run, Will sat in the stadium's stands for a long time, sipping on the water he'd toted along, and absorbing the warm sunshine.

For the hundredth time he went over his plan to tell all to Jensen, and for the hundredth time he battled it. He was convinced he knew the right course, but he could not find in himself the courage to take it. He knew that Jensen would be on his ass, real soon, and that he either had to take the right course, or go back to writing up his fictional thesis, and get it done within a few days. He knew it would take him only four or five days to complete the dissertation. He knew also that he would not be able to live with himself if he were to try to pass it off as a work of science.

It was a little odd Alden Jensen hadn't been hounding him much more than he had. Perhaps Jensen was consulting too much, traveling to pharmaceutical firms and passing on his wisdom for some big bucks. Elaine's isolate of pfaffadine Jensen had personally carried back to NIH, all 20 grams of highly purified compound isolated from the plant material using her highly efficient separation system. Elaine still had quite a few kilos of dried plant material, enough to get maybe another 25 grams of pfaff. This would be necessary only if the next set of anti-cancer studies in lab animals, now underway at NCI, continued to show that the compound might be effective. Jensen had told Elaine that such a success would lead NCI to contract out the isolation of pfaff, at some large commercial lab, and would also lead to a contract for someone else to go out and harvest more plant material. Elaine would probably be asked to help set up her extraction and separation system on a large, semi-commercial scale. In the meantime she was writing up her work for publication, and also getting some patent applications in order. She was onto something really good, Will thought. I can ruin her. I tell Jensen what I did. He wants to know where I got the authentic pfaff I passed off as my synthetic stuff, and he'll know it must have come from Elaine. She is a co-conspirator. She's ruined, just like me. Maybe not. Her transgression is minor compared with my own.

Will threw on his jacket and started off on a slow walk across campus. It was still quiet and uncrowded, and he was somehow able to enjoy the warmth of the afternoon and the peace of the campus. He made his way through Sproul Plaza, stopped to listen to the rant of some born- again Christian who had attracted a small crowd, and then aimed himself up Bancroft toward the apartment.

About a half-block from home he stopped. He saw Elaine standing on the sidewalk outside their apartment building, talking to some guy. Will wasn't sure at first who he was, but then guessed it must be Preston Schaefer. He hadn't seen Schaefer for some time, and it was clear the big guy had lost quite a bit of weight. Will knew he had gone to Guatemala in early October, but hadn't heard word of his return. The conversation between Schaefer and Elaine seemed intense. Will stepped back so that he would not be in their line of vision. He watched the two for a couple of minutes, and then backed away, and headed down the hill toward Telegraph Avenue. He had no desire to confront those two together.

As he settled in for some coffee at the Telegraph Avenue Cafe, he recalled the nutty letter Schaefer had sent to Elaine. Will knew that the nuttiness had spooked Elaine, and that she was worried about running into Schaefer upon his return from Guatemala. The trip he took after ditching Gina. Gina. Where was she now? Will thought about the encounter in the coffee shop, and about how wonderful she looked. Maybe he should do something about Schaefer. Elaine should not have to put up with his harassment. Maybe he was backing off. Maybe that's what the conversation they were now having was about. Schaefer behaving honorably. God, he looked big and strong, where did all his fat go?

Will sat around for about half an hour, and then headed back up the hill toward home. Elaine and Schaefer were nowhere in sight, but when Will entered his apartment he was surprised to find it empty. Where was Elaine? Had she gone off somewhere with Schaefer? Must have. What the hell does that mean?

Will Getz spent the rest of Sunday alone in his apartment, reading, watching TV, doing a crossword puzzle. He called his dad in Boston and exchanged a few pleasantries. He paced a bit, then lay down, to fall asleep for about an hour. When he awoke it was after ten p.m. Still no Elaine. Elaine Callahan had not even called to say where she was.

Will spent the night alone, sleeping only sporadically, wondering at times whether he should go over to Schaefer's apartment, but deciding not to. At dawn he made some coffee and prepared and ate a huge breakfast, compensation for the fact he'd had no Sunday dinner. No Elaine, she'd taken off with Preston Schaefer. This was the kind of person Will knew Elaine was, fickle, promiscuous, ready to follow anything that happened to tickle her fancy. Jesus, how had he ever gotten himself tied up with her?

By about nine a.m. Will had decided to return to his original plan, to go to Jensen and confess his transgressions. He would try to protect Elaine. He would tell Jensen he had stolen the pfaff from Elaine's lab. Jensen would probably not believe that, but Will would try to convince him. If Jensen didn't buy it, Elaine would have to live with the consequences. Will was now trying to save his own soul. Elaine would have to worry about whatever she had that passed for one.

Gina slept solidly but woke up with a start very early on the Monday morning following her Thanksgiving weekend with Marco. It was still dark at about five a.m., the house was completely silent, but something had suddenly disturbed her sleep. She had gone to sleep completely naked, with only a light blanket over her, and now felt very cold. She slipped out of bed to find some clothing and an extra blanket. She bundled up, but continued to shiver for several minutes.

Perhaps she had dreamed of something dreadful. She glanced at the painting her father had given her, standing against the wall. She couldn't make out the colors or much else in the early light, but she sat staring at it while her room began taking on the light of daybreak. Chaos at the center, peace at the edges. She'd seen this theme in several of her dad's recent paintings, and now could not escape its message. Tears came to her dark eyes. She sat, her back against the wall, tears flowing, tormented by the idea of the horrendous disease that was eating at her father's core. For the first time since he had told her about it, Gina came to focus exactly on what was going on inside him and what it would do to him and how it would take him from her. What Marco had said about her mother did not occupy her thoughts on this chilly November morning. She could think only of the chaos at her father's center. She cried for a long time.

Much later she made her way downstairs to the kitchen in search of coffee. The big house seemed deserted; Kay must have left for work hours earlier and the various roomers, most of whom still remained unknown to Gina, had gone off to do whatever duties they had. Gina found only half-a-cup of overheated coffee in the percolator, and decided she would settle for instant.

"How about I take you out for some breakfast?' She turned and saw Chris in the doorway. He was carrying a satchel and was wearing a raincoat. His black hair, now much longer than when she had first met him, was soaked. "It's raining, kinda cold, so bundle up, and get an umbrella." He smiled and Gina was immediately enchanted by that gentle and very handsome face. She went to him and they embraced.

"Did you just get back?" she asked, smiling. She was sure Chris could see that she must have been crying and she looked away from him, then moved away to get a coat and umbrella.

The two found a restaurant on Telegraph they had never before tried, and ordered omelets and coffee. Before eating Gina went to the restroom and washed her face. Her eyes had been swollen by her crying and she thought she looked drawn and exhausted. Her hair was a mess, and she tried to do something with it by wetting it and running her fingers through it. Then she noticed that she'd put on an old flannel shirt that looked as if it had been ripped off some street person. She could pass, this morning, for one of those lost souls who could be seen wandering on Telegraph. She understood, today, what one of those wanderers might feel like inside.

Chris could sense Gina was troubled, but he decided not to ask her directly about what she was feeling. He thought he would talk about his visit with his parents, then ask her about Marco, and eventually she might bring up what was on her mind.

"So, my father and I fought and my mother cried. That was Thanksgiving. They're both completely disappointed in me, and they express it in completely different ways. I think my father never wanted me to enter the priesthood, and he resented my mother's efforts to move me in that direction. But it was my own choice, completely. Early on I felt that religious impulse, it was in me from the day I was first aware of the church in my life. It has never left me. I can't explain it. It's there, it's still there. I just want to do God's work. Of course, my mother would say - - my father, too, I guess - - is that God's work is whatever the church hierarchy says it is. I just got stuck with the most reactionary Bishop on earth. My parents just don't get it. It was not a pleasant weekend."

Gina did not respond, and simply sat quietly, pretending to eat, and sipping at her coffee. She knew her priest-lover, if he was honest with himself, must feel guilty about their relationship. Gina did not have a clue about how he actually saw her, what he felt ... but she believed she had to end their relationship as it now existed. Could they still be friends? She needed to ask.

As these thoughts swirled in her mind she put down her coffee cup and looked directly into Chris' face. He returned her stare and noticed the moistness in her eyes. The two sat in this way for a few moments, and then Gina asked if they could leave.

The heavy rains had ceased but the air was soggy, filled with mist. The sky was gray with low hanging clouds that flooded the Berkeley hills above them. The two walked up Telegraph Avenue to the campus, and then into the Plaza. They wandered aimlessly for a very long time, oblivious to the life of the university, and finally took a seat in a eucalyptus grove. The winds had died down and it was now very still. Gina and Chris had found a place of quiet in the middle of this immense and bustling campus, and in this place Gina told Chris of Marco's illness and of her mother's terrible death and of the reasons for it and of how small and helpless she felt in the midst of this pain. "Your God lets these things happen. Your so-called benevolent God who watches over us. I'm sorry I cannot accept that. I had that religious feeling you talk of, when I was a child, but not now. Not since my mother's death. The church pulls you in as a child and has this way to make you feel guilty about so many things ... so many good things. Like what we have done. Don't you feel guilty about that? Priests don't have love affairs." She immediately wished she hadn't used that phrase.

As Gina related the sad tale of her parents, Chris simply sat, his hands stuffed into his coat's pockets, his head buried in the heavy collar of the coat. The two sat side-by-side, and Gina spoke without looking at him, until she began these last remarks about God and their relationship. When she finished speaking she stood up, and walked slowly about the small grove. Somehow it reminded her, briefly, of that place in the Sierras where she and Will had camped - - - the Refuge they had called it, although that place had no eucalyptus. There was something of its peacefulness here. It was at the Refuge where she had first told Will of the death of her mother.

Chris finally spoke. "I don't know what to say, except, I'm sorry. It's horrible for you. I'm sorry. Priests, of all people, are supposed to be able to help people through times like this, but I feel helpless.... I cannot bring myself to tell you that these painful things are just God's way, we just have to believe they are all for the best, or that they are mysteries we have to live with ...these must sound hollow to you. I feel helpless ... Gina, I'm sorry. I ..." She stopped moving about and turned to look at Chris. He seemed small now, sitting there, so helpless, so caring, so gentle ...maybe she did love him in some way, maybe she did....

The two embraced warmly, and their smiles returned as they clasped hands and continued their voyage around the campus. The skies were still gray but the clouds had lifted out of the hills. Somehow Gina's low spirits had also lifted, buoyed by the fact that she had been able to open up and talk about her pain and anger. She did not know whether she loved Chris as a man or as a priest, and it no longer seemed to matter.

Their stroll around the campus took the two by Boalt Hall, the law school, and Gina stopped to look and wonder about what she might be preparing herself to become.

When Gina and Chris arrived back at the group house, they entered and encountered Peter Weiss in the living room. He rushed to greet them and told them he must talk to them immediately. He looked frightened. His usual confident smile was completely absent. He was agitated, and as he talked, it showed up in his voice and the erratic movements of his arms and shoulders.

"Schaefer. He has done something bad, very bad. I need to tell you, you need to find a way to help, to maybe go to Will Getz, you know him, I do not." He was directing his remarks to Gina, as Kay walked in and took a seat next to Chris.

"I spent Saturday and Sunday at his apartment. By the way he told me something about David which I will get to, but that is not why I am here. It's Elaine. You know ... maybe you don't know. No, you wouldn't. But he is obsessed with her, he has been after her, for months. He spent most of Saturday talking about her. He drove me crazy, but he couldn't get off it. How he was the kind of man she needed. He had to make her see that. Get her away from Getz and let her see what kind of man he - - Schaefer, that is - - was." Peter had taken a seat and seemed a little calmer. Gina moved to the edge of her seat and told him to get on with the story.

"He drank a lot Saturday. He did hash. I never saw anyone take that much hash. Maybe some other stuff also. He finally passed out. I decided to stay over to see that he was okay. He woke up Sunday and told me he was going to get her, get Elaine, away from Getz. He started packing up some clothes and some other things, into a huge duffle bag he has. I tried to get him under control, but no way. He's a big man, no way could puny Peter control him. He looked weird, fierce. I don't know how to describe it.

"He left his apartment finally around three, yesterday afternoon, duffle bag in hand. I saw him toss it into his car and take off, up the hill. I ran out of his apartment building and ran as hard as I could after him. He was on Bancroft, going very slow in heavy traffic. He pulled off after about three blocks, onto a side street. He got out and started walking. I followed at a safe distance. I was really worried. He seemed out of control.

"He stopped at the corner of Piedmont and Dwight Way, and just stood there, staring at an apartment house across the street. I hid behind a bus stop place, watched him for about a half hour. Then I saw him dash across the street. Elaine was there and he grabbed her by the arm. She tried to get away, but he held her, he's really strong.

"She looked angry, maybe frightened, very tense, I couldn't really tell. She was holding a bag, groceries maybe. Then ..." Peter paused, took a deep breath, and went on "... a gun. I am certain. He put a gun to her chest. A pistol. I couldn't see it well, but there, in broad daylight, a gun!" He seemed out of breath, and Chris and the two women were dumbfounded. Peter reached into his shirt pocket and pulled out a nearly empty package of cigarettes.

"He led her away, to his car. Or, forced her, at gunpoint. I'm not making this up. I didn't know what to do. I followed them enough to see them get in his car. He made her drive. He, I guess, he kidnapped her. Kidnapped Elaine Callahan!" He paused to light up and burned his fingers in the process.

The three quizzed Peter for details, trying to see how sure he was about the gun, about Elaine being forced against her will. None of them had ever experienced anything like this, an apparent criminal act. Preston Schaefer, a leading light of the intellectual wing of the New Left, behaving like a freaking criminal. Being a freaking criminal.

"Why are you here? Did you tell the police? This is Monday afternoon. It's been 24 hours. Did you tell the police?" Kay asked, almost in a frenzy.

"No. I couldn't do that to him. I wasn't sure if it really was a kidnapping. I went back to his apartment. He didn't show up Sunday night, and still hasn't. I can guess where he is. But I do not trust the fuzz. This is a good friend, who just lost it. I'm sure he'll get back to his senses, but I'm still worried he'll do something worse ..."

"Jesus, you witnessed a fucking kidnapping at gunpoint, and you don't report it? We need to do this right away!" Kay was frantic.

"No, please. I'm not sure about the gun, I'm not sure she was forced. Please, we need to take care of this ourselves. I came to ask you to go to Will, find out what he knows. See if he has seen Elaine. Maybe she's back home. Kay, you know him well enough to do this. Gina, you too. Please. Schaefer needs help."

The two women and Chris conferred for about five minutes. They decided it would be okay first to see Will, as Peter suggested. Maybe it was over, maybe Elaine was back. Kay volunteered and Chris agreed to go with her. Gina and Peter preferred not to go along.

Will Getz had spent Monday in his lab, waiting to see Jensen. He had resolved to tell the truth, and was determined now to get it over with. Jensen never showed up, and Will finally learned from Brad Mitchell, the new post-doc, that Jensen had gone on from his Thanksgiving holiday visit to Chicago to attend a meeting in Washington. He wouldn't he back until Friday. Will wandered home, dejected, cursing the fact he'd have to hold on another four days. More time to backtrack.

No sign of Elaine. This was good news to Will. Reinforcement of his feeling that he no longer had reason to worry about injuring her by his confession.

This was all fine for him until Kay and Chris appeared and relayed Peter's story. Will didn't know what to think. Was it really a kidnapping? More likely she had just gone along. He had seen the two together on Sunday, but hadn't noticed any gun or forcing behavior on Schaefer's part. Peter wasn't reliable. Chris recalled the fight Schaefer and Peter had had in the Crow Bar, back in September. He told Will about it and said that Peter might be just trying to get back at Schaefer.

"He said he thinks he knows where Schaefer would have taken Elaine," said Kay.

"Where?"

"I don't know. He didn't say. He's back at my house. We can go find out." Kay seemed somewhat relieved, now half-believing that Peter had either made this up or greatly exaggerated.

The three walked back to the group house. Evening had descended and brought cold winds with it. Will guessed he'd come face-to-face with Gina, and half-dreaded, half-welcomed the meeting. He was not yet convinced that Peter's story made sense, and he secretly wished the guy was wrong. If Elaine had run off with Schaefer voluntarily, it would make it easier for Will to go through with his resolution to confess to Jensen, because he would not feel guilt about possibly implicating Elaine in his fraudulent act.

Peter was at the kitchen table, smoking, looking worried, when Will, Kay, and Chris entered. Gina was dishing up some spaghetti and invited everyone to sit down. No one seemed interested in food, but they all sat at the large wooden table. Will and Gina had taken seats just opposite each other, and when they finally looked at each other they exchanged tepid smiles. Everyone at the table knew this was awkward for the two of them, and Kay especially hoped Gina was not too upset. After Kay confirmed that Elaine was missing, Will spoke to Peter.

"So. Where are they?"

"I think I know, though it is just a guess. Schaefer has a cabin, north of Marin. I went there once. It's near a National Forest, up the river from Fort Bragg. It's a small place, very run down. He uses it as a retreat. I went once."

"Can you find it?"

"I think so, but I'm not sure. I know the town, it's Noyo, we can use a map to get there. I think I'll be able to locate ..."

"He has a gun. Are you sure?"

"No. It was hard to see, but it looked that way, something he held like one, up against her. He's not violent. Schaefer is a good guy. He's just ... obsessed I guess. He thinks Elaine, deep down, really wants him. I've never seen him like this. Please. Let's go. I'm sure we can talk him out of this. I'll go. You, Kay, I think he likes you. Will, you can go, but you better not let him see you. I know you need to help Elaine, but you stay hidden while I talk to him. I have no car. Maybe Kay ...will you?" Peter was shaking while he talked, smoking non-stop. Gina watched Will's reaction to the mention of Elaine, and saw nothing to indicate much interest. Will's expression was flat.

Peter stood and raised his arms above his head, and then shouted out, "There's more. I must tell you. Schaefer told me ...he came back from Guatemala without David. David somehow got left behind. Schaefer was angry when he told me this, like he hated David. He thinks David joined up with some local rebels, ran off to fight the revolution. I don't know if any of that is true, I could not tell if he was making this up. Schaefer, maybe you are not aware, makes up lots of things. Kay, have you seen David?" The skinny philosopher seemed out of breath as he dropped his arms and nodded in Kay's direction.

Kay looked horrified. "No, no, I haven't seen him. He moved out of here in September, he joined some commune near Oakland. I saw him a couple of times after that and got the feeling he had joined up with some violent, revolutionary types. I knew he'd gone to Guatemala with Schaefer and some other student." She turned to Gina as she said this, and Gina nodded in agreement, recalling that moment when the big man had discarded her.

"My God, if that's true, about Guatemala ... how dangerous for David. How could Schaefer let him do that?" Gina had an answer for that, but kept it to herself.

Kay still looking alarmed said, "I'll go, but the gun scares me. What if ..."

"I'll go, too ... the three of us. No one thinks we should tell the police?" Will seemed hesitant as he spoke. He felt he should go, he had an obligation to help Elaine if she really had been forced away at gunpoint. He still half-hoped Peter's story was wrong. Elaine had chosen to run off with Schaefer. This would be a relief. But Will was coming to believe that she was probably a victim, not a willing partner. Too bad. Will thought of his upcoming meeting with Jensen, and fear pierced his bowels. He had to go.

Chris volunteered to help. "Maybe you'll need another pair of hands, for something." And so Will, Chris, Kay, and Peter piled into Kay's car. Will asked for the California road map, and he and Peter traced the route to Noyo. It looked like about a two-hour drive. They'd be there about ten o'clock, although there was no telling how long it would take to find Schaefer's cabin. It might be a problem in the dark.

"Maybe it's better if we go in the morning." The four agreed to meet at 7:00 a.m. on Tuesday, and Will went off to his apartment. Peter would camp out on the living room sofa.

Gina surprised Will as he turned out of the driveway to begin his walk home.

"Hello." Will was nervous, and stood back a bit, hands shoved deep into his jacket's pockets. It had turned cold, but the wind had died down, so that it wasn't too uncomfortable. Gina had slipped on her green wool sweater, but she still felt cold. She spoke, calmly.

"I'm worried for you. Schaefer scares me. I think he's cruel. I can't imagine confronting him if he really has a weapon."

Will's gaze fell to the ground. He had not been alone with Gina since the day in May when she had left for Seattle with her father. His last remarks to her were contained in the pathetic note he had left when he deserted her for Elaine. Gina had no idea about the real reason he was with Elaine, and she must believe Will was in love or something like that. Jesus, if she only knew, thought Will.

"Have you been okay? I heard about what Schaefer did to you. Was that true? Your dad. How is he ...?" Will was now looking at Gina, but awkwardly, his body almost at right angles to hers.

"Marco's fine. Yeah, Schaefer dumped on me. I'm through with him. I've decided to try law school. I think I can make a bigger ... have an impact on society as a lawyer. There's so much to do. Kay has influenced me. She's a terrific person. She's taught me so much. I'm going to get a job, take some courses, apply for next fall." The two sat down on the stone wall that bordered the sidewalk. "What about you? I thought you'd be long gone by now. Have you finished up?" She had crossed her arms over her chest, trying to keep herself warm.

"No. I'm having some trouble ...."

"Like last spring? I thought ... someone said ... that you finished up your lab work, completed that synthesis. Is that stuff being tested? I thought it was supposed to be a cancer treatment."

Will would only say his compound was under test, and still looked promising. He talked a bit about moving back to the East coast, teaching or something.

"What about Elaine? Are you two ...?" Gina hesitated, then changed the subject. "I'm really cold. I'm going in. Good luck tomorrow. Good to see you. You look good. Please be careful." Gina hurried off and didn't turn back. She ran all the way to her bedroom and shut herself up for the night. She hadn't eaten anything but a piece of bread, and in fact had eaten almost nothing since her small breakfast with Chris. She tried to sleep, but the hunger was too painful. So she crept downstairs about 9:30 and found a large bowl of spaghetti on the kitchen table, just where it had been left a few hours earlier. While she ate she heard people talking out in the living room. She couldn't make out what was being said, but it sounded like Chris and Peter.

CHAPTER 20

Schaefer had locked up Elaine in one of the two bedrooms of his decrepit cabin. She had screamed and pounded on the door several times on Monday, but there was no one within hearing range. His cabin was off a small road deep in the woods, about two miles from the ocean. It had been shrouded in coastal fog when they'd arrived Sunday evening and it remained that way on Tuesday morning. Schaefer got up at dawn, and rebuilt the fire in his wood stove. With the door to her room closed, Elaine got no benefit from the stove, and was chilled to the bone. Schaefer decided she must be hungry - - he'd passed in some cheese and apples on Monday, some coffee, but nothing else. She still didn't want to see or talk with him, so he was reluctant to enter her room. She'd calm down in a day or two, he believed, she'd be ready to listen to him, would come to understand him, and realize what kind of man he was. He thought of how she looked in her jeans and tight turtleneck. Jesus, what a body.

He fried some eggs and bacon, made some toast, and piled it all on a plate. He knocked on her door and told her he had some food for her. He inserted his key into the door's lock, turned it, and pushed in the heavy door. The room was dark, all the curtains drawn. It took a couple of minutes for his eyes to adjust. He saw her huddled under some blankets, on the mattress that he'd laid out on the floor to serve as a bed. Schaefer went into the room and kicked the door shut behind him. He locked it and then walked to a window and pulled back a curtain. A dull beam of light streamed in and fell upon Elaine's red hair, which was in tangles around her head. Schaefer recalled the night he'd run his large hands through that beautiful hair, and how this woman had responded to his touch. She turned her face toward him and into the light.

"Schaefer. This is fucking weird. You know, this is a crime. You can't imprison another person like this."

"It's warm in the next room. If you just behave, you can go out there. We can talk. Get to understand our situation. I don't think what I've done is a crime. I have a right to talk to you. Maybe not a right, no, but you ... there's no reason not to hear me out."

"Jesus, you talked all the way up here in the car. I listened. Lots of what you said made sense. Look, I do think a lot of you. Your ideas sound really advanced, and novel. But all that has nothing to do with what you want from me." Elaine pulled the blankets tighter around herself, as Schaefer turned to draw back the curtains on the remaining two windows. The fog had lifted a bit, and there was a hint of sunshine sifting down among the huge pines that surrounded the cabin. Schaefer sat on an upright chair and watched as Elaine wolfed down the breakfast he'd made.

"David, David Zaretsky, I told you about him, how he stayed behind in Guatemala. He's dedicated. He had joined a radical group in Oakland. Armed resistance to end imperial wars everywhere, even here at home. The war against black people, against the poor, even against women!" This last made Elaine laugh in disdain.

"Come on, Schaefer, you don't talk about liberating women when you're making them your personal slave, for God's sake."

"David was turning to violence. I knew it was coming. I admire that. He's put himself in danger. Real danger. You're just not committed to anything until you're really willing to put yourself in danger in order to ..." He paused. "I put myself in danger with every article I publish on the evils of American society and on the way to overcome them. They stem from the way we have come to think about the world, the scientific, rational order. It breeds a thirst for political power. Technical power breeds evils. You see that don't you? You see that what David is fighting for down there in the jungles is part of the same war I'm in. The pen and the sword. I reveal the truth. I reveal what is necessary to make our society truthful. I lead the way. My writings are now being cited by all the leaders of the revolution in these United States and will soon be in the mouths of revolutionaries everywhere. I put myself in danger, because the imperial powers will do anything to shut me up. In a way you are part of them. You want to be ... you are ... a scientist. You'll make your contribution to Western imperialism. Can't you see the link? But I smell in you something else. You, at heart, are a creature of the jungle. Feline, maybe. At heart a sensualist. Science is ugly, sterilizing, its only good to serve the power interests. You are a different creature. An artist! I bet even your science is not theoretical. You're a doer. Get in the lab and create. No theory. Just the simple facts of the world, chemicals are like paint is to the artist. I smell something in you primitive, fundamentally out of sync ... I can help you uncover your true self. You can begin to change the world. It takes scientists to put science in its rightful place!"

Although she'd heard some of this stuff before, Elaine now recognized that this guy was really a freak. Who the hell did he think he was? "Schaefer, I don't know what you're talking about. You sound like you think you're some kind of superman, above the rest of us. Why don't you just go back and do what an ordinary professor does? You've got a good position in a great university. Your name is becoming recognized in anthropology. Why are you off in the stars like this? Too much shit in those drugs you take? Please. Can we just go back to Berkeley? We'll just forget this ever happened. I need some coffee." Elaine rose, dropped the blankets and went over to where Schaefer was seated. "Keys. I'll get the coffee myself."

Schaefer stood. He towered over Elaine, and she was not a small woman. He put his arms around her and pulled her close. She resisted, but he just tightened his hold and pulled her closer.

"You can come with me to the other room, have some coffee. It's warmer." Schaefer released her and led the way. He knew she'd try to bolt, given the slightest chance, so he held onto her wrist. She didn't struggle, because his grip would have caused her severe pain. He finally released her when they reached the table where he had set out some cups and the pot of brewed coffee. She went for the coffee and within a few minutes was ready for her second cup. Schaefer poured some for himself and prepared for more discussion. He was persistent.

"So how did you get all these ideas? Not about me. I mean your political ideas. You really think you're all that original?" Elaine thought she'd try his game, seem interested in him, her old way of seducing men who interested her. She had to be careful here, though. She didn't want to seduce Schaefer, no way. She wanted to convince him she could be trusted. Fool him into releasing her.

Schaefer took her question seriously, and went on about his past, his involvement in the early civil rights movement, his growing recognition of the roots of injustice in America. His study of anthropology led to his view that Western science was just one of many ways of organizing man's knowledge of the world, and, finally, to his recognition that it was the most powerful and destructive way. He spoke for a half hour, eloquently, and Elaine couldn't help but admire this part of him. After he finished, with no repeat of his earlier rant about her, it took her a minute or two to recover her sense of where she was and what this creep was doing to her. He seemed, now, more relaxed, more rational, maybe ready to drop his guard a little. She wasn't sure.

While Schaefer went on about his work and his ... his, his, his.... all he really talked about was himself, Elaine's thoughts turned to Will. What a different man. Will was, at heart pretty gentle, modest, completely unlike Schaefer. He had, because of some weakness, some fragility in his character, turned off course, and had started down a path he could now desert only at enormous cost to himself. Elaine knew he wanted to correct his course, but her love for him told her that she had to fight his need for confession. Will was still a Catholic, like his mother --his father's influence had not really changed Will. He still thinks confession brings redemption. Not in science, buddy; in science, confession of wrong-doing brings only death. Schaefer had begun asking her some questions about Will, but because she was lost in her own thoughts, she missed what he'd said.

"You got him away from Gina. I always wondered about that. It seemed to happen about the same time we started this thing."

"What 'thing'? We have no 'thing' Schaefer. It was just a couple of days together. I found you interesting. I still do. But that does not mean ...Jesus, you must understand that. You've had and dropped enough women. People pass through each other's lives pretty quickly these days, and don't feel they have to declare their loyalty every time they sleep together. My God. I thought you were progressive. Maybe ..." She slowed down, withdrew from her attack.

"I stink. I need to clean up. Is there a shower? I want to wash these clothes. Can I? Or maybe, why don't we just pack up and leave? We'll go to your apartment in Berkeley. It's more comfortable. We can be together there."

"You can shower. Here's some of my clothes. Sweats. They're clean. You can wear these. The shower's in there." He pointed to a small closet. "You can undress here and clean up. I'll go outside."

Elaine was surprised at this show of politeness and also relieved. She'd worried from the start that he would rape her. No way could she resist him. But so far, so good. Before he left the room, he turned to her and said, "We'll stay. I think a few days here, we'll be able to clarify some things. We'll begin to see things more clearly. I have some things I want you to try. They'll bring clarity to all this. Then there'll be no need for anything but honest exchange between - - you'll come to see this - - between two kindred spirits. Then we can talk about returning."

Schaefer went outside and locked the door behind him. Elaine spent a few moments looking about the room. It was mostly bare. A few chairs, several piles of books and papers, a small stereo unit, a wood stove, some kitchen appliances. Nothing on the walls. A monk's quarters, though without the neatness. She stripped quickly and walked into the closet where the shower had been installed. She took a quick shower and washed her hair. The soap was harsh, but it did the job. She found some towels, dried off, and stepped out into the empty room. She wished Will were there and that he would caress her naked body and place his head against her breasts. She had to hold on to him, save him from himself, from the weakness in him that he had come to deplore, but that she could not let govern his life. She would do anything to get back to Will.

CHAPTER 21

While Gina was teaching her 101 class on Tuesday morning, the four rescuers were lost. They'd made it to Noyo by 10:00 a.m., but had spent nearly two hours trying to locate the cabin. Peter wasn't much help. They'd tried three different directions from the small downtown area, and had driven miles and miles without coming to a landmark he recognized. At about noon Kay pulled into the town center for the fourth time that morning and parked in front of a restaurant- inn called The Pines. "I'm hungry. I need to eat and go to the bathroom." Kay got out, and the other three followed.

They ate in silence, with no new ideas about what to do emerging. If they could not locate the cabin, they'd have to give up and return. Of course they weren't even sure that Schaefer had brought Elaine to the cabin. Will also learned from Peter the possibility that Schaefer no longer even owned the cabin! He hadn't been here with Schaefer for more than a year.

Chris noticed that one corner of the restaurant consisted of a grocery shop. He got up and wandered over to talk to the clerk. They engaged in a give-and-take for several minutes, and then he returned with a smile on his face.

"Route 72, remember that? Go out about two miles, there's a road to the right, Meadow Lark it's called. We went down it before, but we gave up too soon. Schaefer's cabin is about four or five miles in, toward the west. The clerk knew exactly who I was talking about when

I described him." They were all pleased as hell with their spiritual guide, and took to the road almost immediately.

As they were driving out on 72, Chris spoke up from the rear. "You know, I think Schaefer is, well, unbalanced. Peter took me to one of his lectures, over in San Francisco, last summer. That's where I first heard him talk about his idea that science is the problem with us, too much materialism, too much technology devoted to evil, that kind of thing. I can't explain it very well. Anyway, I was impressed at first."

"Then Peter told me about a group he and Schaefer were organizing. It was going to be some kind of discussion group, maybe devoted to pushing Schaefer's ideas ahead. So I went, two or three times."

Peter turned to look at Chris. He glared at the priest, then snapped, "Enough. All that was done in confidence. You know you promised not to speak about it."

Chris was not dissuaded. "I'm sorry, Peter, but maybe this is relevant to bring out, now that he's done this thing with the woman." He paused, and Peter turned away and put his head to the window to his right. Kay looked into the rear view mirror and saw that Chris was looking agitated, his eyes shifting nervously. After a short pause, Kay urged him to continue.

"Once, maybe in August, we went to this huge old house in Berkeley, right near Oakland. David was there, and there were another dozen guys. I didn't know any of them. Schaefer spoke to the group, and I tell you, he scared me. I thought he'd lost his mind. He just sounded nuts."

Peter, who had started on one of his putrid cigarettes, turned again and yelled, "Shut up! All that is irrelevant. Besides, you left, you ran out. You don't know." Peter was angry and Chris backed off, saying only that he thought Schaefer was unstable.

About four miles off route 72 on Meadow Lark, Will told Kay to stop. "We better not drive up. We don't want to warn him too much in advance. We'll walk. When we locate the cabin, I'll hide out. You guys go on."

"I'm worried," said Kay. "That gun. We don't know what state of mind he's in. Peter what do you think?"

"I'll go first. He won't hurt me. I'll tell him you, Kay, that you want to talk with him. He respects you." The four set out on foot.

In about twenty minutes they spotted the Schaefer cabin. It was set back from the road about 30 yards, maybe more. Schaefer's car was there, and the four dropped to the ground simultaneously as they all saw that the big man was on the cabin's front porch, leaning, with his back to them, against the wooden guard rail. No one talked, but then Kay signaled and she and Peter rose to start up the muddy driveway. The sun had never quite made it to full power, and the forest was bathed in a dull-grey light. Chris and Will stayed low, well out of sight. They could neither see nor hear the first encounter with Schaefer.

"What the fuck ...?" Schaefer turned and stared at Kay and Peter, his face in a rage.

"You shit, what are you doing here? Get out. Now! Both of you!" Will and Chris could hear these last words, yelled out in anger. They didn't stir.

"Preston, we just want to talk. We know what you did. We think you're in trouble, and we want to help. You're at risk, Preston, maybe the cops ..." Kay had not rehearsed her pitch, and all of a sudden she felt she didn't know what to say. "Elaine. Is she okay? Can we see her?"

"Get away. This is my business, no one else's. She came along to be with me. Her own choice. I don't know what this dumb fuck told you, but it's a lie. I don't need any help and neither does Elaine. She's napping. She's fine. Go. We want to be alone here."

"Can we just come in awhile? I need to use the bathroom. It was a long ride. We'll just do that, get a drink, then leave." Peter stepped back, looking down at the ground, as Kay spoke. He was terrified. He had seen that Schaefer was in a rage. The big man paced back and forth on the porch, quickly, waving his arms. "Go. Get the fuck out. We don't need you. Kay, please go. Take that idiot and go!"

At that moment something came flying through one of the front windows, shattering the glass, and landing by Schaefer's foot. It was the coffee pot. With it came Elaine's cry, a piercing shriek, a call for help. This made Schaefer even angrier, and he turned, unlocked the front door, and stormed through it to the inside. In the momentary silence, before Elaine's next scream, Kay heard the lock slam shut. Elaine's next cry was cut off abruptly, and then once again there was silence.

At the second cry, Will jumped up and ran up the muddy drive. Peter was racing toward him, away from the cabin. Kay was climbing the front steps, and in thirty seconds Will was there by her side. Will was trembling, and the two stopped at the top of the stairs, not sure what to do. They stood there, paralyzed. The barrel of a pistol emerged from the broken window. "I don't want to hurt you two. Weiss, if he were here, I'd blow his nuts off. He had no business bringing you here. You two, just do yourself a favor and go. Elaine is okay. She's here of her own choice. We needed some time together."

Then, a loud crack, as Schaefer fired. Kay and Will fell to the porch deck, then saw that the pistol was not aimed in their direction, but toward the driveway, where Peter stood, about fifty feet away. Schaefer had actually fired at him, but there was no evidence he'd been hit. Peter began running toward the road.

"I'm serious, you two," Schaefer called through the shattered window. "Just go away."

Will was still trembling as he lay on the porch, trying to develop a plan. He saw Kay kneeling up, and then heard her speak. "Preston, let me come in. Just to see if Elaine is okay. We're worried. We're all friends here. We don't want to see anyone hurt. Please." Schaefer moved away from the window. There was silence under the midday sun that had finally pierced the clouds. The forest was still, moist and perfectly beautiful. Then a quiet sobbing could be heard from within the cabin, and at that moment Schaefer unlocked and opened the door. He stood, large and powerful looking, in the doorway, his arms hanging by his sides, his pistol shoved into his trousers at the belt line. He finally spoke. "Okay, you two, come in. We need to talk. No weirdness, or else ..."

At first Will was hesitant, but then rose and followed Kay into the cabin.

Elaine was seated on the small sofa, wrapped in a white robe. Her hair was wet, as if she'd just stepped out of a shower, which in fact she had. Schaefer told Kay and Will to take seats, and to stay put. He stood behind Elaine. The curtains were drawn over all of the room's windows, except the one that Elaine had broken and out of which Schaefer had fired. The room was quite dark, except for one strong ray of light that entered through the broken window and that illuminated Elaine's bare legs and feet. Kay could see that Elaine's eyes were swollen with tears, as she began to speak. "Preston, we believe you forced Elaine here against her will. That's not right. You can't do that to someone. You, of all people. Elaine, talk to us, to Will. Are you okay? Did Preston force you here?" Schaefer protested loudly at this last remark, but Elaine ignored him. She turned to Will and said, "Will. I need to get out of here. I need to be back with you. This was not my idea. You know he's been after me, a long time. You know ..."

Schaefer interrupted. "That's enough. That's enough. Okay. I lost it. I only wanted to have some time alone with her. She knows ... we were lovers ...we were ...and then she just cut it off, abruptly, no reason. We were meant to be together, she's the kind of strong woman a man like me needs. She ran out on me, just the way you ran out on Gina. No reason. Maybe you had a reason, Getz, maybe you needed Elaine for your own benefit. You had no reason to run out on Gina and take my woman. Besides, there's other plans for her, I need her to assist me."

"Will, Will, that's bullshit he's telling you," Elaine cried out. "We weren't lovers, that's crazy. His imagination has taken control of him. Please, you can't believe him!"

Will felt a shock at his center when he heard Schaefer's words about how he, Will, had taken up with Elaine only for his own benefit. What did Schaefer know? Could he possibly know what Elaine had on him, her hold over him, her knowledge that he had faked his research? What did Schaefer know? Jesus, if Elaine, in some moment of fear, had told all ... was that possible? Will was in the grip of these terrifying thoughts and didn't hear the exchange that had started between Schaefer and Kay.

"...so what about Guatemala?" Kay had decided to shift the conversation, in an attempt perhaps to reduce the tension, and had chosen the David Zaretsky matter. "Tell us more, Preston. Did David really stay at his own choosing? What happened down there?"

The door to the cabin swung open and Chris Swift appeared. Schaefer immediately went for his gun and howled, "What the fuck are you doing here?" Kay jumped in and said, "It's okay. He's with us. A good friend, a priest, Chris. You've met him before, I'm sure. He's okay, he lives with us in the big house."

"Yeah, I know this guy, a worthless piece of shit. Sit down, you fairy, and just shut up." Schaefer was all of a sudden in a fury again, and he began pacing, the gun now in his right hand.

Will hadn't moved from his chair, but Kay had crossed the room and taken a seat next to Elaine. She put her arm over Elaine's shoulders and spoke quietly, "Elaine, we're going to leave. You come with us. You don't have to stay here, a prisoner. You just get up and come with us. Will, Chris ..."

Schaefer stopped his pacing and turned, aiming his gun in the general direction of Kay and Elaine. "No! Elaine and I have unfinished business. We haven't had enough time to talk. I'm not letting her return to Getz. He's the real slave holder here." Schaefer lifted his arm and pointed the pistol in Will's direction. "He's scum, Getz is. He screwed over Gina, he'll do the same to Elaine when he no longer needs her!"

The room was quiet. Will felt his heart beating, heard it, even, in the quiet of the room. Will had a fleeting thought, in which he saw Elaine dead, murdered at the hand of this madman, and he saw how this would remove a burden from his own life. His secret, that only she knew - - unless she'd told Schaefer - - would die with her. And he would no longer have to pretend he wanted to be with her. Jesus ... what kind of beast am I? And then he saw a movement, out of the corner of his eye. Chris, running across the room, toward Schaefer. What was he doing? Was he crazy? He was only two-thirds of Schaefer's size, and ... a loud crack, like before ... another, louder. The smell of something burning. Chris hustling toward Schaefer and attempting to grasp the big man's arm. Shouting. Elaine's loud cry. A scramble. Will sat, stiff in his chair, a witness ... to what? No! This was all his doing. He, Will Getz, had put everyone in this predicament. He shouldn't have gone to Elaine ... innocents like Kay and the priest (what was he to Gina?) ... and another loud crack followed by a chilling cry.

Will leapt up and saw that Schaefer had fallen. His gun was still in his hand. The two women were heading for the door, and Schaefer was raising his arm in preparation for firing again. He was going to shoot Elaine or Kay, or both! Will sprang across the room, reached Schaefer, and kicked him in the head. He seemed barely to flinch. Will saw that the women were not yet free of the cabin and he fell, both knees landing on Schaefer's gun arm. Will grabbed Schaefer's hand and began wrestling the gun away. Schaefer yelled out some obscenity and then swung his free left arm over his body and landed his left fist squarely in Will's stomach. It knocked the breath out of Will, but he managed to stay put, knees pinning down Schaefer's right arm. Will recovered, spotted a pile of logs next to the wood stove, grabbed one, raised it, and tried to bring it down with the full force of his body against the side of Schaefer's head. Somehow Will lost his advantage and Schaefer managed to turn his body and again plunged his left fist into Will's gut. The big man rose, kicked Will in the ribs, screamed and headed for the open door. On his way out he grabbed Elaine by her arm and tried to pull her with him. "Come on, come on, you bitch, come ..." he snarled. Elaine fell, Schaefer released her, and then ran off, down the driveway to his car. He got in and drove off.

Will rose from the floor, rubbing at his stomach. He was shaking in every muscle of his body. Where were Kay and Elaine? Will walked to the door and looked out. He saw the two women, and told them what had happened.

"Chris. What happened to him? Where is he?" Kay sounded frightened, as she ran back into the cabin. Will followed her in, and saw that she was kneeling beside the priest's body, crying uncontrollably. He was lying face down, stiff, blood at the back of his head and on his shoulders. No movement.

Will saw Elaine, wrapped in her white robe, in the doorway, hair a mess, her face covered in tears. He turned to hear Kay speak. "He's dead. Chris is dead, Will. Not a sign of life. I don't know why he did it. Why did he do such a risky, stupid thing? It was unnecessary. Schaefer wasn't going to hurt anybody. He was all bluff. Chris. God, why ...?"

CHAPTER 22

In early December, a week after Chris' murder and Schaefer's escape, Will told Alden Jensen the whole sorry story of his deception. Will had successfully avoided Jensen for the whole of November and into December, but knew that the Professor had sought him out several times, no doubt to tell him time had run out, that his small stipend would be cut off at the end of December, and that Will would soon be asked to move out of his lab. Jensen needed the space. In the face of protests from Elaine, Will decided that the only course he could take, the only course he could live with, was to tell the truth, take the consequences, and find something else to do with his life. He even considered simply dropping out, as so many in his generation now seemed to be doing, and taking up life on the fringes. He considered this, but knew in his heart he could never live that way. An old friend of his from Columbia, Ed Cheney, had gone this route. Ed was a bright and talented guy so dismayed by the prospect of becoming chained to the type of society America had become that he chose to quit school and take up life in a commune in Vermont. Will had visited him there a couple of times and been intrigued by the apparent ease and beauty, the simplicity of Ed's life.

But Will was not cut from the same cloth. Will was in many ways equally critical of mainstream America, but thought, through a life in science, that he could avoid what he most despised. Science was, in a way, a kind of sanctuary, a home for people who were committed to building a society founded on reason, where there is true competition of ideas, where truth, not power, would finally be the guide. Now, for reasons he could in no way fathom, Will Getz had betrayed science, and he needed to withdraw. He thought Elaine might be hurt, but also hoped Jensen would either not discern her role or would forgive her for it. After Jensen, Will decided he'd pack up and drive back to Boston to reveal everything to his dad. This would be the most difficult thing of all. On Thursday evening he told Elaine of his plans. By this time she had come to expect this news and decided to give up resisting. She'd just wait to hear from Jensen. On a Friday afternoon, at about three, Will entered Jensen's office. The professor seemed relaxed, but immediately started in about Will's irresponsible delays. Will sat and took it for awhile, but then interrupted Jensen and began his story.

Will went into great detail. He started by repeating what Jensen already knew, the story of his first apparent success with the last step of the pfaffadine synthesis, completed the previous January. Jensen was impatient, not understanding why Will was going back over this.

"All the rest of my work was faked. I never repeated the first synthesis. I tried, over and over, but could never find any pfaff. I did it until I ran out of pre-pfaff. I could not bear the thought of going back to synthesize more pre-pfaff. I faked everything. That's the reason I've been unable to write this up. I am not capable of continuing this deception. I have no excuse, except maybe pure laziness and lack of character. I couldn't persevere. I'm not made to be a scientist. I committed the worst offense imaginable. I'm sorry. I'll pack up and leave right away."

It took Jensen several minutes to digest this. The two sat in the office, now darkening with the descent of the late autumn afternoon. The professor said nothing. He sat at his desk, a desk crowded with chemistry journals, half-written manuscripts and letters, materials used in his graduate course on medicinal chemistry, and looked down at his hands, which were folded together at the edge of the desk. He'd never before faced a situation like this. He knew cheating went on, at all levels of science, and he knew it had happened before in this Department, but never on his watch. Jensen liked Will very much, thought very highly of him. This behavior - - could it be true? - - did not fit at all with Jensen's image of Will. It couldn't be true? Jesus, he'd have to go before his peers and withdraw the work. Will had presented it at the ACS meeting. There was an abstract of it published. It's even worse! Jensen had written up a summary of the synthesis for the NCI, had used it as part of his recent grant application, submitted in September. He'd lied! The NCI work on pfaffadine was going very well. They were ready to contract out for the production of large amounts for the next stage of anti-tumor screening. Jensen would be the key advisor, and Elaine, because of her extraction and purification system. Elaine. Elaine lived with Will, what...? Jensen raised his eyes and looked across the room at Will. Will's long hair rested on his shoulders. The young man was sitting stiffly in his chair, looking extremely uneasy. He was staring straight ahead, through the fingers of his hands, which he held before him, fingers touching at their tips, as his elbows rested on the arms of his chair. The room was becoming very dark, but Jensen made no move to turn on the lights.

"I took more than a gram of synthesized pfaffadine to NCI for their first screening test. You gave me that. Last May. Where did you get that? Will, what are you telling me? This can't be true. You're stuck in the writing, that I can understand. What you said, though, that can't be true. Will, tell me." Jensen didn't move from his chair. He seemed calm, his voice was even and relatively soft. He waited.

"I stole the pfaff from Elaine's lab. She'd had her success and had a vial full. I took a gram."

"Not possible. She would have noticed that much missing. She had less than two grams. She would have said something. She helped you in this. She ...but let's go back. Forget about Elaine. What were you thinking? What am I going to do?" Now Jensen's voice was rising. He was agitated. He reached for his desk lamp and put on the light. Will covered his eyes briefly, then recovered and spoke.

"I'll take my stuff out of the lab. I'll do it tonight. You won't see me again. I'm going home. To Boston." Will sat for a moment, then got up and left Jensen's office.

He gathered up his books and the few personal items he kept in his lab, including a small photo of his father, and piled them into two large shopping bags he'd brought with him. He looked around the lab that had been his home for the past two and one-half years. He'd probably never be around this wonderful equipment, the tools of the chemist's trade, again. The dozens of bottles of reagents lined up on the shelves: acetone, glacial acetic acid, chloroform, toluene, diethyl ether, tetrahydrofuran, alumina, silica, on and on. All this gone from his life for a reason he could not explain to himself, and that he could never possibly explain to anyone else.

He wandered down the hall to the elevator and luckily ran into no one except a janitor. As he stepped onto the elevator, the two stuffed shopping bags in hand, he noticed Jensen approaching. Will allowed the doors to close and did nothing to keep them open for his former professor. A joke. Jensen was really the one left holding the bag. He'd have to deal with the professional community that his student had so selfishly wronged.

Elaine was watching the evening news on TV when Will got back to their apartment. She got up, turned off the TV, and went to greet him, the man for whom she still felt a deep passion. She was never sure she'd convinced Will that the Schaefer thing was all one way, that she'd never really been a lover of the madman. After the kidnapping and murder she'd hoped Will would recover his feeling for her - - she truly believed that he wanted her, and never believed he'd moved in with her just because she had something on him, knew his secret sin. She'd felt his passion for her. She had not deceived herself on this matter.

She knew once she saw the full bags Will was carrying that he'd gone through with his promise. She touched his arm, caressed it, looked into his eyes and saw only a dull glimmer of life. He'd done it.

He didn't need Elaine anymore to guard his secret. But that doesn't mean he didn't want to be with her. He'll get a job. They would be together. She would finish up, fly high on her purification system, and land a great job. He'll be able to get a decent job. Maybe there will be nothing on his permanent record? Maybe Jensen will just say Will left, decided he didn't want to do science. That he wanted some other kind of life. No reason for Jensen to put all this on the record. These hopeful thoughts raced through Elaine's mind as she helped Will remove his coat.

He dropped down onto the sofa, took one of Elaine's cigarettes and lit up. He hadn't smoked since June, when he'd taken up running again. He felt he had to tell Elaine about the meeting with Jensen, and even about Jensen's inquiry about Elaine, Will's response to that, and Jensen's denial of the credibility of Will's response.

"I think he'll ask you if you abetted my crime. I denied it. I said I stole your stuff, that you knew nothing about it. You should too. Think of some reason why you wouldn't have reported to him the missing pfaff. You can think of a reason."

"He won't believe me. I'll tell him the truth. I don't think he'll penalize me. At least there's a good chance he won't. A crime of the heart. That's what it was, you know. I knew it was wrong. I wanted you. I wanted to help you. I still want you. I'll do anything."

Elaine was kneeling on the floor by the sofa where Will sat. Her voice was soft, imploring. He didn't recall ever hearing her speak in this way, never had she seemed so honest, so vulnerable. She was on her knees. Hah. He wanted none of this. She could return to the life she had pre-Will. That's where she belongs.

Will put out his cigarette, stood and put his coat back on. "I need to go out. I've got something I need to do." He left Elaine, kneeling on the floor, in the apartment where he had never felt at home.

Will walked the several blocks to the Manse, went to the front door, and knocked. The winds were strong in the Berkeley hills, and the night sky was cloudy and moonless. As he knocked again Will had a brief thought about Elaine and what Jensen would say to her, and then he entered the house as Kay opened the door.

"Will. How are you? Are you okay? We haven't seen you since the police station at Fort Bragg. Are you okay?"

"Yeah. I'm here to see Gina. Is she here?"

"Yes. She's in her room. I'll get her. Or maybe you'll want to go up?"

"Would you ask her? If I can come up? I need to talk to her. It's very important."

Kay turned and climbed the stairs, and in a few moments reappeared at the top of the stairs and called down to Will to come up. He did so, and Kay took him to Gina's room. Will hesitated a bit as he approached her room. Gina was standing in the open doorway, arms folded across her chest. She was dressed in a long heavy, navy blue sweater and jeans, and had her feet bundled in a couple of pairs of heavy socks. Her hair was a little messy, but Will thought she looked great. He'd always loved her face and those deep and richly dark eyes.

"Gina. Could I? Could we talk a little? I need to talk to you."

"Sure. Come in. You want a coke? Or some wine. I've got this bottle Marco gave me. He gave me a whole case, in fact, see?" She pointed to a box sitting in a corner of her room, and upon which she had stacked a pile of papers. "My anthropology students. I'm still T.A. in a course, until the end of the semester. I'm grading those."

"How is Marco? I miss him."

Gina thought all her friends must know. She'd never told Will about Marco, but maybe assumed he would have heard by now. She took up a seat at the head of her bed, and asked Will to sit as well.

"Marco's not well. I thought you must have heard."

"What? No. What's the problem? Is he sick?"

"Very." She felt tears beginning to rise, but held them back. "Very." She looked down at the bedspread and the open space between them. This very spread that she and Will had spent so many nights beneath. Why was she talking to him? About Marco. He'd lost his rights to know anything of her life.

"He has cancer. The worst kind, almost. In his pancreas. He will die from it, probably soon. He's now in pain, lots. I learned just at Thanksgiving. I think he'll have to go to the hospital soon. He's getting worse fast. That's what's wrong with my father." She said all this with a slight tone of bitterness in her voice. She looked directly at Will when she spoke, and anger showed in her face. Will looked away. He had a deep urge to move to her side and to take her into his arms. He then looked into her face and the two former lovers shared a long moment of grief.

Gina and Will sat in silence for several minutes. She finally rose to pour two glasses of wine, handed one to Will, and returned to her seat at the head of the bed. Will had come to tell Gina his story. The story he had just told Alden Jensen, and the story about his departure from her life, the trap he had made for himself that had destroyed the life he had had with Gina. He owed Gina a full explanation. He could then return to Boston and find some new way to live. But now, with the news about Marco, Will felt his own story was trivial by comparison. He'd lost his will to confess.

"Why are you here, Will? What's going on?"

"I ...I was just wondering how you were since, you know, what Schaefer did to your friend." This was not the primary reason Will had come, but it was on his mind. He had not visited Gina after the shooting. Kay had carried the message about the priest's death and Schaefer's escape. The killer had, after ten days, still not been found.

"I guess I've been alright. He was a good friend, a good person who I cared for a great deal. I cannot understand Schaefer. Did he just panic, was he spooked, was it an accident? Or was it intentional? Did he have something against Chris? Peter denied that Schaefer had something against him, but I never trust what that guy says. I hope they catch the bastard, and lock him up forever." Gina turned away from Will and took a moment to catch her breath. "So, is that all you wanted to know?"

Will drank some of his wine and had a thought he should leave. Then, somehow. the words flowed, the truth, finally. He went on non-stop, the whole story starting with the problems he'd had in the lab, his apparent success, the string of failures, his collapse into scientific deception. All this, which he had spent the afternoon telling Jensen, came forth, and Gina could do nothing but sit in silence, dumbfounded ...why is he telling me this? Then Will told her of his meeting with Elaine, their weekend together when Gina was away in Seattle, and her offer to help him deceive Jensen.

"She had me then. I fell for it, I took her up on her offer of a gram of pfaff that she'd isolated, and I gave it to Jensen as if it were the product of my synthesis. She had me then. She wanted me. She'd had this desire to have me with her. If I'd refused her, God knows what she would have done. She knew about what I had done. Maybe she would never have revealed a thing, but at the time I thought I couldn't take a chance. So, I did what she wanted. I moved in with her. Maybe you can't believe me, but I never really felt, you know, close. I admit she, you know, I found her attractive in a certain way, but I can't say I really ... liked her much. Not anything like the way I felt for you."

Gina remained silent, at once angry at him and sad for him, very sad. He went on, about his struggle to write the fake thesis, his presentation in Atlantic City, the continuing failure to complete his thesis, Elaine's constant prodding for him to go through with his deception, and his final decision, after many false starts, to reveal everything and to take the consequences. He ended with the story of his meeting with Alden Jensen of just a few hours earlier.

"I'm going home, to Boston." He got up to fetch some more wine, and refilled Gina's and his own glass. He felt the urge to smoke, but put it aside and sat again, this time close to Gina.

"Telling my father will be hard. I think he will be, I mean, I know he will be devastated. Marco. Do you think I can see him before I go? That's a lot to ask, I know, but, you know, I really liked him."

Gina hesitated, then asked quietly, "Why did you tell me all this? You want something from me? I've gotten by ... I mean I'm remaking my life, I've gotten by you. I'm focusing on a new life for me. I wasn't in the right place, professionally or personally. I've dropped anthropology, I'm going to go to law school. I've got a real good friend in Kay. No men, but I'm way past you, Will. What do you ...?" She stopped what she felt was an unnecessary ramble, subjects that were irrelevant to why Will had come to see her.

"Nothing. I'm not asking you for anything. Really. I just wanted you to know what had happened. Why I had left you."

"You risked your life to save her. That must mean something. You didn't hesitate to go after Schaefer."

"I never thought it would be an armed confrontation. I never really thought he'd have a weapon."

"I think you've done the right thing, Will. Telling Jensen. It must have been really difficult. You'll probably never do anything again that difficult. You couldn't live your whole life, for God's sake, knowing it was built on a lie. Do you have any idea why you ...?"

"None. Some real defect in my character, I guess. I never thought of myself as, you know, an especially admirable person. In fact, I've thought, deep down, that I'm kind of selfish. But I never thought I was that dishonest. Jesus. This is so bad, dishonest isn't even the word for it. I need to figure this out."

"What will you do now, besides go back home?"

"No idea. I'll need to get some kind of job. You know, I even thought about just disappearing, not face my father, just drop out. I have a friend in Vermont who did that. But I don't think I can, it's not in me. Shit, what a mess." He downed the rest of his wine and then went for more. Gina took some, too. She was beginning to feel it. The room was getting warm. She had a passing thought of Chris, remembered the night he'd first stepped into her room while she played her violin. She'd played it nearly every day after that, but not once since the day he was killed.

"Chris Swift. He wanted so much to be a priest, but not an ordinary priest. He wanted to save the world, work with the poor, that kind of thing. He was trying to figure out where and how to do that. He maybe was going to Central American with the Maryknolls. He had this missionary idea. I think he was ... maybe like David, but without the anger. You know Schaefer left him behind in Guatemala with a bunch of rebels, some insurrection. I don't understand Latin American politics, but David's still down there. God knows what's become of him. Schaefer was such a pig, maybe worse. I wouldn't be surprised if he did something bad to David. You know what he ...?"

Will let her go on. She was slightly drunk, but seemed to want to tell him everything that had happened in her life since their separation, just the way he had. She went on, and finally returned to the subject of her father.

"We can go see him tomorrow. He'll be home. I should call him first, to warn him. He always liked you a lot. It'll be good ..." And with these words Gina finally stopped talking. Will wanted more to drink, but the wine bottle was empty. He decided not to open another.

"I'll come by in the morning. We'll call Marco and then go. Okay?" Gina nodded assent. Will covered her with a blanket, turned off the lights, and departed. He walked back to the apartment very slowly, feeling a slight burn from the wine, but clear in his mind, very clear. The cold, dark Friday ended for Will calmly, quietly, and with a peace he had not felt for ages.

Kay had seen Will slip out as she left her own room at about eleven and headed for the kitchen to make some tea. She wondered about Will's visit, but couldn't come up with an obvious reason for it. He'd stayed more than three hours. It must have been important. He'd looked pretty serious when he'd arrived.

Kay worried a lot about Gina. Kay knew that her attachment to Gina was deep, more than ordinary friendship. She felt real desire, but had accepted the fact that Gina did not and would never. Gina had experienced so many dreadful blows - - Will's cruel desertion, her father's cancer, Schaefer's gross unfairness, Chris' sad death, and God knows what new piece of news Will now had for her - - you might think she'd be an emotional mess. It was just for this reason, her possibly heightened susceptibility, that Kay had not pursued Gina more aggressively. Kay did not want to take advantage of Gina's tragic state. Kay had had to restrain herself, mightily at times, because the desire she had for Gina was intense. Kay recognized the force of her desire, the truth about her own sexuality, something that in the past had only weakly asserted itself. But she was not going to try to take advantage of a woman who was so vulnerable.

What was odd about all this was the fact that Kay thought she saw some new strengths in Gina. With each blow she suffered, she seemed to grow, not more vulnerable, but more independent, more determined. Maybe these were just the outward signs. Maybe deep within she was actually weaker, but she didn't let it show. Gina seemed more determined than ever to make an independent and significant life for herself. She had the intelligence, more than enough, as many women did. Had all this adversity really given her the will to succeed? Women needed a lot of will to overcome the barriers that men, powerful white men, had spent centuries building around them. Kay wanted, oh so much, to be with Gina and to witness the ways this woman would grow.

As Kay sat, sipping tea, and letting her thoughts meander in these directions, the object of her thoughts was upstairs, wrapped in sleep. In her dreams that night Gina saw a beautiful young man, tall and slim, maybe naked, running on a sun-drenched beach, free and powerful, kicking up water and sand with each step, not with any specific destination, just moving, in peace ... no, no, not a young man, rather a young woman, slim and slight and dark-haired and naked and free.

The next morning as Gina was waiting for Will to show up for the visit with Marco, she sat in the kitchen chatting with Kay. The older woman had some news.

"By the way ... I got a call at work from an editor at the San Francisco Chronicle. He'd read my series on the Black Panthers, and asked if I'd be interested in talking. I don't know. I'm not sure I can do the same kind of journalism with a paper like that, big, commercial, conservative. I think I'd find it difficult. Anyway, I'll probably go talk to them." Kay seemed pleased with the prospect.

Gina left to respond to the knocking that had just begun at the front door. It was Will, dressed in a thick sweater and a heavy green rain parka. It was unusually cold, and a light rain had just begun.

"You want some coffee? Come in. I still need to call Marco before we leave."

Will entered, removed the parka, and went to the kitchen with Gina. There, after the greetings, he sat at the table and accepted a large mug full of coffee. He wondered for a moment whether Gina had revealed anything to Kay, but relaxed when he saw nothing unusual in her behavior toward him. Gina went to call Marco, and Kay and Will sat quietly for a few moments. Kay finally spoke.

"This is really hard for Gina. Her mother just a few years ago. Now this. And Chris, too. It's dreadful."

"How's she been taking it?" Will asked.

"She's broken down a few times, cried a lot. But mostly she seems okay. It's like she's accepted what the doctors say as almost inevitable with this kind of cancer, but, you know, she's really strong, I think. That crap with Schaefer. She recovered, she's planned a new career path. Did she tell you? Law. She thinks it's something that she can make a difference with. She's a lot more self-confident, I think. Maybe some adversity helps build strength of character, confidence."

Gina returned, dressed for the trip. "We're invited for lunch. It's ten-thirty now, we can go."

The next several hours were very difficult for Will. Marco looked ill, and quite feeble. The vigorous, lively mind that he'd loved being around definitely had lost much of its vitality. Most of all he hated to see Gina, who tried to keep the mood upbeat as they ate the vegetable bean soup Marco had prepared. Marco could not seem to enjoy eating. He took no wine, because of his medicine.

Afterwards he asked Will about his own future. He wanted to know more about why Will had left his daughter, but couldn't bring himself to ask. Will was vague about his plans, and avoided altogether any mention of his and Gina's relationship. It was a mostly quiet gathering, with Marco sitting motionless in his large living room chair, the chair where he'd spent so many hours of his life, his life with Teresa, his life with Teresa and their wonderful Gina, his life alone. He wondered if he would die in this chair.

After a few hours of quiet talk, Marco asked if he could be alone with Gina. Will left the living room for the kitchen, closed the door, and started doing the dishes. His own problems seemed so trivial now. Will recalled how his own mother's departure from his life had felt, and remembered how, as a child, he had had nightmares about losing his father. It never happened, of course, because Will had found a way to convince his father that his mother had been unfaithful-- the story Will had invented about how he had seen her kissing another man had been effective, and helped his father recover. How often had the boy thought that his lie could easily have been the truth? Now Will had to face the kind and gentle man who had devoted his life to him, and tell him the bitter truth about the kind of person he had raised. Will shuddered to think of his father's reaction, and at that moment believed that he could not possibly do what he knew he had to do.

Later that Saturday afternoon, Gina and Will roamed the streets of San Francisco. The rain had let up, but it was still unusually cold. They ended up at Aldo's Trattoria and Coffee House in North Beach, and went in for coffee. The place was crowded for the time of day. All sorts of conversations were underway and the general liveliness of the place was infectious.

"I'm so sorry about your dad. I feel so bad for you. I wish I could do something. It's ..."

"He told me he's going to the hospital soon, to stay. He can't take care of himself. He'll be at San Francisco, the University Medical Center, up on Parnassus Avenue. He's got a good doctor, but there's not much they can do. Just make him more comfortable."

Gina spoke calmly, but Will knew she must be broken up inside. What he didn't know, and what Gina would not tell him, was the story Marco had told her of how he had caused, or so he believed, the death, the suicidal death, of her mother when he forced her to have an abortion. Marco, sitting stiffly in his living room chair, had just told Gina, once again, of how sorry he was to have taken her mother from her. He had cried as he spoke these words, and Gina had wrapped her arms about his head and had felt his warm tears against her arm. He believed that this disease that was killing him must have started within him at the moment he had been so cruel to his wife. Gina had protested this awful self-flagellation, but her father could only cry. None of this could she talk about with Will, the way she had with Chris in the eucalyptus grove, the day before his death. If she and Will had still been together, she would have shared this story with him. But they were no longer even friends. She did, however, feel comfortable sitting here sharing coffee with him. She noticed that Will suddenly seemed more animated.

"I've done the right thing. My problem is so minor compared with your dad's. I feel like a shit for pitying myself about it. But I'm getting by my self pity. I think. I confessed to Jensen and I feel okay, a huge weight was lifted from my shoulders. Even telling you helps me cleanse myself. I'm glad you let me see Marco. I hate to leave you at a time like this, but I think I've got to clear out. I've got to get out of Berkeley. I really dread talking to my father, but I need to."

"You do. The truth, Will. There are so many lies and deceptions, everywhere. The war, it's built on lies, suppression of women and black people, all built on lies. Our generation, you know, we're supposed to reject all that. We can't scorn it in others and accept it in ourselves, our personal lives. You've taken a big step, so keep stepping in the right direction. Your dad, he's great. He loves you, without any qualifications, I'm sure. He'll be hurt, but he'll not reject you. He'll still want to help you, like he always has."

As they drove back to Berkeley in Gina's VW, Will focused on what she had said. He knew she was right. He'd been a coward, but he'd started to rehabilitate himself. He would not turn back.

"I'm going Monday, I think. Just pack up the Chevy and head back to the East. The car is a wreck. I'm not sure it'll make it, 3000 miles, but I'll try. I probably won't see you again."

She didn't like the sound of that, somehow. She didn't detect any particular desire to continue with this man, but there was something ... sympathetic in her toward him. He was a decent guy with a serious flaw somewhere. She couldn't imagine ever doing anything remotely like what Will had done.

She wondered about Elaine as she dropped him off at his apartment. Was Will really through with his co-conspirator? No, Gina would not go tell Alden Jensen about Elaine's role in Will's fraud.

"Write me? Will you write to me, Will? After you decide what you're going to do. I want to know. You know the address at the Manse."

"Yes, I'll write. I promise." Will turned away, and proceeded up the steps to the small apartment he had come to hate so much.

Elaine wasn't in. Will was hungry and made himself a thick peanut butter and jelly sandwich, on stale bread. As he sat devouring it, with a glass of milk, he noticed an envelope on the table with his name on it. He picked it up and stared at it for a moment, then tore it open. The sun had set and the room was fairly dark, so he rose to switch on a lamp. He opened the note that he'd found in the envelope and read it under the lamp. It was from Alden Jensen, and it asked Will to call him, at home, as soon as he got in. It was marked "Urgent."

Will couldn't imagine what Jensen was interested in talking about, but he dialed the number Jensen had written on the note.

"Yes?"

"This is Will Getz."

"Getz, thank you for calling." Jensen sounded calm. "I want to talk with you. Can you come now to my house? My wife's out. It's very important."

"Okay, I guess. Right now?"

"Yes. Please."

At seven Saturday evening Will Getz was sitting in Professor Alden Jensen's living room. Jensen, tall and rail thin in a pair of khakis and a heavy flannel shirt, tried to appear calm, but was pacing nervously. He finally took up a position in a seat directly opposite Will. The large living room was lit only by a single lamp, and Will could not see Jensen's narrow face very clearly. The professor then spoke, quickly and succinctly, as if he had rehearsed.

"You have done something incredibly stupid and unethical. There's no forgiveness in science. It's the unwritten moral law of science. Truth at all costs. Nothing is as important as adherence to that principle. Without it science is just like every other human endeavor. Science cannot become like other human endeavors. It must lead the way. Without complete honesty, it will fail.

"You have learned this lesson. You knew as soon as you had fabricated your results that you had committed the ultimate evil in science. Maybe you could have gotten away with it. I don't know. But you recognized finally that you could not have lived with this on your conscience. Good for you. I didn't even have to ask you to leave. You knew, and offered to do the right thing.

"Your experiment, you say, worked the first time you tried to convert pre-pfaff to pfaff. Okay. You tried three times, and the conversion failed. You then faked it.

"We don't know why you failed. What reaction conditions or isolation procedures were different the second or third or fourth time from the first, successful time. I want to know why the synthesis could not be repeated."

Will stirred in his seat. This was making him very nervous. Where was Jensen going?

"You are a talented guy, Getz. You know you did something grievously wrong. I have a need to know why you could not repeat your work. Here's my proposition.

"I want you to stay on. I want you to work day and night, and repeat the eleven-step synthesis of pre-pfaff. I'm guessing that's three or four months, less if you work your ass off. When you have sufficient quantities of pre-pfaff, we'll get together and carefully work through the last step. You did it once. You're pretty sure about that, and I believe you. You have good evidence about that. That means you can do it again. I will support you. My grant's big enough to support you until maybe April or May. I can't keep you on after that.

"We'll tell the others that I asked you to repeat the synthesis one more time, because we need to provide the NCI with the best possible synthesis procedure. You are working to improve the yields of each step. Not to prove that the synthesis can be repeated. But to improve the amount of pfaffadine that you can produce by synthesis, improve the efficiency. This will be our story.

"Elaine I talked to this morning. I asked her to my office, called her Friday evening, after you spoke to me. I told her I knew about her help to you. I told her she had behaved improperly, but that I would keep her on. I told her that I was going to give you this chance. You are one of the brightest grad students I've had. You screwed up, but there's no harm done yet. We haven't published, except that ACS abstract and your talk in Atlantic City. Minor things. The reaction can be repeated, I'm sure. You have maybe five months. Elaine will say nothing. There's a lot at stake beyond your own professional and personal life. I have established a high standing in my field. I have been at this nearly twenty years. You have jeopardized my reputation. My chances for acquiring continuing funding. My consulting relationships. You need to repair the damage. This is a request of sorts, I'm asking. But in fact, Mr. Getz, you have no choice in this matter. I'm not just going to sit back and let you run away and leave me to clean up your mess. You are not going to be allowed to fuck up my life. Now, go. And be sure to be in your lab Monday morning, first thing."

CHAPTER 23

Gina packed up a pile of the papers she had graded and headed for campus. The class she had to teach at noon was the last of the semester, Anthropology 101, and at its conclusion her obligation to the department would end. Schaefer would never be back and, for entirely different reasons, neither would she.

Gina had a half hour to kill before class, and thought about dropping in to the Teaching Assistant's lounge. As she headed in that direction she passed Schaefer's office on the second floor. The hallway was empty, so she yielded to the temptation to enter his office, the place where, three months before, the beast had told her she wasn't worth shit to him.

She quietly closed the door behind her, and went to the office's only window and opened its blinds. Outside students were shuffling back and forth and the cool December winds were lifting and shaking the long branches of eucalyptus that lined the walkway by the Anthropology Department. Gina wondered for a moment about the lives of these students, their hopes and fears, their deepest torments. How many were, like she, without mothers? Or had deathly ill loved ones? Or had friends who had been murdered? Or had been unfairly treated? Their daily struggles to make places for themselves could be so painful. Yet, maybe most didn't care that much. Maybe most were just occupied with their social lives, with the pursuit of pleasure in drugs and sex and music. For her music was not the Stones or the Doors or even the Beatles. She enjoyed that stuff, sometimes, but her training in music had brought with it a deep love of the classics. Her mother's influence. Oh, what was the truth about her dear mother? Marco, wonderful Marco, suffering the awful pain of his cancer, but hurting more from years of guilt about what he thought he had done to her mother. Gina did not accept his version. She knew she couldn't change his belief about what he had done, that he would probably die with it, but she could not blame him for her mother's death. The parade of students continued below in the cold December sun.

Gina turned from the window and scanned Schaefer's office. She saw the stacks of unfinished manuscripts, his notebooks from the Guatemala trip, a half-finished paper, apparently intended for the radical magazine, *Breaking the Hold*, with the title "Whose Truth?" Probably another of his tirades about the relativity of truth, the value of non-scientific accounts of knowledge, the grip of the technocrats, and how to break out. Schaefer did have interesting ideas. Too bad he was such a moral pig.

Gina opened one of his Guatemala notebooks. The first page, dated October 3, 1967, was filled from top to bottom with detailed plans for the trip, apparently written on the plane ride down to Guatemala City. She looked for her own name, but it was nowhere evident. The rest of the notebook contained observations about the Maryanta peoples. It looked like Schaefer had not worked hard; six weeks of observations barely filled a third of the 100-page notebook. His observations looked messy on the pages and there was no apparent order in them. She turned to the last page. It was dated November 17, and had nothing to do with the Maryanta. She read it in its entirety.

> David is worthless. He hasn't worked well this trip.
> On Day 2 he met this guy, Reynaldo, a local who
> Perea hired to help us. Reynaldo is apparently active
> with some group called "Freedom or Death" (my
> translation). The government in Guatemala is

repressive, as bad as any in Latin America. No doubt supported by the gringos in Washington. The Imperial Monster. The group is a rebel force. Fairly strong, but scattered in small groups throughout the mountains. Government forces have a hard time smoking them out. Their leader is someone called Francisco something, apparently trained under Fidel or Che (poor dead Che, we heard the news up here about ten days ago). Reynaldo captured David's ear, filled it quickly. He now tells me he's going to stay behind, join the rebels. I told him he might as well do something useful with his life. He's no scholar. His political thinking is confused, at best. He's off of my bandwagon, the asshole. Can't understand why what I want is far more important than poking around in the jungle with a rifle. His thinking is a mess, and he won't let me help him. I also know there's some sweet young thing he's plugging, some sexy dark-haired rebel. He's stuck on her, first real ass he's had in his life. I'm encouraging him to stay, do some good. He'll probably get his dick shot off. No big deal.

Gina read the horrible piece through a second time. Preston Schaefer was a bastard. Where did all the hate come from, and how could he reconcile his progressive social and political ideas with his disgusting and retrogressive personal behavior? She struggled to read the final paragraph.

My visions here have revealed to me that my goals are the right ones, and I shall return and renew my efforts. The people I tried to recruit are either stupid or weak or both. David I should never have invited in, too weak, too scatterbrained. No real will. Elaine. She would have been better. Balls of steel. Just not politically or socially involved. Jesus, why can't she see what I've got? I need to get rid of Weiss. The Brotherhood isn't worth shit. The fairy priest is a flake, what a weak sister. If anyone would betray us, it's him. Weiss, the idiot, lost him. I really thought we had something at first. Trouble is I'm the only one with the skill and understanding and strength to carry through. Fuck it. I'm going my own way from now on. My own path...

Gina read it again, but it didn't make sense to her. Schaefer and Peter, maybe some others, had formed, what? a "Brotherhood?" What could that mean? To do what? His own path? To where? Peter had "lost" Chris? Was Chris in the Brotherhood? This sounded weird, but there it was in Schaefer's notebooks.

She realized she would be late to class if she didn't move out immediately. She opened the door, peeked out and saw the hall was still empty, and quickly squeezed out of Schaefer's office. Gina was not the type to snoop like this, but she'd thought a glance through Schaefer's research journals would not really be snooping. As she hurried to class, the information she'd uncovered was all that occupied her, and even during class, as she handed back the students' assignments and discussed them, her mind was still focused on that final page, filled with the cramped, almost illegible handwriting of the strange man who had once been her advisor.

"I thought Will had left Berkeley. I saw him today. I'm positive it was Will. I'd gone to Boalt Hall to interview a professor in the Law Department. He was walking toward the Plaza." Kay had given Gina no time to remove her coat and settle down before she spoke these words. Gina had not been quite paying attention and asked Kay to repeat what she'd said. After Kay did so, Gina told her she must be mistaken. Will had left a week ago.

"No way. I tell you. He's still here. By the way, there's a letter for you on the kitchen table."

Gina removed her coat and made her way to the kitchen. That was strange about Will. Kay must be mistaken. The letter was from Marco. She sat down at the table and slowly opened it. Why was he writing? He'd never done this before.

It was dated the previous Wednesday, December 13. He started by giving some details about his upcoming move to the University Medical Center. Treatments would become more and more intensive, and he would be too sick to care for himself. His insurance probably wouldn't cover all of his expenses. He was worried about this. Then he got to the main point. He told Gina that his house on Green Street, the house he had owned for nearly thirty years, the house Gina had grown up in, had played and studied in, was to be hers. Above all he hoped there was some way she could retain ownership, even if she had to rent it out for awhile if she couldn't find a way to live there now. It was a long commute to the Berkeley campus, but maybe not too bad. The house was all paid for. It could be maintained at very low cost. He loved the house and wanted Gina to have it. If she could not manage, and needed to sell it, he would understand. He closed the letter with a reference to an attorney on California Street whom she should contact after his death. The nearness of his death was incomprehensible to her, a nightmare with no reality to it.

At dinner that evening, which they took to Gina's room on trays, Kay and Gina planned a small party at the Manse for the 21st. It would involve just the other roomers and a few friends. Two of the roomers were moving out and Kay had to find new ones so that she could keep up the monthly payments on the lease she still held. David had also signed the lease, but his departure had made little difference because he'd never paid for anything anyway.

"I'm so worried about David. You know, he went off the deep end and I lost interest in him, but I still care for him. I don't want him hurt, for God's sake. Schaefer the bastard is still on the loose. I wonder where he is. I also wonder if the police are really searching for him. You know I'm thinking of doing a story about him, in depth. About his ideas, the various myths he created about himself, what he did to you, and the kidnapping and murder. There was a lot in the papers when it happened, but no one's done a full story. I'm thinking of maybe a publication in his favorite journal, to expose the brutal fraud he is to his most ardent followers. Great idea, don't you think?" Kay smiled, put aside her already empty dinner plate, and leaned over to start picking at Gina's, which had been hardly touched.

Kay's talk led Gina to bring up her visit to Schaefer's office, and the journals she had seen and read. She related Schaefer's references to David and Peter, and the so-called "Brotherhood," whatever that was. Kay had no idea what he might have been referring to, but it sounded like good, additional story material. Gina did not mention the reference to Chris.

"I think Peter knows a lot more about Schaefer's doings," said Kay. "He's been Schaefer's lap dog for a long time. I'll even bet he knows about David." She continued picking at Gina's food and enjoying the closeness of their two bodies.

"I've always thought Peter's move to San Francisco was a little weird. His story about joining Buddhists never rang true to me. I always thought he was just a lazy wise ass, nosy, always wanting to seem superior, like some kind of advanced thinker. Which he certainly was not - - I never heard him utter anything novel. He just had this smarmy way of appearing to be superior. And his relationship with Schaefer always struck me as a little odd. Though I must admit Schaefer attracts all kinds of weird wildlife." Kay laughed a little as she spoke, but immediately regretted the laugh; Schaefer was no longer a funny subject.

She went on. "I've heard them, several times, talking about Schaefer's ideas, especially about the destructive role of science and technology. Or, rather, I've seen Schaefer talking and Peter listening. I've read Schaefer's stuff. I don't agree with most of it, but it is powerful. You can see how it appeals to some basic human instincts. I think Weiss was some kind of blind follower. Destroy the destroyers. It all seems so anti-reason. Like the world needs more ways to destroy reason."

"So you think the "Brotherhood" might have been some kind of ...?"

"I didn't have that in mind. But maybe it was ... some kind of group they were trying to put together. They didn't seem to like each other much, though maybe that was less important than their need to promote their ideas. Lead the revolt against the madness of a technologically driven society. The madness that leads to every kind of social evil - - the war, racism, the industrial-military shit that ties it all together under the banner of capitalism. I guess there's some kind of coherent philosophy there. You know, I think Peter has access to a lot of money. His parents are really wealthy. I think he's convinced them he's in serious study, and they just keep sending checks. I wouldn't be surprised if he was somehow funding Schaefer."

"You really think Schaefer thought so little of David? The awful stuff in his journals?" asked Gina. Much of what Kay was now saying was new to her, because she'd never been able to understand Preston Schaefer when he spouted off.

"Schaefer, we know, is not a very tolerant human being. He thinks of himself as above the rest of us. Other people can be just used for his convenience, and discarded when they're no longer useful. He's such a mixed bag. I really don't like him much, as a person, but I do think he's a pretty powerful mind. Weird."

"Maybe we should invite Peter to the party on the 21st. Maybe we can get him to talk about Schaefer. Now that Schaefer's gone, Peter might feel free to tell us more. About this Brotherhood, and David." Gina paused. "And about Chris, too."

At the mention of Chris, Kay sat up on the bed next to Gina and slowly put her arm over the woman's small shoulders, and held her close. Kay could see the immense sadness flooding into Gina's pretty face and at this moment Kay knew she had never felt closer to any person. She pulled Gina closer and, after a few moments, said, "Good idea. I'll call Peter, right now."

Gina collapsed onto her bed, dinner uneaten, as Kay left to call Peter Weiss. She thought of Chris and, for the hundredth time imagined what it must have been like that day in Schaefer's cabin, when the priest charged at the man and took two bullets into his body, the body she had known and caressed and that had lain beside her, in fear and in love. He must have feared Schaefer, but he had charged at the man anyway - - did he really think he could subdue that brute? Chris must have thought Schaefer was evil, or something like that. It is incomprehensible. Chris had no reason to sacrifice himself to save Elaine. Will did, he loved Elaine, or had some kind of attachment to her. Was Will really still on campus? Kay sounded completely certain she had seen him...

".... so he'll come. He hesitated a little when I asked, but then said he'd come." Kay had returned to Gina's room, and sat down next to Gina's prone form on the small bed. She ran her hand over Gina's arm and, when she saw that Gina was obviously lost in her own thoughts, Kay decided to leave. "I need to get to bed. I have an early morning interview at the Chronicle, in San Francisco. It's my second one."

Gina caught what Kay said, and it broke her reverie. "The Chronicle. You're really going further with this? Are you sure it makes sense for you? It seems so mainstream."

"I'm not sure. They say they want more coverage of the movement. Black power. Women. Anti-war. The Assistant Editor who talked to me said they were beginning to see the rising importance of the left and they need people who've worked in that milieu. I'm really intrigued, though I'll no doubt get some criticism from my fellow crazies at the Gazette, who'll think I've sold out. I can bear it as long as I know that I'm continuing to report honestly. I'm an advocate for progressive social and political change, but I don't have to be an advocate in my daily journalism. Just a solid, honest reporter dedicated to bringing to light the best of the rising left while not avoiding its less pretty sides. It's intriguing to me. I'm going for one more interview. I'm not averse to the prospect of more money and much more widespread readership!"

Gina spent most of the rest of the evening thinking about Schaefer and Weiss, Chris, David, and the so-called Brotherhood, and what it all might really mean. She also thought about Will and of Kay's mention of him. She hadn't heard from him, although she hadn't expected any news for several days, when he was expected to be back in Boston. Poor Will, having to meet his father and how sad for his father to have to face his son's dismal failure. His only son. She was an only child, too, left now with a single dying parent. She might have had a sibling, not Marco's, but some other man's. Who might that man, her mother's lover, have been? She might ask Marco more about it, but he would have a hard time dealing with more questions on this subject. She had to find some way to get him to believe she bore him no ill will at all, even if his act of forcing an abortion on her mother had actually contributed to her suicide. He should not go to his grave with such a burden of guilt on his conscience. She had to talk to him, and convince him. Soon.

Will. He had tried to save Elaine. He must have felt something pretty strong for her. An attractive, smart, strong woman. Gina passed off into sleep with thoughts of going to speak to Elaine, about Preston Schaefer. Maybe she had something to contribute to the understanding Gina was seeking.

CHAPTER 24

On the following Friday, at about three-thirty in the afternoon, Gina walked into the Chemistry Building on the Berkeley campus and took the elevator to the fourth floor. She walked the fourth floor halls looking for Elaine Callahan's lab. She knew it was here somewhere, because all of Jensen's students were on the fourth floor. She'd looked into four or five labs without luck, and then asked someone who was walking the hall with some weird- looking contraption made of glass. She was successful at getting the information and headed straight for Elaine's lab.

The lab lights were on, the radio was playing something classical - - Schumann maybe - - but Elaine was not in sight. Gina went in anyway. She was amazed by the vast array of glass columns, tubing, valves, recording devices that had been assembled on the main lab bench. Liquids of some type were running through the columns and tubing, and were being collected in little flasks, perhaps 200 of them, that were lined up in some mechanized device that moved the flasks every minute or so, so that the liquid that was being collected would flow into a new, empty vessel after each was about two-thirds full. Gina couldn't figure out what was going on. She'd understood a lot of what Will used to show her on paper about the chemistry he was doing, but the lab stuff had been beyond her. She did see, though, that there was a real art to this lab work, and that it took skills with which many of the best scientists were not well-equipped. A skilled laboratory craftsman was someone to be admired. Everyone had always said that Will was competent in the lab, but not a real artist.

"Don't touch anything, please." A woman's voice came from behind her, and Gina turned to see Elaine. The chemist was wearing a lab coat and had her long red hair tied back so that it hung in one thick braid behind her head. She was wearing rimless glasses and Gina thought she looked slightly cross-eyed behind them.

"Gina? Why are you here? What do you want? Are you looking for Will?" Elaine spoke quickly and there was a touch of rudeness in her voice. "His lab's on the other side of the building."

Gina watched Elaine put down the two large vessels she'd carried into the lab, and walk over to one of the columns on her lab bench and turn a valve at its base.

"No. I'm not. I came to see you. I wanted to ask you something."

"I have nothing to say about Will."

"It's not about Will."

"He's told you about us, how it happened? It had nothing to do with you. Plus, you know, he's gone from my life."

"Yes. I know. He's left. Gone to Boston."

"Is that what you think? He never left. He's in the lab, working like a madman. Go see. He's there now."

Gina didn't know what to say. Why on earth would he be in his lab? Was that all a lie he'd told her, about confessing to Jensen and leaving, to return to Boston? Why would he have lied like that? "I don't understand. He told me his whole story. About his mess, about confessing it all to Jensen. Why is he ...?"

"You see, Jensen doesn't know that you know about Will's problem. He thinks only Will and I and he know. He's threatened me to shut up about it, or he'll say I helped Will carry out the fraud, and have me thrown out. Jensen doesn't know that you know the story. You could hurt all three of us. You could really hurt Jensen."

Gina couldn't quite follow what Elaine was saying. Hurt Jensen? How? If Will had really told everything to Jensen, and was still working in Jensen's lab ... what could that mean? She came to talk to Elaine about Schaefer, but all of a sudden.... She needed some time with Elaine.

"Look, Elaine, I need to talk with you. Will you let me buy you some dinner? Tonight. I really need this, now. Please, do you have some time?"

Elaine recorded some data in one of her open notebooks, checked the liquid level in a large column that was filled with a fine white solid material, and then turned to Gina. "You want to know about Schaefer, right? Okay. Will do. Where?"

"How about that crepe place, on Shattuck. Do you know it? How about 7 o'clock?"

Gina walked across campus in the late December afternoon. She had thought she'd check on Will to see if Elaine's story about him being in his lab was true, but decided she didn't want to chance running into him. Not until she knew more. It was very cold, unusually cold, and she shivered all the way home. Her mind was blank most of the way, and even when she entered the Manse and climbed the stairs to her room, she managed no particular thoughts. There was too much to comprehend, her small world was increasingly complex. She felt herself at the center of so many different struggles and sufferings. They circled around her and seemed to link to each other through her. She had created none of them, yet she was somehow involved in all of them - - Will's disaster, Chris' death and its connection to Peter, Schaefer and David, her father's illness, David's fate, now even Elaine and apparently Jensen. A sea of troubles in the cold hills of Berkeley, California, near the end of 1967. America was itself a sea of troubles, from sea to shining sea a land at war with itself. How much of the trouble that surrounded Gina arose from that larger landscape of woe and how much from the ordinary struggles of individual life? She did not know.

Kay, on the surface at least, seemed outside of all this.

Wonderful Kay. Such a solid, dependable person. Always there with the right idea, always caring yet reasonable, an acute analyst of the landscape of grief. Lonely, though. Deep within, for some reason, Kay had her loneliness to bear. Kay was in that circle of pain that surrounded Gina. Circles. Concentric circles. The closest comprised of friends and family and even people like Schaefer and Peter. But think of all the circles of pain and struggle that are there in the world beyond this immediate one. This cold evening, in her tiny room, Gina Antinori felt herself somehow at the center of all these many rings of struggle and pain and maybe hope.

After waiting twenty minutes Gina convinced herself that Elaine was not going to show up for their dinner. Before coming to the restaurant Gina had called her dad and learned that he was going to enter the hospital on the following Friday, the day after the party at the Manse. She made arrangements to visit with him on Friday at about noon and to help him check in. She'd spent twenty minutes nursing a beer, trying unsuccessfully to come up with a clear line of questions for Elaine, and worrying about Marco and how he must feel. God, where is thy mercy? The circles of pain and suffering. She was not the "center" of this. What a strange, arrogant idea, she thought. It's like I'm really separate, at the center, everyone else is in some orbit around me! How God-like. Drop it.

Elaine entered the restaurant.

Gina looked at her closely as she removed her black leather jacket. She was dressed in a wool sweater and jeans, her hair now flowing loosely over her shoulders. Elaine was a strong, even voluptuous-looking woman. Gina could see how she would appeal to men, she was very sexy. She still wore those rimless glasses that were not especially flattering to her rather ordinary face, but she moved her body in ways that intimidated Gina. Small, delicate Gina, at the center of the world's sufferings.

"Sorry I'm late. I got stuck at the lab later than I expected. The lab controls, a lot, you're its slave." Elaine sat down and smiled at Gina. She seemed immediately more relaxed than she had been earlier in the lab. Gina was pleased to see that, and felt herself relax. She returned Elaine's smile and handed one of the menus she was holding to her. The two ordered and exchanged small talk until the dinners came.

"I was totally shocked to learn about Will. I don't understand. Look, I'm over him, a long time ago. I'm holding no hard feelings about you. Okay?"

"Well, I guess I can believe that. I did ... you know, did kind of ... go after him." Elaine was looking down at her food, playing with it with her fork, as she spoke these words.

Gina thought she'd follow up on this, but decided not to. "Okay. Fine. That's all past. But I am worried about Will now. He told me everything he'd done. He told me what you did to help him. But he also told me that he'd confessed everything to Jensen, cleared it all up, admitted to himself that he could not go on with this deceit. He was on his way out when I saw him last, maybe around two weeks ago. We went to my father's house. My father is dying of cancer. Will wanted to see him, so we went. We walked around San Francisco. He was going home to Boston."

"Well, things changed fast. Here's the deal. Jensen called Will. Told him to get back in the lab, to repeat the work. You know, Will was sure he had completed the pfaffadine synthesis once. He'd got the last step to work, but he couldn't repeat it. Then he ran out of the stuff he needed, so he faked it. Didn't have the patience, the will to go back and run through all those long, tedious steps again. Jensen told him to go back and do it, to work until he got it right. Jensen wasn't ready to tell the world that fraud had been committed."

"But, isn't that wrong? How could Jensen do that? He knew Will had committed fraud. They even gave a presentation at a scientific meeting. How could ... and how can Jensen hide this? This is unbelievable."

"He's convinced the government, the National Cancer

Institute, that he's got a synthesis of pfaffadine. They're funding him. The compound is looking good in some anti-cancer testing. They want more." Elaine paused to eat a few mouthfuls, then continued. "Thank God I've got a way to prepare the stuff by isolating it from its natural source. If I didn't have this, the NCI would be trying to synthesize the stuff using Will's method. They'd find out it didn't work. So I'm Jensen's safety valve, my method for getting pfaff. The NCI might contract with some commercial lab to scale up my system, all that shit you saw in my lab this afternoon."

"But why would Will agree... he had convinced himself, I think, that he could never go back. Now he's trying to ... go back?"

"Jensen threatened him, or at least scared him enough. Plus, I think Will probably saw it as a chance to "go back," as you put it. To redeem himself. I don't think that's really possible in science. Science is unforgiving. Once you cheat, you're out. If you're found out, of course. Jensen is finished if anyone learns what he's doing. He threatened me. He came to me, told me he knew what I had done to help Will. Said he'd get me thrown out of science unless I kept quiet. I can tell you this, because you know what Will and I did. Jensen has no idea you know. He would shit his pants."

Gina couldn't digest all this, she didn't know what to think. What was in Will's mind? How could he ... backtrack like this? "So what is Will saying? Why is he back in the lab?"

"He's telling people Jensen had a need to give NCI more synthetic pfaffadine, and that Will agreed to go back into the lab to do it. That's their story. It's plausible. Will doesn't have a job lined up, so this gives him some more time. I go back to my lab, just shut up, and do my thing." Elaine completed her meal and ordered coffee and some dessert. Gina declined dessert and ordered just coffee.

"By the way. Will did walk out on me. He told me about Jensen and that he was going to stay and do as Jensen said. He said he wanted no more of me. He's got some room, way up at the top of the hills, in some rooming house. Really cheap. Jensen's giving him slave wages. I wasn't surprised. I knew he was through with me after the Schaefer thing. Even before. I came to accept it. I don't give up men I want easily. Maybe you could've guessed that."

Gina still needed to talk about Peter. Elaine seemed in no rush to leave, so they made some small talk. They told each other a little about their families, their years in college, and shared some stories about Will and some of his habits. Gina found Elaine more interesting than she had imagined, tough but straightforward and open. She could see how some men would be drawn to her, and how others might be intimidated. Chris would have been scared to death.

"So, how about Schaefer? I'm trying to figure out why Chris did what he did at the cabin where Schaefer took you. I'm suspicious of that Weiss guy. He's creepy, at the least. I think he controlled Chris, somehow. I thought I should talk with you, maybe more came out when you were with Schaefer at the cabin."

"I don't know anything about Chris. Schaefer told me nothing about him and I don't know why he did what he did." Elaine looked away for a moment, and then turned back. "Why do you think Peter had something on Chris? You knew him, I didn't. I know Peter pretty well."

"You do?" Gina was surprised to hear this and looked inquiringly at Elaine.

Elaine paused, then said, "What the hell. No big secrets here. Yeah, I met him at Northwestern, my first year at grad school. He was a junior, undergraduate. I got to know him. He was an interesting guy. I kept in touch. I put him in touch with some people here in Berkeley. A philosopher. He was in Philosophy here. I don't know why he quit."

"He never talked to you about Chris?"

"No. Never. I didn't know they even knew each other."

Gina sensed that Elaine was telling the truth. She wasn't going to be of any help. Maybe there was nothing here to explain. Chris acted on his own, just trying to be a hero, trying to do something good. That's what he wanted, a life full of good deeds.

"So what was he like, your priest?" Elaine smiled as she put the question to Gina. "Just a friend? More than that? A real priest or just pretend? Sorry, I wasn't being facetious. I just mean, was he really a working priest?"

Gina found herself pleased to have been asked about Chris, and responded enthusiastically. She told Elaine just about everything. Sex apart. She wasn't going to talk about having sex with a priest. But everything else just poured forth. She let Elaine know about his kind, gentle spirit, his commitment to the word of Christ, especially as it concerned the poor, lost souls of the world, and his yearning to find a home for himself somewhere in the complex institution called the Roman Catholic Church. Elaine listened intently, apparently honestly interested in Gina's tale of the dead priest. Elaine did suspect that Chris and Gina were more than just friends but she found no reason to pursue her suspicion.

"So what could he have had in common with Peter? Nothing I could see. Peter was a complete atheist, as far as I know. He had ideas that seemed sort of mystical, about secret paths to the truth. He was like that when I knew him at Northwestern. I only saw him, except at a few parties, two or three times since he came to Berkeley. He had this real superior attitude, like he could see things others could not. He was also close to Preston Schaefer. Closer to Schaefer than to me, by far. They both did a lot of drugs, I'm pretty sure, and not just pot, but some serious stuff. The last time I saw Peter I asked him to talk to Schaefer. The bastard had been hounding me for months. I couldn't get rid of him. I asked Peter for help. The next thing I know, Schaefer has a gun in my face."

"But Peter helped rescue you. He came to us and told us what happened and asked that we help find you and Schaefer. He even led the group to Schaefer's cabin."

"I know. I think he just wanted to keep Schaefer out of trouble. He just hoped you'd convince Schaefer to give up. No troubles with the law. It didn't turn out the way Peter hoped. I'm sure of that. Maybe he hoped Chris could help. Asked him to go into the cabin and help. Maybe he thought ..."

"But he knew Schaefer had a gun. Remember? Schaefer even fired it, at him. If he urged Chris in, it was like sending a lamb to the slaughter." The two women left the crepe house at about 9:30 and walked together toward the Manse, which was not far off the route to Elaine's place. Gina talked about her own ideas about law school. Elaine found herself warming up to Gina. She'd always thought of Will's ex as a weak sister, passive and withdrawn. The Gina she'd spent the last several hours with seemed anything but.

"Look, I have an idea. I'm no friend of Peter. I don't even like him, and have mostly avoided him since he came here. But I ...know some things. Things he doesn't want others to know. His parents. They're rich, really rich I think. They support him because they think he's doing serious things. I'm sure he's not. Probably spends most of his time on drugs, LSD and stuff. Peter was an early devotee. Still is, I'm sure. He's pursuing mystical states, higher states of consciousness, that bullshit. He probably doesn't do much else. I'm not sure, but I'd have no problem threatening to write to his parents about his decadent habits. He'd worry they'd cut him off. I know other things too, I'd rather not talk about. So, if you want me to help get the low-down on his thing with Chris, I'd be glad to help."

Gina didn't like threats, even with people like Peter. What "other things" was she talking about? His homosexuality, no doubt, she thought. Chris had been right about this, and Elaine knows about it too. Immediately, Elaine confirmed this thought when she said, "Peter, he was ... queer, I guess they call it, homosexual. He keeps this a deep, deep secret."

The two sat for a moment on the steps outside the Manse, but it was too cold, so Gina invited Elaine in. She needed a few moments to think about Elaine's proposal. They went to the living room, which was deserted. Kay was in the kitchen making up lists of things to buy for Thursday's party. It wasn't going to be a big one. They'd invited a couple of Kay's friends from the newspaper. The remaining boarders at the Manse would be there with a few of their friends, and Peter had agreed to come. Now, thought Gina, a new factor had been introduced. Elaine might be able to help pry some information loose. How would they ever know the truth? It was probably not ever possible. Peter was not likely to admit anything that would implicate himself in the priest's death, even under threats from Elaine. But it couldn't hurt to try, could it? Could it?

"Elaine. There's a small party here, Thursday evening. Peter is coming. Can you come? Maybe you can help." Without hesitation Elaine said, "Sure. What time?"

Gina told her the time, and Elaine turned to go. Then, she paused and turned to face Gina.

"Look, I'm feeling pretty lousy about what I've done to you, and also to Will. I had my eye on him and I took advantage of him when I had my chance. I've always thought of myself as someone who was not going to let anyone stand in her way. I was not going to behave like most women and back off whenever I thought someone - - a man, usually - - disapproved. I still think women have to stop behaving like passive little lambs. But I guess I never thought enough about limits, the line between selfishness and honest self-interest. I'm sorry, at least I hope I'm the kind of person who can be sorry, about what I did to Will, and to you. I think it was destructive to Will. I should have never enabled him to find a way out, a foolproof way to deceive. He couldn't live with it. I judged him to be, maybe, the kind of selfish person I am, but he isn't." She smiled faintly, wrapped her coat tightly around herself, and left.

CHAPTER 25

The 2,4-dimethylaniline solution dripped slowly into the reaction flask, into the stirring solution of 4-methoxybenzaldehyde that had been dissolved in tetrahydrofuran. Equimolar amounts of the two reactants would over the course of the next two hours create about 150 grams of reaction product. The reaction system would be dismantled, the tetrahydrofuran solvent stripped off, and the yellowish sludge at the bottom of the flask would be purified by multiple crystallizations and recrystallizations. This was the simplest reaction in the series that was designed to lead to pfaffadine. The purified product would be combined with another compound Will had spent the last week preparing. That combination would get him about 250 grams of the third compound in the series of twelve, the twelfth being pfaffadine , if, of course, the conversion of compound eleven --pre-pfaff--to pfaff could be successfully carried out. That huge question could not be answered until pre-pfaff was available. Another three or four months of drudgery.

It was the afternoon of the Thursday before Christmas, the first day of winter, 1967. A clear, windy day in Berkeley, the last school day before Christmas holiday break. Will sat and watched the reaction in progress. There's not much else to be done while the two reacting chemicals do their thing. They follow their natural course. They do exactly what all molecules like these do when they meet each other. Molecules with these particular groupings of atoms always interact in the same way. Discovery in synthetic chemistry came when chemists put together molecules that had never previously been introduced to each other, and watched how they interact. Not easy work, figuring these things out. But that was the fun, the excitement of this science. New molecules were created, never before seen on earth. Or molecules were created in the laboratory that were identical to what nature had long ago learned to make, molecules like pfaffadine. No chemist was as remotely efficient or creative as nature. The molecules created in plants and animals and other life forms were seemingly endless in number - - they'd never all be known - - and could be complex almost beyond imagining. The act of determining the structures of nature's molecules required enormous knowledge of basic chemical science, exquisite laboratory skills, and a kind of creativity that was hard for chemists to describe, even to each other. Then, to try to design and execute a laboratory synthesis of these complicated molecules - - this was almost an even greater challenge. It required a thorough understanding of basic chemical reactions, the predictable ones, and careful analysis of the conditions under which new reactions could be forced to take place. It was never just a question of putting two molecules together. The course of many reactions was influenced by many factors - - the solvent used, the reaction time, the presence or absence of other chemicals that in one way or another assisted in the reaction process, the other atoms present in a molecule - - and unless these other factors were understood and controlled, the molecules would not do what you wanted them to do. Will assumed that his failure to repeat the final conversion of pre-pfaff to pfaff was due to his failure to understand these factors. Why hadn't he gone to Jensen after the first failure? Maybe he had come to doubt the reality of his first "success" and was afraid to tell Jensen that he'd been wrong the first time. He didn't even remember. God, it was almost a year ago that he'd had those few milligrams of pfaffadine in his hands ... he was sure, damn it, that it really was the authentic stuff.

Darkness settled outside his laboratory windows. The reaction was well underway, most of the aniline compound had been added. He left his lab and headed down the hall to the coffee machine. It was going to be a long night.

These halls. How many extraordinary scientists had wandered these halls? All the great discoveries made here that had been recorded in the professional journals. Not only in organic chemistry, but in physical chemistry, analytical chemistry, inorganic chemistry, biochemistry - - so much accumulated knowledge. Knowledge that doesn't excite many people, but that is powerfully exciting to those who love the subject and work to learn it. Jesus, it's tough, especially physical chemistry, the interface of chemistry and physics, along with analytical chemistry, the most quantitative of the chemical sciences. The energy that creates the chemical bond and how it can be transformed and transferred. The nature of the chemical bond itself. Shit, that last ester linkage in pfaffadine, why couldn't he make it form? That last bond, the two groups of atoms in the pre-pfaff molecule that needed to interact to create the new ester bond should have done so. Shit, what did he fail to do? Maybe the bonds did form, but then something happened when he tried to isolate and purify the product, something that caused the pfaffadine to degrade. The true scientist would have pursued the question, pursued it until he had done everything imaginable to understand the problem and correct it, if possible. The true scientist would have, in fact, been challenged, intrigued, made more curious, and then just plunged onward.

Damn, Will thought, he was back where he should not be. Back where Jensen should never have forced him. He could not erase what he did before, but now he was attempting, again, to cover it up. It'll be in him, his conscience ... Jesus ...but maybe this is a chance to redeem himself ... Jensen's given him a chance ... it's to protect himself, mainly ...but so what? Gina. Will would never be able to explain this to her, after he had told her about what he'd done and how he had decided to take the right path. That's how he had left it with her. He couldn't really expect not to run into her. What could he tell her? Will had no story, no explanation for her. The little ruse, that he was here just to make some more pfaffadine, that he's just an employee still looking for work ...this holds up with others. But Gina. God knows what he could say. She could squeal, but that's not like her. He was going to have to face her. She'll call his father and find out Will never went home! Maybe she's called already! Will had not heard from his dad, so she probably has not called. She'll know that Jensen is now part of the scheme. Maybe he should tell Jensen Gina knows about the fraud. He'll go out of his mind.

Will returned to the lab and for the next several hours he worked up the new reaction product. Two crystallizations, the first rapid, the second requiring more care and time. The crop of colorless crystals seemed to have completely formed by about ten in the evening. He collected them on filter paper and introduced them into a vessel for overnight drying. It looked like a good yield, with more to come in the mother liquor as it evaporates slowly overnight. A successful day. He'd of course have to verify the composition and purity of the reaction product before proceeding to the next step, but he'd have that done by Saturday evening. Seven days a week, no rest for the wicked.

At about ten Thursday night Will took the long walk across campus and then began the longer walk up into the Berkeley hills, to the sad room he'd rented. The first day of winter was not so cold, not like in Boston. His dad would he sleeping, it was after one in the morning back there in the place where he'd grown up, where he'd learned to love science, where he'd fallen in love with the chemistry lab in his high school, where he'd lost his mother, on the first day of winter in 1953. Such a cold, cold winter day.

By midnight on Thursday evening everyone had shown up at the Manse, maybe a dozen people, a few unknown to Gina, friends of the three roomers she'd never gotten to know very well. Peter did not arrive until one, with some skinny, bearded guy he introduced as Zoltan. Gina was sure Zoltan was stoned on something. With Peter it was never possible to tell. The guy was dressed in a heavy white sweater, white jeans, and sandals. He looked even skinnier than the last time she'd seen him, cheeks so sunken that he looked sick. But he still wore his enigmatic smile and behaved as always - - smoking heavily, not saying much, staring at people as if he were trying to get inside their heads and was being successful at it. He and Zoltan got some wine and sat down on the floor near the fireplace. The living room had a very large fireplace and Kay had been successful in getting a fire going, the first time in the more than two years she had been at the house. Although it was the first day of winter, it wasn't especially cold in the Berkeley hills. The fire nevertheless was welcome and the guests tended to migrate toward it.

While Gina was greeting Peter and Zoltan, Kay was in the small den, just off the living room, talking with Elaine Callahan. Gina entered the den and told them that Peter and his weird buddy had arrived. She leaned up against the wall next to Elaine. "I think we just cool it awhile, then slowly gather around him and get him talking. I don't think it'll be hard, he's got such an ego. Elaine, you'll help right?"

"You bet," smiled Elaine, as she put out her cigarette.

The women slowly migrated into the living room. The large area was dark except for a couple of small lamps and the glow from the fireplace. About a dozen people were spread out on the sofa, chairs, and the floor. Dylan provided the recorded entertainment as several passed a joint. There wasn't a lot of conversation. The mood seemed relaxed and friendly but lacking in much social interaction. No heavy topics up for discussion.

Kay collapsed onto a couple of large pillows on the floor, in possession of a large tumbler full of wine. She had not seen much of Elaine before this evening, and hadn't formed a clear impression. Elaine had been pretty quiet the whole evening. David used to say she was very aggressive, sexually and in other ways. He used to hear that from Schaefer. Kay guessed that's how he knew. She wondered if the Elaine thing was totally Schaefer's fault. Was he the real predator? God, she thought she sounded like a male chauvinist. Sexually aggressive women bring on their own troubles, right? She deserved what she got, the temptress. You can't expect men to behave right when these sexually aggressive women are around. Let's excuse the poor anthropology professor. Let's put Elaine in jail! Kay downed half her tumbler of wine.

She then saw that Peter and his buddy had taken seats on the floor by the fireplace. At that moment someone knocked at the front door. Kay thought everyone who'd been invited was already present, but she got up and went to open the door. Gina was in the kitchen on the telephone, probably talking with her dad.

"Will. What ....?" Kay was a bit shocked to see Will Getz standing before her, staring in over her shoulders.

"I'm looking for Gina. I just wanted to see her for a few minutes. Is she here?"

"Ah ... yeah. We're having a little party. Just some friends. You want to come in?" Kay wasn't sure she should be doing this, wasn't sure Gina wanted to see Will just now, but she ushered him in anyway.

"I was just on my way up the hill, going home from the lab. But I had this idea I should see Gina. I've got some things to tell her."

"I guess. She thought you'd left, gone back to Boston."

"Did she tell you why I was going to leave?"

"No. She just said you were leaving. I never asked more."

Will followed Kay into the living room and immediately spotted Elaine seated at the end of the sofa, engaged in conversation with some bearded guy who wore a beret and had a large scarf wrapped around his neck. Elaine turned and saw Will, but immediately dropped her head and turned away from him.

"Sit down. I'll get you a drink. Wine or beer?"

"Beer's fine." Will said as he lowered himself onto the large cushions that Kay had occupied. Kay went off to get the beer, and to locate Gina. In a moment the two returned and walked directly toward Will.

"Hello, Will. I see it's true. You never made it back to Boston. Change of plans? You're good at changing course. Hard to stay on the path, right?" Gina sounded hostile, something that didn't come easily to her. She'd had some wine, but not much ... she'd vowed to keep a clear head for the Peter confrontation. But she knew the lie Will was now living, and for some reason she was angrier about this than she had been six months earlier when he'd left her for Elaine. Later, when she'd come to understand how Elaine had trapped Will, she had even felt a little pity for him. But now, after he had confessed, had said he would do the right thing and never backtrack ...this made her angry.

"I'd hoped to talk to you, alone. I need to tell you ..."

Gina cut him off, turned away and walked across the room toward Peter. Elaine had already moved in and taken a seat beside Kay, on the floor in front of Peter. Will returned to his seat, not knowing whether to leave now or to wait for another chance with Gina. He had to get this over with, so he stayed put. The little gathering across the room, around the fireplace, around Peter Weiss, puzzled him. He drank from his bottle of beer and tried to guess what the big deal was.

"What do we have, a little party of worshippers gathering around me? A tribal gathering? Shall we pass the peace pipe? Zoltan, please, the peace pipe!" Peter's skinny, bearded friend complied and passed to him a small pipe full of smoking hashish, from which he immediately took several deep draws. By now Elaine, Gina, and Kay had gathered on the floor in a semicircle in front of Peter Weiss and his friend. The fire was now roaring and cast so much heat that the little tribe had to move a few feet away. Across the room Will Getz sat, alone with his beer, staring at the group, and glancing from time to time at the guy on the sofa who had been moving in on Elaine.

"Chris. We want to know about Chris." Gina spoke, directly into Peter's eyes. He'd offered the hash to Elaine, who was seated to his immediate left, but she turned it down, as did Kay and Gina. Peter took a couple more draws and returned the pipe to Zoltan.

"No takers. I am disappointed. This is a peace offering. I am sincere. We have all been such good friends. This tragedy that we have all suffered. The horrible, accidental death of one of us at the hand of another member of our little tribe ...we need to deal with this ... tragedy."

The room was fairly quiet, just some Thelonius Monk, solo piano, on the stereo and a little chatter in the background. The group that had gathered around Peter was silent, apparently expecting a response from him. He drank some more wine and lit up a cigarette. He let the cigarette dangle from his lips, and puffed continuously to create clouds of smoke. He managed to retain a smirk through all this.

"Yes, Chris was a dear friend. I have had great sorrow for him, and for Schaefer as well. I have been so saddened by all this. At least the great man, wherever he is, is out of the grasp of the law. None of us, I am sure, wants to see Preston Schaefer in the hands of the law. We wish to have him back among us. We may disapprove of what he did to the good priest, and to Elaine here, beautiful Elaine, who was fortunate enough to command the great man's most heartfelt attentions, but I am sure we think his importance as a leader of the new order of things overshadows all that, and that we would like to see his return ...n'est-ce pas?" Peter smiled from behind the cloud of cigarette smoke that surrounded his head, drank some more wine, and accepted another toke on Zoltan's pipe. None of the women said anything; they knew he was beginning to open up. All they had to do was look as if they were intensely interested in what he had to say, despicable as it was.

Peter paused and looked around, waved in Will's direction and asked him to come closer, to participate. By this time Gina began to feel that a little more prodding might be useful. She accepted Zoltan's offer of a toke on the hashish pipe, took a small one, and then said, "The Brotherhood, Peter, that must have been interesting. All men, I guess? Why not women, too?"

Peter looked surprised at this, drank some more wine, and put out his cigarette on the bricked floor by the fireplace.

"You know, Schaefer and I used to ...we assembled a group of like-minded fellows. Yes, all fellows. You must know this, Kay. Your David used to attend. We usually met at Schaefer's. We also went to that place near Oakland where David moved, to bring in some of his people. I thought you all knew this, or at least you, Kay. Schaefer must have told you, Elaine. You two were very close." Peter smiled at Elaine as he said this. "We were never close. That's bullshit. Schaefer's fantasy. Not any reality, you asshole." Elaine spoke these words calmly, as if she hadn't been upset by Peter's remark. Gina broke in and said, "So, why don't you tell us about your meetings. Sounds interesting."

Peter put out his cigarette, and asked Zoltan to light up some more hashish. As he did this, Will arose and wandered slowly across the room, and leaned back against an arm of the sofa that was near where Kay was seated on the floor. Gina glanced up at him and frowned. Will saw this and guessed she didn't want him to hear what was going on, but he decided to stay anyway.

Peter took a couple of drags on the freshly lit hash pipe, and then leaned back against the wall. The fire had peaked, and was beginning to die. It was well after midnight, and the room was getting darker. Most of the others in the room had cleared out, except for a pair of couples who were making out in a far corner, and the guy in the beret and scarf who was still sitting on the sofa, no doubt hoping to resume his conversation with Elaine. It was Elaine who spoke next.

"We have all night. We'd like to hear about you and Chris. Maybe if you'd tell us about these meetings ... maybe we'd understand. I would like to hear. There are no secrets here, right? We like everything out in the open, right? I personally would be most willing to follow these rules, about getting everything out into the open."

Everyone turned to Elaine as she calmly spoke these words. Peter stared into her face. Gina knew immediately what he must have been thinking, what he knew Elaine knew that was, at least for now, still their secret. Peter lost his ridiculous little smile, returned the peace pipe to Zoltan, and raised his head to stare at the darkness above him.

Gina decided to add a little more fuel to whatever fire Elaine had started. "Chris told me all about you. Among other things, he said your Buddhist stuff, your story about studying in a monastery was phony. You are just living in some kind of commune over there. Doing nothing, just living off your rich parents. A rich hippie, wasting away, like so many others, except you've got that steady stream of money pouring in. A serious student of religion and philosophy you are not. I don't think Father Swift would have lied to me."

Peter was still staring up toward the ceiling. He was leaning back against the wall, his arms hanging by his sides, hands, palms up, on the floor, legs crossed in front. For a moment it seemed he was in a dream-state. He was no doubt completely stoned from all that hash. Everyone sat in silence, staring at him. The fire had nearly died, the stereo had gone off, the two couples had climbed the stairs to locate a bedroom. Only the guy on the sofa remained, mystified by the little gathering.

Peter, head still raised, spoke. "Tell that guy, the one on the sofa, to go." The members of the group turned their heads in unison to see who Peter was talking about. Will made a move, walked over to the sofa, and politely asked the guy to leave. "Private business. Please." The guy seemed reluctant, but finally complied. Before he left he walked over to Elaine, bent over, and slipped a note into her hand. She turned her head in his direction, smiled, and shook her head in a silent "yes." This seemed to please the stranger, who waved goodbye and left.

"You are right, Elaine, we have no secrets. My life is an open book, at least open to those who are true comrades and believers. Our little tribe. Too bad our inspiring leader, the great Schaefer, is not here with us." The silly smirk was back on his face. He seemed completely relaxed as he lowered his head and surveyed the small group circling him. He had a brief flashback to some night, back at Northwestern, when Elaine was naked and locked in sex with his beautiful former, long lost, probably now dead lover. Those beautiful times when he would watch and then, after, bring such satisfaction to that beautiful man, satisfaction Elaine could not bring.

"So, Mr. Weiss, please, inform us," interjected Kay. "We await your revelation."

"There is little to reveal, I am afraid. You all know Dr. Preston Schaefer. A great mind, a committed mind. The best schools, back East. A real leader, passionate, but with a difference. He understood like no one else the root of the problems this country, the whole developed world - - so-called developed world - - faced. He saw deeply. He described the problem, at its deepest level, as resulting from the so-called scientific revolution. A European phenomenon, imported into America and, like most things imported into America, made bigger and better. Schaefer saw how the kind of thinking, the way scientists go about understanding the world, brings enormous power. These countries grew to be enormous powers on the huge tidal wave that the scientific revolution caused. Every other way of thinking, every other way of knowing the world - - the religious, the mystical, the intuitive - - was discarded. Or given only token recognition, to appease the masses that the power structure depends upon for life support. But science, objective knowledge, came to dominate. We in the West have built enormously powerful societies based on the scientific way of thinking." Peter paused and looked over his audience. They were paying very close attention, and he loved this. Jesus, how can someone so completely stoned speak so clearly, thought Gina.

"So," continued the smiling Weiss, "so, so, we see, we must recognize ..." he stumbled a little, paused, and then reached for a cigarette. Zoltan lit it for him. He was clearly wound up and ready to spring open.

"Schaefer saw how important it is for the elite of the West to preserve the scientific world view. Maybe the politicians and business leaders and Wall Streeters and their lawyers and bankers don't understand this clearly, but at some deep level they recognize the importance of preserving the scientific mentality. And so they bring some good things to at least the privileged among us - - never to the poor - - but with this comes enormous destructiveness. They go to war to suppress cultures that have different values, different ways of understanding the world. Vietnam is just the worst example. Look just to the South, in those miserable societies of Latin America, where we murder and put down every attempt by the natives to make their own way of life, to be independent of our system. So we make wars or we hire thugs to fight them for us. We make wars at home here against our own black people. Our great leaders do this so cleverly. They teach the poor whites how to take advantage of the slight power they have over poor blacks, to make it seem that racism is caused by the poor whites. In fact it is a plot with deep roots in history, a plot devised by the power structure, the white male trash that runs the world. This is not just capitalist, it's white male communist and socialist trash as well. All these bastards build nuclear bombs, by the millions, and scare the hell out of us underlings. And they all, consciously or unconsciously, lean upon the modern religion we call science. Is this clear?"

The audience sat, fascinated not so much by the words and ideas - - at least some were familiar to Kay and Gina and even Will, who had listened to or read some of Schaefer's writings - - but by the clarity with which they emerged from the mouth of this guy they had come to see as something of a buffoon, or at least a fake.

"What's all this got to do with Chris? With your group?" Gina asked.

"Patience my pretty little one. You wanted the book of my life opened. I am doing that." Zoltan got up and started to leave. "I need to piss."

"Strange guy. I think he is schizophrenic. I think he was locked up once, somewhere." Peter chuckled.

Kay decided the room was too dark, so she rose to switch on one nearby small lamp. It was enough to allow everyone to see Peter's face, to see the liveliness in his eyes, the great smile that he displayed. He was enjoying his chance to show his stuff.

"So, thought our great Schaefer, we must begin to disassemble the underpinnings of modern Western society. This will be the only way to save the world from the hell that the power elite, capitalist and communist, is building to preserve itself. If we learn not to trust science, if we see that its way of understanding the world is the cause of our modern hells, why then we have a chance. Science makes the world and everything in it an object, for study, for manipulation. Those who understand its methods can rise to great power. No other way of understanding the world brings such power, either for good or, especially, for evil. We need to return to the pre-scientific world. That was our project. Schaefer was our leader, though I have to say that many of his ideas, at least in the fine details, came from me. You may see me as weak, lazy, decadent, but I have ideas, insights. Some come during periods in which I study the great minds and spirits of the past. Some come - - I admit it freely - - during drug states. LSD, discovered by a Swiss natural products chemist, someone like our friend Will and our friend Elaine, allows the mind to penetrate deep into the human past. The pre-science past, the past explored by the great mystics and wisemen ...the truth is found there. Science is an evil. Its goods are greatly outweighed by its evils. It is insanity. It separates us from God, from the natural world, from our very selves. We lose our deepest feelings - - try sex sometime on LSD, it's like you never did it before. LSD brings you to the world we, our little brotherhood, wanted to recreate."

Will had never paid much attention to Schaefer in the past. He'd read some of these ideas in Schaefer's articles for *Breaking the Hold*, but never took them as more than intellectual curiosities. The story Peter was now weaving seemed more interesting. Will felt the urge to start challenging the guy on his ideas about science, because his own ideas were completely different.

Will, of course, saw science and its method of understanding the world the best hope for improving the condition of the world, for overcoming superstition and irrational beliefs and the fears they engendered. Completely off base, these ideas he was now hearing, dangerous. But Will decided not to challenge Peter. This gathering had a different purpose and Will had no intention of getting things off track. Will also felt he no longer had legitimacy, a right to speak for science. His own acts were far more dangerous to science than some wacky, bullshit ideas about the superiority of mystical insights. So Will just listened.

"So, you and Schaefer gathered some potential fellow travelers around you, and began indoctrinating them? Is that it, your so-called Brotherhood? I assume all of you were boys," Kay exclaimed as she returned to her seat on the floor. It was approaching 1:30 am, and Gina had collapsed onto her side, but was wide awake and listening. Zoltan returned just in time to light another cigarette for the animated speaker. These French butts really smelled putrid.

"You are exactly correct, Miss Hooper. David was a student of Schaefer's, and so he was brought in. Another priest Mota, Robert Mota, came, far more intellectual than Swift, but not as passionate ... and much less handsome. Oh, how beautiful Father Swift was, how passionate! But like a child in his mind. This was all about a year ago. We usually met at Schaefer's. And you are right, all boys. Twelve of us, after Swift joined last spring. And you are also right, whoever said it earlier, I do have some money. My parents - - my father is a high prince in the power elite - - they supply me. Schaefer knew this and I was only too pleased to help underwrite our project. One other gentleman in our group, an older man, maybe he was about 60, named Dexter - - I never got his last name - - also had money. Came from some rich California clan, railroads or something. Robber barons we used to call them. Barons. We don't have aristocracy here in the same way they do in Europe. In Europe it's all blood, and the aristocrats are not really in the modern power elite. Just kind of show pieces. Here the aristocracy is not about blood relations. It's about the kind of power, so very destructive, that science has brought, and that our little project was designed to begin systematically disassembling."

"So our little Brotherhood of Twelve was going to bring down that power structure by teaching the world that the scientific way of knowing, the religion of that power structure, had to be dissolved. It was a false way of knowing, or attempting to know, the world. A false religion. We would begin a new religion. It would be like Christianity overthrowing the false religions of the past. Our new religion would draw upon all the best of the pre-scientific past, draw upon all the great mystics and poets and priests and shamans and Buddhas and pagans and artists and musicians and poets and ...poets ..." Peter began slurring his words and slowing down ... but then resumed in perfectly enunciated tones. Everyone gathered there in front of him seemed awake and listening, although all were now sprawled about on the floor. Gina wasn't sure they'd get out of this what they wanted, but Weiss was spewing forth and who knew where it might lead.

"All these types would come to replace the generals and the politicians and the financiers and the industrialists and the technicians and their lawyers and bankers. Imagine this!"

Gina imagined Chris sitting in one of these Brotherhood meetings. She couldn't believe he would fall for these insane ideas. Chris was no great intellect, and was driven by religious passion, but he would never have believed all these things ... that there could ever be a return to a pre-scientific time. A completely ridiculous idea. She then thought about her dad and her promise to be at his place tomorrow by noon. Weiss showed no signs of letting up and she had to hear him out. Kay, too, was clearly determined to hear this guy out. Gina saw that Will was still present, sitting on the floor to her left, back to the wall, eyes closing and opening, trying to fathom what he was hearing.

"And so, we were twelve when I introduced the good Father Swift. It was one beautiful night last spring. I remember because the two of us, the priest and myself, walked home from Professor

Schaefer's abode together, late at night." He paused and asked, "Is there wine? Any more wine?" Zoltan had fallen asleep, so Kay volunteered to fetch some. She returned from the kitchen with a full gallon jug of Cribari, and proceeded to fill everyone's glass.

"Father Swift - - your very good friend, my pretty Gina - - the priest with such striking good looks. Black hair, thick and wavy. Slim, just perfect in his kind face. I would think that women would have been in pursuit all the time, collar or no collar. How could he resist? But I digress. Chris did not speak out at our first two or three meetings. Of course, no one could get much in when our great leader was lecturing ... or preaching. What a powerful figure he presented. Such a large man, with a huge deep voice, fierce looks, small but intense eyes that could captivate. And those powerful magnetic ideas....

"The members of this Brotherhood came from all over the Bay area. You all know David, the one-time friend of our sister Kay. David, I must say, was the first of our group to break away. I don't think he ever understood what Dr. Schaefer was saying. David, if you can pardon me, was not as ... clear-thinking as you might have thought. He was very narrowly political, I believe - - destroy the militarists of the right! Destroy the capitalists! No higher vision. Incapable of understanding the roots that Schaefer and I and several others in the group had uncovered and were ready to dislodge and destroy.

"One evening we ventured to the house near Oakland where David eventually moved, and our leader captured the minds of several new men, people with more vision than David. David just could not comprehend this great vision.

"But Chris. Poor Chris. He kept coming to meetings ...he moved in with me, my place off of Bancroft, where we lived several months together. We became very good friends, I instructing him in the ways of the counter - scientific revolution, and showing him the way to deeper levels of meaning in his personal life."

Kay poured herself another glass full of wine and also refilled Peter's glass. She asked, "What was your plan? How on earth did you all think you could ...revolt, cause such a revolution? There's nothing there that can be brought down with guns or protests. There's nothing there that can be caused to collapse under the weight of more powerful ideas. What was your ... plan?"

Peter stood now, wine glass in hand, and stepped over the several bodies strewn in front of him, and strode to the center of the large living room.

"Every great revolution begins with an idea. You all know this, Kay better than most! We decided we needed to show in very concrete ways how destructive science was. Education was part of it. We planned a series of bulletins, just like every revolutionary group of the past. But ours would go to every level of society. We would write them for students at every level. The power of our ideas, if they could be disseminated widely, would gradually fill the hearts and minds of students, even the youngest. So we planned a series of bulletins. Bulletins from The Future. Bulletins from The New Eden.

"But we all knew this would not be enough. We had to strike in other ways, at the heart of science, at the guts of the vast scientific establishment. We had to show how all the evils of our society emerged from technology and how technology could not exist without the scientific way of knowing! We had to show the world that all the beauty and harmony and grace that is the natural world has been grievously injured by the inquiries of science, and that there is an elite that has profited from these injuries. Destroy the source of injury!"

Weiss was now pacing furiously, back and forth. His audience had begun to rise from the floor and soon each had found a seat. It was nearly three a.m. and the grand master showed no signs of slowing down. His words poured forth.

"How could people be made to see in concrete ways the beauty, the desirability of the pre-scientific way of being? One way was the way some of us in the group had used to see the truth of Schaefer's vision - - LSD. Doctor Leary, Timothy Leary, with whom our leader studied, has of course been teaching his vision, his quest for inner light.

And he has convinced many to follow his way. Perhaps some of you here have followed Dr. Leary's great ideas. But, you know, they are not put into the right context. For him, LSD was the way to some truth. Schaefer's view and mine - - please do not underestimate my role here - - was almost the reverse. We understood the truth about the need to rediscover the pre-scientific world through the strength of our intellect and creative intuition, like great artists. LSD was simply a tool for allowing us to experience first-hand that pre-scientific way of knowing, its beauty. Dr. Schaefer, because of his vast knowledge of the medicinal fruits of the Central American jungles, went beyond LSD, and found even higher truths than Leary could ever imagine!

"So, because there is no reason to hide these ideas, the intent of our project, from my good friends here - - I'll tell you why later - - I shall go on." Peter seemed in a half-manic state, completely absorbed in the sound of his own voice, self-mesmerized. He tore the thick white sweater he was wearing over his head, and then stripped away his white trousers and kicked off his sandals. He was completely naked. He collapsed onto one end of the sofa, next to Elaine. He turned to her and said, "You remember, don't you, don't you Dr. Elaine? Remember my body ... ha ... ha ...ha."

Elaine moved off the sofa, away from Peter and dropped to the floor. No one was exactly sure what these last remarks might mean. Will immediately thought she must have slept with him, one of dozens of men, no big surprise. Peter rose from the sofa, and asked for some matches. Gina ran to the kitchen, brushing by the skinny, white-skinned maniac on the way, and returned with a box of matches. He proceeded to move about the living room, lighting every candle he could see. After he'd lighted about ten candles, he ran around the room and turned off the three small lamps. The room took on an eerie character, perfect for the madness that was on display. The skinny naked creature fell to a kneeling position, and went on.

"Each of us pledged to go into the hearts and minds of our closest comrades, and become evangels, to bring the word and the vision. We would seek the vulnerable, the intelligent doubters. We would bring the new gospel. It would become a lifelong quest ... to spread the gospel. LSD and other revelatory medicines would be one of our tools. But this crusade would be too important to rely only upon these means."

Peter laid his hands, palms up, upon his boney thighs. His thin penis lay tucked neatly between them.

"So, so - - and here I must ask for your complete trust - - we decided that our evangelical passions would be accompanied by some kind of demonstration, something that would symbolize our vision for the world. And so ...I shall get right to it. We planned, and please do not be shocked because the plan was never executed, we - - Schaefer and I and two others in The Brotherhood - - last summer, we planned a series of symbolic ... executions ...there, I have said it. One after the other, we planned to bring to trial and to execute ... scientists! Imagine the absolute brilliance of it. And, moreover, the symbol would come in the manner of execution. Crucifixion! This was my brilliant addition. They die for the sin that is science. Scientists, pay for the evil of your ways! A few would be selected to die for the sins of the many! Ha! Ha! Brilliant. I remember the night we conceived it. Wine, please, my cigarettes! Where is that feeble-minded pest I brought with me? And please, do not fear my feeble-minded ... prick. It is feeble. It does not stand, since my beautiful priest ... my beautiful cowardly priest, who turned from our brilliant plan, ran away crying, and left my prick feeble."

There was silence in the dark, candlelit room. The clock in the kitchen struck four, four a.m. The small group of friends and near-friends and ex-friends and ex-lovers who had gathered to hear this story sat in stunned silence. The story master, naked, shivering, hands still resting on his thighs, bowed his head. His puppet Zoltan came crawling up, cigarettes in hand, but stopped a few feet away.

Gina saw, as did everyone in the room, save the numb Zoltan, the complete insanity encapsulated in the naked, shivering body there before them. It was Will who crawled up first, to Peter's side.

"Elaine. That was it, wasn't it? Schaefer's first victim? Was that his plan for her? Execution? Crucifixion? Tell us!"

The shivering Weiss burst into tears at this, and dropped his head further, folded his whole upper body over his legs. "Yes. Yes. Yes." ....he sobbed. "Yes. Elaine. I could not let it happen. I was weak, so weak, and I could not let it happen." He rose and wiped the tears from his eyes.

"Any others? Did the Brotherhood do any others?" Will continued the questioning.

"No. The plan went nowhere. Schaefer and I and two others, Virgil and Cicero, they called themselves, plotted it all. We would bring our victims to some isolated place, and gather our comrades - - the Brotherhood and all those we could convert - - for a ritual execution. The hallucinogens would let us see the wisdom of our act. We would capture scientists. All kinds. Mathematicians. Chemists like Elaine. Physicists and biologists. We would begin with minor figures and progress to more influential ones, all the way to the holders of Nobel prizes! They would be kidnapped and indoctrinated, made to see the evil consequences of their world vision, their rotten way of taking apart the world, the beautiful world, and breaking it into fragments, their cold atoms and molecules. They would be doped with LSD and some of Schaefer's rich collection of pharmaceuticals, and every other means would be used to get them to understand... and then they would be tried, convicted... and crucified! Before our Brotherhood. And they would leave behind a written denunciation of science, the evil method of science. They would go to their deaths willingly, to save humankind!"

The madman was shivering now so much that Kay arose, found a blanket, and wrapped it around him. He muttered into Kay's face as she wrapped him up, "Crucifixes would be found month after month, all over the land, and they would continue to be found until we saw evidence that the scientific establishment began to act, to disassemble itself. Our Brotherhood would grow and grow, and these symbols of our sacred quest - - crucified scientists, Christ-like, dying for the sins of their whole enterprise. Such a brilliant plan. No revolution in human history would ever have had such an effect upon civilization."

Will asked, "So, what happened? Why did this grand plan fail? And what about Schaefer and Elaine? Tell us."

"I am exhausted. I must stop. I must sleep." Peter whispered as his frail body collapsed into Kay's arms. He moaned, "Cowards, David, the priest, all the others, deserted, they could not take the next steps. Cowards."

After a few moments Kay saw that Peter Weiss, the pathetic, mad, hallucinating, visionary, had fallen asleep, so she released his limp body and let it fall gently to the floor. Zoltan lay down beside Peter and embraced him. The group sat for several minutes, staring at the pathetic pair wrapped together on the floor.

Gina rose first and dragged her exhausted body to the kitchen. The others slowly followed. Kay circled the living room and blew out all the candles. They gathered in the kitchen, and sat around the big wooden table. The lights in the kitchen were at full blast, and shocked their emotionally drained systems. Several moments passed before anyone spoke.

"How about some fried eggs and toast? I'm completely famished. Weak as hell. I think we all need some food." Kay finished speaking, got a bowl of eggs, and started scrambling then, while Gina and Elaine began slicing bread for toast.

"It all collapsed, somehow. Thank God," said Will quietly. "Maybe the four couldn't convince anyone else. I can't believe Chris would have gone along with murder, for Christ's sake. Gina, he couldn't possibly ..."

"No way. He split from Peter. You all know. He lived here until he died. He never said anything to me about any of this. The most he said was that he thought Schaefer was deranged."

"I also see," said Will, who was sitting opposite from Gina, "why he went for Schaefer. I'm guessing he knew Schaefer's plans for execution, and he probably guessed that Elaine was to be his first victim. Chris couldn't let it happen and, not knowing what was going on in the cabin, came charging in. He also knew what Schaefer and Peter had in mind - - a series of executions. So he went for Schaefer. And died ... this makes sense, doesn't it?"

"Yeah, it does ... but it also makes sense that Schaefer had it in for Chris, that he thought he might go to the police, or something like that, with the story about Schaefer's brotherhood. Schaefer had a motive to wipe him out," chimed in Kay.

Gina also now knew that it was likely that Chris had homosexual tendencies, that Peter had probably gone after him and maybe even had him, and that Schaefer knew this, told by Peter. Schaefer hated "that fairy priest" - - she remembered the notes in his Guatemala journals.

"Jesus, Elaine, did you have any idea he planned to do this to you?" asked Kay. She began dishing out the eggs and toast as Elaine spoke.

"Not really. He started in on me up there at the cabin, but I thought it was all about, you know, him and me ... he thought I, like wanted him as a lover or something. He did keep saying he had things to go over with me. Things he wanted me to understand. But then it all ended. Jesus, I could have died ... nailed up on some cross. For my sins. Which sins? Trying to be a good scientist? That is so fucking weird.

"But Peter was not mad enough to go through with it. He chickened out and tried to rescue Schaefer, keep him from acting. And he knew Chris could be counted on to try to stop Schaefer. And Schaefer's still alive and that quiet, decent priest is dead."

254

The small group sat around the table for another hour, recapitulating what they'd heard from the madman sleeping in the other room, guessing about the collapse of the Brotherhood and about Schaefer's intentions to go on alone, or with some new cast of adherents. God knows, the times were ripe with disaffected, vulnerable, lost children who could easily be captivated by the big man's words. At one point Elaine wondered aloud whether the whole story they'd heard was a fabrication, Peter just acting out some fantasy. No one rejected the idea, but neither did anyone pursue it.

At about dawn they decided sleep was necessary. They doubted they would ever get more out of Peter, but, at this hour of the day, in a state of utter exhaustion, they seemed to think they knew enough.

Will found his jacket and started for the front door to make the walk to his apartment. Elaine also wrapped herself in a shawl and asked if she could walk with him. As the two were about to leave Gina approached, and grabbed Will by the arm. "Will. I ... do want to talk with you. I'm sorry I brushed you off earlier. Please. I want to hear what has happened." Gina then explained that she had to spend Friday afternoon getting her father checked into the hospital, but that she'd be back in the evening. Could Will come to dinner that evening? Or have dinner out with her? They agreed to meet at 7:30 at Chico's.

Will and Elaine walked slowly down Prospect and then paused at the corner of Bancroft to go their separate ways. It seemed unusually warm for dawn of a late December day in the Berkeley hills. The first rays of the sun were becoming visible over the hilltops just above them.

"Jesus, you would have been ...the first female Jesus. Sacrificial lamb, or whatever. Daughter of the great God Science. I can just picture you, up on that cross. You know, I'm the one he should have chosen. But for different reasons. My sin is against science. Science is not the evil. Science is the only really honest way to truth. I committed the greatest sin of all. You did too, small as your sin was. Now Jensen, too. What he has me doing is wrong. I gave into him out of fear. Three crucifixes are needed, me in the center. The modern ... God, it's all so completely insane."

He grimaced at Elaine, turned, and walked up the hill toward the small cell he called home.

CHAPTER 26

"Your father is a very handsome man, such a kind, warm face."

Gina was surprised by Kay's remark as she settled in behind the wheel of her VW. She and Kay had spent Friday afternoon getting Marco into the University Medical Center. Marco had resisted the move, but Gina knew that his condition had deteriorated badly, and that he had no choice. She was surprised by Kay's observation because she thought her dad looked terrible, thin and old and weak. He had always been robust, full in the face and, in Gina's eyes, powerful-looking. He was not a large man, but that big, square head sitting firmly on broad shoulders made him appear larger than he was. And he certainly had been handsome, this Gina knew and had always been proud of it, always happy to be seen with him in public. Now, this horrible disease was eating away at him, taking his heart and soul and mind ... God, who can explain this to me? Gina turned to Kay and said, "I can't begin to tell you what this cancer has done to him, physically and mentally. It's like he's a completely different person from the man I know as my father. Except in his eyes. I still see him there. Who said the eyes were the doorway to the soul..? It's true. I feel him still present when I look into those eyes, but what I *see* is not Marco. Jesus, I'm not going to be able to deal with this. You," she turned to look at Kay, "you are just great. I love you ... thanks for being here."

Neither said anything more until they were halfway across the

Bay Bridge, heading back to Berkeley. It was Gina who broke the silence as they turned up University. "God, I'm bushed. That was one long, weird night. I couldn't sleep afterwards. That guy is completely whacko, if you ask me."

"Peter or Schaefer?" asked Kay. "Schaefer was behind all this. One weird combination of genius and insanity. His writing and his thought can sound so brilliant, and novel. But he apparently takes all that far too seriously. It's way, way out, this brotherhood of maniacs. I can't believe he really convinced anyone to go out and commit murder in the cause of ... whatever ..."

"Kay, you didn't really fall for that stuff, did you? Peter was just play-acting. He just made all that up. That's what I think anyway. It can't be true, all that crucifixion stuff."

"No. I believe it. Schaefer, I think, is a crusader and is power-hungry, wants to create a new world. I believe he'd do anything to start a mass movement behind him."

"But Kay, no one in his right mind could believe a cult of murderers, no matter how powerful their ideas, could pull off such a monstrous plot. Too weird."

Gina had spent the earlier part of the day trying to make sense of Peter's story, to see if it helped explain Chris Swift's suicidal action. She thought it could, but she still believed Peter tortured Chris with threats about revealing his homosexuality. Peter would never admit to this, of course, because to do so would bring out his own sexual predilections.

She knew Chris had other reasons to dislike the kind of person he was. His homosexual inclinations, regardless of what Peter might threaten, no doubt brought on a lot of self-hatred. It appeared that Schaefer knew or guessed and threatened Chris. She recalled the notebook in Schaefer's office, where he referred to Chris as a fairy. Maybe it was Schaefer, not Peter, with the threats. And he would also feel guilt about his thing with Gina. He must have been a mess inside, but somehow she had never seen anything but a calm soul, disturbed only about his inability to find a home for his priesthood. Chris Swift would probably always remain a mystery.

As they turned up Bancroft toward the Manse, and as darkness began to settle into the Berkeley hills, the rains came, and came in torrents. Gina slowed way down and the little VW beetle crawled the last mile. Gina had promised Will that she'd have dinner with him at 7:30, and she noticed it was already well past 7:00. She'd drop Kay at the house and drive to Chico's; these rains had no intention of stopping soon. As they pulled up to the house Gina's thought turned back to Marco and the fear and pain that must be in him. She felt tears beginning to flood her eyes as Kay asked if she had an umbrella in the car.

"Sorry. I know I should ..." and tears welled forth as Gina broke into uncontrollable weeping. Kay leaned over and awkwardly wrapped her long arms around Gina's shoulders. The two friends sat in the small car, for several minutes, under the rain's thunderous pounding.

When the rain let up a bit, Kay moved to get out. "You've got to go."

"Yes. To see Will."

"Don't let him ..you know ..."

"I know."

"If you need me, just call. I'll be here, just having some dinner." Kay smiled at Gina, and squeezed her hand before opening the car door and leaving.

"Thanks for coming with me. I don't think I could have ...." But Kay was already gone.

Gina arrived at Chico's about 7:45. It was virtually empty. Will was seated by himself in one of the booths, and Gina took off her wet parka, hung it, and quickly slid onto the seat opposite him. Her hair was wet and she knew she looked a mess. Tears and rain. Will looked good, rested, and relaxed. Gina couldn't help taking a glance at his perfect blue eyes, but then quickly lowered her eyes and focused on the tiled table in front of her.

"Sorry I'm late."

"I thought you might not come."

"I thought so, too. I'm not real happy to be here."

"What did you do today, after that incredible performance last night?"

"I had to move my dad into the hospital. He needs daily care. Intensive care. He's declining fast. I told you, he's got one of the worst cancers. In his pancreas."

Will was silent. He looked at the half-empty glass of beer in front of him, and then whispered, "I'm sorry. I don't know what ...and his voice trailed off.

"Maybe you can, you know, write me a note about your thoughts, here. You're better at writing notes than at direct conversation, I've noticed."

Will flinched. He felt the pain of that remark in his gut. He had it coming.

"You know, Will, you are a real coward. I don't know any other word for it. We lived together almost a year, I've known you maybe two years, and I never realized it. I try to think back on the time we were really together. You'd have your moods, you know, where you'd clam up, just get lost in yourself for days on end. But this behavior, toward me and, even worse, toward your research ...God, you told me just a few weeks ago you were quitting. You were going to confess to Jensen, and just depart, clear the air and take the consequences. I was happy about that. It's like you had found yourself again. But, now, you're still here! And working in the lab. What is going on?"

Will sat staring down at the table. There were several minutes of silence. He'd planned what he was going to tell Gina, but couldn't recall where he was going to begin his story. The truth. Yes. He was still capable of telling the truth. And so he did. He told Gina of his meeting with Jensen, his confession, and Jensen's unbelievable response. He told it directly, looking Gina straight in the face.

"So, he scared the hell out of me and I went back into the lab, half-glad that he'd given me a chance to go back and try again. See, I know I completed the synthesis once. I'm sure of it. With another try, with a more careful set of experiments to identify the crucial factor that was missing on the second and third and fourth tries, I can be successful, do what I need to do to get back on track. I'm a good chemist, I know it. I love this subject and I know it well, exceedingly well."

Will's story about Jensen matched the one Elaine had told her, except that Gina now perceived that Will had not gone back to the lab because he was afraid of Jensen, but because he really thought he could put things right, successfully complete the synthesis and put things right.

"Will. Jesus, you know what he did was wrong. Couldn't you just tell him that you couldn't go along with such a thing? You confessed your errors. You cleared the path for yourself, and then just fell back into an even worse morass. Will, for God's sake, don't continue this. You're killing yourself."

"This morning, walking home from your place, I made up my mind, again, to do the right thing. After that incredible night, I was completely exhausted, walking home at dawn. I saw myself whole. Just the way you see me. Cowardly. I was that with you. I was that with my research. Now with Jensen. I don't understand where this comes from. Never in my life before have I behaved this way. I avoided the draft, that's about the worst. I have not before lived a life of lies. I think, maybe, my mother ... I mean ... my father was such a good man, a wonderful model for me. When my mother ran off, he just ... I became everything to him. He dealt with the pain of losing my mother by giving everything he had - - everything - - to me. And I grew up in his sturdy, honest, hard-working, world where science was everything."

"You're all of a sudden talking about your parents? You're searching there for some answer? To who you really are? Maybe ..." Gina paused. All of a sudden she felt extremely hungry. She hadn't eaten all day. She grabbed up a big handful of chips and went at them ferociously.

"I need to eat. I feel faint." She took a swallow of Will's warm beer.

They took time out to order some food and then took up where they'd left off.

"Okay, Will. Do you mean it this time? What you decided this morning? Are you going to hold onto that idea now? Jensen can't do a thing. He's now in the wrong." She paused for some more chips, and then stopped while the waiter served them.

"I'm still ... worried. Jensen's career is on the line. He'll have to go tell his sponsors at NIH he doesn't have a synthesis. He might lose his grant. Sure, he can blame his lying grad student, and maybe the government will buy that. But, you know, maybe they'll say he wasn't doing his job, not monitoring me close enough, always off consulting for some drug company. Besides, he wants to make a deal on pfaffadine. Some juicy grants from a drug company, maybe even a share in the profits if pfaffadine makes it to the big time. It's possible he's thinking big time bucks. This story comes out, and it's over for him, possibly."

"Elaine has her way to get the stuff. She told me. I saw it. I was in her lab."

"You were? Why on earth ... it's okay, none of my business. Yeah, but her way requires that there's a good supply of the plant, this Guatemalan plant, and maybe there isn't. Maybe it can't be cultivated. I'm sure Jensen's thinking all this. And so I come along and pull the rug out from under him. I can see why he did ..."

"Bullshit, Will, I don't buy that. Look nobody's holy, nobody's beyond some dishonesty. But this is really different. I can't imagine ... you go back, complete your work. It's successful. Ph.D. On to great things. But you'll know, always, what you did. An ugly blackness at the center of your life. You know, and I do, Jensen, Elaine, me ... but... you... you think you can live with it? And, Jesus, what if you can't repeat your first try? What if all this new effort just shows that your "success" was, in fact, not a success, that you never ...."

Will stopped eating, and looked into Gina's eyes. "Gina. I'm sorry. I did to you something so completely wrong and, like you said, completely cowardly. There's no way I can correct what I did to you. You'll survive me, looks like you already have. You're a strong, good person. What you're telling me is the truth. Maybe I'll now have the strength of character to do the right thing, finally. It's ironic, you know, they teach us God forgives everything and, if he exists, I'm sure that's true. But science forgives no transgression. Humans invented science and made the rules about how it operates. It's the only thing we have that demands complete honesty. That's why Schaefer and his weird friend are so completely wrong. Completely. I think I have the will now to do what's right and remove myself from where I do not deserve to be. We're all weak, somewhere, I guess. Look at Jensen, now, scared to death, willing to cheat because something beyond science is at stake - - his status and maybe even his income! So, I'll finally do the right thing and save him from himself."

Gina smiled and raised her head to look at Will directly, into those wonderful blue eyes. She flashed briefly back in time, to a hike the two had taken in the Sierras, when she had first noticed his beautiful eyes there in the clear and luminous mountain air.

"Will, you're right about God. I'm sure he, or whatever God is, is there and all he needs is for you to get onto the right path. Please, also, I'm not saying all this because I have any special right to. You don't have to listen to me. I'm just saying what I think is the right thing."

Will reached across the table and put his large hand over Gina's small one. The two former lovers looked at each other and smiled. Will squeezed Gina's hand and quickly got up and left the restaurant.

Gina remained at the table for several more minutes. She felt as though some long fostering disease had just been eradicated, some wound had been healed, some cancer had ... Pfaffadine. She wondered if Will's chemical would kill her father's cancer. Dr. Barrett had him on all kinds of chemotherapy, but the only hope, he said, was to slow down the spread of these cells gone wild. Cells out of control, and murderous. That's how Dr. Barrett had explained her father's terrible disease. Something sets them off, and over time they become deranged. But they don't die, not all of them. They just keep reproducing, out of control. It's like Will, who can't seem to keep from reproducing the bad things in him. They grow and grow and grow and just suck the life out of the person carrying them. They even break away from the tissues where they're growing, and start traveling around the body to other tissues, where they take up residence and begin to reproduce and crowd out all the good cells. Doctors can try to kill the cancer cells with certain chemicals, and with radiation. But these treatments are so damaging they usually kill good cells too and don't get all the bad ones. Pfaffadine. Maybe Will's chemical, the one he wishes he had, would be better at killing cancer cells than anything that came before. Gina remembers Will talking about this possibility, last year, maybe it was at Christmas dinner, at Marco's house. That very happy time when Will was another man and when she loved him and when her father was full of joy and the spirit she so loved. What had happened to these two men she loved so much? God, she thought, if Dr. Barrett is right, Marco had had some cells turning cancerous way back then. Just a few maybe, nothing he could notice. What could possibly have set them off? An act of God. What could have set Will off on his journey of self destruction? An act of God? Does God direct the cells in our bodies in this way? Something, maybe all that paint Marco came in contact with. Maybe ... maybe somewhere ... in one of the cells of his pancreas ... somehow, the pain that was in him, the pain that began to grow when he first realized - - or at least began to believe - - that he had injured Gina's mother, by forcing her abortion, and had caused the agony that led to her death. Whether her father's belief had any real basis no one would ever know, but it was a fact that Marco believed he had sinned in this way.

Had he ever confessed, received communion, did he believe God had forgiven him? Who knows? Even if he thought God forgave him, the pain never left him. The pain that caused those cells to turn bad. Will has a pain in him now. He may do the right thing, but that doesn't mean the pain will ever leave him. The pains we inflict on ourselves, because we do things we know are wrong, those pains never leave us. Maybe they destroy us. How Catholic she still was, god damnit?

Chris, poor Chris. Was he fated in some way, because he did things he knew were wrong, to develop his own deep wounds, wounds that would cause him to want to disappear from this earth?

Like the war in Vietnam. It's a horror this country is inflicting on itself. We'll never get over it. It'll grow into a huge cancer. America has cancer. Marco. Will. Chris. Gina's thoughts began to degenerate, began to collapse. Jesus, Will didn't even pay his share of the bill. Gina paid up and walked out into the black Berkeley rain.

CHAPTER 27

Gina moved her possessions into a recently abandoned and much larger room of the Manse on the morning of Sunday the 31st, the last day of 1967. The rains had continued almost non-stop since the evening she'd spent with Will. Christmas had quickly come and gone. She'd spent several hours at her father's bedside on Christmas day, but he was not able to carry on much of a conversation. He looked dreadful, and scared. Gina's mind had been blank, a kind of numbness settled in, when she was with him. The rest of the day she'd spent with Kay, cooking, eating, talking about the future. Kay was to start her new job at the San Francisco Chronicle right after the first, and her substantially bigger paycheck would easily cover the loss in revenue from the two departed boarders. Besides Gina and Kay only one other person, a junior faculty member, now lived in the Manse, and Kay hoped to leave things this way. Gina's last paycheck from the Anthropology Department would come in mid-January, and she had been talking about a job with a woman who headed a small, local law firm. It seemed like a perfect position and Gina hoped it would be offered to her. She had some savings, maybe $1200, so she wasn't yet worried. Her share of the rent was only $175 a month. Gina was planning to sign up for a course in the law school, but had no other plans except to earn some money, have some fun, and prepare for full-time law school in the fall.

Gina had not really put the Chris Swift matter behind her, and probably never would - - she believed there was no way to get at the ultimate truth. Gina could think of so many reasons why he might have done what he did - - including that it was simply an act of bravery - - that she had come to believe that no certain answer would ever emerge. In fact every reason might have had some influence.

In the midst of her move to the new room the phone rang, and Gina ran to pick it up.

"Is this Gina?" The male voice on the line was very quiet.

"Yes. Who's this?"

"I don't know if you remember me. Tom Silva. I was a student of Schaefer's, with you."

"Tom, of course I remember you. I haven't seen you since you left for Guatemala. You went with Schaefer and David. How are you? I haven't heard a thing about your end of the trip."

"That's what I want to talk to you about. I got your phone number from the Anthro department files. I hope you don't mind. I've been wanting to talk to you for some time. I even tried to get to you a couple of weeks ago, after the class you teach, but I missed you."

"Well, sure, I'd love to see you. You know, I'm dropping out of Anthropology. It's a long story, but I've decided there are more important things to do."

"Oh. I hadn't heard. I wondered what you would do after Schaefer's thing. I'd assumed you were not too happy about the way he treated you, how he screwed you out of your trip to Guatemala."

"You bet I wasn't. But that's only part of the story. Look, you want to meet? Maybe I can meet you later, or you can come by our place in a couple of hours.

"Okay. What's the address?"

Gina gave him the address and agreed to see Tom at lunch. While she continued to move, she recalled what little she knew about Tom. She had always liked him. He seemed kind of shy, but really bright. He had asked her out once, but that was when she was living with Will.

Tom arrived exactly at noon.

"God, I invited you for lunch, but I haven't made anything. Are you hungry? Maybe we have to go out," Gina exclaimed as soon as she opened the door for him.

"No, not much. If you want to, we can." Tom was seated on the huge living room sofa. He wore a heavy rain parka and boots. His hair was dark, almost like Gina's, and it curled about his head - - a large head, a little like Marco's. His face was attractive in a rugged kind of way.

"Maybe in a while. I've got some soda." She went to the kitchen and returned with two bottles of coke. The two made small talk for awhile, and then Gina asked Tom what he was going to do now that Schaefer was out of the picture.

"I'm not sure. I really want to continue. I'm going to talk with a couple of other possible advisors. Hayward I kind of like and maybe Caruso. They're both possibilities and at least Caruso has enough interest and experience in Latin cultures to make the transition easy. And you? No more anthropology?"

Tom finished up his coke and leaned forward toward Gina. She also leaned forward, elbows on her thighs, and propped her face up with her hands. She liked Tom, and also liked his looks. He was dark-haired, like Chris, but taller, almost as tall as Will, but broader, more muscular.

"I've done a lot of thinking over the last couple of months. It's been a fairly dramatic time in my life, a lot of changes. When Schaefer gave me the shaft on Guatemala, it just turned me off. You don't know the other stuff, like I was a good friend of the guy he murdered. It's complicated. But, anyway, I gradually began to see myself in a different way. With Kay ... I began to see myself as maybe not so weak and passive. I always thought of myself as ... sort of a quiet, shy mouse. I'd be a school teacher, teach anthropology at Humboldt State or something. Hide out. But I've come to realize there's a lot to do in our society, all kinds of good causes to be fought for. Kay is a journalist and is very perceptive. She understands a lot. She's progressive but balanced and sane. Not one of these hare-brained, adventure-seeing hippies.... my God, I'm going on like ... I don't know what. Sorry ... anyway, I'm going into law. I think that's a great way to have an influence. Move in on the elite and bring some new ideas ... begin using the law in ways that benefit people other than those in power and ... okay, okay, I'll stop preaching. Please, I want to hear from you." Gina felt herself blushing, and turned her head downward so that Tom wouldn't see what she thought must show on her face.

"Hey, no, that's great. I like that. I'd like to hear more."

Gina thought she ought to get to the reason for Tom's visit, the Guatemala trip. "Please, what can you tell me about David? Why did he stay there? What do you know?"

"Okay. I don't know everything, but there's some things ... I called because I wanted to find out myself more about Schaefer and the killing. I thought it might tell me, or help me understand about Guatemala. Also, I knew you knew David better than I did, and might lead me to his family. This might take some time. Maybe we should go find lunch."

"Yeah, sure, lunch is good. But no, I don't know his family, but my roommate here, Kay Hooper, might. David lived here at one time."

They put on coats and walked down to Telegraph. The Avenue was crowded and later that day, New Year's Eve, it would be completely jammed. The clubs, bars, and restaurants were all offering New Year's Eve specials, and no place in America was going to be as filled with the wild uninhibited spirit of the 1960's as Telegraph Avenue in Berkeley, California. The weather was great, and a liquor- and drug-crazed frenzy of delight would pervade its every nook and cranny. As Tom and Gina ate lunch at the Telegraph Avenue Grill, they made plans to maybe join the frenzy. "Kay's out of town, visiting her mother in Palo Alto. I wish you could meet her."

"I'm sure I will. Look. What I know is this." Tom pushed aside his plate. "David and Schaefer fought, all the way down there and most of the time we were there. I was there to work. I didn't pay attention at first. Believe me, I knew David was not prepared for that trip, and Schaefer knew that, too. Why he took David instead of you, I never figured out. I knew it was wrong.

"Anyway, there was this guy down there, a friend of Schaefer. A college professor named Perea. He met us in Guatemala City and arranged our visit to Chimaltenango. We stayed two days with Perea in Guatemala City before we went to the hill country. Perea and Schaefer and David would get into these deep conversations. I was not invited in. They'd go into Perea's bedroom in his apartment, close the door, and have Perea's wife - - a real nice woman, Veronica, an American - - entertain me. Or they'd send me out to get supplies for the trip.

"Every once in a while David would break away, steaming mad. But he'd never tell me what was going on. Anyway, we went up to the hill country, settled in, and planned the work. Perea stayed with us. We four shared a house, a shack, really, that Perea had found for us. I went to work as planned, but David did not. Schaefer went through the motions for a couple of hours a day, but he really wasn't involved. I couldn't get any real help from him, and I wasn't happy about that. Anyway, I did my best.

"The place is real interesting. I know you would have found it completely fascinating. You know, I was interested in concepts of property and ownership, and I collected terrific amounts of information. David did nothing for a week, then he disappeared.

"When I asked Perea and Schaefer about it, they said they'd sent him for supplies. I knew that was bullshit, because David couldn't possibly find his way around. Plus it was fairly dangerous up there. There's guerilla warfare. We could even hear gunfire from time-to-time, natives trying to overthrow the government. It's a wicked, military dictatorship, no question. David talked about it a lot, and I got the impression he was ready to join in on the side of the insurgents. I can see how that would be tempting, I'm pretty sympathetic myself. The miseries of Latin American peasants are about the worst you'll find on earth. And it's true that our Washington big boys, the same boys who've brought us Vietnam, are on the side of the devils down south of the border."

Tom paused to order some more coffee, and Gina sat quietly opposite him and waited for the story to continue.

"David did not return for three days. I was panicked, but couldn't get anything out of Schaefer. Perea had taken off. On the day after David's return, he and Schaefer cornered me at dinner and that night I heard the most fantastic things I've ever heard in my life. Most of it came from Schaefer. David said almost nothing. In fact, I thought David really didn't go along with Schaefer on this. I couldn't believe anyone in his right mind would go along with Schaefer. I knew some of his ideas. I'm sure you do, too. You've read some of his political and social writings. *Breaking the Hold*, all that stuff about the dominance of science and technology and how it's created huge injustices. How it has put so much power into the hands of a few. How it destroys every way of life on earth that does not adhere to its life-defying rules. It's interesting stuff, but way, way out there. You know what I'm talking about?"

Gina nodded. God, was this another Peter story coming? Had Tom heard this fantastic plan about "crucifixions" directly from its author, Preston Schaefer? Was it really true?

"So, Schaefer started in on me, in that shack way up in the Guatemalan mountains, as night settled in. It was hot and humid, and Schaefer kept getting up and splashing water all over his face. We lived by candlelight. Can you just sort of picture the scene? So, he forced me to listen to his whole grand thesis, about the origins of oppression and the destructiveness of the west with all its scientific way of studying the world and how that way brings power to those who support it. Not to the scientists, but to those who pour money into their work. Those are the owners of the world, he said. He went through his whole argument,

271

some of which I'd read, some of which was new. It's a fantastic thesis. The owners keep the scientists happy by feeding them, the scientists provide a kind of knowledge that can create the technical means whereby the owners can stay in power. Also, he says there are many other ways of knowing about the world. Science is only one of many. But science is different from all the rest because of this power thing ... I'm not sure I've got the argument right ... and anyway, the only hope for mankind is to destroy science and to bring back pre-scientific ways of thinking and seeing and believing. He ties all this to specific things in Guatemala, as examples. He's got the whole history of U.S. involvement down there at his fingertips. He sounds ... brilliant, I must say. Can you picture the scene? I'm drawn in the more he talks, it's maybe two hours straight of talking, the more I'm drawn in. I'm transfixed. I feel myself believing it all. I've never heard such a perfectly reasoned picture of how things work in the world. I mean, I know his ideas are extreme and bizarre, but at the time they sounded right. We were drinking a lot of wine. Except David. He just sat quiet and looking to me nervous."

Gina listened intently. This was about to overlap with Peter's story, and might be some kind of verification of it. Gina also found herself transfixed by the way Tom was telling this story. He seemed more and more interesting to her as he talked, she enjoyed his manner, the movement of his lips, his soft, clear voice.

"I'm guessing Schaefer is stoned or something. You know he experiments with lots of drugs - - not our kind of stuff, but stuff from plants and even mushrooms, that he's picked up during his travels down there. He told me his greatest insights come when he'd experiment and I think he was whacked out on some powerful stuff, like, everyday down there.

"He makes these trips to renew his insights, that's what he said. The drugs he takes give him visions, and that's where his insights come from. The more I think about it, the more I recognize that it was the real reason for his trip.

"Anyway, finally, Schaefer tells me he knows I understand what he is saying. He knows I'm bright, aware, and all that stuff. He knows I can deal with what he's about to say."

Tom went on to describe Schaefer's grand scheme, almost the way Peter had described it during the endless night at the big house. Except, as Tom heard it directly from Schaefer, there already existed a network of comrades, adherents to the mad professor's cause. It was even international, and Perea was one of them. According to Tom, Schaefer claimed a brotherhood of maybe a dozen people he considered peers of his, each of whom had brought together a small group of supporters. Perea was a peer, and others existed in Boston, New York, Washington even.

"Mostly academic types, who communicated regularly, and who were slowly working up to these completely bizarre crucifixions of scientists. It was all to be coordinated and they'd take place simultaneously."

"He then said I needed to join him on one of his journeys, his mind travel. He said there was a series of four drugs, straight from God, he said, that I needed to take and that I would see the world and the truth of the Schaefer vision, and never return to the world I now know. This scared me, I did not want any of those drugs. I'm not a pharmaceutical virgin by any means, but I did not want to venture into such completely unknown territory."

Tom continued into the late afternoon, talking about how Schaefer tried to convince him to take his mind journey and to join the Brotherhood. "He said he knew I could understand the wisdom of his thesis and he also believed I would appreciate the beauty of his "solution." He also, I must tell you, threatened me. If I ever revealed any of this he said the Brotherhood would do me great harm, without hesitation. He said they were serious people with a serious purpose, to restore truth and sanity to the world, to recreate the glorious, pre-scientific past. The way the hill people, the indians, lived there in Guatemala was one of those Edens that had been partially destroyed by the power structure of America and its band of military police in Guatemala City. It was okay to support the kind of revolt going on in Guatemala, but that was only going to represent a temporary solution. The roots of all that oppression go much, much deeper, to the way of thinking about people and nature that western science has brought."

Gina looked at Tom in amazement. She'd heard it all before. It had to be real. Tom did not know Peter and his whole side of it, or of his place in Schaefer's gang. "Tom, I know this story. I need to tell you how. But first, David. What happened to David down there?"

Tom related how Schaefer had gone on until the early morning hours. He told about how he was spending most of his time in Guatemala writing and preparing for the upcoming holocaust, which was to begin soon, and reach full implementation in 1968. First, as Peter said, some minor figures in the scientific community, and then more and more prominent figures, and finally some of the greats would be made to see the truth and die for it.

"The next day, when I finally woke up and in the clear light, I was both appalled and scared. I thought Schaefer must have been making all of that up. I knew the guy was extreme. But this was nuts beyond belief. I was sure it was just the drugs talking.

"I finally was able to spend some time alone with David. He told me what Schaefer said was at least partly true. He did have believers, this network of like-thinking people. But David then told me that Schaefer's attempt to form a group around him in the Bay Area wasn't working. Schaefer had recruited a bunch of guys, David, some other students and so on, and had brought them together. But it wasn't holding together. David wanted out. When he finally realized what Schaefer really had in mind he thought it was just crazy, and he wanted no part of it. But Schaefer had threatened him in the same way he threatened me.

"David knew that most members of Schaefer's Bay Area gang wanted out. They'd all stayed with Schaefer for a few meetings, but when he pushed them to start plotting these murders, they wanted out.

Several, I guess, argued with Schaefer, just told him "no way." David argued and argued, tried to talk Schaefer out of it all, but the arguing just made Schaefer madder. He accused David of moral weakness. One day near the end of our stay in Guatemala, David just took off. He told me he had connections with a band of local insurgents, and that he was going to join them. It was, I know, partly out of fear of Schaefer. He thought Schaefer was going to hurt him. David told me that the night before he took off. He said he had threatened Schaefer, told him he was going to reveal Schaefer's murderous plan. He immediately regretted saying this, because he believed Schaefer was insane and that his life was in danger. So he took off."

Tom went on about his own feelings, about how he wanted no part of this, but that he didn't know how to get out. He tried to tell this to Schaefer several times, but each time Schaefer had come back with a combination of arguments and threats. "I finally just told him I'd been convinced. Just to get him off my case until we got back to the U.S. What I'd do then, I didn't know."

"Did David tell you anything else about his plans? Like how long he would stay?"

"Yeah. He said he'd made no long term commitments. He just told the rebels he wanted to stay to understand their cause, help a bit, and then return to the U.S. to publicize their activities. To fight for their cause back here, where their real enemies were. That's all he said."

"I'll bet he'd come home if he knew Schaefer was locked up!" exclaimed Gina. Tom shook his head in agreement and went on to say how Schaefer had been really pissed over David's abandonment of him.

"Then came the worst part." Tom paused, and Gina could see he was trembling all over. "As we were leaving, we encountered a large contingent of government forces. Schaefer told them about the location of David's band of insurgents. He wanted David destroyed. I hate to tell you this, but it's true. I was terrified and I have been ever since. I couldn't figure out what to do. It's like six weeks since we're back. No word about David?"

"None" said Gina, clearly horrified by what she'd just heard.

Tom went on. "The rest of the time down there Schaefer just did drugs. He used the roots of some plant and made a thick paste from them, just like the Maryanta. Except the indians used this stuff only for certain ceremonies, like a couple of times a year. I swear, Schaefer used it almost everyday. He'd go into these stuporous states, just sit under some tree. He didn't eat much, that's why he lost so much weight. I think he'd get bad diarrhea, he'd vomit a lot, I think what it was - - it was the plant he said his girlfriend in Chemistry was working on. So anyway, he did this and then he'd do some writing, God knows what. It certainly wasn't research stuff."

The two finally left the Grill and wandered out onto Telegraph Avenue. It was near five o'clock, New Year's Eve. The Avenue was already crowded and they strolled slowly down it, lost in the sad, frightening tale of the mad professor. Gina's thoughts turned to Chris Swift, Schaefer's first real victim, and then to David. Should Tom tell his story to the authorities? What authorities? No one was going after Schaefer because he'd ratted on a rebel force. David must be dead, she thought.

Tom wanted to hear Gina's side of the story, so they decided to pick up some groceries and return to the group house to make dinner and continue talking.

And so they did, late into New Year's Eve. Gina told the story of Father Swift, the kidnapping of Elaine Callahan that had led to his death, Schaefer's escape and his continued absence, and, finally, the weird night with Peter Weiss. The stories overlapped. The only thing that was unclear was how great Schaefer's delusion was about the size, strength, and dedication of his peers and followers. They must have assumed that with Schaefer in flight from the law, whereabouts unknown, his "movement" would just die. Tom had simply stayed away from Schaefer after they returned from Guatemala. "I was pretty scared most of the time, but I didn't know what to do. I was incredibly relieved when he disappeared from campus. Now you tell me he was going to murder that woman, Elaine; her death was to be his first symbolic act? God, the only victim was a priest! That's ironic. He wanted to save the world for the priests!"

The two sat around after dinner, drinking wine, listening to music on the radio, and making small talk. Gina had intended to drive to San Francisco to visit her father, to be with him as the new year came, but all of a sudden a great tiredness overcame her. When she tried to rise from the sofa, where she was seated next to Tom, the combined effect of her exhaustion and the wine overwhelmed her and she collapsed. Tom raised her legs off the floor, and made her comfortable on the sofa. He found a blanket in one of the closets off the living room and covered her with it. He turned off the living room lights and, as midnight came and went, and 1968 was born, Tom Silva smiled and quietly crept out of the large old house where he hoped he would be spending lots of time in the new year.

The phone woke up Gina. Dawn had not yet fully arrived. The ringing seemed unbelievably loud and Gina rolled off the sofa and crawled quickly across the living room to pick up the receiver.

"Is this Gina Antinori?"

"Uh, yes this is ... yes."

"Miss Antinori, we're sorry to wake you at this hour." It was the hospital. Dr. Barrett was then put on the line. Gina knelt on the living room floor, by the small table that held the phone and, at the first dawn of the new year heard the news of her dear father's death.

"He passed away about an hour ago, about five a.m. I was there. He did not seem to be in pain. He seemed at peace, Gina. I'm very sorry, but you knew this disease he had would not be overcome. He was a good man. I liked him very much. He loved you more than you could possibly know."

Gina hung up the phone, wrapped the blanket she had carried from the sofa closely around her small body, and sat on the floor, back against the wall. The early morning sun rising over the Berkeley hills gradually awakened the room around her and then, somehow, brought warmth and light and peace.

CHAPTER 28

Alden Jensen arrived at his office early on Monday, the eighth of January. He had spent three days between Christmas and New Year's in Bethesda, Maryland, at the National Institutes of Health. All of his government research support came from the NIH, specifically the Cancer Institute, and because the NCI was seriously interested in pfaffadine, Jensen had been asked to participate in several long meetings about the compound. The Deputy Director of NCI had been at one of them, but Jensen's principle contact was Virgil Goode, Chief of the Medicinal Chemistry Branch, and several other senior and mid-level scientists also participated. They'd had several reports from the Chief of the Chemotherapy Screening Branch, Bill Winslow, on the results of the tests they'd run on the last batch of pfaffadine, the one Elaine had isolated in October from the dried plant material Schaefer had arranged to have shipped from Guatemala. Every screening test was positive, a couple dramatically so. The compound was effective against three kinds of cancer cells in "test-tube" experiments, and looked highly promising in some relatively short-term screens in tumor-bearing mice. "We need lots more material," Winslow told Jensen. "We need to do some long term studies and also some toxicity tests in mice." Every chemical available to kill cancer cells was also toxic to normal cells. Side effects, some relatively serious, were a normal part of cancer treatment. The search for more effective and less toxic cancer drugs was high on NCI's list of priorities.

The group had spent a lot of time discussing the pros and cons of chemical synthesis of pfaffadine and of Elaine's isolation and purification system. The disadvantage of Elaine's system was that it relied upon a consistent and reliable source of the plant from which pfaffadine derived. This was troublesome, highly so. Also, if Elaine's approach were to be selected, and pfaffadine proved to be a successful drug, it would mean setting up some means to cultivate the wild plant, perhaps in Mexico or Costa Rica. Guatemala was just too unstable, offered Virgil Goode. All during this discussion Alden Jensen was in a state of serious anxiety, and he knew he was not contributing much to the discussion. He of course knew that there was no synthesis. He knew that that stupid, dishonest graduate student of his had faked it. At one point in the discussions Jensen had been tempted to reveal what he knew, but just couldn't manage to get the words out. When it became apparent to all that he was under stress, he simply offered that he was feeling a little sick, some flu was coming on.

Virgil Goode had pressed for pfaffadine synthesis. "It's only a 12-step synthesis. Some, I know, are tough, but we've handled more difficult ones. The molecule is not as complex as some of the other natural products. I propose we set up some contracts with a major pharmaceutical company and have them scale up Dr. Jensen's synthesis. Alden, you can consult on it under your grant from us. I'd also like to recruit Mr. Getz, William Getz. Has he finished up his work, has he graduated? He'd be a great asset here. A post-doc."

Jensen had been stunned by Goode's unexpected proposal to use the synthetic path, which had apparently been accepted by all at the table. He leaned over the conference table, looked up and down each side at the half-dozen scientists sitting around it - - scientists who could not be fooled, scientists who would be highly influential in any future grants Jensen might receive - - and simply said he wasn't sure of Will Getz's plans. No, he was still writing up his thesis, and would probably not be finished for a couple of months, Mr. Getz had not been particularly diligent in getting his work written up but he, Alden Jensen, would be glad to bring Virgil Goode's proposal back to Berkeley.

The meetings had ended on the morning of the 29th and Jensen had immediately flown back to San Francisco after promising to get full write-ups of each step in the pfaffadine synthesis delivered to NCI as soon as possible.

On the flight back and for the next several days, through New Year's Day and into the week following it, Alden Jensen shut himself off from contact with his wife and everyone else. He had never in his life been faced with such a dilemma, although he fully realized that it was of his own making. He knew that he should have immediately dismissed Getz, retracted in some journal the Abstract of the synthesis published for the ACS Meeting, and revealed everything to the NCI. The consequences could be severe, even loss of government funding. No matter that he was completely ignorant of the fraud, he would have been blamed for lack of sufficient vigilance. Perhaps that was true, but he'd thought he had stayed pretty close to Getz's work. A student who wants to fake it, especially one as bright as Getz, could easily get away with it. How many others had there been? Getz was to be the 21st Ph.D. student Jensen had produced, and he had had about a dozen post-docs, including that Elaine Callahan - - she'd probably helped Getz out of love or whatever it was between them. How many of these had faked it?

Jensen couldn't fathom Getz's behavior. He had had in his own professional career a scrupulously honest record. Solid research. A string of significant if not major contributions to his science, and respect from his peers. At age 49 Jensen was just entering what could be his most productive decade. The work on pfaffadine, if it were real, could have elevated his standing even more. Now he faced the possibility of a significant descent. Nothing catastrophic would happen, he would not be dismissed, but his professional stature, maybe even his grants, would suffer.

He was also concerned about his grants from the two pharmaceutical firms, and his juicy consulting arrangements with them. He stood to make more money out of pfaffadine, as would the holder of relevant patents, the University of California. Jensen had been thinking that Elaine's approach, isolating pfaffadine from its natural source, would be the preferred one. But now that NCI was clearly interested in pursuing the synthetic pathway, Jensen's assumption that Will's and now his own transgression would never rear its ugly head was invalid. Damn, he should have argued more strongly for Elaine's approach!

By the time Alden Jensen arrived at the chemistry building on Monday morning, he had made up his mind about what he would do.

Will Getz arose very early on that same Monday, but sat around in his apartment until after nine, drinking coffee and trying to read from the novel he was finding difficult to stay with. On Christmas day, which he'd spent alone except for a phone call from his father, he'd picked up Melville's *Moby Dick*, for the third time in his life. The first two times he'd failed to get very far; he had no doubt been too young to really grasp it. He was now well into, yet bogged down in, the long descriptions of the whaling life. But he'd stuck to it, because he now seemed to fathom Melville's real message. How powerfully he communicated the immense uncertainty that seems to underlie all of human striving, and the great fear it creates in all of us, a fear we sometimes try to ignore, a fear we sometimes try to overcome in both good and bad ways. The novel ran along at so many different levels, and said so much about the experiment that was America and the struggles of personal life. Maybe even all this detailed whaling stuff was essential to give the story depth. The daily struggles of life, the mastery of craft, all played against an underlying sense of uncertainty and despair. That great white whale. Will had his own whale in that elusive chemical compound.

Will arrived at Chemistry at about 10 a.m. and went directly to Jensen's office. The professor was seated at the table he used to prepare manuscripts.

"I'm writing a retraction. A letter to submit to the Journal, retracting your pfaffadine abstract and the ACS talk you gave. I'm saying we have been unable to repeat the pfaffadine synthesis. The last step, the cyclization of pre-pfaff, I'm saying is the problem. We did it before, but now can't. We're *both* going to sign this. Then, in a week or two, we'll tell NCI and submit this letter at the same time."

Jensen stared down at the paper on which he was writing as he said these words. He didn't look up at Will, who was standing, leaning against Jensen's desk, his back to the windows, his face in shadows. The professor liked to work in natural light and keep only a small desk lamp lit. Will stared down at Jensen, trying to assimilate what he'd just heard. The professor had done his job for him, he was doing the right thing, finally. But why should he sign the letter with Jensen? Shouldn't the whole story be told, about his deception, his dismissal from grad school?

"I was going to tell you today that what we were doing was wrong and that I should leave, that we should stop perpetuating my crime."

"That's not what this letter's about. It's just a retraction. I'm saying we haven't been able to reproduce, but that we are going to continue trying. You and I. This way, we let everyone know the synthesis hasn't been completed, or that for some unknown reason we can't get the last step to go as it did before. No blame here for fraud. We get the scientific truth out. I believe you when you say you did it once. The only lie is a white one. That we just recently, maybe the last few days, found out you can't reproduce the last step."

Will was stunned. This was a continuing deception, just dressed up in more digestible language, and for some reason designed to ignore his own inexcusable behavior. Why was Jensen doing this? What had happened during Jensen's meetings at NCI?

When Will asked for an explanation, Jensen at first simply stated that he believed Will's story, that he had once had a successful synthesis and that it could be repeated with more time and effort. Jensen was willing to forgive Will's having gone off the path. The letter was a way to ensure that the public record was corrected. It was only after Will kept pushing for further clarification that Jensen told him about the NCI meetings and the decision to go with Will's pfaffadine synthesis. Jensen was prepared to go back to NCI and explain that more work had to be done before a set of protocols for pfaffadine synthesis could be delivered to them. They'd be disappointed but would understand. These types of problems were not uncommon and did not suggest fraud. Many chemical reactions, especially those involving complex molecules, were highly sensitive to factors such as the solvent used, the temperature, the catalyst, even minor contaminants. The isolation procedure can sometimes result in destruction of the product. Sometimes, even in the hands of the best lab scientists, reactions or isolation procedures failed even after they had been verified, because one of the variables contributing to them is inadequately controlled. Jensen's letter was not at all implausible.

"Your behavior, Will, is just between you and me. I need you to complete this synthesis. I know you have been working. Where are you now?"

Will didn't know what to say. This was not the outcome he was looking for. Besides, his crime wasn't just between him and Jensen. Elaine knows, and Jensen knows she does. Gina knows, and Jensen has no idea she knows.

"I don't know. I came here to do the right thing. I should not be allowed to continue. My behavior should not go unpunished. I did the worst thing a scientist can do. I shouldn't be forgiven." Will got the words out, slowly and almost in a whisper.

Jensen had finally looked up at Will and listened carefully to what Will said. His student's face was still in the shadows of the unlit room, and it was as if the words had emerged from some inanimate object. Will's long, lean body - - he seemed to be leaner than ever - - was completely still as he spoke.

"Will, I think that you are basically a decent person. You for some reason got off track, did some things that are not really consistent with your basic character. We are all weak sometimes. We come into temptation. I don't know why you did what you did, but I believe it was only a minor lapse. Your suffering has been great, I know that. I want you back as you were. You are a good scientist who strayed temporarily from the right path. I see no reason to ruin your life. The retraction letter sets the scientific record straight. On the science we are deceiving nobody. NCI will be disappointed but will accept the story. I can keep you on under the grant until the synthesis is complete. It simply requires lots of hard work from you. I'm confident we can get the synthesis right. I know you believe that, too. Pfaffadine, as I said, looks really promising for cancer therapy. We need to get lots more material. We can't rely on the natural source. Maybe some way can be found in the future to get the plant and cultivate it, but we're not there yet. Your synthesis can be completed in, what, another six weeks, maybe eight? NCI will go straight to scale-up. Will, you need to do this. Your whole professional life is at stake."

Will stood in silence. He heard Jensen's words, and at first it seemed as if the professor was forgiving him, offering him an honorable way out. But within minutes he realized that what Jensen was now asking him to do was simply to continue the lie, in some new form. Will left Jensen's office without a word.

CHAPTER 29

A week after Marco's death Tom called Gina and asked her out. It was then that she'd told him about her father's recent death and funeral. Tom said he was sorry and assumed she was probably in no mood for a movie or a night out. She agreed and suggested he call back in a couple of weeks, which he did.

The two went to dinner at a small French restaurant on Shattuck and spent the evening telling Schaefer stories and making small talk about their lives and plans for the future. Tom asked a lot of questions about Marco and Gina's mother, but Gina wasn't prepared to discuss her parents' grief. Gina did talk a little about her friends, Kay in particular, and even mentioned Will, but only briefly. At one point Gina mentioned the house on Green Street and the paintings it still held, and Tom asked if he could see it sometime.

"Sure, I need to go there soon. Maybe I'll go tomorrow. Want to come?" Tom readily accepted her invitation; he seemed unusually interested in her life. Tom walked Gina home under an umbrella to protect her from the rains sweeping at them from across the Bay.

The next morning, a Sunday, they drove to San Francisco, to Marco's house on Green Street. Gina's father had left the house and everything in it to her. Marco's attorney had suggested she had three choices. She could live there, sell it, or rent it out. The house was completely paid for, and was probably worth $80,000. The furnishings might be worth a few thousand more. Gina did not want to sell the small home where she had been raised, where her father had painted, where her mother had cooked and cleaned and listened to music and played the piano and graded school papers, where she had learned to play the violin.

She had decided she couldn't live there either; it was too far to drive to Berkeley for law school and work. She'd guessed Kay would love it, because she was now working in San Francisco, but she'd have to break the Berkeley lease. Gina had decided to rent it out, and had engaged a real estate broker to arrange for this. The broker would take a fee, but Marco's lawyer had convinced Gina that this would take a burden off her, and she'd still do well financially. The place would rent for $500 a month, at least, and she'd realize maybe 90 percent of this. This was more income than she'd get from her work at the Berkeley law firm. She also had about $6,000 from Marco's savings account. She would be in great shape financially. This is what death can bring. Thank you, God.

Gina showed Tom around the house and shared some of its history with him. They even made some food from what Marco had left behind when he'd entered the hospital six weeks earlier. It was near the end of January and the Bay Area rainy season was in full force. Tom and Gina ate in the small dining room as the cool rains lashed at the large window that faced Green Street. Here, in this place, Gina felt a need to talk, to relate the story of her father and his struggle to create and to live in his creations. At first she spoke only of Marco and not of her mother. Tom listened, quietly and with attention, entranced by the way Gina expressed herself and captured in words her feelings for her father and how he had, in his own quiet way, come to have such a profound influence on her. Gina felt, in the way Marco expressed himself in his paintings and in his attitudes, the importance of intimacy and of emotion, and the importance of distinguishing true intimacy and emotion from the kind of superficial and passing states that seemed so pervasive in the lives of so many in her generation. It was like Mozart or Van Gogh as against so much of popular culture, even the component of popular culture that was in the sixties associated with all these movements for freedom and justice and liberty for all. "We shouldn't mistake the medium for the messages, I think. The messages are important, there's so much injustice on earth and we need to overcome it. That's why I'm going into law. But there's a frivolous side to it all, I think. It's choking off real intimacy and emotion. I think you fight injustice with reason and the law, not with drugs and rock-'n-roll and sex." Gina had never before said things like this to someone, they'd been thoughts she'd kept to herself. How would Tom take them? But she went on.

"Real intimacy and emotion, the things that really enrich life, are things you have to work to find. Understanding these things, whether in music or art or in everyday life, or even some aspects of science, is not easy. It takes hard work, and maybe you need to experience tragedy in your life. And the most important, maybe, comes with real love for other persons. Or, maybe, another person." Gina had stopped eating and was just going on, half-afraid of how Tom would find all this, and at the same time feeling the need to get it out.

"Marco never said them directly, all these things, but I felt it in the air around him. He was a great man." Gina felt tears somewhere in her, but she smiled over them. She saw Marco's large smiling face, his thick moustache, his bright eyes.

Tom nodded, sat back in his chair and he smiled as he replied, "Yeah, maybe you're right. I think I agree with you mostly, but I think all these cultural changes are kind of important, too. There are so many kids in revolt against the way they were brought up, they're just not going to grow up and get jobs and buy a house in the suburbs and raise two kids and watch TV and put two cars in the garage. I think there's more to sex, drugs, and rock-'n-roll than just fun for fun's sake. Although I sometimes wonder. But, for me, like you, what's important to fight for are the real injustices. I hate this war more than anything.

I've worked on several anti-war efforts and I won't give up. It's a wicked, senseless thing."

The rains hammered at the windows behind Tom as he spoke and the room became suddenly dark in the late Sunday afternoon. The woman sitting across from him had, in her words and in the smile on her beautiful soft face, brought forth feelings in him that he had not experienced many times in his life. She was like some fresh, warm wind that suddenly appears from nowhere and brings with it the scent of new possibilities. She can't have been unnoticed by others all this time. He wondered about Will and how he possibly could have abandoned this woman. Maybe he was reading too much into this. He should not rush to conclusions too soon. Tom Silva was more cautious than most guys his age.

"Come on, let's look around some more."

They spent an hour in the upstairs room Marco had used for his studio. There was a half-completed oil on the easel, not very interesting, perhaps something started when his pain had begun to grow. Maybe a priest ... hard to tell ... a young priest ... unusual for Marco. There were another ten paintings standing around, but nothing remarkable. Gina told Tom about the Palo Alto show, and Marco's relative success there. "He made about $15,000. Got rid of all his debts and still had maybe $6,000 left. But most of his paintings are gone, the good ones. Except for the two in the living room. I'm going to take them. I love them. Everything else I'll sell. We'll empty the studio and it'll be another bedroom. Make the house easier to rent."

The two left the studio and went to the master bedroom. Gina hadn't been in it for several years. This is where her lonely father had slept since her mother's death. How many nights had he lain awake here thinking about Teresa, and suffering under his belief that he had caused her death by forcing her to have an abortion? Gina wondered now about her mother and the other man in her life. Why had she done this? It could not have been an impulsive action. Her mother was not driven by impulse, though she was a passionate woman with strong desires. But she was not frivolous, not just out for a good time. Could she have loved two men at the same time, truly loved? Gina had read some book last year by a psychologist who claimed we were all capable of loving more than one person at the same time, that we could have the same depth of feeling going out in many directions at once, if we'd just learn to get by the inhibitions our repressive cultures imposed on us. Gina didn't buy it.

They moved about the bedroom, not talking, just looking at all the small things that Marco and Teresa had accumulated. On the bedside table, Gina found a book entitled *Bread and Wine*, by some Italian writer; it was in an untranslated version, and it appeared, based on a piece of paper inserted in it as a marker, that her father had not read more than the opening chapter. Gina then noticed that the paper he'd used as a marker had handwriting on it, Marco's handwriting. Only a few lines, dated December 1, 1967

Dear Gina -

Such a wonderful Thanksgiving with you. My last, I fear. I cannot understand why this thing grows inside of me. Only God knows and He will never tell, at least while we live. He never has explained, really explained, pain and suffering. It's the main reason I doubt he exists. I'm not sure how much doubt I have. You think I am not to blame for your mother's misery and death.

I live with it everyday. It is in everything I paint. It is now inside of my body, this I believe. You cannot accept this. But you must not blame your mother. Talk to Aldo, my friend....

An unfinished letter, intended for her, but never sent. Did Marco know she would find it? Aldo, the restaurant in North Beach, the Trattoria where she and her parents had spent so much time when she was a child. A very happy place. Talk to Aldo. Yes, she would, but not tonight.

Gina and Tom drove back to Berkeley that Sunday evening. The rain had not let up and the winds were very strong. As she drove, Gina could barely see the road and other cars. All was a blur of dim lights and rain moving in all directions around them. Gina wondered what Tom was thinking and wished he would say something. Instead he sat quietly with his left hand resting on his thigh, his fingers tapping gently at it. He said nothing until she pulled into the parking lot adjacent to his apartment complex. She didn't turn off the engine, and sat waiting for him to leave. When she turned to him there was a slight look of hostility in her eyes, and Tom sensed this.

"I am sitting here, like a dumb guy, afraid to speak, afraid I'll say something stupid. Whatever 'this' is, it's something wonderful for me. I'm almost afraid to say it, because it's, like, sure to sound silly to you. Maybe it doesn't. Is there a chance I've got this right?" He knew it must have sounded awkward, but his only wish that moment was to take her into his arms and hold her to him. She didn't turn off the engine and sat looking at him as if she just expected him to say goodnight and leave.

"I need to go to my house, Tom, now. I need to do some things and get ready for work tomorrow. Kay will wonder where I am. The day was very nice. I feel like I did most of the talking today. I kept wondering all day what you were thinking, whether you thought I was some sappy romantic or just silly. I like being with you, but I need to go now."

"I'm sorry. I was just fascinated by what you said, how you talked about your life and Marco and everything ... I'm not usually so quiet. I'm not the opposite either, but, believe me, I just wanted to listen. You don't realize how rare you are."

"Tom, I ... call me later, tomorrow, okay?"

She clasped his hand and Tom started to get out. "I'll see you tomorrow. Maybe I'll come by your office and walk you home. What time ...?"

"I'm done at five o'clock. Please, come then."

"I will. I'm seeing Caruso about my Ph.D. thesis and a seminar I'm helping him teach this coming quarter. I'm really excited about it. He's so refreshing after Schaefer. I mean, Schaefer was interesting and all, and smart, but his down sides were really down, and now we know they were really evil, too. I'll see you tomorrow."

On the following Friday evening, early in February, Kay brought home a friend, Lily Valmont, who worked with her at the Chronicle. Gina was preparing dinner and begged Kay and Lily, who had said they were going out to eat, to stay and eat in. There was plenty of food, rice and beans and a big salad and some shrimp. Gina had received her first full paycheck the day before and had splurged on the costliest shrimp she could find in the city. Kay and Lily agreed, and the two women opened a couple of bottles of chardonnay and joined in on the cooking.

"Lily's from Louisiana originally. She came to do journalism at UCSF. Got a master's there. She does basic reportage and is really good at it."

Lily Valmont was a black woman, about Kay's size, with a modest-sized Afro, and the prettiest eyes Gina had ever seen. She was dressed in jeans and a heavy, colorful wool sweater. Her speaking voice was quite lovely, and carried just the lightest touch of a Louisiana accent. Kay's friend seemed completely at ease as the women talked about the food they were preparing and Kay's upcoming trip.

"Cesar Chavez has announced a hunger strike, beginning next week. The guy is amazing. I'm not sure he's another King - - his goal of unionizing farm workers isn't exactly as ambitious as King's - - but he comes from that same philosophy of non-violent resistance. He's

Catholic, strongly religious, I think. I'm down to Delano Monday morning to interview some of his people, if not him." Kay had taken up a seat at the table and left the remaining food preparation to the others. Within a few minutes they were all seated and began digging in.

"How can you be objective in a story like that?" Gina asked, her mouth full of rice. "We know how you feel about Chavez and his cause. You can't possibly say anything good about the big, corporate farm owners and be honest."

"I think I can. I need to. That's my job. That's what journalism is. Just covering the story is what's important. I took this job because I was going to be allowed to cover movements like his, and do it in-depth. The wide public exposure, that's important. Of course I need to give the owner's side, but that doesn't really lessen the impact of the union's story. I'll just keep covering social and political movements like that and try to tell the truth about them. Lily is going with me, we'll spend about 3 or 4 days."

Lily nodded, smiled, and spoke up. "Hunger strikes can be powerful. Did you ever read about Gandhi? His main weapon, in a way, was the hunger strike. It's a spiritual way of bringing attention. Chavez wants a nationwide grape boycott and I'm guessing he'll get it."

Although she had read a lot about Cesar Chavez and was highly interested in his cause and methods - - he was a frequent topic of discussion at her law office - - Gina didn't contribute to the conversation. She couldn't keep her thoughts from wandering away, to Tom and the times they had spent together. She'd seen him after work every day and three times they'd gone to his apartment in the late afternoon. They'd spent several hours just sitting around talking. Perhaps her happiest moment came when he told her about his lifelong passion for music and his skill at the piano. They'd talked previously about music, but it wasn't until their last meeting that she'd learned about his musicianship - - jazz, primarily - - and he'd immodestly claimed a pretty fair talent for himself at the keyboard. She couldn't wait to hear him play and before she'd left him, they'd made a plan to go on Sunday to the music department where students had access to instruments and practice rooms. Although she enjoyed his company, she had little interest in moving their relationship beyond that of friendship. She wasn't sure what was in Tom's mind.

"So maybe you'll do a story on Preston Schaefer and his cult." said Lily. "There's another movement worth reporting, right? An expose?" Kay must have told Lily about the Schaefer matter.

"You know, if you forget about all the crazy human sacrifice shit, and just think of his theory, about science and power and all that, it doesn't take much effort to see how completely preposterous it is. Schaefer has this following and people talk about his insights and his brilliant writings. I say it's bullshit. He's got one little germ of truth - - the stuff about the power structure and how it holds on by appeasing the masses, deluding them into thinking they've got power - - but all that other stuff about scientific ways of knowing and how other ways are just as legitimate but don't provide the means to evil forms of power, and about the need to recreate the pre-scientific world ... it's pure nonsense. It's like the jerk has no conception of human history. The germ of truth he's got came from Marx and everything else is mystical bullshit. The so-called pre-scientific world was mostly fear and famine and disease and murder and mayhem, with a little spiritual beauty thrown in, like the so-called Third World is nowadays. Shit. I always thought he was interesting in an amusing sort of way. But this cult he tried to build ...I guess you can get some people to believe anything. And the more extreme and crazy the idea, the easier it is to get sick minds to do anything to further it. Like that crazy Weiss guy, who I guess is a coward of sorts who couldn't follow through - - thank God for that."

Kay held the undivided attention of her two friends. Gina had reached conclusions about Schaefer very much like Kay's, and she was pleased to hear Kay affirm them.

Gina had told Kay the story Tom had related about Schaefer and David, and about Tom's guess regarding David's fate. Kay had no idea at first what could be done about it, but eventually decided she should at least report the story to the U.S. State Department, which she did through a consular's office in San Francisco. The bureaucrats there dutifully recorded what she told them and, a couple of days later, called to tell her they had had no reports of an American found to be fighting alongside the insurgents in Guatemala. "We'll keep our ear to the ground on this, Miss Hooper," was what she was told. Bullshit was what she thought.

During cleanup, Kay turned on the radio and the three were immediately drawn to a newscaster's announcement that the North Vietnamese had launched a massive and unexpected invasion of the South. It had begun on Tet, the Vietnamese New Year's, and it appeared that the invasion could be a serious threat to the South and to American forces.

"God, maybe it's the beginning of the end. You think?" Lily asked, of no one in particular.

"One can hope," answered Kay. "Course, our Washington war machine will probably think it's necessary to dig in our heels and we'll end up with a lot more dead boys who will die not knowing why they were sacrificed. Let's pray this gives more fuel to the anti-war effort. Tet. New Year's. I wonder if the timing is historically symbolic or something? Maybe this'll give some push to the Dump Johnson campaign. You know, Gina, Lily's younger brother is there, missing."

"That's right," said Lily quietly. "Missing in Action. Vincent. My big little brother. 24 years old. M-I-A."

The three talked late into the night about the war and pledged to get more involved in the anti-war movement. Gina had strong convictions about the evils of the war and had participated in a few marches and rallies, but always somewhat passively. It was time, she thought, to act and Tom's fervent anti-war views would no doubt provide incentive. Her life had been sheltered in many ways, but she had had a rich inner life, both intellectually and emotionally. The joys and sorrows she'd experienced, the time she had devoted to learning and to her music, the closeness of her family life, had been immensely meaningful and fulfilling, but mostly inwardly. But, somehow the traumas of the past year - - the loss of Will, of Chris, of her father, even David and all the strange stories that surrounded these losses and the even stranger story about her mother - - had somehow brought strength to the woman around and within whom they swirled. She was feeling more and more ready to plunge headfirst into the whirlwind that American society was becoming, or had become. The whirlwind would not be stilled until justice was everywhere evident, and she and women like her were the new force that would make it happen. Some more wine! The women toasted to peace, justice, and love.

CHAPTER 30

Will was out running at dawn on Saturday morning. He ran through the cool winds of the Berkeley hills, first down Piedmont Avenue and up to Canyon Road, back across the whole campus and then like a bullet downhill all the way to the interstate, about five miles. He then turned around and made the long slow climb back toward his apartment. The whole thing took about 90 minutes and he finished up at Copp's where he bought two bagels slathered with cream cheese and a giant coffee. Because he was a walking dish rag soaked through with sweat, he ordered out and consumed his food sitting on a street bench that faced the sun. He had been occupied with two streams of thought during the run: resentment for Alden Jensen and the hold he had on his student, and the incredible success that student was having with his experimental work. During the near month since he'd surrendered to Jensen and took up the pfaffadine synthesis from step 3 - - where he'd been when he'd last made up his mind to quit and then backtracked under Jensen's new proposal, or rather his directive - - Will had worked exceedingly hard and almost nonstop; on some days he'd be at the lab at 7:00 am and wouldn't leave until 9 or 10 at night. He'd taken the synthesis from step three to step ten. Every step had proceeded exactly as Will had described it in his notebooks from 1966 and early 1967.

Exactly reproducible, in some cases with even better yields. His experimental skills now operated superbly. Every manipulation of his experimental tools seemed perfect. He felt at times as if no one could match his techniques in the laboratory, and he may have been right. He never faltered, he worked with supreme confidence and with intense concentration. He was sometimes amazed at how he so easily managed four or five complex tasks simultaneously and with perfect coordination. He did it all with a certain amount of grace. Grace under fire, whose phrase was that?

No one witnessed most of this. Since Bill Kane had graduated Will had had no lab mate. A few of the new grad students, the crop from last September, popped in on occasion, but Will showed little interest in them, and most never returned. But if a film had been made of his performance, the community of Will's peers viewing it would have been mightily impressed.

He was now at step ten, and had about 75 grams of the compound that, under mild acid treatment, should lose a hydroxyl group and a hydrogen atom to form pre-pfaff. He would take on that reaction later on Saturday. He'd run it on a small scale first to be sure there were no hitches, and then go back and convert maybe 50 grams to pre-pfaff. According to his notes from more than a year ago, this reaction should go smoothly with greater than 90% yield. By the end of the weekend he expected to have more than 40 grams of pre-pfaff. He thought he might take Monday off, maybe read some more Melville, and then get to the last, problematic step. He'd go at it systematically, using no more than one gram of pre-pfaff at a time, and varying the reaction conditions until pfaffadine showed up. He was not to be taken down by this white whale of a compound, the one that had wounded him a year ago. Not Will Getz, not hungry, determined Will Getz who had swallowed Alden Jensen's venomous scheme and been thereby liberated from his guilt. Science required good skills and intelligence, that's all, and Will Getz had those in spades. Nothing else mattered. Preston Schaefer's characterization of science as only about technique was right on target. Technique in the service of power. Ahab, the great whaler, such superb technique.

Jensen had followed through with his letter to the journal, *Drug Chemistry,* retracting the synthesis, and noting that strenuous efforts were being made to identify the recently identified problem. The letter ended with a confident statement about being able to reproduce the initial result in the future. The letter went in with Jensen and Will as signatories. No mention, of course, of the fact that Will had failed several times to reproduce his results and had perpetrated a fraud until he caved in and revealed it to the good professor, who then covered all that up. For his own benefit, not Will's, though Will would nevertheless benefit from the professor's fears about losing status, grants, contracts, and consulting fees.

Jensen had also written to NCI and had sent the letter in mid-January. The NCI letter had explained that when Jensen returned from his trip to Bethesda, his wonderful student had informed him that he had *just* discovered that he could not reproduce the last step of the pfaffadine synthesis. His wonderful student had successfully reproduced the synthesis, earlier in the year, but in two recent tries had failed to do so. His wonderful student had immediately reported the problem, and the good professor, after carefully checking the wonderful student's work and notebooks, had regretfully concluded that the wonderful student was indeed correct, and the honorable professor was now regretfully but dutifully informing the federal government. The letter also expressed confidence that this was only a temporary glitch, and that the wonderful student and his good professor would be working night and day to identify the source of that glitch. Regretfully but Sincerely, Alden P. Jensen, Professor of Chemistry, University of California, Berkeley.

Jensen had spent a couple of hours on the phone with Virgil Goode, going over the situation in detail. Will had sat by listening to Jensen smoothly and calmly explaining the situation and giving assurances. The NCI scientist seemed to accept the story; he was disturbed but there was no evidence he suspected fraud. These things happen and the only recourse was to dig in and solve the problem. With the right technique, all problems can be solved. Jensen appeared in Will's lab almost every day at about 5 p.m. to check on progress. Otherwise he wasn't around. Full professors don't mess around in the laboratory. They just guide the student and go on to more important activities. The fucker has turned me into a freaking Techno-Machine, a robot, perfect for the modern laboratory, and I turn out to be a Master. These last thoughts had possessed Will as he was completing his run.

After downing his coffee, Will sat awhile in the sun and then began walking up Dwight Way in the direction of his apartment. After three blocks he came to Piedmont, where he paused, then moved onto Piedmont and walked two blocks. He looked up into the second floor of the apartment house, into the apartment where he'd lived for part of last year. He paused a few moments, looked to his right and to his left, crossed the street, and entered the building. He pushed the buzzer for 202.

Elaine opened the door and stood, speechless, as Will asked if he could come in. Elaine, dressed in a heavy robe, ran her hands through her just-slept-in hair, yawned, and waved Will in. "What the hell do you want? Jesus, you smell. Running, huh? Cute legs. You need some new sneakers. Same old shorts. Have you washed them since you left here? You look skinny. I'm brewing some coffee. Have a seat. You know where the cups are."

Will entered Elaine's apartment.

"Well, I asked you, what do you want?"

"I was out running. Passed your place. I just had the urge to see you."

"I'm just down the hall and around the corner in Chemistry. You've never come by."

"Neither have you." Will sipped his coffee.

"I've seen you at work. Still at it, huh? I heard about Jensen's letters. It's all over the Department. They don't implicate you. In fact, they make you sound like an honest, diligent guy. Do they give Nobel Prizes for honesty? So what's your scheme now? What have you and Jensen cooked up?"

"It's all his doing. I'm just his tool."

"I see. So, what happened to your attempt to restore your dignity? That's where you were when we last spoke." Elaine's robe slipped a bit, exposing her knees and some of the thigh above one of them. Will glanced down at her thigh and felt an urge to touch it.

"The fucker convinced me, we needed to clear the air, get the scientific truth out. We are confident we had the synthesis, and that we can do it again. We just didn't want the wider community and the NCI to believe everything was okay. We are solid scientific citizens."

"Jensen told me NCI was going with synthesis rather than my system. That's okay with me. My system is versatile. It has many applications. I'm talking to two big pharmaceuticals on the East coast. I think I've got some interesting offers coming, good positions, a chance to grow, and even some big bucks. You see, Mr. Getz, I may have slipped when I helped you swindle the scientific community, but all of my scientific work is completely honest. And good. That's what's important."

Will smiled at Elaine, and this caused her to look away. She reached for a pack of cigarettes, took one and lit up. She was obviously distressed, uncomfortable in Will's presence. She knew she wasn't over him. He was for some reason still immensely attractive to her. She'd gone out with and screwed one guy since Will had left, another post-doc named Brad Mitchell. He was a very good-looking man, sexy, well-built, but both times she'd been to bed with him had been far from satisfactory. Almost for the first time since she'd become sexually active she felt less than enthusiastic about the act. A weird feeling for Elaine Callahan, the sex cat, the voluptuary.

"So, the work. How is it?"

"Really good. I'm going to make pre-pfaff today and tomorrow. I'll be ready soon to get to the pre-pfaff-to-pfaff conversion and figure

OFF TELEGRAPH

out how to make it work. I've never felt so competent in the lab. It's like sex sometimes. Isn't that weird. It really gives me a wonderful satisfaction, knowing that my technique is so good. Grace under fire."

"Hemingway," remarked Elaine.

She looked squarely at Will, and felt an urge to embrace him. At the same time some deep sadness possessed her, and tears seeped from her eyes. She looked away, put out her cigarette, and wiped her eyes with a napkin. Will saw her tears and put out a hand and covered one of hers. He squeezed it and Elaine turned again to look at him, her lover, the one she wanted.

She didn't mind the sweaty flesh. She wanted him, now, in a gentle way. It was not what he wanted. He was hard quickly in her hands, and he tore the robe away from her body so that he could possess her completely and quickly and with all his power. She collapsed beneath him without resistance and let him have what he wanted. She accepted him completely, accepted the pain in his fierce movements. It was over quickly. She did not reach orgasm, but that did not matter to her. She had what she wanted, not in the way she wanted it, but that turned out not to matter. She cried as Will collapsed in his coming into her and she cried as his penis grew soft and slipped from her and she cried as she felt his warm breath on her neck and his fingers in her red hair.

He was a perfect automaton in the lab and he was equally perfect in bed. A sex machine. It is a fine feeling, being technically so skilled. Ahab.

Will Getz was in the lab every day, plugging away at the conversion of pre-pfaff to pfaff, trying to recreate what he was sure he'd observed more than a year earlier. He'd turned out almost 50 grams of highly pure pre-pfaff, a remarkable accomplishment. The 11-step pathway was, by the standards of most natural products syntheses, not an exceptionally long one, but several of the steps required very

302

tight controls on reaction conditions, and isolation and purification of the products required extraordinary experimental skills, at least if large yields were to be achieved. Will's achievement - - 50 grams of highly pure pre-pfaff - - was truly impressive. He had completed that work by early February. He'd taken a day off, and then plunged into work on the synthesis of pfaffadine.

He planned to experiment with one-gram quantities of pre-pfaff. Those amounts were sufficient to determine whether he could successfully convert the compound to pfaffadine. He began by setting up reaction conditions exactly as he had recorded them in his notebook on January 5, 1967. Reaction solvent, time, temperature, amounts and rates of addition of the reagent that should cause the conversion, all exactly as he had recorded them the time he thought he'd achieved the synthesis. Of course, his three subsequent failed attempts, the ones that had resulted in the consumption of all his available pre-pfaff, had also involved these same conditions. But, it was a reasonable place to begin his new attempts.

At the completion of the reaction, which he'd allowed to continue for one hour after he had completed addition of the reagent, boron trifluoride, to a solution of pre-pfaff in an ether-like solvent, Will began work-up. Following the procedure he'd recorded a year earlier, he stopped the reaction, evaporated the solvent under a vacuum, and then began the work to isolate pfaffadine, if indeed it had formed, from the yellowish solid left in the reaction flask. He set up a chromatography column, dissolved the yellowish residue in a small amount of solvent, and passed it through the column. Chromatography was a technique based on the differential physical adsorption of chemical compounds to a chemically inert material, usually alumina or silica. Chemists and biochemists used this technique frequently for isolation and purification of chemicals from mixtures. The reaction product, the yellow residue, contained not only pfaffadine - - assuming that it had actually formed during the reaction - - but some leftover, unreacted pre-pfaff and probably small amounts of other, undesired reaction products. Complex molecules like pre-pfaff contained many groupings of atoms, so-called functional groups, that could undergo chemical changes, and thereby produce different products. Alden Jensen had shown, through years of research with other compounds, that the reagent boron trifluoride, BF_3, was very efficient in causing the change in a specific functional group in pre-pfaff that would cause it to convert to pfaffadine. Of course, the change in the functional group was not always assured - - other factors could influence the change - - and attempts to cause the change in previously untested molecules containing that same functional group did not always work. That was not a problem with Jensen's BF_3 procedure; it just meant that you might not get the same result with every chemical molecule that contained the particular functional group that, in some molecules, was changed by BF_3. The reaction caused by BF_3 addition to certain molecules containing the functional group could not be guaranteed to occur in every molecule containing that functional group. Other factors, often having to do with atoms and groupings of atoms in the molecule that were neighbors of the functional group of interest, could alter the course of BF_3 treatment, and sometimes completely prevent its influence. So, at the end of the reaction time, Will could not be sure that pfaffadine was actually present in the yellowish mixture.

Will had used the particular chromatography system he had previously used to purify small amounts of pfaffadine that had been isolated from the plant. Jensen had received small amounts of "dirty" pfaffadine from his colleague, Joel Atkinson at UCLA, who had first isolated the compound from the plant, and who had then determined its chemical structure. Will had had success with the purification procedure, and had later used it to purify the product Elaine had given him, and that he had passed off as the product of his chemical synthesis. Elaine's isolation and purification system was designed to deal with exceedingly complex extracts from plant products, and was both conceptually and in matters of scale and mechanization, completely different from Will's simple, but completely effective chromatographic procedure. Because Will had had success in purifying pfaffadine using his column, the problem was probably not in it - - it was more likely in the reaction conditions themselves.

Will's first attempt, using one gram of pre-pfaff, again resulted in failure: he could find no pfaffadine in the fraction off the chromatography column that he was sure should have contained it. In fact that fraction contained nothing at all. The yellowish residue consisted of some unreacted pre-pfaff, and several other compounds of unknown chemical structure. If he could identify the structures of these other products, he might have a clue about what was going on in the reaction. Was BF_3 under the reaction conditions preferentially acting on some other functional group in pre-pfaff? Was it somehow causing one functional group in pre-pfaff to react with a second one? Was one of these other products some kind of intermediate chemical that would, if enough time were allowed, eventually convert to pfaffadine? Was the solvent influencing the course of the reaction in undesired ways? Was pfaffadine actually forming and then breaking down during the reaction? All of these were real possibilities, and identifying the chemical structure of the reaction products that were actually present might lead him to the correct explanation, which he could then deal with and overcome. But identifying these structures would be very difficult and time-consuming work. It was better to go back and rerun the reaction, varying one reaction condition at a time, until he got it right, the trial and error approach. Of course it was still possible he would never be able to produce pfaffadine in this way.

And so Will plunged ahead, day after day, night after night, experimenting with the reaction conditions, trying every variation he could think of. Each try, including the chromatography, took three or four days; the column work was slow and tedious but it had to be done. He was in the lab early, every day, and hardly ever left before seven or eight in the evening. He'd started going to Elaine's place every night and would sleep there. He went at Elaine sexually the way he went at his work in the lab, in a kind of robotic frenzy. He was a machine working at the top of its form, smoothly and efficiently, but in overdrive. He slept little, ate little, smoked a lot, did pot frequently, and used Elaine to try to relieve the tensions that had taken control of him.

Elaine didn't like the situation, but suffered it, because she thought Will was caught in some temporary situation from which he would be relieved before too long. He was either going to be successful with the synthesis or, at some point, have to decide it was all futile. God knows what would happen then. With the letters to *Drug Chemistry* and NCI, Jensen had paved the way for Will to come out of the situation, even if he failed to synthesize pfaffadine, with his honor intact. No one would suspect he had cheated; rather, he was just the victim of some bad luck, and because he had discovered and dutifully reported the problem, he would not be held to blame - - it was just one of those unexplainable things that now and then turns up in even the best laboratories. Of course, he might not be awarded his Ph.D. It was possible Jensen might be forced to conclude that Will would have to come up with another thesis topic and spend a couple more years with that. It was hard to know what would happen if all this work failed.

So Elaine accepted Will's behavior, his moodiness, his increasing hunger for the soothing effects of marijuana and hashish, his constant desire for sex that had begun to be so mechanical. After a couple of weeks of this, she could not enjoy the sex, and simply serviced his desires. She became increasingly despondent, but was nevertheless able to keep up her own lab work. Her complex isolation - purification system for natural products was proving to be fabulously successful. She'd extended it from plants to fungi and to some fermentation products. She had enough experimental data for at least two publications, and Jensen had urged her to wrap up her work by the end of March and spend the next month or so writing. She'd opted to make a job decision in this same time period, and to leave Berkeley by the end of May. Her preference now was for a position she'd almost certainly be offered at a large pharmaceutical house in New Jersey. The pay was exceptionally good, and she'd be working in one of the premier medicinal chemistry labs in the world. Jensen had said nothing more about her foolish attempt to help Will perpetrate his fraud. In fact Jensen had become more friendly to her than he had ever been. No doubt, with his name on Elaine's papers, he saw opportunities for himself in areas where he'd not previously worked; the University's patents on her technology would also create a revenue stream for his lab. Of course, the fact that Elaine's system was almost entirely her own invention was not relevant to the question of the benefits he would receive.

Jensen was not particularly friendly to Will during all this frenzy of experimental work. He'd stop in and check on progress almost everyday, but offered no assistance, brought no ideas to Will. The wayward student would make his own way back. He was smart enough to know what to try; he just needed to work his ass off, and he'd finally nail down the synthesis.

And so the cycle of work and drugs and sex and smoking and drinking went on, nonstop. Fortunately for Elaine he worked so much she was forced to deal with him only for a couple of hours in the evenings, from the time he arrived from the lab until he'd finally drop off to sleep, usually at midnight or a little later.

Will's ability to concentrate on his experimental work was astounding. It was as if almost nothing else occupied his mind. He was totally engaged by the hundreds of experimental manipulations he had to undertake every day, and he could do no wrong. He could work on several difficult tasks simultaneously, and handle them without error. The perfect technician at work.

The only emotion that seemed to possess him during these days and nights had to do with Jensen - - the loathsome professor who hated him and whom Will now resented deeply. The professor who had forced Will to continue in his sinful ways, who used Will's weakness, his lack of power, to rescue himself. It was usually in the walks to and from the lab that these thoughts came to Will, caused knots to grind in his guts, caused him to walk with fists clenched, shoulders and back hunched. This was all Jensen's way of making Will pay for his sins, and avoiding the consequences of his own complicity.

Will ignored letters and calls from his Dad. He made some small talk with Elaine, said a few words to make her feel good, but otherwise she was simply relief for his anger and resentment. Her beautiful body still aroused him, but she could have been any woman with a beautiful body. He gave no thought to what she meant to him, what he might mean to her, or to what the future might hold for them. He gave no thought, in fact, to his own future. He was locked into the abysmal present, and moved from day-to-day like a ravenous mechanical creature and a very quiet one at that - - through all this he rarely spoke. He was on a quest and anything that detracted from that quest, except for inconsequential moments during which the tensions that quest brought could be relieved, was to be ignored.

One evening, near the end of February, Will collected the column fraction that should have contained pfaffadine. He had been through eight tries, variations on the pre-pfaff -to -pfaff conversion, and all had failed. As he was evaporating the liquid solvent from the flask in which he had collected the pfaffadine fraction, he noticed that a solid material began to appear. He had not seen this before. A white solid began to appear and as the solvent evaporated, more solid material became visible. Will stared intently at the evaporation process. He felt nothing, there was no excitement in him, but he knew something different was happening. In fact he knew that this ninth attempt must have produced pfaffadine. He would have to do the work to prove that the compound was indeed pfaffadine, but in his gut he knew. The solvent's evaporation was complete in about 15 minutes, and there in the bottom of the flask sat a colorless solid - - what the layman would call 'white' the scientist called colorless - - that was almost certainly pfaffadine.

On this ninth attempt Will had controlled reaction time. He had stopped the reaction immediately after the BF_3 addition had ended, by turning off the reaction system and plunging the reaction flask into a dry ice bath; the temperature plunged, of course, and all reactions were quenched. This approach was based on the hypothesis that pfaffadine was forming quickly under the influence of BF_3 on pre-pfaff, but that continuing the reaction time somehow caused the pfaffadine to decompose. It now looked as if the hypothesis might be correct.

If this was, in fact, the key parameter - - reaction time - - it was hard to explain Will's initial success of a year ago. Why hadn't pfaffadine decomposed that first time? Maybe he had put the reaction flask in an ice bath and just forgot that he had done so. If he'd done something like that the first time, the lowered temperature might have stopped the reaction in time to preserve at least a small amount of pfaffadine. The yield of product that first, successful time was, in fact, tiny. Nothing like tonight's yield. He'd never be able to explain that first observation, but if the powdered material he was now shaking about in the flask was pfaffadine, he was back on the path. Not the moral path; he was off that forever, he could never justify his actions. But that's not the path he was thinking about now. His only interest now was achieving the synthesis of pfaffadine. He couldn't wait to show this to Jensen, to shove it down the bastard's throat. Jensen the lab rat. Too bad he doesn't have cancer; he could be the first human test subject.

But Will had to prove he had pfaffadine. That meant subjecting it to a number of spectroscopic studies; he would measure its infrared spectrum and its nuclear magnetic resonance spectrum. Neither took more than a few milligrams of compound and, in fact, neither technique resulted in destruction or loss of the compound. He would perform a few other tests as well, but those spectra would pretty much tell the story. He first weighed the flask containing the powder - - 15.841 grams. He checked back in his notebook for the weight of the specific flask he had used to collect the pfaffadine fraction off the column - - 14.902 grams. Difference: 0.939 grams. He had started with 1.05 grams of pre-pfaff. The theoretical yield, if every molecule of pre-pfaff had converted to pfaffadine, should have been 0.97 grams. His yield was stupendously high, if the whole 0.939 grams was pfaffadine.

He did not go home that night. He did not call Elaine to tell her any of this. He just worked. First, a melting point: 279 C, right on target. He spent the next three hours getting the IR and NMR spectra. They were also right on target, identical in every way to the recorded spectra of natural pfaffadine. He would have to wait for the next day to get a mass spectrum run, he couldn't do that himself. He decided to run another couple of grams of pre-pfaff, to repeat the reaction with the same time and dry-ice treatment. He stayed the whole night, lost in his work, no other thoughts in his mind, steady, on course, he'd got it just right, he was perfection, he was a real chemist, doing better at it than anyone on earth, his skills in the lab unexcelled. His hands manipulated the flasks and columns, and solvents, and fractionation system with ease and without error.

By noon on the last day of February, 1968, Will Getz had successfully completed a second run of the synthesis of pfaffadine and had a total of 1.85 grams of highly purified compound. His 12-step synthesis was reproducible, he knew, by anyone, and was near optimum. Little work would have to be done to improve yields on the scale-up to commercial synthesis. NCI would almost certainly adopt the Getz synthesis. Jensen would no doubt brag about how he got it back on track, how he had guided his temporarily lost graduate student back to success. All the past would be forgotten. Will quickly put a label on the vial containing pfaffadine. This time the label described honestly the contents of the vial. He set it down on his lab bench and went home. This great scientist, the killer of white whales, needed some food and some pot and some womanly flesh.

CHAPTER 31

Gina asked for an extra hour for lunch on Monday and left for San Francisco at noon, sharp. She wasn't sure about what she would say to Aldo, what she would ask him. She just assumed that she'd mention Marco's unfinished letter to her, with the note urging her to talk to his old friend, and that would be enough to get him going. She parked a couple of blocks away on Columbus, and walked hastily to Aldo's Trattoria. She couldn't remember when she had first eaten there. She just thought her parents must have taken her there when she was an infant. So many meals, so many laughs and good times. She knew that Aldo really loved Marco and her mother, and that they loved him. Aldo had never married, and Gina had always felt that he treated her like his own daughter - - gifts on Christmas and her birthday, attendance at her recitals and school functions, and endless hugs and kisses. She felt bad that she'd not visited him more often once she'd started college, but when she did visit, Aldo was as warm and loving as he had been before she'd gone off.

"I am sorry I did not help more with the funeral. I was so devastated; I found it hard to do anything. I was just there, but I felt so ... dead myself ... I don't know the right word. You seemed to handle it all so well, Gina, I am sorry I have not visited. Also, please, I need to know where you live now, your phone number. You look so beautiful. I miss you ... please ... you must have some lunch."

Gina detected moistness in his eyes as he ushered her to an empty table, and went off to fetch her some food. The Trattoria was nearly full with the regular lunch-time crowd. Aldo had an incredibly loyal following and his small restaurant was, as Marco used to say, "A gold mine, a much more lucrative business than painting pictures. At least the pictures I paint!"

Aldo had plenty of help on hand, so he was able to sit with Gina and share some linguine with clam sauce. He hadn't forgotten that Gina had always been crazy about this dish. "Simple food, that's the best, no complications, just pure joy on a plate." The dish was as good as ever, and she ate ravenously.

"You seem very happy, my dear Gina. You are ... not over ... his passing, I am guessing. But you still seem happy."

"No, I am not over his passing. I think of him every day, some memory comes to me. I loved him ...I *love* him ... so much. He was so gentle, so caring. If everyone could be like him, if every man.... but I cannot understand why this happened. He was not old, the same age as you, you who are sitting there eating, looking strong and alive, all that life in your eyes ... dear, dear Aldo, my dear, dear ... friend."

"There is no way to understand. God knows but we cannot."

"I am angry at God. He allowed this horror to infect Marco's body, to kill him, for no reason. Why not me? Or you? Or that guy over there, the one who looks so mean? I am angry, but somehow, I will get beyond that. It's so terrible, that this happens just when Marco has a success with his painting. His first halfway big success. All last summer and fall, he painted like crazy, and he sold most of them. I have one, he gave me one. I see him in it, I have it hanging where I can see him, talk to him, everyday." Gina looked around the restaurant and eyed two of the earliest paintings Marco had done for Aldo. She remembered standing by, as a child, as her Dad and Aldo argued about where they should be placed, and how her mother had finally stepped in and made the decision for them. The four of them had celebrated the hangings with a big meal and Gina recalled that Marco had consumed too much wine and that Aldo had had to drive them all home. Her old Dad loved wine, but just couldn't handle too much. Just like Gina. Teresa, her mother, was somewhere in one of the paintings, Gina always felt that.

"Aldo, he told me to talk to you. Or, he wrote me a note saying I should talk to you. He didn't say about what. Something he wanted me to know. I guess about my mother."

Aldo was sipping some coffee. He paused and reached for his cigarettes, offered one to Gina, who declined, and lit one for himself. It was after one o'clock, and Gina felt she couldn't spend more than another 20 minutes. She didn't want to get back to work too much later than two o'clock. She pushed Aldo to tell her what he might know, about her mother and father and maybe about her death. Was there something Aldo knew that Marco would want her to know?

Later, on her drive back to Berkeley and throughout the remaining afternoon at work, she was preoccupied with thoughts about what Aldo told her. Her father's friend knew about Teresa's love affair; in fact, he'd known about it before Marco had. Aldo didn't hesitate to bring up this subject, because Marco had told him that Gina knew, that he had told Gina about it recently. Aldo told Gina that Teresa had come by the restaurant one day, he thought it was about a year, maybe nine months, before her death. She had confessed to Aldo that she was involved with another man, and that she wanted to leave Marco. She was scared to death that if she went through with this she would lose Gina. She was torn up about this and didn't know what to do.

Aldo was saddened by her revelation but was convinced that Teresa truly felt she was in love with the other man, whom she referred to as Terrance. She had met him more than a year before and their affair had commenced when they had an opportunity to spend a whole day together at some meeting - - Aldo wasn't sure what the meeting had been about. Teresa had described how it evolved, how she thought she'd managed to hide it from Marco, and the enormous guilt she felt about it. The human heart is such a mystery. Here was a sensible, sensitive woman, completely honest in every way, married to a good man, a loving, dedicated husband and father, and suddenly she is filled with a passion and desire for another man that completely overwhelms her, takes possession of her, and leaves her helpless to do anything about it.

Aldo had told Teresa she could not continue in this deception, that she should either end the affair or tell Marco about it and take the consequences. She'd left their first meeting without committing to take either course. Aldo had assumed she would continue in the deception and that the situation would only get worse.

Following that first meeting, Aldo saw her many times over the next six or eight months, but always in the company of Marco and Gina. Aldo couldn't tell whether she was continuing the affair but he guessed that she was. She seemed increasingly shut off from Marco, was not communicative, and Aldo had sensed a deepening inner sadness. At one point Marco had come by and expressed concern about Teresa; he thought she was depressed and he didn't know why. Only when she was with Gina did she seem her old self. Aldo did not think Marco suspected anything about another man.

The other man, Aldo came eventually to find out, was a priest, Father Terrance Flaherty, who taught at Gina's school. Teresa had confessed this to Aldo when she visited him alone for the second time, about six months after her first visit. She had been completely distraught during the visit, and managed through her sobbing to tell Aldo who her lover was and that she was carrying his baby. She had revealed that both she and the priest had tried over and over to end the affair - - they were both married to others, he his church, and both felt tremendous guilt about their infidelities. But none of this was sufficient to overcome their love for each other. She'd told Aldo that she intended to run away with the priest. She intended to leave her family and he intended to break his vows and leave the church.

When Gina heard this story she was deeply saddened. She had always believed that her parents had loved each other, and it seemed impossible that either one of them could love someone else. Another priest - - there must be some genetic thing that attracts them to the Antinori women! But no joke here. God, how could Gina not have noticed that there was something so wrong between her parents?

Father Flaherty had ended the affair soon after Teresa's second visit with Aldo by killing himself with a large overdose of some drug. He'd left a letter for Teresa explaining his intention to do this - - his sin was just impossible to live with. He could no longer bear to live in sin and he was too weak to stop it. His suffering just had to end. And so it did. The priest died and left his child growing inside of the woman he could not cease loving.

Gina remembered. She had been in 9th grade. She had not had Father Flaherty as a teacher - - he'd taught only high schoolers - - but she remembered his death. No one had been told it was a suicide, but she remembered there had been rumors about that possibility.

Aldo told Gina that Marco had come by a few days after the suicide and, for the first and only time, had been angry, very angry at him. Teresa had confessed everything, including the fact that she had confided in Aldo. Marco had accused Aldo of being disloyal for hiding all this from him. But his anger faded quickly, and it wasn't long before he'd turned it toward himself. Marco began blaming himself for what had happened. "He said that Teresa must have some need he could not fill. He loved her so much, she could do no wrong in his eyes, and any blame must be his. I told him there was no blame here, certainly nothing he should bear ...but I could not persuade him."

What Gina learned next was deeply perplexing. Marco had told her that he had forced her mother to have an illegal abortion, and that going through with it was so distressing that she couldn't live with herself, and so took her own life, in a way much more violent than the way her priest had ended his. Marco blamed himself for her death, and died - - or so Gina had thought - - with this self-inflicted wound buried inside his conscience. Aldo had a different story to tell, and was certain that his version was the truth. In fact, Aldo was startled to hear Gina tell him what Marco had, for some reason, wanted her to believe.

Aldo knew that Marco had wanted her mother to have the baby. He was not only willing to forgive her in every way, but he thought that accepting this child would help to bring her out of the deep depression she had been suffering since the priest's suicide, and also back to him. Marco's love for Teresa had been unshaken by her actions, it was that strong. The only thing that had been shaken was his confidence in his own ability as a husband and lover. Aldo remembered a painting Marco had done, a portrait of Teresa embracing a small child; he thought this might bring her back to life. Aldo had seen the portrait on a visit to Marco's studio during this time. Gina had no recollection of such a painting, and Aldo did not know what had happened to it. "It was as good a painting as he ever did. Your mother looked serenely beautiful, the way I had always seen her."

Nothing Marco did helped. Teresa wanted an abortion and found someone to do it; Marco could not stop her. Aldo believed her accident was, in fact, a suicide, but it had nothing to do with the abortion. "Teresa was seeking her lost priest," was the way Aldo had put it.

At dinner that evening, Gina told the entire story to Tom, including her own memory of her mother's death and how it had affected her at the time. "You know," Gina said, "what's puzzling is why dad would have given me one version, and then wrote that note for me to see Aldo. He must have known Aldo would have known the truth, and that he would not verify what Marco had told me. That's a mystery."

Tom put down his beer, thought a moment, and then replied, "Maybe he wanted to protect your mother. He didn't want you to know the extent to which she'd brought all this on herself - - she was, after all, the responsible one here. So blaming himself for her death was just an extension of blaming himself for her love affair."

"Yeah, I understand that. That's obvious. What isn't clear is why he wrote that note to me, telling me to see Aldo."

"He didn't send it. Remember, you just found it in the bedroom. It wasn't even finished. You don't know he ever really intended to ..."

"He must have known I'd find it."

"Maybe. I just don't know. Your father was maybe a simple man on the surface, but from all you've said about him, I think he was pretty complex. I'd have liked him, I'm sure."

"Yeah, you know you kinda look like him." Gina got up and started clearing dishes from the table.

Later they turned on the television and Tom was immediately into some western. Gina pretended to pay attention but was virtually lost in thoughts of her mother. She wondered how, as a sixteen-year old, she could have been so completely unaware of the strains in her parents' relationship and of the depths of her mother's sadness. Gina had often thought of herself as having her mother's body and soul. She was small like her mother, quiet in the same way, sensible, orderly, but also inward-looking and even spiritual. Her father had, of course some of the same emotional qualities, but he was more outgoing, friendly, welcoming of others into his life and willing to share his feelings and beliefs. Gina knew her mother had felt deeply about many things, above all her music and also her God and church. She'd also thought - - but was now not so sure - - that her mother felt equally committed to her dad and to her child. But, although her feelings were profound, her mother did not display them except on rare occasions. Now, before her was the previously inconceivable vision of her mother losing herself totally to romantic and erotic passion, willing to give up her family and quiet, sensible way of life for love, illicit love. How mysterious are the ways in which we can be so totally transformed! Or, maybe it isn't really transformation, maybe it's more like awakening. We are for some reason unaware of the powers that lie asleep within us. Why do they seem to sleep forever in some of us, and why, in others, are they shocked awake? Shocked? Is that the word?

Gina saw that Tom had fallen asleep on the sofa. She rose and turned off the TV, then decided she needed a walk. The weather was spring-like, cool but inviting. She threw on a sweater and left the house. On her silent stroll through the dark, cool streets of Berkeley she pondered once more her own awakenings, her recognition of the many powers of her mind and heart and spirit and will that, she understood now, would turn an inward-looking soul into a healing force in an outer world that was so wracked with pain and disease. She was happy, completely happy, for herself and for the mother who had more than eight years ago so suddenly vanished from her life.

CHAPTER 32

"That was a really great series you did on the Farm Workers Union, Kay. Chavez you made come to life; and it was very well written. You rarely see stuff that good in newspapers." As he said these words, Tom accepted a beer from Gina, and began to help himself to some peanuts. Gina was in the kitchen preparing more refreshments for the small crowd gathering to celebrate Kay's birthday, February 25. She was turning 30, and was the oldest of those present. She looked great. She'd cut her hair very short and appeared to have lost a little weight. Both changes did her some good and, with the riskier clothing style she'd begun experimenting with, she had created an outwardly more arresting presence than Gina or the others had ever seen. Kay was no great beauty and had often appeared physically ill-at-ease in her tall, largish body. She'd not been fat, or even overweight, but she'd not carried herself well, and so sometimes appeared to be. No more. She was also openly at ease and affectionate with Lily, at least among her small crowd of friends. No one talked about their relationship, but everyone recognized it and appeared to be accepting of it.

"So, you think Bobby Kennedy will go for it? That's the rumor. He's looking at how well McCarthy's doing. He's picking up steam. Bobby would be a better candidate. He'd have a better chance of knocking over Johnson. I'm not so sure he's as anti-war as McCarthy. But I like him." Kay came out with this as Tom, Gina, and Lily, and the two friends from the newspaper Kay had invited, Peter and Geoff, settled in for some serious snacking and drinking. Tom had brought some of his jazz albums and, although he wasn't sure anyone but Gina and he could handle it, started with some Thelonius Monk stuff, quietly in the background to be sure. Gina had not listened to much jazz in her life; she was mostly interested in the classics, but she appreciated the musicianship of the jazz greats and, because Tom loved it so much, she was becoming increasingly engaged. As Tom was in classical. Friendship leads to this sort of thing, she thought, as Thelonious struck a series of chords that, she was certain, no one in the room but Tom and she could possibly appreciate and marvel at. From her position, cross-legged on the floor she smiled across the room at Tom and caught his smile in return.

"I think he's more liberal than his brother. He really pushes the civil rights stuff. Johnson hates him and vice versa. But if he's strong on the war, and goes for the nomination, we should all be out working for him," Lily responded. "Although I'm still a little partial to McCarthy. I think McCarthy might even call on Mr. Martin L. King as his running mate. What do you think, too weird?'

Everyone laughed. "No way. Even McCarthy believes that choice would cost him about 200 million votes!"

"But, Jesus, if Johnson comes back, what then?" asked Tom.

Kay spoke up, "We'd have to see the opposition. If it's Nixon, God help us. Even Johnson'd be better. Besides, now that his warriors are leaving - - McNamara is just the first, I think - - and lots of his people think the North's going to win, he might withdraw, even before the election. If Johnson did that, just pulled out, he'd win a second term in a second."

"Maybe. But keep in mind that this country's war machine is not used to defeat, and what's he going to say? That we're no longer anti-communist? Remember all the dominoes? The great domino theory? You lose one country to the Commies, then its neighbor falls. And the next neighbor, and so on and on," Tom said forcefully. "So how would Johnson explain to everyone that his great domino theory isn't right anymore? He'd never do that. He'll want to just keep sending troops."

"I think Johnson's a tragic case," said Gina. "His civil rights legislation is remarkable stuff, and he's doing things with it politically that JFK could never do. LBJ is a master at getting his way in Congress, and these laws, these civil rights laws, are terrific. They're going to remake this country, believe me. If the guy didn't have this huge blind spot. I'd love to get into the White House and talk to him, person-to-person. I'd love that. He's a ruthless politician, but I think that he's a decent person, who really believes in his civil rights stuff. That's why I say tragic."

"So, speaking of civil rights laws, how's our budding law student?" asked Kay. "On the road to being a rich lawyer, are we?"

"Money has nothing to do with this, you know that Kay," Gina responded, somewhat defensively. "I'm taking a course, legal history. It's really good, the teacher is wonderful. Just the one course. One next summer. I hope to start full time in September."

Gina continued. "This professor, Atkins is his name, really made crystal clear the power of the ideas behind the Constitution. Those people, our Founders, the people who came up with the idea that America should be governed by some words on a piece of paper - - you know where they got this great idea? They got it from the philosophers and scientists of the Enlightenment, the minds who promoted the power of reason and objectivity. These are the people who tried to drive out superstition, and arbitrary political power and even religion. Reason and objectivity. That's what our friend Schaefer was saying is what destroyed the world. What a fool Schaefer is, what an evil fool." Gina was proud of what she'd said and of how she'd said it. She got up, got another bottle of wine from the kitchen, and returned to sit next to Tom.

"Well said."

"No, wait a minute," said Lily, her index finger raised in

protest. "So, if our Constitution is the law of the land, if it rules, then how do we have this war? How do we have the racist laws and customs of the South? How come we have so much injustice, so much that our beloved Constitution and all its wonderful Amendments prohibit? How come?"

"So, we're not perfect. We have imperfect, even some evil people who don't want to live under our laws. And we don't always know how to stop them, or ... oh, I don't know ... you know what I mean," Gina replied, angry with herself for not getting it straight, but then she went on.

"So, we'll keep trying. We can change the country if we keep trying to find ways to live by our laws. And find ways to make new laws where the existing ones don't help." Gina was now speaking authoritatively. "Like, I've been thinking about abortion. We have all these laws prohibiting it, so we've got all that going on illegally, and unsafely for the women involved. I see the consequences in some of the work our law firm does. Dreadful cases. There's no reason abortion should be illegal. That takes away a fundamental right of women. To choose whether or not to have a baby. And then to have access to safe medicine when she needs it. The anti- abortion laws were made by men who don't have babies, and they're wrong. They are UN-constitutional! That's what they are, and we need to change them. That's politics and that's the law and that's where I and lots of other women from our generation are going to be!"

Tom loved hearing Gina speaking this way, and so, apparently, did everyone else. "Gina for the Senate. How about that? Senator Antinori. That's where you're going!"

The evening went on in this spirit for another hour, when Kay's birthday cake was brought in and cut. Everyone wished her the happiest of birthdays, and no one seemed to find it odd when Lily kissed her square on the lips, as a true lover would. Kay kissed her back, and then offered a toast to all her dear, dear friends. The evening ended with the lights turned down, and everyone listening to the serene saxophone of Coleman Hawkins and his rendition, one of his dozens of different renditions, of "Body and Soul."

Later that evening Gina walked Tom home, and on the way they talked about their possible futures, not their future together, but their hopes for themselves and each other as they moved through school and on into the "real world," as if the worlds they had known up to now were somehow less than real. Their experiences until recently had been quite different. Tom had come from a large family; he had two brothers and three sisters, and had grown up in Los Alamos, New Mexico. His dad, the son of a Mexican immigrant, worked as an engineer at the large government facility there that designed and produced parts for weapons, including nuclear weapons. Los Alamos had, of course, been the home of the A-bomb. The original facilities had been constructed during World War II, and the scientists and engineers working there under J. Robert Oppenheimer had produced the bombs that ended the war in the Pacific, with such devastating consequences for the citizens of Hiroshima and Nagasaki. Los Alamos and half a dozen similar facilities around the country, the homes of what was called the Manhattan Project, were to become the homes of the modern American nuclear weapons industry.

Tom loved his father but grew to hate what he did for a living. In his high school years he'd occasionally debated his dad on the matter, but generally avoided the issue because he did not want to create friction in his otherwise very close family. Besides, his father had come from a background of near poverty, and had managed to become a professional through long years of very hard work and study.

Tom's mother, like Gina's, was a school teacher, but her students were Los Alamos first graders. She'd done all this and raised six kids. Two, including Tom, had graduated from college, two were in college now, and two were still in high school. Tom loved them all.

He'd gone to the University of New Mexico, and managed nearly straight A's. He'd also managed a music minor while graduating with honors in history. He'd become interested in archaeology and anthropology while hiking the ancient indian areas that were everywhere in his part of the world.

"I'd love to take you there. To meet my family and to hike and camp the area. There's just so much wilderness and those Anasazi ruins are spectacular. It'll make you want to go back into anthropology! Plus, those areas, the high plains and mountains of northern New Mexico, from Santa Fe north, are as beautiful as any place in America. Believe me, you'll love it!"

Gina got excited. All she knew about the area was what she'd read about the Indian cultures there in one of her anthropology classes. She'd also been completely fascinated by Willa Cather's *Death Comes for the Archbishop*, her novel based on the life of a priest who wandered the Southwest seeking to win converts to Catholicism. After years and years in an unending effort he becomes archbishop of Santa Fe. She remembered Cather's wonderful words about how the archbishop "died of having lived." Gina couldn't wait to go, so they made plans for mid- April, during school break, to drive down and spend a week.

Several times when they were together Tom had expressed to Gina how fond he had become of her, and had tried to embrace her. But Gina had resisted; she cared very much for Tom but romance was not in the cards, as far as she was concerned. Tom seemed disappointed, but okay with that. As she left Tom to return home, she had second thoughts about agreeing to the trip to New Mexico, but decided it would not be a problem, and that Tom was not the kind of guy to take advantage of that kind of situation. Her excitement about going returned.

CHAPTER 33

He had, unlike the foolish Ahab, overcome *his* white whale. He had it trapped in a small glass vial. It was a white powder, pure, free of any color, perfection itself, and Will Getz had conquered it and had it within his control. This compound that was somehow synthesized by cells in an obscure plant from Central America, that must play some role in the life of that plant, could now be synthesized by a human being. A human being with great knowledge and skill. It mattered not, not at all, that the compound might have some medicinal benefit. Will no longer cared about that; in fact, he may never have really cared. That was all an ancillary benefit. What was important was the fact that he had found a way to manipulate a series of molecules in the lab, without any assistance from the living cells of that plant, to create this unique molecule. He was now among the elite, a master craftsman.

The great beast that had tormented him for a year was now under his control. To gain that control he had - - what? - - allowed some black malignant creature into his being. Now this creature had control of him, from the inside. Wasn't all this like some old moral tale? He did not care. That was the course he had chosen for himself. He would be Doctor. Doctor of Philosophy. The temporary glitch, the retraction letter, would all be forgotten. A piece of last year would be ripped out of his life and buried forever. Hah.

Will did not want to meet with Jensen and tell him about his success. Instead he wrote a note, explaining that he had successfully converted pre-pfaff to pfaffadine two times, with identical results. He had identified the source of the problem and found a way to overcome it. He was confident that the synthesis could be reproduced, with very high yields. He still had about 39 grams of pre-pfaff. What should he do next? And maybe the letter to *Drug Chemistry* can be withdrawn - - it had not yet been published, and wasn't scheduled to appear until the April volume was out. He could also tell his comrades at NCI that the recently discovered problem had been solved, in only seven weeks! His wonderful graduate student had fixed everything. What should his wonderful graduate student do next?

Will didn't return to his lab for four days after he left Jensen his note. He'd spent the time at Elaine's place, sleeping, smoking pot and cigarettes, and occasionally reading. He took a walk or two, visited Cody's Bookstore a couple of times but bought nothing, and even tried running once. He gave up after a half mile. He couldn't think about anything at all, he just lived in a zombie-like state.

Elaine avoided him most of the time and, except for one night, he seemed to have lost his sex drive. She was thankful. She thought she must be losing it herself, a once inconceivable thing. But she wasn't ready to throw him out. Somewhere in her she believed he'd recover and that he'd see that her patience and caring had helped him. He didn't speak much with her, but he did tell her he'd got it, he'd made pfaffadine, twice, no uncertainty. Elaine understood that his success was a mixed blessing, because he had convinced himself that he deserved none of it, that he should not have been given a second chance - - or was it a third, or fourth? She knew he hated what he had done and hated himself even more for letting it continue. God knows what he feels about Jensen. She knew the defeat Will felt at Jensen's hands and thought this explained his increasing moodiness and obvious depression. Mania, too, sometimes. She let it be. She had faith he'd return, maybe forgive himself, and see that what Jensen had offered him - - a second chance - - was not just for Jensen's own benefit, but also for Will's.

Will had returned to his lab on a Saturday afternoon after he'd been out for a walk. Elaine had spent the day in the Chemistry Library, writing. She'd told him she'd be home by six and would make him a special meal. He needed to get off his steady diet of sandwiches and beer.

Will sat at his small lab desk and saw an envelope addressed to him, in Jensen's handwriting. He opened it and found a note, dated March 7, with no greeting.

> I want to see all the spectra and other evidence that you
> have produced pfaffadine. Let me know when. I am in
> all next week, except for Friday. If you have the
> compound, you will need to make immediately another
> 5 grams. The NCI needs to do some test for toxic
> effects, involving mice. If it's not too toxic they will
> gear up to get our synthesis underway at a contract lab.
> They will need complete, detailed write-ups of each
> step. Leave nothing out. You will also use up the
> remaining pre-pfaff, except maybe 5 grams, which
> should be reserved, and make as much pfaffadine as
> possible. I guess another 25 or 30 grams.

> If your work is sound I shall retract our letter and call
> NCI. But I will not do this until I have reviewed your
> data, and until you have run the 5 gram batch.

> Do not stall.

> A.J.

The bastard, the unbelievable bastard! What an asshole, what an evil asshole. 5 grams and then more! My Christ, Will thought, I'll have to scale-up the chromatography system, way up. Or run the shit a few grams at a time until it's used up. This is not a god damn commercial lab. More work. More tedious work, just repetition, the same stuff over and over. Any fool technician could do this. But of course that's what he was, a perfect fool technician, a master of the test tube. It will take another month to make all that shit.

He ate little of the big spaghetti and meatball dinner Elaine had made for him, and never explained to her why. She didn't understand, but complained only a little. After dinner she served ice cream and apple pie she'd bought at Brewster's Bakery. He nibbled at it, and thanked her for her efforts.

"So, when will you write? I hope you saved all your write-up from last year. You shouldn't have much more to do to finish the dissertation." Elaine was cheerful, but not overly so. She wasn't sure he'd take this well.

"I dunno. I guess soon. I'm sure I'll have to do some more lab work."

"Why? What's to be done?"

"I dunno, I'm just guessing. He'll want a shit load of the stuff for his NCI people."

"So, maybe that's good. They'll have enough to do some significant anti-cancer testing. You can make enough with what you have to do a lot of testing, I'm guessing. It'll take, God, months and months for them to get large-scale synthesis in place."

"I'm in no mood to slave anymore for Jensen's benefit. I hate the bastard." Will left the table, and went to bed.

He didn't return to the lab until the following Wednesday, and then took all his spectra and other data to Jensen. The mass spectrum and elemental analysis had been completed by that time, and completely confirmed his other evidence. The meeting with Jensen was straightforward, emotionless. No congratulations. Remember, you stupid cheat, you're here only because I was good enough not to throw you out on your ass. That's what Will felt from Jensen. He walked away from the meeting with the same instructions Jensen had put into his note. And he confirmed he would not retract the letter or contact NCI until Will had produced 5 grams of pfaffadine, identity confirmed in Jensen's presence. The bastard wants to see the final isolation step from the column, the purification, and wants to watch the spectra run, first hand. He knows, the fucker, the angry, ugly, lying creature who owns me. The fucker rejuvenated the black creature that's eating me up, gave it new life. I was ready to kill it. I hate the fucker more than I hate myself. Jesus, there is no end to this misery. It is a growth within me.

These thoughts occupied Will Getz everyday. He worked, not the very long hours of February, but long anyway. He took off weekends, and mostly slept and read. He ran out of his large stash of marijuana on the first day of spring, and asked Elaine to buy him some more. She resisted at first, but eventually caved in to his request. She believed there were signs of recovery in her man. He'd become more talkative and had turned from sleeping all the time to at least watching TV or listening to some music. They engaged in sex several times, but it wasn't much for either of them, nothing like their earlier days.

He hadn't risked the lab scale-up. Instead he ran the reaction and chromatographic clean- up five times, each on one gram amounts of pre-pfaff. He'd done two of them under the eyes of Jensen. The professor was satisfied, and agreed to contact the journal where the retraction letter was to be published, to tell them to pull it. Instead, in a couple of months, he was happy to report, he'd submit a full manuscript of the complete synthesis. He also called Virgil Goode at the NCI and relayed the good news. He told Will to get the write-up, the detailed description of the experimental work, completed as soon as possible. He should also continue producing more pfaffadine. "We'll talk about your thesis and Ph.D. later." That's all he'd say.

And so the dreadful, tedious labor went on, and the laborer did his duty, suffocating in his dark, satanic laboratory. He also began to write up his work in detail. He found his written material from last year, but it wasn't adequate, nor was it complete. He'd put in minimum effort back in those days when he'd truly felt guilty over his misdeeds; he'd had no will to write up his work. And so he began again, almost from square one. It would take him a month, well into April, before he'd have the experimental work written down in sufficient detail for submission to NCI. Working up the full Ph.D. thesis would take until the summer. Jensen, the detestable bastard, would probably not be willing to keep him on the payroll that long. His income now was bare bones. The bastard had Will not only a slave to the devil, but had him in financial servitude as well.

He had produced 5 grams of pfaffadine by the end of March, and Jensen had immediately shipped it to NCI. Will felt completely exhausted at this time, and quit the lab for more than a week. To hell with Jensen. Let him get pissed.

It was during this time of rest that he had for the first time in many years a dream he could remember. It did wake him, and he couldn't remember much of it, but what he could recall shocked him, to his core. An older woman, dressed in some kind of gown, silk maybe, and wearing lots of jewels. She had red hair that flowed in thick waves over one side of her face and everywhere down to her shoulders. Someone offstage called her name - - Angela. His mother's name. Was it his mother? The woman who vanished from his life when he was only 12? The woman who never returned, who left his father for some other man. Yes, another man, the boy had seen her kissing another man and had described this to his father and his father had believed and the boy was happy he had made up this lie.

He wasn't sure, he couldn't remember her face, he didn't recall her hair as so long and he'd never seen her dressed like this. She seemed to be dancing, but alone, looking around at a crowd, a crowd of indistinct faces, mostly men. Now many were calling for her. A boy, a young boy, in the crowd. He recognized his old Red Sox jacket, with the missing button right in the middle. The young boy called out the woman's name, his voice rising and rising and rising, finally above all the others. Jensen. He was there, the other man! He stepped around the boy and walked out and took the woman in his arms. They danced. He kissed her and she hungrily kissed him back. They both turned to the young boy, who had collapsed to the ground, who began to fall away, into a rapid free-fall, darkness everywhere, the woman's face large above him, and laughing. Angel. Angelarum. Angela. "Come back my son. I'm here for you now. I'm here for you. Daddy and I will help you, care for you, make you see ..." And the darkness around the falling boy was shattered by a huge lightening-like flash that became a jagged crack, brilliant as the sun, that divided the blackness. Down into the crack the boy fell, into the blinding light.... It was out of a grotesque painting by Bosch he had once seen, exactly.

And so it ended as Will struggled into wakefulness. It was his mother. The mother who ripped something out of him, and left some hole, now dark and wicked. That's what Will thought as he woke. Nothing more. He did not want to think about his mother, the woman who left that vacancy in his spirit. That's how he had always thought about her. She'd taken something out of him and...

He became occupied with thoughts of Jensen. Each day, as he sat around Elaine's apartment, or wandered about the campus, or drove aimlessly around the Bay Area, he tried to understand why the professor did not simply kill him, the student who should have been chained and whipped. Instead he just put him in a hair shirt and chained him to his lab bench. At other times he was able to put aside such thoughts. Instead, he found himself accepting the professor's generous forgiveness. He thought of his degree, of moving on to the good life, a year at NIH, helping to get pfaffadine made in large quantities, guiding the contract lab, telling them exactly how to do it. He would be a star at NIH, working on some chemical derivatives of pfaffadine, looking for slight modifications in the molecule that might make more effective drugs. He would be a true leader in the search for new therapies for the most hideous of human diseases. Dr. William Getz. How proud his father would be! His father. He hadn't written or called his father. He hadn't answered at least two letters.

He would do that. Yes, soon. He could forget his transgressions. All would be lost in the dark past. Now he felt he'd broken out into a bright future. Like in his dream.

He finally returned to the lab in early April and began to work up the conversion of nearly the entire batch of pre-pfaff that he still had. It would be long, suffocatingly tedious work, but he'd do it, he'd persevere. He'd also complete writing up his experimental work and begin the final assemblage of all the parts of his thesis. He had been too self-punishing. He was a good scientist. He would just get on with it. Jensen was okay.

One evening, a few days later, Elaine showed him a story that appeared in the San Francisco Chronicle, front page, bottom left. Most of the rest of the front page was devoted to Martin Luther King's assassination on the previous day.

UCSF PROFESSOR ABDUCTED
Scientist escapes unharmed.

Friday, April 5. A University of California, San Francisco professor of physics, Arnold Stroheim, was abducted Wednesday evening by three men who approached as he was getting into his car at the University parking lot. They forced him into the car and threatened him to follow their instructions. According to Stroheim, he was ordered to drive out of the city and across the bridge to Marin County. The abductors then ordered him to stop, and they blindfolded him and moved him to the back seat. They drove for about 2 hours, mostly north the professor thinks, to an isolated area.

"The entire way one guy was talking about how they just wanted to talk to me about science." One of the abductors did all the talking. "He wasn't very clear.

I really didn't follow him."

The article went on about how the group had taken him to a small house in the woods where they'd locked him in a bedroom. He'd spent one night there in complete ignorance of the motives of the group or of their intentions. The professor had managed to escape early the next morning. He described the three "hippies" as heavily bearded and unkempt, and as "incompetent, clearly not experienced criminals. I have no idea what this was about."

Will read the article twice. Then he put it down, and stared at Elaine. He grinned but said nothing.

CHAPTER 34

Gina had returned from her late afternoon class and was beginning preparation of dinner when she was surprised by a call from Elaine. She asked if she could visit, and Gina invited her for dinner. Gina had not seen Elaine since the infamous Peter Weiss night, and was eager to have the chance to visit with her again. She'd liked what Elaine had said to her about Will and what she had learned about herself as she witnessed his agony.

Kay had departed for Memphis on the fifth, the day after King's assassination. She intended to do an extended series on the man himself and on what might be expected of his movement now that he was gone. Her first story, about King and his wife and their personal histories, had appeared in the Chronicle on April 8. As she waited for Elaine, she read the piece and marveled at the quality of Kay's writing and at the fact that she'd learned and understood so much in such a short period of time.

Elaine showed up at about 7:30. The two caught up on things and then turned to dinner. Elaine seemed a little strung out through all this, and had little apparent interest in the homemade tacos and beer. Gina thought Elaine looked thinner, especially in her face, and really tired. Elaine had said nothing about Will and her current relationship with him. She brought up the Chronicle article.

"Did you see it, last Friday, front page?"

Gina had not. She surely would have remembered it if she had. All the news that day was about King's death. Elaine had clipped out the piece and now gave it to her to read. As she read it Elaine nervously pulled out a cigarette and lit up.

Gina looked at the paper in disbelief. "It has to be ..."

The two talked about going to the police. "Schaefer's still at large, as they say," Gina noted. "I doubt the cops are even looking for him. Could he be behind this? It seems pretty risky for him to do such a thing. So maybe it's Peter and some of the stragglers who stayed with him after the Brotherhood broke up. It has to be them."

Gina was hesitant to talk to the police about what they knew. "The police would probably think we're crazy, that the Schaefer plan was too far out to be real. Who knows?" Elaine said she'd been thinking a lot about the matter, and had convinced herself to report what she knew. She feared the Peter Weiss gang would try again, and maybe they would succeed - - somebody would get hurt, or would die. She said she was going into San Francisco soon, maybe the next day, and was planning to tell what she knew. "I hoped you would come with me. The fuzz might think one person was crazy, but two of us - - we were both there for that long weird story. Maybe Kay would come, too."

"But why would Peter do this? He told us all that night about this idea, so he knows we all know about it. So why would he go ahead now, why would he risk doing this? He's a little crazy and he's a manipulating guy, but he's cautious about his own life. He's smart and he puts Peter first. Maybe it's some other group Schaefer recruited, or some group Peter now has nothing to do with. So we send the cops to investigate him, and he's completely innocent. I despise the guy, but I don't want him hung if he's really innocent." Gina sounded so rational and even-handed about this, she almost convinced Elaine to back off. But it seemed Elaine was determined to go.

"You know, I'm with Will again." The words seemed just to erupt from nowhere. They came with no enthusiasm; just facts, plain dumb facts.

Gina was startled. So the guy was still around. She had been assuming since December, when she last saw Will, that he was gone forever from Berkeley and her life. She had put him away, locked him in a past she wanted no part of. She didn't really want to hear this.

But Elaine went on. She told the whole story, about Jensen and how he'd dealt with Will. About the chemistry professor's participation in Will's fraud, and the clever way he was wriggling out. About Will's real success with pfaffadine. About his despondency over it all and about how maybe he was coming out of it.

Gina could barely stand to hear this. She knew now how extraordinarily weak and empty her former lover was, but she did not want to think about it. She wanted it all locked away in her past. She could not understand how Elaine, a strong, independent woman, could put up with him.

"I feel, as you know, partially responsible for his predicament. I'm there trying everyday to think of how to help him now. I feel helpless but I keep hanging on." Gina detected a hint of moisture in Elaine's eyes, partially shielded by her eyeglasses. Yes, she looked exhausted.

After Elaine had gone, Gina called Tom and told him about Elaine's visit. He immediately suggested a visit to the police was mandatory, and that he would be willing to go along and add what he knew about Schaefer, based on the Guatemala trip. Gina couldn't dissuade him, and he began to convince her that she should probably do it.

"Kay will be back on the 11th; we can talk with her and then, maybe ... we're still leaving for New Mexico next Saturday, the 13th, right?"

"Yes, and I can't wait, you'll love it."

As Gina said goodnight and returned the phone to its cradle, she thought she heard an unusual noise, from outside, from the front porch. She was alone in the big house and the sound made her nervous. When it happened again, louder the second time, she decided to investigate.

Gina turned on two lamps in the living room and then walked to the front door. She paused and listened. When she heard nothing she moved aside the curtains covering the small window that was next to the door and peeked out into the darkness. Prospect Street was quiet and nothing unusual was visible. Then, someone knocked on the door and Gina, startled, hopped away from it. She wore no shoes and felt a splinter, or maybe a small piece of glass, cut into the bottom of her right foot. She swore out loud, then called out, "Who's there?"

There was no answer, only another knock; it seemed louder this time. She hopped forward on her left foot and opened the door, chain in place, just a crack. She peeked out and saw a very tall man wearing a rain coat, standing stoop-shouldered with his hands stuffed into the coat's pockets. She could not see much of his shadow-covered face, but what she saw was not familiar.

"Gina ..." he said softly. The pain in her right foot was increasing, and she was anxious to sit down and remove whatever it was she'd stepped on. "Yes ... who?" She looked up into the man's face.

He was clean-shaven and wore rimless glasses. She could see that under his raincoat he wore a necktie. A necktie! She knew nobody who wore a necktie. Maybe this guy was selling something, but that didn't explain how he knew her name.

"It's Preston ... Schaefer. No beard, new glasses. You've never seen me this way. Invite me in, won't you?" and before she had a chance to slam the door on him, which had been her immediate impulse, her former professor, this escaped murderer, barged in, slammed the door behind him, and locked it. He took off his raincoat, walked quickly into the living room, and turned off all the lights except for one small lamp that sat on the bookshelf by the fireplace.

"Something to drink, please, I need some beer or wine. Please." He spoke gently, not in the gruff way she remembered. He wore a suit, dress shirt, and tie, and looked nothing like the Schaefer she had known. He was also quite thin, he had lost a huge amount of weight. Gina hobbled to the sofa, and told him he'd find some beer in the refrigerator. She had to work on her foot. It was now hurting so much that she thought of nothing else, including whether Schaefer had come to do her harm.

He returned from the kitchen with a bottle of beer and a piece of cheese. He took a seat in the large chair opposite the sofa and began to eat and drink.

"What's the matter with your foot?"

"I stepped on something just as you knocked. It hurts." She located the offending agent, which seemed to be a piece of glass that had embedded itself into her sole. She would need something to get it out. "Please, Schaefer, I need tweezers to get this thing out. There's a pair in the medicine chest, in the bathroom right at the top of the stairs. Also, bring band-aids and some peroxide." Here she was talking with a madman and killer about how he had to help her deal with her wound. How absurd. But Schaefer put down his cheese and beer and headed for the stairs. He was back in a minute and offered to help remove the glass; Gina thought this would just increase the weirdness of the moment and so agreed to let him help. He was gentle and executed a nearly painless extraction and treatment. He then returned to his chair.

"You don't need to be afraid, Gina. I'm not here to cause problems. Believe me, I just want to talk and find out some things."

"Where have you been since ... last fall, since that day ...?" Gina now began to feel fear and a tenseness come over her; she felt a chill and wished for a blanket or sweater.

"I'd rather not say where I've been. Let's just say I've managed to hide out. You see. I've changed my appearance, I even have a respectable job. I wear a suit and tie. It's a perfect disguise."

"Why did you come here? I hate you, you killed my friend ... you bastard. We all hate you."

"Look, that's one thing I came here for. You need to hear me out, please." The new Schaefer, asking permission, of a woman, yet. "That was purely accidental. I never intended to hurt him. I had the gun, sure, but I panicked. He charged at me, I panicked, I fired off. It was purely accidental."

Gina took this in but said nothing. She had to keep calm, she had to not let the tenseness in her body control her mind. Let him speak, Schaefer had always liked to control the conversation. He was still that way, no doubt about it.

"I came back to you to say this. You, the priest's best friend. I felt I needed to say it to you directly. To say I'm sorry. I really am, I never intended him harm."

She spoke up. "So, why didn't you turn yourself in? Why don't you now? If it was accidental, you have nothing to fear. You see, I'm becoming familiar with the law. I'm going into law. That's because of what you did to me. Remember how you rejected my trip to Guatemala? That set me back months and months. Remember that? But maybe what you did was okay, in the long run maybe I'll be much better off, doing something really useful for society. So maybe I should thank you for shitting on me." She felt good when she said this, and she felt a little of her fear evaporate. Schaefer sat back in his chair, rigid, with his long arms spread over those of the chair, his knees raised high with his calves tight against the chair. He was beginning to look a little tense.

"I don't recall ... I ... didn't mean to set you back ... what ...?"

"Didn't mean to!? Like you didn't mean to kidnap Elaine, like you didn't mean to have a gun, to shoot Chris? Who else is to blame? And David, where is David? You took him to Guatemala instead of me, even though he wasn't the least bit prepared. And you left him there. You turned him in, didn't you? He's probably dead." She was feeling better all the time, but then a thought came to her that she might be provoking him, and that she had to remember he was a dangerous man. "So, what do you want from me?" she asked calmly. "So what if I accept what you say. What then?"

Schaefer shifted his body and relaxed his legs so that they spread out from the chair.

"Look, I thought about turning myself in, but I'd get massacred. The fuzz and the law would come down so hard I'd be sent up forever. Remember what I am. Remember, I am a leader of the new order of things, I'm dangerous to the state. They'd find some way to hang me. No way will I turn myself in.

"Second, I did nothing to David down there. I don't know what you heard, but if you heard I had anything to do with what happened to him, it's a lie. David was the master of his own fate. You know, he wasn't all that bright. He changed his views every week. I couldn't track him.

"Third, I'm here because I still have important work to do. I'm still writing. I've got a book in the works. I intend to publish it from exile. I have associates who can help me do this. My book will have the effect of a nuclear bomb, it will just incredibly weaken the science-based power structure and a new order of things will begin to emerge. I need to continue this work; the future depends upon it."

He paused and waited for a reaction. Gina thought it might be time to bring up the Brotherhood and its insane program, but she decided she didn't want to provoke him anymore. Now she just wanted him to leave.

He leaned forward, and for the first time his face came out of the shadow. The small lamp just a few feet off to his right faintly illuminated his face, and Gina could see how extraordinarily plain-looking this monster of a man really was. His beefiness, his long hair and mammoth beard, and his bullying style had always made him seem as extreme and fierce in his looks and manner as he was in his ideas. Now, without his beard, with his hair cut short and neatly combed, and in his new skinny body, he seemed as plain-looking and inoffensive as some accountant or high school math teacher. It was not possible that someone who looked like this could have the ideas he has and could have acted the way he did, impossible.

"And fourth, you mentioned Elaine. You said I kidnapped her. No way. She was there with me voluntarily. Completely. When things went bad, she got scared and changed her story. But I did not force her to do anything. I had the gun out to ward off Getz and that freak Weiss." He was now sitting on the edge of the chair and leaning as far forward as he could. What a geek, she thought. If Elaine could see him now she'd probably laugh. Gina decided to remain silent. It was possible Schaefer was now getting to the real reason for his visit. Gina's foot was sore, throbbing in fact. The glass must have cut deeper than she'd thought.

"You see, she was trying to get rid of that ex-boyfriend of yours, Getz. She had hooked up with him and at first thought he was an okay guy. But she saw in no time at all how *boring* he was. She needed to get away, so she came to me. We had had a thing for several months, but it had kinda died a little. She came back. She needed help."

Gina couldn't believe the fantasy world this guy must live in. Too many years into too many weird drugs.

"I'm not saying she loved me, but she did respect me, my ideas. She knew I was going to be a leader of the new order of things. She wanted to be there ..." Schaefer paused, and then stood. He started pacing nervously.

"Then that Weiss, that fucking idiot, that disloyal shit, goes and makes up this kidnapping story. I know he led Getz and the others to my cabin to "rescue" Elaine. What a conniving son- of-a-bitch. He ruined my plans, but I'm coming back. I'm coming back. I'm coming back!" He was waving his arms wildly as his voice rose in anger, and he looked like a deranged used car salesman. Gina thought she should fear

Schaefer, but she perceived him to be nothing but a poor, demented soul who should be locked up somewhere. Then, she spoke, calmly and with a tone of genuine caring.

"Schaefer, she does like you. I've gotten to know Elaine pretty well. She did something bad to me, but she now knows it was wrong and she's even apologized. She learned some things from her experience with Will. So I've put all that behind me.

"I can see how you would be attracted to her. She's said some very good things about you. She thinks you're the most interesting man she's ever known." Schaefer stopped pacing and turned to look down at Gina. He plunged his hands into his pants pockets, scowled, and then twisted his face in an odd way so that, in the dim light, it looked as if it had just cracked down the middle.

"Bullshit. No, I don't believe you." He yelled and then dropped his big body onto the sofa next to Gina. She didn't flinch.

"No, it's true Preston. Why didn't you go see her? Why did you come here?"

"I told you, I wanted to tell you about Chris, directly. I wasn't sure Elaine would welcome me. I thought she might still be in denial."

Gina got up from the sofa. Her foot hurt like hell, but she began walking around the room herself.

"I am sure she would like to see you. She mentioned you to me only last week, wondering out loud where you could possibly be."

"My God, if that's true ..." Schaefer seemed to be smiling. "Maybe ... I'll ..."

"You want me to tell her you're here?"

"Would you ... maybe that would be better than me just barging in. If she's still in denial, maybe she'll shut me out. Maybe, if you tell her first what I've told you - - about Chris, David, the new order I'm writing about and that I'll be leading, and how I still want to be with her, that I don't hold against her what she said, about the kidnapping. Call her, go ahead. She'll listen to you." Schaefer was elated and couldn't sit still.

"I'll do that, Preston. Maybe I'm wrong about you. I always admired you and I was so puzzled by what happened. Your stories make sense to me. I need to think about you again, in new ways. Maybe I can be of help to you in some way."

"Yes. Yes. I'm sure, and you can begin by calling Elaine."

"Okay ... but wait. I think this is too complicated for a phone call. I'll go to her apartment. I'll explain all this, and then I'll bring her back here. This house is safe. Kay's traveling. You can go upstairs. There's a room just beyond the bathroom, on the right. It's across the hall from my room. It's where Chris stayed. Just get yourself some more food and beer, go there, and wait for us. I bet she and I will be back here in an hour. I need to get some shoes on."

Schaefer seemed uncertain for a moment, but then rose from the sofa and followed Gina upstairs. As she opened the door to her old room, the tall, skinny used car salesman entered the former room of the man he had murdered.

In her room Gina threw on a sweatshirt and the thickest socks she owned. Her foot was still throbbing and she needed to protect her wound as much as possible. She pulled out her sneakers, put them on, and limped out of her room, down the stairs, and out of the big house. She entered the cool spring evening, took a deep breath, hobbled down the steps to the sidewalk ... and started running.

She ran as fast as she could down Prospect to Bancroft Way, and then turned east. She had to slow down at every intersection to watch for automobiles, but she kept running. Down Bancroft, as fast as she could go and not bump into pedestrians, all the way to Oxford, where she turned north and now picked up speed. She ran as if her life depended on it, to University where she took a left. After a block she slowed down to catch her breath and to get her bearings. She was certain it was on University, but how far down it she wasn't sure ...was it on the right or left? She began running again, cutting through traffic at the intersections, her heart racing.

She had not moved this fast for a long time. Each time she felt as if she'd have to stop and walk, she denied the feeling and she just kept going. She hardly noticed the pain in her foot until she spotted the place and stopped. She was completely out of breath and could feel the sweat accumulating under her shirt. Now she felt the pain. My God, it was awful. She raised her right foot and leaned against a column that was at the foot of the stairs of the building she was about to enter. In small, block print the letters appeared on the glass of the door she limped toward --Police Department, City of Berkeley.

CHAPTER 35

"It took four cops to pin him down. That's what they told me. He was screaming and yelling like the madman he is. He 'cussed me out for hours afterward, in the lock-box at the station. I just told my story, and then the cops let me go. They even thanked me. The worst part for me was my foot. It just throbbed all night. I couldn't sleep. I went to the free clinic the next morning, and they treated it. It's already much better."

"You weren't just terrified while he was there?" asked Tom. He was driving Interstate 5, south, toward Bakersfield; from there the plan was to head toward Las Vegas, across Nevada and southern Utah, and then down toward Farmington in northwest New Mexico. From that point it was just a couple of hours to Tom's parents' home in Los Alamos.

"No, for some reason he didn't frighten me. In fact, he looked pathetic, like a completely innocuous thing, the kid you always ignored in high school, geeky. You'd never believe what he looked like. Did you see the Chronicle Friday morning? They had his picture. Escaped Killer Captured -Berkeley student turns him in. They had my name; I cut it out of the paper so I can show you when we get back. They're going to do a big story on Schaefer, and want to interview me. I want to do that and tell all I know. Kay is going to do a background piece on the Brotherhood and on Schaefer's ideas and what he wanted to do. She's trying to interview some of the guys who were in it, hoping they've come to their senses."

Gina felt, in the two days since she had tricked Schaefer, as if she had discovered something new in herself, a kind of strength she had never perceived in herself, but it was accompanied by a return of the sorrow she had felt at the time of Chris' death, although it seemed, unaccountably, more profound now, as if her recognition of how utterly insipid the killer really was made Chris' death even more tragic. A life obliterated for no reason, just like her father's - - and her mother's.

"It's unbelievable, how you were able to fool him. How were you able to think of that? I would have been terrified."

"I don't know, it just came."

It took the rest of the trip for Gina to put Schaefer behind her, and her good spirits had pretty much returned when they arrived at Tom's parents' house in Los Alamos, late Monday evening. His parents, Carlos and Violette, and his two younger brothers, Anthony and Edward, greeted them quietly but joyously, and they gathered for a late evening dessert of homemade cake and ice cream. Tom's parents almost immediately reminded Gina of her own, not in the way they looked, but in their quiet manners and their slight shyness. The six talked for several hours until Carlos begged off. "Tomorrow's a work day, I'm afraid."

Gina was taken by Violette to their daughter's bedroom. Rosie was away at college, and her room was to be Gina's for the week. She crawled into the bed wearing pajamas, something she hadn't done for several months. She thought of Tom in his bedroom down the hall, and wondered how he really felt about her. He had done nothing on the trip down to suggest he was interested in more than friendship, but there were times when the way he looked at her conveyed a deeper interest. She had become certain that anything deeper was not for her.

Her thoughts turned then to Schaefer, and his menacing grin. God, he could sound so convincing. She hated him. At the same time she hated this feeling of hatred within herself. Forgiveness. She had always been taught to forgive. Could she possibly do that for Schaefer? It didn't matter, she guessed. Will. What about him? He needed forgiveness, from someone. Not her. She had nothing to forgive him for. God forgives.

The week was grand, just wonderful. The two friends roamed all over Los Alamos, and Tom showed her some of the historic buildings where some of the smartest people on earth had gathered to create the deadliest weapon ever. They drove out of the town to Bandelier National Monument, where they hiked one of the most beautiful trails Gina had ever seen down to the Rio Grande. Tom knew a dozen other trails in the mountains around Los Alamos and Santa Fe, which was just an hour's drive to the southeast. Gina had never done much hiking, though she had done some camping with Will in the Sierras. These mountains were different, somehow, and Gina found them more arresting, more dramatic. The northern New Mexico landscape was blessed with an infinite variety of colors that coated the desert floor and the cliffs that rose from it, the scents of pinyon pine and sage and other herbaceous wonders, and the largest imaginable spans of sky, in a blue that seemed miraculous. They hiked for hours each day all over this landscape, and Gina still couldn't get enough of it. She was not in great shape, would need frequent periods of rest, and in the evenings ended up soaking in hot baths to ease her sore muscles. "Okay, so I'm going to do lots more of this when we get back home," she'd tell Tom, determined to become more physically active. Tom had always been an athlete, straight through college, but had slacked off in graduate school. "Okay, so I'm with you," he promised.

Gina fell completely in love with this indescribably beautiful land and sky. She could understand how the characters in Willa Cather's novel felt spiritually enlivened by being here. To be alive in such a beautiful and soul-filling place with someone you think is alive in the same way - - there is no greater joy to be found on this earth.

Deep in the forest, off the trail and under a stand of quaking aspens, near the edge of a cliff overlooking a valley dense with pines and juniper. and birds sailing above them, in the cool, scented air, Tom reached for her and pulled her close. He pressed his lips against her cheek and held them there. Gina felt both paralyzed and excited by his gesture. She did not want a romantic bond to develop between them, but she treasured Tom's friendship and wanted it to continue. At the same time the beauty of the place and the quality of Tom's gentle touch aroused her passions, she experienced a yearning for physical contact with the flesh of a man. For perhaps the first time in her life her hunger grew purely out of a desire for pleasure. Love, romantic attachment, was, on this day not necessary, and Gina turned to Tom and embraced his strong body and kissed him and soon they became naked. Gina felt no shyness, and opened herself wholly to him, as a complete woman in search of the deepest pleasures of her body. Their bodies, sweaty from a long hike, were alive to each other, and their hands and lips caressed in hunger every particle of each other's flesh, but when they joined, Tom smoothly and quietly lying between Gina's soft thighs and sliding with no urgency into her warm spring, there beneath those leaves that shivered even without the slightest breeze, a billion of them under the sun's warmth, they seemed to be at one with the beauty that surrounded them.

The two sat later, naked and in each other's arms, on the blanket that had been their bed under these trees, and looked out together across the canyon, to the cliffs that reflected the sun's dying rays, flashing colors and light too complex to describe, but completely understood and appreciated. There might have been no other people on the planet. If there is a God, thought Gina, this is what he is.

An hour later as they dressed, Gina felt for the first time that what they had done might have been a mistake, that Tom would read it as something far beyond what she had intended. She said nothing, though, and the two made the long walk back to their car, in the late high desert afternoon, in complete silence. At the car, as they were putting away their gear, Tom spoke.

"That was completely beautiful, Gina. I will have this afternoon in my memory forever. I know you are worried, though, I can tell - - you think I'm going to make too much of it, or maybe expect that we've just taken our relationship to some new level. I know that's what I would like, but I am not going to do anything to force you there, if that's not where you want to go. I promise." Gina could say nothing, but it was clear to Tom this is what she wanted to hear. He understood the meaning of her silence.

Something like normal life returned that evening, back at Tom's home. Gina and he ate huge dinners and then almost immediately Gina succumbed to the press of sleep. She apologized for having to cut out early, but she was so tired she just could not do anything but go off to bed. She was on her way to dreamland when she heard from downstairs in the living room the sound of a piano. She pictured Tom at it, and absorbed the faint vibrations that he set off by the play of his fingers across the keyboard. Those fingers that had caressed her dark, smooth skin under the whispering aspen leaves.

Later, Tom helped his mother clean up the kitchen. When they were done, his mother removed her apron and spoke. "Tom, I have some mail for you. It came a couple of weeks ago, but I didn't send it on, because I knew you would be coming home. I held it all week, because I was worried it might spoil ..." Violette handed him the envelope, and turned away to hide the tears she expected would come. She began putting away the clean dishes.

Tom stared at the envelope that was addressed to him. Postmarked, April 12, 1968. It was from Albuquerque, the Selective Service Board. He opened it and read to himself an invitation to report for military duty in Albuquerque on Friday, May 31.

CHAPTER 36

There were more dreams of the woman who could have been his mother. The woman laughed. The man cried. The boy smiled. The boy was triumphant. Long, long days and nights, filled with the odors of solvents, reagents, the sweet, poisonous fumes of the laboratory following him everywhere, even into his dreams. He had a kind of happiness in him through those days and nights, except for the dream time. The man whose face was twisted into a silent scream, and the woman who laughed, and the boy, who could have been the dreamer, falling away, into darkness, the woman finally wrapped around him, holding him close, like a baby. The man crying far above them, as they fell away. "You stole my boy. You stole ... my only ..." with the stench of the laboratory penetrating his sleep, waking him, as the blinding light swallowed the boy and his mother.

So it went day after day, as the chemist continued to amass more and more compound, all of it pure and colorless and crystalline and authentic. No invention was required now. He just had to plug away, like a good soldier, repeating the same manipulations again and again. Near the end of April the chemist had manufactured and purified 36.78 grams of pfaffadine. He stored it all in one large vial, carefully double-sealed and labeled.

During this same period he completed writing up and typing perfect descriptions of his "Experimental Methods;" any skilled chemist could reproduce his work by following these descriptions, no variations allowed. The "Methods" would be sent to the NCI, and would also become the centerpiece of his doctoral dissertation. Except for his dream time, the chemist, the future Dr. William Getz, went through this period in relative calm. He did become more aware of the chemical stench that seemed to trail after him. At first he had thought it was just something he'd spilled onto his clothing, but its persistence throughout the month, indeed its increasing intensity, made such an explanation unlikely. Elaine, who had the nose of a chemist, didn't notice any unusual odor. He could not wash it away, and eventually concluded it must be an odd psychological reaction to some noxious substance, and that nothing could be done to expunge it. In time it would no longer be noticeable. He could do nothing but live with it and try to ignore it. In his dreams - - how many dreams had he had this last month? Maybe six or seven? - - the man who could have been his father sometimes emitted this odor, and it appeared as visible fumes around his shrinking body. The woman laughed and the boy held her hand and pulled her away from the smelly old man. Who could have been his father.

His father. Will had to call his father. He had not spoken to him since Christmas. He had a half dozen unopened letters from his father stacked away at home, or rather at Elaine's place. He had to call, or at least write. He'd completed his lab work and the typing of his "Methods" paper late on the last Friday in April. He considered delivering it all to Jensen, who he'd seen only a couple of times the whole month, but decided to wait until Monday morning. So Will locked up the vial of pfaffadine and his manuscript in his desk, and then spent another hour cleaning up the lab and organizing his desk. He read again the letter from the NCI, dated April 19, that Jensen had left on Will's desk. It congratulated Jensen on his success and requested a copy of the complete experimental methods as soon as possible. The 5 gram sample of pfaffadine that had been sent earlier in the month had been put through its initial toxicity screening in mice. The NCI toxicologists found that pfaffadine was toxic to the liver, and that a dose of 500 milligrams of the compound per kilogram of animal body weight was the minimum lethal dose. Based on the earlier screening tests for pfaffadine's potency in knocking out cancer cells, this toxicity dose did not appear to be a problem - - it was perhaps 50 times greater than the amount that looked to be therapeutically effective, at least in the NCI's experimental test systems. So far, so good. As Will closed up his lab for the weekend, he whispered to himself words of hope and optimism. On the walk across campus he recalled that Elaine had announced to him a few days earlier that she had accepted a position in a New Jersey pharmaceutical firm, and that she would leave early in June. He had not reacted one way or another to her announcement. He had no idea where he would be going after he completed his degree. She reminded him that he probably would have no trouble landing a post-doc at the NCI, where he could get in on the ground floor of cancer therapies based on pfaffadine chemistry. Bethesda was only a few hours' drive from where she'd be in New Jersey. Elaine continued to have hope in Will, and had detected some signs of improvement in his mood over the past several weeks. She did not know about his dreams, and he had mentioned the odor problem to her only once in passing.

Will wrote to his father on the weekend; he did not have the courage to call him after such a long time. He felt he had first to apologize and explain himself in writing. The letter Will wrote did not, however, explain much. He simply chose to outline the story of his troubles in the way Jensen had explained it to the NCI. And now Will could claim victory to his father; his son was on track. He would call soon, and explain his plans for the future. Upbeat.

Will mailed the letter Monday morning on his way to the lab. He arrived early, made some coffee, and sat around waiting for Jensen. The professor finally arrived about ten a.m., and Will was in his office within five minutes, asking to see him. Jensen begged off until noon. He had a class at eleven and wasn't ready. So Will sat in the lab for a couple of hours, reading a journal and trying to figure out which chemical, out of the dozens stored in bottles all over the lab, including what used to be Bill Kane's side, might have penetrated and screwed up his olfactory nerve. The stench was still there, and it was really beginning to bother him.

At noon Will explained to Jensen where he was in his work. The professor spent the whole time shuffling through papers on his desk and apparently only half-listening. Will found this irritating. "Do you want me to come back later?" he asked.

"No. Just go on."

There wasn't much to say. Will ended by asking whether he would have financial support through May. "I'm pretty sure I can get the entire dissertation written and typed in the next month. Also, I'd like your help in getting an interview arranged at the NCI with Dr. Goode."

Jensen shuffled some more papers, looked up something in a book, and then asked Will to sit down. He complied.

"Getz, your work has been good over the last few months. You have delivered, as I assumed you could. We have met our obligations to the NCI. But I must tell you ... I have given a lot of thought to ... what you did last year. It was completely unacceptable. On further thought I have decided this University could not possibly award you a doctorate. That would be wrong. I intend to inform the Department Chair today what I have now discovered - - that you faked your research last year, and intended to complete the fraud last winter. I shall inform him that you came to me with another lie this past January, when you told me you had just *then* discovered that you could not repeat the last step. I then immediately contacted the NCI, sent a retraction letter to the journal, and set you to work to find and correct the problem. At that time I never suspected fraud. You have been successful in getting the synthesis completed these last few months, but I have now discovered that you had never completed the work last year, and that you tried to fake it. Knowing now what the problem was, I realized you could never have gotten the compound before. I pressed you on this point, and you finally confessed your fraud. So I can do nothing else at this stage. I have thought long and hard about this, and I have decided I have no choice but to ask the Chairman to discharge you from the University immediately. Now, please give me your pfaffadine sample and write-up. I then want you to get out of this building, and not return."

Fear came first and it caused him to slouch away, to vanish from the professor's presence. He crept down the corridor, walking close to the wall so that no one would notice him. He'd shaved and showered that morning and had dressed in clean, well-pressed chinos and a blue polo shirt. He'd combed his hair back. He looked good, no longer the unkempt lab tool of the past four months, no longer smelly ... the stench ... where was it? Even as he entered his lab the stench did not return. Victory over the stench.

The professor was, of course, correct.

He had finally done the right thing.

He had canned the fraud.

Good for the professor.

But he was not going to have the product of Will's genius, the fine, microcrystalline white powder that Will had captured, tamed, bottled up. No. The professor could have the write-up. Okay.

Will found the bottle of compound that he had, a year ago, used as fake pfaffadine. The compound he and Bill Kane had synthesized for another purpose. He found an empty vial, and weighed out 36.8 grams. He sealed it and labeled it "Pfaffadine, synthetic, April 29, 1968." He pocketed the vial of authentic pfaffadine, to take with him. He then pulled a file full of papers from the bottom drawer of his desk. He extracted a portion of the papers, the recently completed "Experimental Methods," and he took that write-up and the vial of fake pfaffadine to Jensen's office, where he left them outside the door. With the file of the remaining papers under one arm and the vial of authentic pfaffadine in his right hand, Will walked quickly to the stairwell, and ran down the four flights of stairs and out of the

Chemistry Building.

He was scared, not angry. The campus was in full spring bloom, the scent of eucalyptus was everywhere. The bell in the Campanile tolled one o'clock, April 29, 1968, a Monday, and Will Getz no longer existed. He had been extinguished. He wanted this freedom last winter, and the professor had denied him that. The professor got what he wanted, the only thing he cared about. But Will had the product of his great search in his own pocket. Others might reproduce his work, but he would always have what his own hands had produced, what no other living soul had yet produced. Will was unique.

And frightened. His letter had gone to his dad, and there was no way to retrieve it. As soon as Jensen discovers that I gave him fake pfaff, he'll come searching for me, to get the real pfaff. This thought further frightened Will. Through Sproul Plaza and Strather Gate, he exited the campus. The great University at Berkeley was his home no more. He had to get out, right away. No, not to Boston. He ran to Elaine's place.

Will found the little book Elaine used for addresses and phone numbers. The address was there, and Will wrote it down. He knew Elaine kept some money in her drawer in her bedside table. Will took all that was there, nearly $150, and left without even locking the door.

He returned to his own apartment, packed up the few items of clothing he had, got into his car, and drove to San Francisco. He knew what he needed to do. The feelings of fear began to evaporate and the fierce black creature began to return. He was nearing Page and Ashbury when that happened. The dreams of his mother and the stench seemed to have drowned the great creature, but now he realized they had just masked it. The creature was still there, the one his former master had planted last winter. Will remembered that moment. He remembered how the creature had grown and grown as he had worked with such skill to produce and capture the whiteness that was now in a double-sealed vial, in his pocket. Maybe when the boy took his mother away from his father, maybe that was when the creature.... The professor had just discovered what was still alive in the boy, what had brought the boy to him in such a state of sin. The boy is father to the man. Did Ahab say that? Or did Will just make that up?

He parked, grabbed his suitcase, and walked the three blocks to Page and Ashbury. The number was at a door placed between two stores. He entered the door and climbed the stairs to the second floor. It must be above these stores. There was only a single door at the top, so Will knocked. Nothing. He knocked again. He might have to come back later if no one.... The door opened a crack. Although it was mid-day, it was very dark inside the room. A hand crept out and its thin fingers grasped the edge of the door.

"Yes. Who's there?"

"Is this where Peter Weiss lives? I'm a friend of his."

The door opened. It was Peter himself. His eyes widened and a smile appeared from deep within what had become a large beard. Peter's hair was now very long, its thin dirty blond strands and those of his beard falling over his shoulders and chest. He was dressed in white pajamas and gold and silver bands, several of them, ringed his skinny wrists.

"You are ... Getz. Yes? You look different. I haven't seen you much. Aren't you Getz? You live with Elaine, my very good friend Elaine. Come in. Please."

Will entered the dark room. Some music of a type he'd never heard before was playing. There were some other people in the room, but it was too dark to see them or even to count how many there might be. The room was very large, huge in fact. The whole place seemed to be this one large room. The kitchen area was in some light and as Will's eyes adjusted he began to make out the rest of the place. Mattresses were scattered about the room, maybe five or six. Now he counted four people, one woman, three men. No one moved to greet Will and no one even seemed to acknowledge his presence.

"To what do I owe this pleasure?" Peter asked as he lit a cigarette.

"I need a place ... to stay. A few days."

Peter hesitated, then asked, "Elaine, did my good friend give you the shaft? I thought ..."

"No. We aren't together anymore. It's a long story. I just can't be in Berkeley for awhile."

"So. My friend Doctor Getz - - are you a Doctor yet, are you a certified scientist? My friend is in trouble with the fuzz. You look awfully ... neat."

"No, nothing like that. It's other shit I'm going through. I'll tell you about it. I want your help with something. You and what remains of the Brotherhood. Remember, I was there the night you explained all that. You remember the night, up at Kay's ..."

"I do."

"So, can I stay?"

"It's crowded already. Do you have any money?"

"Some. I can get a job."

"You said a few days."

"Yeah. Okay. I can support myself. I just need a place to hang out, and I need to talk with you and your friends. Do they live here?"

"They?"

"The Brotherhood, remember?"

"Oh. Yes. Well, maybe."

Will tossed down his bag and the file full of papers, and asked for something to drink. He had been sweating profusely, and also needed to use the bathroom. Peter got him some water and showed him the way.

As Will used the bathroom, his host called out, "Listen, my friends. We have a visitor who needs a home for a few days. We shall welcome him here. He is an old friend. A scientist, but he seems human anyway. You shall welcome him. He is called Getz. Will Getz."

CHAPTER 37

Will would often wake up several times in the middle of the night. The large dark room was sometimes filled with people who were sleeping or sitting or wandering about, but at other times there appeared to be no one else present. More than once he awoke to the sounds of people having sex and he would try to locate where they were coming from so that he might watch. He usually lost interest in a matter of minutes and would try to return to sleep.

Sometimes he would wake because of a dream, but he usually lost his hold on it and could not recall its content and that was okay. Once or twice the woman who could have been his mother was there but what she might have been doing he could not grasp.

It was different when he tried LSD. "This wonder was discovered by a fellow chemist. Did you know that? He was a chemist, like you, my friend. It is a passage to truth, inner truth. Did you know that, my friend? These chemicals, some of them open paths within that are normally blocked. This chemical, lysergic acid diethylamide. Many contemplatives spend years in meditation trying to go where this wonder drug takes us in minutes. It was out there in the natural world, inside a fungus called ergot, waiting for someone to find it. A chemist, Hoffmann, did that. You will learn much from it, my friend."

Will rejected Peter's offer several times. He was content with pot, which was in plentiful supply in the apartment, or "monastery" as Peter preferred to call it. The entire place was rented by Peter who, it appeared, still had a steady flow of income from his wealthy parents. "I am studying. I visit with the Buddhist monks in their temple, just a few blocks away. I am contemplating a visit to Japan, to a Zen monastery." Will did not observe much "study" in the monastery, though there was a lot of quiet discussion among the strange people who came and went all day and all night. Only a couple of them bothered to introduce themselves to Will by name. Many would try to talk with him, asking why he was there, what journey he was on, but usually gave up because he was not responsive. A couple of young women approached him seductively, but he showed no interest.

It was about ten days into his stay that Will agreed to try LSD. Peter and another guy, Herman or Heinrich or something like that, talked with Will about what to expect, how to keep calm when strange things began to happen, how he had to just accept it - - it was, after all, only the awakening of what was already in him.

The first trip was not very eventful. He felt himself drifting, as if afloat on a calm sea. The sky, or whatever it was, spread above him, infinite in all directions. It was a strange color, something he had never seen before and that he could not compare with any other color. He drifted, it seemed, for days, until everything above and below him dissolved into a vast, colorless emptiness.

Will had not come to Peter simply to lose himself in this way. The experiment was interesting, and he would do it again, but at some point he had to bring up what he had come to talk about. Days passed, he lost track of time, and still he could not bring himself to talk or to do much of anything at all. He would wander the city streets, but usually not for long. Jensen would be searching for him. He had to recover the prize that Will had walked away with, the beautiful vial filled with his own wonder drug. Will kept the vial in his pocket at all times. It was immensely valuable.

Will took his second LSD journey very early on a Sunday morning, a perfect May day. He went with Peter and his friend, and a young woman whose name he did not know, to Golden Gate Park.

The four found a grove of eucalyptus, and settled in for their mutual voyage. This time the trip seemed shorter to Will. He was more aware of his surroundings during it than he had been the first time. The large trees around him seemed to pulse with life. He had never known that plants were so alive and he felt the energy, the life-force, that was in them. He lay back and swallowed the clouds, one after the other. But this was not something he liked, and he felt fear. He was being filled, the clouds were darkening and filling some giant cavity within him, the cavity was enormous. He turned his head and saw the young woman, saw through her clothing and all of a sudden there was nothing in his head but her breasts and smooth skin and her laughing eyes. Her long red hair seemed to reach out to him and he wanted to embrace her.

Several days later Will awoke feeling that he could not simply remain in this place much longer. His hideaway had become, for how many days or weeks he did not know, an excuse for laziness and lethargy. He simply drifted in and out of sleep, and occasionally into a drug- induced state. He ate little, thought about still less, hardly ever cleaned up. It seemed, although he couldn't be certain, that he had not changed his clothing since his arrival. On this morning he awoke with the strong feeling that this existence could not continue, that he had to find his way out. So he tried to plan. He returned in his mind to the reason he had sought out Peter in the first place. Yes, it was time to bring that up.

By the time Weiss showed up later that day Will had lost interest again, and had returned to his state of lassitude. He tried to read some of the books that were strewn around the monastery, but couldn't concentrate for more than a few pages.

During a walk one day in Golden Gate Park he managed to recall his last meeting with Jensen. The professor had finally, it seemed, understood what the student had tried to tell him - - that the student's sin should not go unpunished. And so the professor had finally inflicted the punishment the student deserved. But now that that was done, what should come next? The student had been expelled from the community of scientists, and this was proper. But was there nothing more? Was the student - - actually a student no more - - simply now an empty space? No, he was not. He had been filled with some venomous dark creature and the professor had, at first, allowed this creature to grow, like a cancer, inside his student. The professor should not have done this, he should have ripped out the creature the moment he first recognized it in the student. For this the professor should be punished, even though he ultimately did the right thing. But it was too late for the student, because the creature was out of control. The creature had devoured his host, the student. There was now nothing but the creature that had devoured the student. It was time.

The third LSD trip was not good. The chemical opened parts of him that allowed the black venomous creature to emerge, in all directions, and to be seen face-to-face. Face was not right, it was something unfaceable, but it was a darkness visible. Will sat calmly in the monastery and allowed the creature to writhe about. The stench returned, that was the first thing. He knew it, without question. The odor of decaying life, a compound produced when proteins are broken down by certain bacteria. Some ghoulish chemist gave it the common name putrescine. Will had once worked with the compound. The stench was wickedness itself. The woman who could have been his mother flowed out of the writhing creature, her thick dark red hair shining and long, long enough to reach her naked buttocks. The woman who could have been his mother was naked and he saw a body he knew. A body he had caressed and made love to, not his mother's, but Elaine's. He saw Elaine's perfect body, but the face and eyes and smile and hair were of the woman who could have been his mother. She reached for a bottle of perfume called *Putrescine*, and she took some and dabbed it on her neck and shoulders and breasts and on her thighs. Will sat, completely still, as the lysergic acid derivative worked these miracles. And then there was the miracle that was a small boy who became a genius. The woman molded the small boy with her perfect hands and gave him the hands that could create scientific wonders in the laboratory. Then crystals began to appear, fine, colorless micro-crystals, falling from heaven, settling around the boy genius and the boy captured them and made a large pile of them, and showed them to the woman who could have been his mother and she was proud and she wrapped her arms about the small boy and took him into her nakedness.

"The killer awoke before dawn, he put his boots on," Jim Morrison recited the verse from his song, *"he took a face from the ancient gallery, and he walked on down the hall* ..." and it all ended with his insane screaming, the Doors to another world now open. The music from this album was everywhere in the air, non-stop, day and night.

The vision finally dissolved, and there sat Will, calm and whole, but enclosed within him was a small black thing, hard and painful. A pain, sharp, like a billion needles directed at a single point. Nothing else. The stench was gone, the naked woman who could have been his mother, the writhing creature - - all now captured in this point of pain.

He could not eat after that. He drank water, lots of water. Maybe he could drown the pain. Peter noticed a change, noticed that Will was increasingly agitated in his manner, that he'd stopped eating, that he drank incessantly. He asked Will what was happening.

"I want to be the next victim. The first successful symbol," Will said, his mind all of a sudden completely clear.

"What are you talking about?"

"I know about your attempt to implement Schaefer's plan. The physics professor you kidnapped, but who got away. It was in the paper."

"I had nothing to do with that."

"That's impossible to believe, Peter. Impossible. It is exactly what you described that night at Kay's house. Exactly, except you couldn't pull it off, the guy escaped."

"It was not I. I never bought into this insane plot. I just pretended in order to please Schaefer. It was just a way to make him think he was our leader."

"Now is your chance. I want you and your friends, whoever they are, to execute ...me. Just in that way. Crucifixion." Will had come with this idea in his head. That is why he had come here in the first place. He had in mind at one time that he should get them to take Jensen, but he knew this was wrong. Will the ex-student was the real sinner.

Will told Peter the whole story. He explained in detail the huge fraud he had almost carried off, the roles of Elaine and of Jensen, and his own unending guilt. He talked with some pride of his accomplishment of the past several months, and then told of his final defeat. "The final emergence of the truth. I need to be punished, now, and I am ready to be the symbol of the evils of science that you are looking for."

Peter listened with astonishment. The smirk that was almost always on his face was not in evidence anytime during Will's long recitation of his confession. Peter denied again that he was involved in the failed kidnapping and execution, and stated firmly he could not participate in such a thing. Certainly not if the victim was Will. The physics professor had probably been taken by some of the others Schaefer had recruited and who had remained true believers.

"You are too hard on yourself, my friend. So, you screwed up. So you won't have a degree. It's a simple thing. You find something else. You are a bright guy. Besides, you would not be the kind of symbol Schaefer was talking about. His attack is on the institution of science itself, science at its best. He would probably think that what you did was a way to undermine science, and so it would be something to applaud. You would be a lousy symbol. He was looking for the best, not the worst."

This hurt Will, because he knew it was true. He began to lose his power of concentration, his train of thought, but he managed to say, "Listen, you fucking shit, you do this, or else. I need this. Or else it means I tell what I know. I go to the cops with your story. Remember, there were many of us who heard you that night. So I tell them about that, and about the kidnapping of the physics professor. They'll put the two together and come after your ass." Will put his fists against his own mid- section, where the pain was exploding, and pressed against it, hard, harder. He screamed and collapsed onto his mattress.

Will slept and did not stir from his dirty mattress for two days. When he awoke he was ravenously hungry. He found a pint of ice cream and consumed the whole thing. He drank five or six glasses of water. He packed up his few items of clothing, grabbed the file full of papers, put the vial of pfaffadine in his pocket and prepared to leave the monastery. Before he left, he looked around him, and saw that only one person, not someone he recognized, was present. He searched for and found a piece of paper. On the kitchen table there were some crayons. He took an orange one and painted in large letters: GINA - THE REFUGE. He put the note on Peter's mattress and left.

CHAPTER 38

Lily and Kay, and Tom and Gina were sitting around the living room of the big house, reading the Saturday newspaper, drinking coffee, and listening to a new album from Cream. Kay all of a sudden was totally in love with Eric Clapton, and couldn't stop playing "Sunshine of Your Love." After about the sixth repeat Gina told her she had to turn it off.

"We're going to Los Angeles, Lily and I, for the Kennedy campaign," Kay said. "We're going to his victory celebration, assuming he'll win the California primary. And I'm betting he will. It'll be a big night. This is very important. I hope all you guys are out for Kennedy. Gina's still hot for McCarthy, I'll bet," Kay said, cheerfully. Gina just smiled and, as she returned to the paper she was reading, said, "I'm still making up my mind."

Kay had published two very successful series of articles in the last several months. The first had been devoted to Cesar Chavez and the Farm Worker's efforts to unionize. The second, even more ambitious series, had focused on the probable fate of the Southern Christian Leadership Conference in the wake of King's assassination. For the last four-part series Kay had spent more than a week in the South, and interviewed everyone with a significant tie to or position in

SCLC, including King's widow.

Lily had gone with Kay to cover the Chavez story, but had other assignments that prevented her from going to the South. "Just as well," she'd said at the time. "We couldn't be seen together the way we like to be together. We'd both end up lynched, or worse." An interracial pair still provoked tension in the South, and in other parts of the country, but if it became known the pair consisted of lesbian lovers, watch out. Things were bad enough for such a pair in California, and Lily and Kay were careful not to broadcast their relationship beyond their closest circle of friends.

Kay Hooper was fast becoming a star at the Chronicle. Besides having superb writing skills, which improved with each story, she was extremely hard working and meticulous in her investigations. Everyone knew that her own political and social views were left-liberal, but when she was reporting she managed to find just the right balance. Her personal politics influenced only the stories she elected to report on. She had been lured to cover the new political and social forces that were, in the 1960s, everywhere evident, and she worked everyday to get people to take notice. Lily was also a reporter, but did mostly local news. She also assisted others, including Kay, in doing some of the necessary leg work. She was always happy to be around Kay, and admired her skill. "You're my role model," she'd say, and Kay would smile and maybe kiss her.

But not in public. They showed the deep affection they held for each other only when they were alone together, or when they were among the friends they trusted. They obviously made each other very happy. Gina knew that Kay was emotionally a new person, that she now fully accepted the truth about her sexuality, and that she would become a major force in the world of journalism. Gina was proud to know her.

Tom and Gina went for a walk around noon, but didn't get far before Tom complained of hunger and the need to get some lunch. They went into the Telegraph Avenue Grill and ordered burgers and cokes. Tom had two orders of fries. "That's good, Tom, you need some fat. You're getting too skinny," Gina scolded, in fun. Tom, however, seemed serious, and as they finished eating he broke the news he had been hiding since they had left New Mexico a month before. In that time he had appealed to his draft to the Board, and his appeal had been rejected. He was to show up for induction on the 31st of May, in Albuquerque. Next Friday. He could wait no longer to tell Gina, and so he did.

It was a bolt of lightning and it seemed to shock every nerve in her body. When she realized this was not a joke, that his words were real, that he was to be ripped away from her, she broke into tears. She did not cry out, but simply sobbed. Tom passed a table napkin to her, and held one of her hands in his as she wiped her eyes. Later, when she learned he had known this for a month, she became angry, and this brought more tears. "Why didn't you tell me right away? I thought you were…" she shuddered in anger as she spoke.

"I … thought I might have a chance on appeal. If that worked, you wouldn't have to know anything about it. I didn't want you to worry. I just got the rejection letter earlier this week."

"Worry? Why shouldn't I worry? You are a dear, dear friend, someone I care for a lot." She could not continue, and motioned to Tom that she wanted to leave the restaurant.

Telegraph Avenue was very crowded on this completely lovely, warm spring day. Gina wanted to get away from the crowd, and led the way up Bancroft, over to Canyon Road, where they reached the small park where, she knew, Will liked to rest during his long runs. She sat on the bench where her former lover, the weak, dishonest former friend, had probably sat many times. He was the type the draft boards should come after. Not this wonderful, gentle man, her friend, who was now walking slowly toward her, and taking a seat beside her. The two sat with several inches between them and did not touch each other.

Finally, after several minutes of silence, Gina asked, "What will you … when will you leave?"

"I'm not going."

She looked at Tom, puzzled, and then turned away, to wait for an explanation.

"I have a friend, from college, who was drafted, right after graduation. He left the country. He's in Canada. Vancouver, British Columbia. I called him earlier this week. He's there still; he can't come back to the U.S. or he'll be arrested for draft evasion. But he's very happy there, he likes it. He's got a decent job, and he's working on a Master's degree of some type, part time. He says I would do well there. Maybe work awhile, and apply to the doctoral program at U.B.C. I've decided to go, to Canada. I cannot accept a draft."

Gina didn't know what to make of this. They had had many talks about the war, and she knew Tom objected to it, was as passionately against it as she and her friends were. But she would not have expected him to take an action as extreme as this. She was also partially relieved by what he'd said. On the long walk up the hill she had had visions of Tom in battle, thrown into the jungles of Vietnam to be chopped to pieces, another casualty in the never-ending American nightmare. Her friend ground up like the hamburger they'd just eaten. The horror of these possibilities made her, almost at once, urge him to follow his instincts, and leave the country.

After the New Mexico trip, Tom and Gina continued to see each other, two or three times a week, but he had done nothing to promote his desire for her. For some reason she did not want to move their relationship beyond friendship; he could not be sure whether she did not want him as her lover or did not want to enter a romantic relationship with anyone. She increasingly devoted her time to study, to preparing for law school - - she'd aced the Constitutional Law course and was in the process of doing the same in her new course - - and was also spending long hours at the law office where she was employed. Gina was cutting a path for herself into the future and love affairs were, for the time being, off course.

They talked no more about Tom's decision to emigrate, and,

after a few moments of embracing, they walked hand-in-hand down the hills of Berkeley. A chilly wind had come up, and the sun, now beginning to drop in the Western skies over San Francisco, passed behind some clouds. This brought a further chill, and the two began walking quickly back to Gina's house.

They arrived at about four in the afternoon. They entered and immediately saw Elaine Callahan sitting at the table in the dining area. Kay and Lily were also there. Elaine rose to greet Gina, who introduced her to Tom. Elaine seemed to be in distress, and asked the two new arrivals to join her at the table.

Elaine started over, telling Gina and Tom that Peter had visited her with news about Will. She then backed up and related to them the story of the ordeal Will had been suffering since January. She told what she knew, and she knew most of it, about Jensen's threats and of the phony retraction letters to the NIH and to the journal: "Phony, because Jensen knew that Will had faked it a long time ago, but he pretended that he and Will had just discovered a 'problem' that they would work to solve. No hint of fraud." She told the four of them about Will's endless hours of work, from January through April. She described his moods during this time, and admitted she wasn't sure why she hung on with him. "He was living some horror, but he seemed to have it buried, he became like a machine, running on empty."

Elaine went on in detail about his great success in the lab, and about how he had solved the problem. "Will was right, in a way, all along. The first time he tried the last step in the synthesis, he did, in fact, get it to work, to a degree anyway. But he did not understand what really controlled the reaction, so he could not repeat it. He tried several more times, and couldn't get pfaff. He was out of pre-pfaff, and was so completely discouraged he could not go back and go through the long and very tedious synthesis of pre-pfaff. That was his failing. That's where some weakness in him took over and it put him in a terrible place. He has suffered ever since. It's very sad for me, but I realize it's his own doing. Will, I think, had in his heart and mind the real scientific spirit, but something in him defeated that spirit."

Elaine went on about Will's disappearance at the end of April. "He just left, not even a note." Gina recalled the pathetic note Will had left for her when he had moved in with the woman who was now speaking. "I assumed he was going back to Boston, to his dad or something. At that time I thought he was going to finish his dissertation and go on to his doctorate. He had completed everything Jensen had asked him to do. And he had made a sizable supply of synthetic pfaffadine, far more than he needed to prove his synthesis."

Elaine had not known at the time that Will disappeared that Jensen had thrown him out. After she had received a letter from Will's dad, asking her whether she knew where Will was, Elaine started to worry. She asked Jensen if he knew anything, and the professor simply waved her off.

"Just a few days ago, last Monday in fact, I heard from Jensen's secretary what had happened. In fact, the story was all over the Department. Jensen had talked to the Chairman, and his action against Will was no longer a secret. I was the last to know about it, for some reason."

Elaine told them all of Jensen's cruel act - - of how, once Will had produced what Jensen needed to restore his own standing with his sources of funding, the professor had disposed of him "like lab waste." Elaine had at first wanted to meet with the Department Chair and tell him the whole truth, the part about Jensen's role in perpetuating the fraud until he got what he needed.

"My Irish temper was at fever pitch, I was ready to tell all. But I held back, because I realized I might not be believed. The Chairman would probably find it hard to believe that Jensen, a full professor after all, with an excellent record, would do these things. Of course I also knew that this wouldn't save Will - - he still committed fraud, after all. I was just wanting to fuck over Jensen. So, I cooled it, tried to figure out how to do this and get the effect I wanted. All the while, I'm terrified about Will. I couldn't imagine where he'd gone. His father back in

Boston is dying of fear. Then, last evening, Peter Weiss shows up."

By the time Elaine had reached this point in her tale, it was nearly seven o'clock, but no one moved from the table. The weird Weiss was back in the picture, God knows what was in store. Peter had told Elaine everything. He told her about Will's arrival at his place, about his behavior during the three weeks he was there, his acid trips, and his generally sunken state of mind and body. Weiss even told her about Will's pleading with him about what he wanted the Brotherhood to do. "Jesus, he wanted to be the next victim. He wanted for us to crucify him! I told him I had nothing to do with that. He pleaded several times. I finally told him he could not be a good symbol, because he was anything but a good representative of the scientific tradition."

Finally, Elaine got to what had recently happened. "Peter told me Will left four days ago. He hasn't seen Will since, like, Tuesday morning. Then he gave me this." Elaine pulled a piece of paper out of her purse, unfolded it, and held it up for Gina to see. "What is that, Gina, do you know? The Refuge?"

Gina stared at the lettering on the note. It was done in crayon, orange crayon. She saw her name, in large letters, printed by this lost man who had once shared her life.

The Refuge. It was the name she and Will had given to that wonderful camping spot they had discovered in the Sierras, more than two years ago. They had camped there three or four times. They had made love there several times. Her first realization of how extraordinarily powerful and wonderful sex could be took place there, in a moment she could not help but remember. Yes, she knew about the Refuge.

Gina explained to her friends and to Tom. "We used to camp there. It's near a town called Dardanelle, near Yosemite. We named the camp ourselves."

"So why did he leave this note? He must have gone there," said Kay. Elaine agreed, and said, "Please. He needs help, I'm sure. That's why the note. I want to find him. Gina, do you know ... could you get us there?"

Gina hesitated, then said, "It's been a long time, but I think I could find it."

Will must have left the note because he wanted them to know where he was. What they would do when they located him they would think about on the drive out.

Later that evening Gina went to her room, stripped off her clothing, and put on a very large t-shirt. She sat on her bed with the lights out. The window shade was up, and the moon's unusually brilliant light illuminated her room and cast soft silver-blues everywhere. The painting her father had given her hung facing the window, and it seemed under that unusual light to take on new meaning. She had always thought of the painting as depicting chaos - - chaos at its center, surrounded by ever-widening concentric and more peaceful images, with complete harmony finally attained at the beautiful gold-green-white perimeter. Tonight, under the silver blue of the moon's light, light reflected from the sun and cast through her window, here in the streets of Berkeley, California, her father's creation seemed to shimmer as if in pain - - no chaos, no harmony, only pain. And the daughter sobbed and asked her God to bring peace to that poor lost boy who had been encapsulated, massively, in his own fear and pain.

CHAPTER 39

He slept on the ground with nothing between his body and the earth. Three nights like this. It was cold, but the cold and the winds did not bother him. The place was high, near the edge of a cliff, but safe, a refuge, just made for him. The winds could be fierce and cutting when he stood near the edge of the cliff, but all he had to do was turn around and walk down a little hill into a cove, a small grassy area surrounded by fir and alpine spruce. The trees were not tall at this altitude, but they were densely packed around the cove that became his refuge from the winds. Each night was brighter than the last; the moon seemed to expand and cast more light with each passing night. During the day he walked some of his old trails, but often he would crawl into some warm sheltered area and sleep. Or try to sleep. It rarely came. Sometimes the pain at his center was all that he felt.

One morning he remembered the woman. He had been here in this place with the woman. She was small and dark, oval-faced, prettier he now believed than he had thought back then. She played the violin. She had told him that, but he did not think he had ever heard her play. He did not sleep at night, not much. Some dreams came. The man who could have been his father cried and the boy laughed. The man could not love the woman, the woman with hair that flowed in all directions, ruby-red in the sun, violet under the moon. And the woman ran, laughing, away. The moonlight was so intense he could not go to sleep.

He wrapped his sweater around his eyes, but he still could not sleep. The pain seemed to be scratching and crawling around inside of him.

Beautiful friends.... of our elaborate plans ... of everything that stands....

On the fourth day he removed a small glass bottle from his pocket and set it on a flat stone. The bottle was tightly sealed and contained a pretty white powder. He read the label. He knew what it was. He could write out its molecular structure; he knew every atom and how it was bonded to every other atom. He had made all those chemical bonds come together. What a struggle. 36.78 grams. Pure, so pure.

Waiting for the summer rain ... and all the children are insane....

He thought of his lost love, the woman who had made love to him here. When he had first known the woman she had seemed frail, uncertain, timid, a little girl. He knew she had grown in her time with him, and she had captured a part of him, the clean, soft, healthy part of him, at this very place, under this very moon. She did not know about the creature that crawled around inside of him. She would come to this place, he knew she would. He had to prepare.

Desperately in need of some stranger's hand ... in a desperate land....

And so on the fourth night he opened the vial that had the label that said "Pfaffadine, synthetic." He knew, good chemist that he was, that the amount he needed, nearly everything in the vial, would not dissolve in water. So he opened one of the cans of beef stew that he had bought at the store in Dardanelle, on his way up to The Refuge. He had eaten only canned stew since he arrived, and five empty cans lay scattered in the grassy area around him.

Above him he saw a bat fluttering about in the moon's vast beam. An immense silence had settled around his refuge. He could make out in the distance the mountain that he had always desired to climb. He would have to train for that, he was not in the best of shape.

Into the can of stew, when he got it open, he emptied most of the contents of the vial. He stirred the white powder into the stew until it was no longer visible.

The end of laughter and soft lies ... the end of nights we tried to....

He was the first human being to create this substance, this pfaffadine - - he loved the name - - and he would be the first human being to be cured by it. This wonder drug, first created by God and now by this man, so potent it could kill the most evil, most deadly, living cells, cells that had gone wild and out of control, and that might be immortal were it not for this pfaffadine . Think of all the people it would save, how it could destroy the evil cells in them, like those that had killed the woman's father. He who created this substance would be the saver of multitudes. Consume the life-saving host. Now here, in this refuge, under this brilliant moon, it was time to eliminate the venomous beast that was crawling about inside of himself, and by doing so he would end his long pain.

Beautiful friend, the end....

CHAPTER 40

Although it was a fairly steep climb, Tom, Gina, and Elaine did the three-mile Motahwa Trail from Timberland Road to the camping area in under an hour. They had driven in Elaine's Mustang since dawn, and had arrived at the small town of Dardanelle by eleven on Sunday morning. There was only one road out of town that led up into the surrounding mountains, and Gina recognized the trailhead immediately when she saw it. They carried with them a couple of canteens of water and some candy, and in the coolness of the Sierras the climb was not especially difficult for all three. During the long ride from Berkeley they'd talked mostly of Will and both Gina and Elaine were relatively open about their relationships with him. Gina was sufficiently frank to create some anxiety in Tom, although she made it clear that, while she still thought he was decent at heart but terribly flawed in some tragic way, she had lost whatever emotional attachment she once might have had. At the same time, it was apparent that Elaine was still hooked on him.

"I find him very attractive in many ways, but I'm sure I could not remain with him if he continued to stay in this dismal, self-pitying state. I'd hoped he might pull out, once he finished up with Jensen and got out of here. I didn't approve of what Jensen had him doing, his hiding of what he knew was fraud, but I still thought Will might work his way back from that, especially when he had such a huge success with his synthesis. What Jensen did to him in the end was just plain dreadful. He just shit on him, pure shit. I still need to find some way to get the truth out and be believed."

Gina listened intently to everything Elaine said, and her fondness and respect for the woman grew.

The three were silent during the hike. Gina led the way, and when the trail reached a turning point at the edge of some cliffs, she recognized that they were not far from The Refuge. She stopped and looked around. She recognized a stony area just after the upcoming bend in the trail, and immediately knew that the place they were looking for would be just beyond that area, and down a small hill. She remembered the little cove-like setting amid the spruce and fir. She whispered to Tom and Elaine that the place they were searching for was just ahead. The three paused and looked around and at each other, worried looks.

It was very quiet. High noon, and not even bird songs could be heard. A pleasant wind rose from the valley below them and curled over the edge of the cliff. They moved ahead about ten yards, and stopped again.

"Will ... Will ..." called out Elaine.

The silence remained. All of a sudden Gina felt very warm, she felt the rays of the overhead sun almost scorch her head and shoulders. She removed her sweater and tied it around her waist. Elaine wished she'd worn a t-shirt under her sweater, so that she could also strip down. Instead she just suffered the heat.

Tom crept slowly ahead. Gina followed, and when she recognized the hill leading down to the cove - - The Refuge - - she grabbed him by his shirt and led him toward it.

"Look, there," said Tom. He pointed to a couple of tin cans that were lying on the ground. They both looked new, only recently opened. Gina saw the cans of beef stew and instantly remembered that Will used to bring along half-a-dozen of them during camping trips, and that he'd often eat right out of the cans, cold. She'd thought it was disgusting, and always poked fun. When she saw them now she shivered with fear.

Then she saw his feet, shoeless and bare, and his long, jean-clad legs. His torso and head were hidden behind some shrubs, but she knew they were his legs. She stared at the motionless limbs for several seconds before she spoke up.

"There ...he's there, on the ground!"

Tom and Elaine quickly turned and ran together with Gina down the small hill toward the body that was sprawled, face-down, on the ground. Will wore only a ratty-looking t-shirt. His long, unwashed hair was all that was visible above his shoulders. In unison, the three fell to their knees around his body. The sun was at its highest pitch in the cloudless sky and its heat was intense. Gina saw two flies buzzing near Will's left ear. Elaine's hands were wrapped over her mouth and cheeks, as if she were trying to muffle the piercing shriek that came as she collapsed at Will's side. He was completely motionless. Gina looked at Tom and he understood he needed to turn the body over. When he did Elaine cried out in pain and both Tom and Gina drew in deep breaths of horror.

His dirty blond beard was caked with blood. His half-open mouth was filled with clotted blood. His skin was tinged a sickly yellow. A blood-red liquid floated in his wide open eyes. He did not breathe. Will Getz was dead. His death must have been hideously painful.

How? Gina wondered and, when she finally was able to speak, she asked that question out loud. No one responded. Elaine pressed his eyelids downward, to close his eyes. Tom looked around for a blanket or something with which he might cover the body, but there was nothing anywhere visible. All he could see was a bag that must have been used for food and drink, and some open cans of beef stew, one of which lay about four feet from the body. A spoon lay on the ground next to it. Then he spotted the small glass vial. He walked over to it and picked it up. He saw the label: "Pfaffadine, synthetic. 36.78 grams.

April 29, 1968. WG" The cap was on, but there was only a small amount of the compound in the bottom of the vial. Tom showed it to Gina and Elaine.

"There's not much in there, maybe half a gram," said Elaine, as she held the vial and shook it. "There's nothing like 36 grams."

"You don't think he..." Gina said, in shock.

Elaine nodded. "That's what it looks like to me. He poisoned himself."

"But this was a medicine, I thought NIH was testing it as a drug against cancer," Gina said, as she rose from her kneeling position and stood next to Elaine.

"Sure it is. But these medicines are all toxic if there's enough. The NIH had tested it in mice. They have to be sure the toxic amount is greater than the amount they need for medicinal use. Plus, the lethal amount has to be way above that level. I know they tested it in mice. I saw a letter they wrote to Jensen. Will brought it home once. I forget what they said the lethal dose was. The letter's probably still at home somewhere."

"My God," said Tom. "He killed himself with his own creation. Is that what this looks like?"

"It does. I have no idea what the medical examiner might say. If he thinks it's a poisoning, there's no way he could ever tell it was due to pfaffadine. There's no test for it. Will had the only supply available. Except for NIH, the guys at the Cancer Institute."

The three walked around the cove looking for any other clues.

Nothing appeared.

"We need to get the police," Gina said. She untied the green sweater she had around her waist, and placed it over Will's head. The tears came as she did this. Elaine sat on a rock a short way up the hill and held her head in her hands. She was numb, as if the experience simply sapped the life from her.

"Look."

Gina looked over at Tom. He held something in his hands. She walked over to him and saw that it was a folder. Tom was pulling papers out of it. It was jammed with papers with writing on them, some typed, some handwritten. There were also graphs and spectra of various types, and pages containing calculations. Some had complex chemical structures drawn on them, and reactions showing the conversion of one compound to another. These were Will's notes and some of the pages that would comprise his Ph.D. thesis. There were several hundred pages crammed into the folder.

Tom was reading from a page that was on top of all the others. Large print on the yellow- lined paper: May 25, 1968 Sierra Nevada.

Dear Father

I want you to see what I have accomplished. I never got it all written up. At the bottom of this stack there are 42 pages of typed experimental methods. They describe exactly how to make pfaff. They are my creation. They are completely accurate and true. I did all that.

I'm sorry I could not do more for you. I'm sorry.

Love Willy

Later, Tom went to notify the police, and Elaine and Gina stayed behind with Will's body. They sat together, at one point embraced each other in sorrow, and talked about the man with whom they had both been lovers. "I did a lot of this, my selfishness, I hurt him more than I will ever understand. I'm so ... sorry ..." Elaine sobbed and took Gina's hands into her own.

Later, after several moments of silence, Elaine asked Gina about Tom, and Gina told her of his draft notice.

"He even asked me to go to Canada with him, but I can't do that," said Gina. "I do not want to leave the U.S. There's a lot to do here, I feel more strongly all the time that I'm on the right path in my life to really change things. I think women are a huge asset for this country, an untapped resource of tremendous power, and a power to do good. I'm not one of these women who thinks men are all destructive, and that they can do no good. But I do think that, on the whole, a greater role for women in society will mean less destructiveness. I want to be part of that, I see cracks opening all around us, cracks in our social structure, our culture, that will let women in. We better not ignore it.... You know, men seem sometimes as self-destructive as they are socially destructive." She looked over at the corpse of the man who should have been something great and good, and she wished he would move, come back from wherever he was.

"Yeah, you may be right, but I'm not so sure about women being such a force for good," replied Elaine. "Maybe so, but I have a hunch power corrupts, and that's true no matter what the sex."

"I guess we'll see, won't we?" Gina smiled.

It took more than three hours for Tom and the police to arrive. Tom had briefed the cops on the way up the trail. They took statements from Tom, Gina, and Elaine, and said they should stand by. The county medical examiner and his equipment would be driven in by way of a fire road that was a quarter mile away, and he would want to hear what they knew about the poison.

It was nearly eight in the evening before Tom, Gina, and Elaine were told they could leave. By the time they arrived back at the car it was near nine, and night had settled in. They decided they'd never make it back to Berkeley that night, so they took a room at a local motel. The three crawled into bed together and all fell to sleep within a few minutes.

In the morning they ate a very early breakfast and took off for Berkeley by eight. They drove in silence for a couple of hours, and then Elaine spoke.

"You know, I'm going to tell this story. I am going on Thursday to New Jersey, to look for a place to live." She had told Tom and Gina on the trip out about the position she was taking at the New Jersey pharmaceutical firm, and they had been impressed. "I think I am going to fly to Washington first, and go visit the NCI. The group there that Jensen works with, they know about me. They know about my isolation and purification system and how I used it to prepare pfaffadine from the plant. All that's in Jensen's annual report to them, it's in his grant write-up. You know, that's where almost all his funding comes from. I'm going to tell them this whole story, including the part about how Jensen hid the fraud from them and then how he treated Will. I'll also tell them about what we just saw, what happened to Will. I don't know if they'll believe me, but it might be enough to concern them. I don't know what they might do ... but I think I have to do this."

Tom and Gina both thought this would be the right thing to do, and encouraged Elaine to proceed.

"What about his dad?" asked Gina.

"I'll take the file containing his thesis with me. The police will contact him about Will, right away they said. I'll call him and try to meet him, if not on this trip, then when I go East permanently. That's only three weeks away. I'm going to fly back here after my trip to find a place to live, finish my work here, pack up, and then drive east. Maybe I can get to see his dad this trip. I'll call him before I fly."

The three drove the rest of the way back to Berkeley in silence. Elaine dropped Tom and Gina off on Monday afternoon, and then drove back to her apartment. As soon as she entered she stripped off her clothing and took a steaming hot shower. She wrapped her wet body in a robe, and seated herself at her kitchen table. She picked up the small plastic bag, one she had used to carry some candy up to The Refuge, into which she had emptied a small amount of the white substance that had remained in Will's vial. The vial and what was left of the substance had been taken by the medical examiner, but Elaine had taken just enough to allow her to determine whether it was, in fact, authentic pfaffadine. She believed Will had produced pfaff, but she wanted to be able to take the proof of authenticity with her to the NCI. It would take only a couple of hours of lab work. She also decided she'd leave a day early, on Wednesday morning, for Washington.

She dressed and prepared to go to the lab. As she gathered some papers from her desk, she noticed the letter Jensen had received a month earlier from the NCI, and that Will had brought home. The letter reported the results of animal toxicity tests on pfaffadine, run with the five gram sample Will had first synthesized, and which had been sent by Jensen to the NCI in early April. The NCI had verified that the compound was indeed pfaffadine, and congratulated Jensen on his success. They reported that the minimum lethal dose of the compound in mice was 500 milligrams of compound per one kilogram of animal body weight. These were the usual units in which doses were expressed.

Elaine did a quick calculation in her head. 500 milligrams was half a gram. Will weighed maybe 150 or 155 pounds at the time of his death - - he'd lost maybe 15 pounds over the last year. In kilograms his weight was about 70, so if he were as susceptible to the toxic effects of pfaffadine as were the NCI mice, it would take about 35 grams to cause his death. 35 grams per 70 kilograms was equivalent to 0.5 gram per kilogram. Perfect. That's the amount he had taken from the vial; he'd left about a gram out of the 36.78 that had been in there.

The NCI report described briefly how the mice had suffered severe and massive liver injury leading to liver failure and rapid death.

CHAPTER 41

Elaine took a taxi to Bethesda from Washington's National Airport late on Wednesday afternoon, and checked in at a Holiday Inn for the evening. She had realized at the last moment that the upcoming Friday was Memorial Day, and that the NIH would be shut down, so she felt lucky to have moved her flight back from Thursday. She wanted to be in New Jersey for the weekend, and back to Berkeley by Tuesday at the latest.

She had called Will's dad on Tuesday evening, worried at first that the police might not have yet contacted him about Will's death, but realizing almost immediately when he answered that he had been told. He asked a few questions on the phone, but when Elaine told him she would be in Bethesda on Thursday, he said he would fly down to talk to her. He'd be down on the shuttle and Elaine agreed to meet him at Washington's Union Station in the late morning. From there she would take the train to Newark, where the pharmaceutical company people had arranged for her to be picked up.

On Thursday morning Elaine walked to the NIH campus and located the Cancer Institute, Building 35, easily. She thought she would start with Dr. Virgil Goode, Chief of the Medicinal Chemistry Branch; she knew he knew her name and work. His office was on the third floor, and she walked the stairs to it. She arrived at eight o'clock, and it was not yet open. She wandered for awhile in the corridors of the third floor and wondered where the labs might be. She found a small library and entered. She leafed through some journals and newsletters for a half hour, then returned to Dr. Goode's office.

Virgil Goode was a tall, thin man, probably in his late fifties. He had an international reputation in his field, bolstered by a very long history of publications involving the synthesis of a wide range of chemical types used in medicine. He had for the past dozen years directed a lab of top-flight scientists, and was a central figure in the worldwide cancer research community. He was also a key player in decisions about research grants, including those held by Alden Jensen.

He was extremely gracious toward Elaine, and it took him only a few minutes to recall what he knew of her work. He told her he was highly pleased to meet someone who had done such excellent work, and welcomed her into his office where he offered her a seat and some coffee. Elaine was so excited and gratified by what he said, and how he behaved toward her, that she almost forgot why she came.

The two chatted for about ten minutes, during which time Elaine told him about her career plans. He told her he wished he'd had a chance to talk to her about an NIH career. Goode finally asked Elaine the reason for her visit.

She paused, gathered her thoughts, and began to tell the tale she had rehearsed in her mind a dozen times. "I have a terrible story to tell you. I fear you may not believe me, but I have to take that chance, because I have to tell it."

This got Goode's full attention, and he listened as she related to him the entire story of Will and pfaffadine and the professor who had abused him so wickedly. Goode became increasingly uncomfortable as her story went on. Will's fraudulent acts, his terrible dishonesty, angered Goode, and Elaine's own role in abetting Will he found troublesome. But when he heard of Jensen's scheme to cover up the fraud, to perpetuate it, his stomach churned. The final abuse of Will and the ghastly tale of Will's suicide simply stunned Goode into silence. He had no idea what to think, except that the whole affair, if true, represented a major ethical infraction against the scientific enterprise.

He wondered if it all were true, and could not fathom why Elaine might make up such an incredible story. Did she have something against Jensen? Her own complicity in Will's fraud should be condemned, but she had freely admitted it. There was no reason for that - - she could have incriminated Jensen if she wanted to without fabricating the story about her own small role. Goode also knew that what she told him seemed to fit with something else he had learned just a week ago. He felt he needed to talk with the NCI's Director or his Deputy about this.

"I did something else that I thought might support what I'm telling you." Elaine pulled some graphs and spectra from her briefcase. "I took a small amount of the compound in Will's nearly empty vial back to Berkeley with me. I ran NMR and IR spectra on Tuesday, and had a mass spec confirmation run. There's no doubt that what Will had in the vial was pfaffadine. I can show you with these spectra."

She also told Goode that she thought the weight of pfaffadine Will had written on the label was accurate, and went through her calculation of the amount he must have ingested. The thought of the young man, whom Goode knew only by name, forcing this amount down his throat, and of the agony he must have suffered, probably over ten or twelve hours, made him nauseous.

"Dr. Callahan, this story is just awful. If it is true, I think we need to investigate. But I need to talk to the Director of the Institute, or maybe his Deputy. Could you wait here? They may want to speak with you directly."

"Yes, sure. Also, one more thing. You should have received Will's write-up of his Experimental Methods, from Professor Jensen. I have a copy here, in this folder, if you haven't. I think they will he found to be completely truthful, and that synthetic pfaffadine can be produced in large quantities using them. I think what I found in Will's vial proves that."

Goode nodded, solemnly, in apparent agreement, and left the room. He did not return for nearly an hour. Elaine sat all the while full of anxiety and worried they would simply dismiss her and what she had told Virgil Goode. She had never felt so anxious in her life, and at one point even felt an urge to leave.

But she held on and, at about eleven, a secretary came by and asked Elaine to follow her to the Director's office. This increased Elaine's anxiety, but she complied. At the huge office, filled with books and journals, papers piled everywhere, she was introduced to the Director and Deputy Director of the NCI. They asked her to be seated at the conference table, and with Virgil Goode still present, she was asked to repeat for their benefit what she had told Goode earlier. It all came out over the next hour, almost word for word.

"This fits with what little we know, Dr. Callahan," said the Deputy Director. "About a week ago, we finally got around to beginning the next series of tests on pfaffadine. We had received from Professor Jensen a vial, early in May, labeled "Pfaffadine, synthetic." It was labeled as having 36.78 grams. Is that right, Virgil?" Goode nodded in agreement. The Deputy went on.

"We had earlier received about five grams, the first batch of synthetic. We checked it and confirmed its authenticity. That's what we used for the toxicity tests in mice. A week ago, as we were planning some tests with the 36 gram batch, we checked it. It's fake. It has no resemblance to pfaffadine, except that it's a colorless, crystalline material. We have tried four or five times to reach Jensen about this, but have so far been unsuccessful. We think what you have told us squares with what we know. Evidently Mr. Getz took with him, when he left, the authentic material, and gave Professor Jensen this fake material. Jensen never checked it himself. He just sent it on to us. He assumed that since Will had produced authentic pfaffadine once, there would be no need for him to fake it again. In fact, he'd have to assume that Will would be a complete idiot to try that again. By the way, we do have Mr. Getz's write-up of his "Experimental Methods." I think we can have confidence in them. We still have great hopes for this compound in cancer therapy."

Elaine felt more at ease when the Deputy finished. She saw that
Virgil Goode was looking more comfortable and that he even smiled in
her direction. The Director looked lost in thought. He was clearly
disturbed by what he had heard, but said nothing until the Deputy said
that they should meet and decide what to do.

"I think I know," said the Director. He was a small man with
thick brown hair and an equally thick mustache. He sat in a slightly
hunched posture, with his arms on the conference table and his hands
folded. His eyes, seen through thick, horn-rimmed glasses, seemed to
be focused on his hands and did not move as he spoke.

"I believe we need to investigate this matter fully. I am pleased
we now have, apparently, a reliable synthesis of pfaffadine. I am,
however, uneasy about using this synthesis if its origin is as filled with
deception as Dr. Callahan wants us to believe. We can tolerate no
deception of the type we have heard about. Even your small role,
Doctor, is unacceptable. Science, the essence of science, is scrupulous
honesty, complete fidelity to the facts. Nothing less. Science is just
about the only institution we have that does not tolerate dishonesty.
We accept that there will be honest error - - we are, after all, humans
only. But not deliberate deception. Never. I am not sure exactly what
we will do, but we will investigate. We shall probably he back to see
you, Dr. Callahan. The fact that you have come forward in this fashion,
we appreciate. We have noticed, at least I have, that you have a motive
for wanting to damage Professor Jensen - - he hurt someone you have
told us you cared for. I think you will have to acknowledge that we
cannot ignore this.

"In any event, we shall investigate. You seem to be ready to
embark on a potentially excellent career. I am worried about your role
in this business, but I'm not sure that it's significant enough to damage
your career. If we issue a report on our investigation it will be a public
document. I am concerned about what you have told us, deeply, and it
is my responsibility to see that nothing done under the grants issued by
this Institution is based on fraud. We thank you for coming, and we

wish you luck. From what I have heard from Virgil, I think you might have been a real asset here in Bethesda."

Elaine took a taxi from Bethesda to Union Station. She was relieved to have this behind her, and was not worried about being further investigated by the NCI. She knew she had the truth on her side. It might be extremely difficult for the NCI to develop convincing evidence of Jensen's complicity, and he would no doubt continue to lie to them. But he would still have to live forever with the knowledge of what he did, both to his science and to his student.

Before she'd left the NCI she had told Virgil Goode that there was someone else back in Berkeley, another friend of Will's, who knew the story of what Jensen had done, and who, Elaine was certain, would be willing to tell what she knew to the investigators.

Because it was nearly three o'clock when she arrived at Union Station, she was worried that Will's father would have given up and returned to the airport, but she found him sitting on a bench near the entrance. They had met once, at Atlantic City, and she recognized him easily. As he stood she realized that Will had his father's body, but that his handsome face must be mostly his mother's, his lost mother's. Elaine was completely famished, so they walked out of the station and across Massachusetts Avenue to a restaurant, deserted at this time of day. They took a booth and Elaine ordered two cheeseburgers and coffee. Will Senior ordered coffee. He looked deeply sad.

Elaine had thought a lot about what she should tell Will's father. She at first thought he need not know about Will's fraudulent work, but in the end she decided that the full truth needed to be told. And so, for the third time that day, Elaine related Will's story, in all its detail and without gloss - - the plain, sad truth. The only thing she added to the story was more about her feelings for Will and his feelings for his father, as she understood them. She refrained from offering much detail about what Peter Weiss had told her about Will's dreadful three weeks at his place and his several acid trips.

Will Senior was quiet during all of this, and expressed little emotion. The first sign of sorrow came to his eyes when Elaine turned over to him the folder containing Will's thesis materials and the note to his father. After reading it, Will's father lifted the paper-jammed folder to his chest, embraced it, and then burst into tears. He cried for several minutes and continued to hold close what remained of his only son. He would never understand what had led Will in the direction his life had taken, but he would surely find the blame to lie within himself.

CHAPTER 42

With Gina driving, she and Tom were on the last leg of their journey to Portland, Oregon. They had left Berkeley on Wednesday morning and it was now approaching three o'clock on Thursday afternoon. They had spent Wednesday night at a motel in Medford and were now about an hour away from their rendezvous spot, a small town just west of Portland called Aloha. Tom's friend Bert had picked the spot and had sent his Canadian girlfriend, Louise, to meet Tom and Gina in front of the town's only service station. "I was there, last year, on my way up here," Bert had said. "I think it's a Chevron. Anyway Louise's car is a green '59 Chevy," and he gave Tom the British Columbia license tag number. Tom told Bert he'd be arriving in Gina's green VW Beetle, California tag number CXI 423.

The two friends, soon to part, drove in silence in the warm June afternoon. Both windows were open and the sound of the wind blowing by and through the VW was loud enough to make conversation difficult. Just as well. They had probably said to each other everything that had to be said.

Gina had wavered in her opinion about Tom's choice to abandon ship. She certainly didn't want him to be in the military if there was any chance he might be shipped off to kill Vietnamese or to be killed by them. But she was uneasy with his decision to take flight. He might never be able to return to the U.S., or he'd be arrested if he did. Why not just refuse to be drafted now, and take his punishment here? No choice was good and in the end she told him she'd support whatever he wanted to do. Women did not have to face these horrible choices. Of course, in Gina's mind, it was wrong that men should, either.

Tom had urged her several times to come with him, and it became clear that he wanted Gina in his life for more than friendship. She did not give the option serious thought. She had a course mapped out for herself, not only one that included law school at Berkeley, but one that looked beyond that time into a future that held open the possibility that someone with her intelligence and will and talent and values could be a force for change in America. She wanted to stay on this path. She had talked about all this endlessly with Kay, and she knew where her heart was.

She had experienced, she had to admit, some perceptible loss of feeling for Tom in the time since he told her he was going to emigrate. Perhaps it was the loss that inevitably comes when an unavoidable event over which neither person has control scars a relationship like theirs, and as the two gradually come to recognize that it is not just a scar but that it is perhaps an irreversible injury, the feeling of loss causes each person to turn inward, and away from the other. In this, to prepare for the inevitable separation, the heart finds a way to protect itself from even greater damage. About this neither Gina nor Tom had talked. They talked instead about staying in close contact, writing and calling, about finding ways for Gina to visit, and about the possibility that she might one day change her mind and join him.

At the Chevron station in Aloha, Oregon, on the afternoon of June 6, 1968, Tom and Gina embraced, kissed each other and separated. She leaned against her green VW Beetle as her friend walked away, two suitcases in his hands, to get into the '59 Chevy with the B.C. tags, driven by the Canadian girlfriend of Tom's friend. Gina stood in the same position as the Chevy drove off, and with her hands stuffed into her jeans, kicked at the ground a couple of times with her right foot, turned and got into her car, and drove off.

She'd driven for about thirty minutes before she realized she hadn't been watching the roads and that she was lost. She stopped, pulled out her road map, and eventually figured out that she had driven north to Route 26. She and Tom had driven up from California on Interstate 5. Now looking at the map and recognizing where she was, she decided to head west on 26, swing down on 6 toward Tillamook, and Highway 101. She would take 101 southward along the Pacific Coast, all the way back home. She had traveled some of that highway in California, but had never seen the Oregon coast or, in fact, most of the California coast. Gina was in no great hurry to get back to Berkeley, so she thought she would make a little adventure of her drive. She swung south on 101 at Tillamook and in about forty-five minutes the ocean was in view.

For the next several hours Gina lost herself in the drive and in the magnificence of the Oregon coast. On her right were cliffs plunging down to sandy beaches out of which emerged ocean-washed boulders of many shapes and huge sizes, and on her left grew dense forests of pine and fir. Within three hours the sun had descended to a position over the ocean that was directly in Gina's line of vision and the beauty of the seascape took her breath away. She had not seen much of America, but she knew there could not be many places more beautiful than this, except, maybe, the northern New Mexico landscape she had trekked with Tom. The ocean and the desert and the forests and the great mountains she had experienced in these few places made her apprehend that its landscape was one of the most wonderful things about her country.

She pulled into a motel just south of Coos Bay at about seven-thirty, and registered. The motel was not situated in the most beautiful of locations, but she was able to walk to an ocean wayside and watch the sun in its final descent. She was feeling very tired, so she went to a grocery store and bought a sandwich and a carton of milk, and went to her room to sack out. She showered and then got into bed.

She hadn't brought anything to read, and so turned on the TV.

Robert Kennedy, she learned almost immediately, was dead. He had been shot by someone in the Ambassador Hotel in Los Angeles in the early morning hours, as he was walking away from a huge celebration of his victory in the presidential primary election of the California Democratic Party. Gina felt she must have been the last person in the country to know; she had not turned on her car radio all day. She thought of Kay and Lily who, she knew, had attended the Kennedy affair, and hoped they had not been in harm's way. The newscast made it known that the assassin had been immediately captured and that Robert Kennedy had been the only one injured. He had died very early on the morning of the sixth.

Gina turned off the TV after about twenty minutes of this, and returned to her bed. She sat against the headboard and cried.

The tears came uncontrollably and she made no effort to contain them. She cried for a very long time and the tears were not just for the second dead Kennedy, but for her beautiful, kind father, and for her gentle, lost priest, and for the sad damned boy who had once shared her bed. She cried for the man who became her dear friend and who had to flee from her and from his country. For the confused, angry boy lost or dead in the sorrows of Guatemala. For Lily's little brother, still MIA in that weary country in Southeast Asia. Even for the professor who had become twisted into an unrecognizable form and had descended into his own hell. The skinny rich boy who had dropped off into a drug-laced misery, the selfish chemistry professor who had so ravaged his student, the priest who had betrayed his church for love of her mother - - all these were in her tears. All these men who had swirled around and through her life, who in these restless, turbulent times had been consumed, obliterated, deformed even, for reasons that are ultimately beyond human comprehension, mysterious. The mystery that is at the core of life and that is, she had to concede, grasped only by the mind of God. Only the mind that comprehends these mysterious events and acts is truly capable of forgiving them. God may not be necessary for anything else, but for this ... there's nowhere else to turn.

She cried herself into the edge of sleep and so laid herself down under the blankets and turned off the tiny bedside lamp.

As she passed into sleep Gina heard somewhere the voice of Teresa, her mother, who so long ago had driven off some cliff to end her own pain. Gina could not make out what her mother was saying, but then her face - - a face even more beautiful than that of her daughter - - came into focus. She was smiling and a song came from her. Her sleeping daughter recognized the melody and knew she had heard her mother singing this same song many times. The words did not make any sense but the beautiful melody was clear and filled the daughter's night.

The dream seemed to have gone on for a very long time, but in the morning she could remember only her mother's face and the fact that she had been singing, and that she seemed to have found some kind of peace.

After coffee Gina's adventure continued. For some reason food was unnecessary. In the cool morning hours, with the sun still hidden behind the trees of the forests, she drove south. With no sun above it, the ocean cast an entirely different spell, more somber and mysterious. In some places it seemed almost menacing.

The sun eventually rose up above the forest line and the entire mood gradually began to change. As Gina approached the California state line she noticed that the cliffs became steeper and the drop to the ocean more precipitous. She slowed down. She was alone on this stretch of highway. The forest was no longer immediately to her left, but off in the distance. She saw an enormous butte and several mountain peaks in what looked to be a very wild area. But she spent most of her time contemplating the ocean and the great cliffs that bordered it. She drove carefully.

Just before noon she entered the coastal redwood forests through which Highway 101 took her. For several stretches, the highway carried her away from the coast and deep into these great stands of redwood trees. She felt in awe of them, like anyone else who had ever seen or touched them or walked among them. She stopped at a roadside parking area to go to the bathroom, and then decided to spend some time wandering among and beneath these breathtaking giants. Gina had gotten over whatever feelings of inadequacy she had because of her physical slightness. Among other people she no longer felt small; among these trees, though, no one could feel anything but. And reverential.

It was remarkably cool in the redwood forest, so she spent only a half-hour. She continued on her drive south and by early afternoon passed through Eureka. She stopped to refill her gas tank, bought a coke, and drove on. South of Eureka Highway 101 veered eastward, well away from the ocean. She drove through the Humboldt region of redwoods and the small towns that had grown up, many as lumbering centers, along the great highway. As she neared Leggett she noticed a directional sign indicating she was approaching the turnoff to California route 1, which would take her westward and back to the coast. The route 1 sign also told her that it was the road to Fort Bragg and Mendocino.

Mendocino. She knew it well. Her parents had visited that small town almost every year, and Gina remembered spending many happy days there. Her parents had both loved the place, and she remembered her father painting in the streets and on the nearby hills, where they would picnic. Her mother would read and Gina would just wander about and pick wildflowers and, when she was older, read alongside her mother. Those visits to Mendocino were, at least in her memory, almost idyllic and, in fact, they probably were. She headed down route 1.

The road was not a divided highway, like much of 101. It was small and winding. She could not drive very fast, but that was fine. A half hour south of Leggett the ocean came back into view. The ocean and coast were gentler here than they were to the north.

About an hour north of Mendocino she drove into a fog bank. It came on so suddenly it startled her. The sun's rays, coming in the late afternoon from over the ocean, were barely able to penetrate. The fog was thick and the air filled with heavy mist. She could make out some of the nearby forests, but soon the ocean was lost to her vision. She had to slow way down and put on her lights.

It was like this all the way to Mendocino. She arrived in the town about five and stopped for gasoline and to ask directions to the Gloucester Inn. She remembered the name of the inn where her parents had stayed so many times. Its name was the same as the fishing town in Massachusetts. Mendocino was a fishing village, and most of its buildings had a New England character to them. The town had been settled by New England fishermen and their families, and they had built the village in the style of the places they had left behind.

She was able to get a room at the Gloucester Inn - - she remembered the name because she had never understood the relationship between the way the word was spelled and the way it was pronounced. As a child learning to spell, the name was completely confusing.

She hadn't been to the Inn since she was fourteen or fifteen - - a year or more, maybe two, before her mother's death - - but it seemed completely familiar. She wondered if the owners she had known, a man and woman who may or may not have been married to each other, were still here, although she did not remember their names or even what they looked like. She might recognize them if she saw them.

There were only a half dozen rooms, and Gina took the smallest and cheapest of the three available. The room she took was very small and had only a single window, but through it she could look downhill to the ocean. The street leading away from the inn to the ocean was lined with cottages, and all of their yards were filled with flowers. The fog was still heavy and Gina could not really see beyond the cottage-lined street. The hovering sun lent a faint red glow to the misty air but it could not be seen.

Gina showered, and put on some clean clothing. She had brought along a long black skirt and a heavy gray cotton sweater, turtle-neck style. She decided to wear no bra beneath it, because she loved its softness against her skin. She brushed her dark hair until it hung thickly and in soft waves down to her shoulders. She put on her sandals, and went down to the Inn's dining room to eat. She felt beautiful and fully present in this wonderful setting. She was also extremely hungry.

The dining room did not look that familiar to her. It was still only six-thirty and none of the other guests had yet come for dinner. She took a table adjacent to a window that looked out onto the street. A few people were wandering by, but would disappear in a block or two into the heavy fog.

Gina ordered a bowl of fish soup and a glass of wine. Along with the perfectly made, fresh-baked bread the huge bowl of soup was enough to satisfy her hunger. She had finished eating by seven-fifteen, and ordered coffee and some apple pie.

As she sat drinking her coffee, she turned in her chair to look about the dining room. Almost immediately she saw it, hanging on the wall, not more than ten feet away, next to the entrance to the kitchen. It startled her. This could not be! She set her coffee down, rose, and walked over to it.

She stared at the painting for several minutes, taking in its every detail. It was without doubt her father's and, without doubt, it was the painting Aldo had told her about, the one Marco had done when he had learned that Teresa was pregnant with the child of another man, her mother's priest-lover. Marco had done the painting to show Teresa his love and to convince her he wanted her to have the baby. Her mother was at the center of the painting. Her beautiful face stared back into Gina's. Something like deep sorrow was in it but there seemed to be something beyond that, deeper than sorrow, maybe it was love. A small child was present in her mother's arms. It was not possible to tell whether it was a girl or a boy, but it was very happy. Gina saw in the child her father's eyes, she was sure of it. And to her mother's left stood or, rather, floated, a young girl. She held a violin in her left hand and her right hand rested on her mother's shoulder. The relative proportions of the figures in the painting were not realistic, but the emotions were. Gina knew this perfectly. Marco had not worried much about the background or the border of the painting, but had simply set the figures into an abstract pattern of soft and harmonious tones.

Gina moved to a chair just below the painting. She could not stand, her legs would not support her. She stared up at it and let it sing to her and her quaking heart filled with something joyful.

"You like that?" someone asked.

When she finally understood the question was being asked of her, she turned to find the speaker. It was a woman, gray-haired and with glasses, wearing an old sweater and pants.

"Yes... I do... where did it come from?"

"An artist we used to know. He lived in San Francisco. He came here for many years, with his wife - - that's her in the painting. They had a daughter, I remember her and I think she's there, with the violin. The other child, I don't know. The artist's name was Marco. Italian."

"But where did this come from?" Gina pointed to the painting as she asked.

"Marco came here, maybe seven, eight years ago. He was by himself. His wife had recently died. We - - Frank and I, he's my husband - - hadn't seen him for a couple of years, and then one day he shows up. He didn't stay long, but he left us this painting. We have two other paintings of his here, but we like this one best. He said he had done it just before her death, and for some reason it was one painting of her he just didn't want to save. So we benefitted. I love it. He stayed a couple of days, did some painting in the area, then left. We got a letter from him some time after that, but haven't seen him since."

Later, Gina walked out of the inn, and spotted a street that seemed to head up a hill that overlooked the sea. The fog was lifting but was still fairly thick. The air was damp and cool, but Gina felt fine in her heavy sweater. She walked slowly up the narrow road northward toward the bluff, and away from the village. As she passed the last house on the road she entered an open, wind-swept area of tall grasses and wild poppies. The sea was to her left, and its grey-green looked heavy and dark beneath the low clouds that stretched across the distant horizon.

Gina sat upon a large rock scattered among many near the top of the bluff. Cool winds rose from the sea but were gentle against her body. The sun must have been just above the horizon, cloud-hidden, and a quiet darkness permeated the world around her. She sat for several minutes, letting herself be absorbed by that darkening world.

Moments later, at the far horizon she noticed a thin opening in the clouds, a band that stretched horizontally across the length of the sea's border with the sky. The band widened slightly and through the crack that was created came the brilliant light that was being cast by the sun at day's end. The dark clouds were illuminated from beneath and the long rays of orange-red light played over the restless surface of the great ocean. The young woman sat upon the rock, and let the world bathe her in this uncommon light.

When the sun finally disappeared and the moon appeared full and silver-blue in the eastern sky, she rose and walked down from the bluff and found the road back to the inn. She walked quickly, but not because of the cold damp mists. She had to get to bed and get a good night's sleep. She would get up early for her drive back to Berkeley. There was so much she had to do.

THE END

Made in the USA
Las Vegas, NV
03 October 2023

78518641R00223